IN THE HOUSE OF THE LATE PETROU

Cover design: ConnorCorcoranDesign

IN THE HOUSE OF THE LATE PETROU

Louka Grigoriou

MOBUK
PRESS

"History is only the register of crimes and misfortunes."
– Voltaire

"Those to whom evil is done, do evil in return."
– W.H. Auden

For my good friend, Sotiris,
and for moonlit stories on the terrace
at Apostólikou…

Epilogue

(Ἐπιλόγιον)

Summer
2018

The gates to the house called Douka, on the road to Anémenos, are chained and padlocked now, a For Sale sign fixed with black plastic zip-ties to its rusting wrought-iron spears. Beyond these gates the sloping driveway is cluttered with weeds, and littered with the curled leaves and peeled bark of the eucalyptus trees that line it.

Further on, unseen, the lawns are dry, browned by the sun; sprinklers disconnected, vines and orchards untended; fruit left to drop and rot, or scavenged by village children who dare to trespass.

The swimming pool where the body was found has been drained, and the upper cistern is just a tangle of bent grasses and tilting lily pads set on fathomless black water.

On its rise of grand terraces the home of the Contalidis is empty. Its doors are locked and every window is tightly shuttered, its rooms bare and silent, the air still and stale yet lightly scented with distant notes of citrus.

A hollow, shadowy space.

But for all this emptiness, for all its disrepair, there is a sense of history here. Something living, breathing. A whisper in the air, of people and ages long past.

And when the early morning sun strikes its lofty limestone walls the house called Douka glows with a golden life.

The Douka Estate

Press Release (Immediate)
January 2018

"The Douka Estate, on the Greek island of Pelatea, is one of the finest island homes to be found. Built in the early nineteenth century by the freedom fighter, Admiral Ioannis Contalidis, and occupying much earlier foundations, this remarkable property has been in the same family, with one brief exception, for more than two hundred years.

Surrounded by the Admiral's own vineyard, orchards, and olive groves, this magnificent estate covers ninety-two hectares, with elegantly terraced gardens fully stocked with specimen plantings, all set within edging stands of well-established cypress, pine, palm, and eucalyptus. An easy walk from the house is a private beach and cove, with a boathouse, and Balinese-style pavilion.

The main accommodation is set out over two floors and comprises: a grand entrance hall of polished concrete flooring and high stucco walls, with a beamed ceiling and central 'floating' stone staircase; two formal and spacious Bauhaus–Belle-Époque salons that overlook terraces, gardens, and sea; a study and separate library to the rear that enclose a gravelled and fully-stocked courtyard; a dining room with original ship-timber half-panelling; and a state-of-the-art kitchen leading into a walled herb garden.

On the first floor is a master bedroom with dressing rooms, wet-room shower and bathroom, with five further fully-provided guest suites, all floored in rare Mexican Honey Oak.

Beneath these two main living areas lies a brick-vaulted basement, equipped with numerous workshops, storage facilities, and featuring an extensive wine cellar with original racks and bins.

Beyond the main house a number of outbuildings have been converted into additional guest-suite accommodation and studio space.

Redesigned and rebuilt in 2016 by Athens-based design architects, ConStav Associates, Douka is on the Register of Greek Historic Houses.

For further sales particulars, and serious enquiries, please contact…"

Pelatea and Athens, Greece

Summer 2017

Mischief

(Σκανταλιά)

1

THEY STAND on the quay at Tsania, three of them. Huddled around their bags, in a gusting breeze that smells of drying nets and slick seaweed steps. The last spiteful tatters of an early summer storm snatch at their hair, billow trousers, flick at the hem of the woman's skirt. The quay stones are shiny wet from a flurry of earlier rain and puddled at uneven corners, the sky is still dark and menacing, and across a restless chop of white and bruised blue lies the brown smudge of Pelatea.

"I'm tired," says Dimi.

"Not long now," says Nikos, pulling the boy closer, peering out to sea.

Electra is silent, stands alone, irritated. "You said he'd be here by four," she says at last. Wishing they'd caught the ferry. Wishing she'd worn flats, not heels. Just cork wedges, but they still tilt dangerously.

"He'll be here soon, you'll see. But it's rough. If he wasn't coming, he'd have left a message with Kosta."

When Manolis arrives an hour later, only Nikos remains on the quay. He catches the line, helps secure the boat.

"*Yassou*, Niko," the old man calls up. "Welcome back. It is good to see you again."

"And you, too, my friend."

"Where's the family?" he asks, noting an edge to Nikos's voice. He's not surprised.

"At Kosta's. I'll fetch them. Can you manage?"

"I'm not dead yet," says Manolis, and as he sets about the luggage he watches Nikos hurry to the harbour-side taverna.

Electra and Dimi are sitting at a corner of the bar. An empty wine glass, an untouched bowl of wrinkled black olives; a Coke bottle, a crumpled wrap of chips. The floor is gritty with sand, the air close and damp, and Dimi rocks his stool.

When the bill is settled, the three of them head for the quay.

The boy, Dimi, races ahead.

"Is that our boat?" he calls back to his father.

"That's our boat."

They are twenty minutes from the old port of Navros when a low sun breaks through the clouds above a distant ridge, and shifting beams of evening light gild a path across the waves to the island ahead of them.

"The sun is showing us the way home," says Manolis, pushing up the throttle as the swells settle, his passengers perched beside him in the wheelhouse. "It is good luck, the storm passing and the sun returning to welcome you like this."

Nikos gives a short grunt of a laugh. "Of course it is, Mani. Just like you tell all the *xenia* who come to Pelatea. But you're talking to an island boy; a Contalidis, remember? I know the lines."

"You're right, my young friend. But sometimes…" Manolis taps his head below the band of his tilting cap. "Sometimes this old boy forgets."

"Won't it be dark by the time we get there?" asks Electra. She doesn't need to look at her watch. She is fretting.

Nikos seems not to hear her.

But Manolis does. He knows. He's been waiting for it. Another story to tell in the *ouzeri* tonight. The Athenian. Madam. Up to her old tricks. Yannis, Costas and Mavrodakis will lap it up.

"So stay in town," he tells them. "Stay with Lysander, in the old place, and leave for the house tomorrow. It's not going anywhere."

And he laughs as the bow suddenly dips, and a bubbling white wash of spray splashes over the wheelhouse.

"Here, little captain," he turns to Dimi. "Take the wheel. The ship is yours."

"I want to stay," says Electra, and she turns to count their bags on the Navros jetty. She can't help it. She's Athenian. She doesn't trust islanders, even if she is married to one. "It's too late to drive all that way, my darling." *Agapi mou*, she says, firm but pleading.

"Ella, it's thirty kilometres. Nothing. It'll take no time at all."

"Niko, I want to see the house as much as you. For you to show it to me. To be there, at last. But not tonight. And not on that road. It's been a long day, and Dimi is tired."

"Doesn't look tired to me," Nikos replies, sensing once again the moment slip away from him. Always the same, he thinks. Nothing changes. Down in the *caïque*'s wheelhouse Manolis takes a two-euro coin from behind Dimi's ear, much to their son's astonishment and delight.

"Say we're staying, please, Niko."

Nikos sighs. Knows the old boy is watching, listening. And knows he has no choice. Leans forward, catches Electra's arm above the elbow, firmly, and lays his lips to her forehead. "Of course we are," he whispers.

And she can feel the warm breath of his words on her cool skin.

That night, in Lysander's house, on a stepped lane above the harbour of Navros, Nikos and Electra make love. The first time in a long time. Softly and quietly. As though they are dreaming the moves. Sliding together like sleepy eels beneath the sheet. Just sharp intakes of breath and a squeaking screech of bedsprings at the end. Which makes Dimi, asleep in his bed by the door, whimper and stir.

In the warm silence that follows, from somewhere far off, there comes a low rumble of thunder, like a distant chesty snore. And moments later a brief soundless spill of lightning flares across the sky, whitens the muslin drapes, and sends shadows flickering across the bedroom walls.

Slipping from their bed, Electra goes naked to the window, draws aside the curtain and looks out over a sleeping town. Feels a cool breeze on her flushed skin. Across a black pelt of sea, she sees the pinprick coastal lights of Attica.

Somewhere in the gardens below a cat wails, and another rumble of thunder rolls down from the north. Another long, distant groan; like rocks tumbling into a bottomless ravine.

Go home, the sound seems to say. *Go home*; *and go now*.

Like a whisper, close enough to make Electra start, and shiver, and look behind her.

For the second time that day, she feels a sudden, unexpected weariness; the soft, deadening weight of despair. Turning from the window, she goes to the sink; finds her pills, swallows one dry. And with its bitter chalky taste in her mouth, she returns to their bed.

There will be dreams now, but at least she will sleep.

2

OLD MAN Contalidis is not happy.

Just before midnight, and once again at a little after three in the morning, he becomes fretful; gets out of bed to rattle the handle of his walking stick along the cast-iron ribs of the radiator below his window.

On both occasions the duty nurse at the Navros hospice comes hurrying down the corridor. The second time she bustles through his door with a brisk but kindly, "Shush, shush, old man, or you'll wake the dead."

To which Theo Contalidis replies, "He's already awake, Mother."

He says it again as she steers him back to his bed; straightens the sheet on his scar-webbed bony chest, and smooths down wisps of damp white hair.

"Already awake, Mother," he tells her once more, in a fractured, croaky voice. "All of them. Already awake."

When she has him settled, the nurse slides a needle into the shrivelled crook of his elbow, counts to seven, then leaves the old devil to his demons.

3

THE PREVIOUS day's bluster has swept itself away. Not a cloud to be seen. The morning bright and warm, the island sky a wide cavernous blue.

"Admiral Contalidis had two homes," Nikos tells the boy. "One in town, his fleet headquarters, where we stayed last night with Lysander. And one on the other side of the island; where he grew up, and where he moved when he stopped going to sea. The house where I was born, and the house we'll come to every summer when it's too hot to stay in Athens."

"So we'll have two homes as well," says Dimi, leaning between the Jeep's front seats. "Just like Admiral Contalidis."

"Just like the Admiral," says Nikos. "One in Athens, and one here."

They are driving along the shoreline, a four-kilometre stretch of sand-swept blacktop. Cactus, windbreak bamboo and crumbling stone walls on their left; low dunes to their right, a strip of beach beyond, and a glittering cobalt sea.

Athens, thinks Electra, gazing out over the dunes. So close, yet now so far away. She feels a tightening in her throat. She's homesick, that's all; that was why she'd felt so low the previous day. Leaving the city, the house in Kolonaki; her garden, her friends.

And last night's dream hadn't helped.

Chased by a dog… Falling, getting up, falling again… An endless struggle to keep on her feet and run – from where to where, she couldn't say. And behind her that angry barking and those excited, hungry yelps; growing louder, coming closer; always closer. Until she'd woken with a start, sweaty and exhausted.

And she had been so excited at the prospect of coming here. To their new home on Pelatea. The whole summer away from the heat and the dust and the clamour of the city. And Dimi would love it: all those snakes and lizards, the creepy-crawlies. That's what she'd said to herself.

Yet now that she's here, she misses her other home, and the city; wondering why she'd been quite so enthusiastic about spending the summer on Pelatea. Had she really thought it such a good idea? Or was it just to please Nikos? For Dimi?

But she's here now, so there's no going back; no chance to change her mind. She knows she'll just have to make the best of it.

For Nikos, for Dimi. And for herself, too.

And Nikos is right. It is a good thing to do. It's his home, after all.

And now, their home.

Up ahead the beach comes to an end in a tumble of black rocks that rise into a bookend bluff; where the road swings left, inland, away from the coast. Nikos slows, turns the wheel with an open palm, and follows the dusty grey strip between thick stands of rustling maize and silvery groves of olive. Up through Falanistis and Calamotí, then round to the left into the first of the hairpins leading up to Avrómelou and Akronitsá.

As always Electra tries to decide which she likes the least – going uphill on switchbacks, or coming down on them. A narrowing road curving into thin air whichever way you go. Both seem equally hazardous. Turning the last corner out of Akronitsá, where the road begins its descent towards the island's southern coast, Nikos brakes hard for a herd of goats that have strayed onto the road. Their bells tinkle, dust from their hooves and the Jeep's wheels rise around them, and through her window Electra looks down at the rocks and the sea far below.

"Sit back and put on your belt, *agapi*," she says, glancing at Dimi.

It's as if the boy hasn't heard.

"Dimi. Seat-belt. Now. Niko, tell him."

"Do as your mother says, or there'll be trouble." He reaches out a hand and rests it on her leg. She sees his reassuring smile; tries to smile back.

"Not long now," he says, passing the last goat and putting his foot down. "You won't believe it."

"Does it still smell of smoke?" she asks.

"Only when you light the fire." Nikos glances at her, smiles again. "Don't worry. There's nothing. I had Spiri put resin on all the surfaces before replastering – timbers, too. There's nothing. You'll see."

"And Ariadne?"

Nikos chuckles. "Well, what do you think? She'll be there to greet us, but then she's away; visiting her cousin on Aegina. We'll have the place to ourselves. A week at least. Time to settle in."

4

SHORTLY after ten o'clock that morning, the housekeeper Ariadne Papadavrou crosses the hallway at Douka, her tight black shoes tapping on the polished concrete floor. When she reaches the front doors, she pulls them open, secures the latches to stop them slamming shut, then sits herself down on a straight-backed tapestry chair. Arranges her black skirt, straightens her shoulders, and clasps her hands in her lap. Soon they will be here, following the driveway from the Anémenos road, down those steps and along the path. From where she sits, she will see them before they see her. Nikos, her own little boy. And darling Dimi… Just like his father. The same brown eyes, the thick black hair that turns to a wave when it grows too long. The pirate in the pair of them. And that smile. That big, wide Contalidis smile.

And her self, of course. The wife… Electra. Ella. Always the centre of attention, or else.

Mummy. Darling. Mainlander. Athenian. Madam. Milady. Cow.

With her skinny shanks and flat chest, that haughty look, the tight little smile… A writer. Pah! The scrawl of her name on a cheque or a credit-card slip, that's as close as she comes to writing, thinks Ariadne.

Three times Madam has visited since the house burned, staying at the hotel in Anémenos. And each time a performance. A drama. The last visit, more than a year now, the wrong flagstones in the kitchen herb garden, the wrong blue dye for the concrete floors in the hallway, the wrong handgrips on the sliding salon doors. Too much of this, too little of that. A nightmare. How the poor man puts up with it? she'll never know.

And this time, no different by the look of things.

There they all were, the night before, up from Kalypti and Anémenos, with the lamb roasting on the spit. In their best, waiting to welcome the family home.

And then the phone call from Nikos.

Held up in town…

As if…

Just her ladyship not wanting to drive all that way with night coming on. And the sun still to set!

She should have known, thinks Ariadne; tightening her lips, working the joints in her swollen fingers. She should have seen it coming. And not bothered. But the lamb had been good, and there was wine from the cellars. Good wine, too. Contalidis wine. And the past hour, with Lina and Aja to help her, the three of them had cleaned up the mess from the night before – the kitchen, the herb garden, the terrace. The house like a pin – bright and sharp and shiny.

Everything ready for them.

It is then that Ariadne hears the car. Beyond the steady buzz of cicadas; the distant beep of a horn as they turn through Douka's gates and start down the drive. Windscreen glinting through the line of eucalyptus. The Jeep sweeping down into the forecourt, crunching to a stop on the gravel in a passing cloak of dust. The engine switched off. Silence, for a moment, until the cicadas start up again. And then the opening and closing of doors. A shout from Dimi…

Pushing hands onto knees, Ariadne gets to her feet, brushes out the creases in her dress; and sees, along the stone skirting, the scorpion.

Skorpíos.

Flat as a coin. Black as night. Scuttling for the shadows beneath the Admiral's desk. A big one. The size of her thumb. The third she's seen that morning, but the only one inside the house. Come in through those glass louvres above the skirting, he has. That's her guess. She can almost hear its sharp little feet on the concrete floor; sees the reddish bulb of its stinger on the curved tip of its quilted tail.

Ouch, but it hurts, that sting. Hot, hot, hot. Worse than a wasp, worse than a hornet or horsefly. But never a sting on the foot. Always the hand. Dipping into a dark place for something; a drawer, a cupboard. Reaching, feeling; without thinking. Or putting on clothes without shaking them first. Just the briefest flutter had them out. Not like spiders, holding on tight. You'd think, with those spiky legs and pincers and hooked tail, that they'd be the devil to shift. But they aren't. Just tumble out, they do, to scuttle away.

Ariadne watches this one swing round to back past the desk's shadow line. Pincers raised, threatening; sliding out of sight, seeking the dark.

She'll find a matchbox, she thinks, as she walks to the open doors to greet the new arrivals.

Catch one, put it somewhere.

Which makes her smile.

5

"YOU WERE right, Niko. I don't believe it..."

Nikos watches Electra kick off her shoes and step barefoot onto the balcony outside their bedroom, her shadow slanting thin and long and dark, moving over the stonework behind her. The last stop on her tour of inspection. The entrance hall with its light blue floors and floating staircase; the two grand salons either side with the limed beams and sliding teak doors; the dining room with its half-panelling and bare stone walls; the German kitchen sleek and stylish with grey Arkon work surfaces; the study and the library facing each other across the rear gravelled courtyard; Dimi's set of rooms; the four guest suites, the linen rooms, the bathrooms. And finally their bedroom, while the housekeeper, Ariadne, keeps an eye on Dimi.

Electra goes to the balustrade, the sun above the palm tops. He can see by the way she walks that the stone is already hot beneath her feet, but a cool morning breeze whispers across her neck, shifts through her blonde hair. Beyond, the gardens slope away to the sea: terraced lawns shaded by palms; with orchards on one side, vineyard and olive groves on the other; a bank of twisting pines on the lowest slopes concealing the beach beyond.

"It's so beautiful, Niko, simply beautiful. In just a year... A building site one minute, and now... this! You've done a brilliant job, *agapi mou.* You must be so pleased."

And he is. At last.

So happy with Douka.

For the first time since leaving their house in Kolonaki, Electra feels her mood change, lighten, and suddenly she remembers how much she loves this place. Nikos's home, where he lived as a boy. The Venetian-style manor house the Contalidis family had lost, and found again. First built by Ieroklis Contalidis, the Admiral's grandfather, when Pelatea was one of the region's richest trading islands, and the Contalidis its wealthiest merchants. This was where the Admiral had come in the last years of his life, to the headland of Douka where he had grown up, to live with his memories on this south-facing slope with its green lawns and distant sea. Living long enough to plant a vineyard, an olive grove, orchards of lime and orange and lemon. Putting in stands of fig and peach, eucalyptus, palm and cypress, all the way down the hillside to the sea, a shimmering, sun-winking strip of blue above a line of pine and tamarisk that hides a narrow cove of powdery sand and turquoise shallows.

Electra had fallen in love with the house the moment she saw it. On a summer's day, like today. A strong, bold, noble home built with mighty limestone blocks from the island quarry at Effoutsi. Painted wood ceilings, ship-timber panels and flooring, carved stone lintels, faded red roof tiles. With the headland of Douka rising behind it.

That first visit Nikos's father, Theo, had shown her around. The house of the Contalidis, owned by them for generations until Xandros Petrou had taken it.

Petrou, the shark; Petrou, the moneylender.

But now Petrou was dead, and Douka was back where it belonged, the old boy had told her. A twenty-year gap in more than two hundred years. Sixteen years with the loathsome Petrou in gloating residence, and four years with the nephew he'd left it to, a trader on Wall Street. Just so the Contalidis wouldn't get it.

And every summer this nephew had come to Pelatea with his wife and children to spend a month on the island. He'd put in the pool, turned some of the old storehouses into a row of terraced guest cottages, and was waiting for permission to extend the main house when the Crash came and the money stopped. The apartment in New York went, the house in Greenwich. The cars and the yacht. And, of course, the house of his uncle, the late Petrou, on Pelatea.

It had gone to auction and he, Theo, had made the winning bid.

So now this house is theirs. Their summer home.

Three months. Twelve weeks. Monday to Thursday with Dimi, and Nikos at weekends. How hard can it be, she thinks? With so many friends who want to visit. Her good friends and neighbours, Ilias and Ana, in Kolonaki; the Stavrides, Iphy and Vassi, Nikos's partner at ConStav; her agent, Chrysta. Even her mother, Gina, had promised to make the trip.

So she won't be short of company, unless she chooses to be. It really won't be so bad, she tells herself.

And she has the book to finish. Her biography of Admiral Contalidis. To take up where she'd left off

The time will fly.

In this gorgeous house, on this glorious headland, on this wonderful island.

Nikos comes up behind her; slides his arms round her waist, pulls her against him. Still so thin, so gaunt. She puts her hands on his; as he leans down, nuzzles her neck, whispers in her ear.

"It's all for you, *agapi mou*. Away from the city. In this beautiful place. You can finish your book, and enjoy the summer. And rest."

"Just what I was thinking."

"And Dimi will love it. So much to explore. Like me, when I was his age. Like all the Contalidis."

"Is he safe?"

"He can swim, so he won't drown. There are no cliffs, so he won't fall. And everyone knows who he is," he replies, squeezing her tight. "He'll meet up with a village kid, and you won't see him dawn to dusk…"

"Scorpions?" Electra loosens his grip, turns in his arms. Lifts her hands round his neck, pushes her fingers through his hair. She can feel the heat of the balustrade stone in the small of her back. "There was a scorpion downstairs, under the Admiral's desk."

"Inside the house? No, no…"

"There was, I'm telling you. And you know how I hate scorpions."

Nikos shakes his head, laughs; leans down to kiss the side of her mouth. "Scorpions live outside. Under stones, urns, in old walls. But never inside. Not in this house. Ask Dimi."

"Niko, I know what I saw…"

"But just in case…" he sighs, "I'll have Ariadne and the girls do a sweep. To make sure…"

"*Baba, Baba*!" Dimi's voice, calling for his father, rings up from the pool. "Can we go to the beach?"

"You want to swim?" he asks her.

"You promise?" Electra grips his hair, tugs it. "About the scorpions?"

"I promise."

"Then, yes. I want to swim," she says.

Their first lunch on Douka is a picnic at the beach, in the small pavilion that Nikos has built among the tamarisk. Bamboo walls, shingle roof tiles, and curling oriental eaves; with a raised teak deck and stretch of scarlet sail to shade it. They carry the food in a hamper – pearly pink fillets of *barbounia* brought up that morning by Ariadne from the quay at Anémenos, to grill on the beach; a salad of green leaves from the kitchen garden; tomatoes, *feta*, and olives; tubs of Ariadne's home-made *taramosalata* and *tzatziki* with pita bread; plums they pick along the path to the beach; lemonade for Dimi, and a bottle of the Admiral's own wine, a frosty white as dry as garlic skins. Afterwards, they swim out to the raft, sunning themselves on its raffia deck; their salty skin tightening and prickling in the drying heat, while Dimi patrols their floating wooden square in mask and snorkel.

That first night in the house of the late Petrou, in the old home of the Contalidis, they make love again. Two nights running, thinks Electra, as his tongue pushes into her mouth, and his fingers reach between her thighs. The first night in Navros soft and sinuous, this second time here in Douka swift and fast and breathless. Rough and urgent. Like a punishment. Flipping her over so her face presses into the pillow, his body so heavy on hers that her arm is trapped and she cannot use her fingers. And she knows she's being taken for his own purposes. Selfishly, thoughtlessly. Whether she likes it, or not. But she makes no complaint. She's grown used to it. Sometimes that's how Nikos is. And sometimes, too, she likes it.

In the settling quiet that follows their lovemaking Electra senses footsteps in the corridor, hears the soft click of the bedroom door handle, and bare feet on Mexican oak.

Small, sticky footsteps…

Dimi

"I had a bad dream," he whispers, sliding beneath the covers, burrowing into her embrace, shivering. "I was frightened."

"Then you'd better stay here, *agapi mou.*"

6

AND SO THEIR first summer on Pelatea begins. In the old Contalidis house at Douka.

That first week they make the house their own. Put their mark on it, she and Nikos. With Lina and Aja, the two girls from Anémenos whom Ariadne has found to help. While Dimi plays in the pool, or searches for lizards and snakes in the gardens.

Numbered crates and cardboard boxes in every room. To be opened, unpacked. Books on shelves. Paintings hung where the sun doesn't reach. Ornaments unwrapped and placed: the four alabaster elephants with gold-rimmed eyes they bought in Beijing, on her father's blue Murano dining table; the demon masks from Lombok on the pillars between the salon windows; her sister's bronze bust of Dimi in the hallway; and, hung behind it, the foxed mirror she and Nikos had found in Rome, in that echoing arcade on Trastevere. Lamps set out, plugged in; rugs unrolled, laid down – *kilims* and *kayseris* from Anatolia, *Ardabil* prayer mats from Iran, Electra's favourite *Chobis* from Pakistan, and roughly-woven Indian *dhurries*; audio, TV and Wi-Fi connected; study and library arranged, and the kitchen properly organised. A home to be found for everything. Ground floor first, then bedroom suites. Day after day, the house takes shape. Until, finally, all the empty boxes and crates, the wrapping and padding, have been removed. Floors swept, everything where it should be.

Electra has no doubt that Ariadne tried her best with the furniture, (and smiles kindly at her efforts). But nothing is as it should be: two of the sofas from Milan, still in their plastic covers, set against bare walls; another two facing each other, not a metre apart, in the middle of the main salon; her mother's mahogany music stand too close to the fireplace; armchairs in a nest by the window, for the view. She is only glad the old housekeeper is away. Electra can see the thin lips and that stiff-backed disapproving look, as she re-positions the sofas, the armchairs, the side tables, the music stand; sets it out as she wants.

At the start of the second week a white van from Athens arrives on the first ferry. From Zephyros, Electra's favourite florist in Kolonaki. All the houseplants she has ordered. Enough to fill the van. And the house.

The driver rolls up the slatted back with a runaway rattle, pulls out the ramp and trolley, and sets to with his partner. Unloading the tubs and pots and urns, wheeling them into the house, placing them where she tells them: two towering ficus trees with thick braided trunks for the hallway; parlour palms from Guatemala for one salon, and spreading ferns from New Zealand for the other; broad-leaved philodendrons and striped aphelandras; succulent flowering crassulas, spikey aloes, and sabre-shaped sansevieria; and *sadap malam* and stephanotis for their delicate blossoms and night-time scent.

And the orchids, of course. What Electra has been waiting for. Her favourite flower. Fifty plants in cream pots. Fringed cattleyas, clustered ascocendas, and curved maxillarias. Reds and golds, blues and purples. Spotted, striped and mottled. All of them on slender budding green stems. For the bedroom suites, for the corridors, for the library and study. For shade and sun. And for the main salon, an impulsive whimsical extravagance, another fifty phalaenopsis. Broad-petalled white blooms and swollen opening buds, their leaves like lolling green tongues. To be set out in a corner of the room; a massed single group on terraced shelving. The slanting side of a snowy pyramid.

By two in the afternoon the job is done, the van emptied, the plants positioned to Electra's satisfaction, and a sweating driver and his mate offered a late lunch. Which they take in the kitchen with Lina and Aja, finally departing for the drive to Navros and the last ferry back to the mainland.

Nikos, who has spent most of the day in his storehouse studio, comes in to see what Electra has done. He nods and smiles as she leads him round the house.

"Beautiful," he says, standing in front of the shelves of phalaenopsis. "You've done a wonderful job. Really wonderful."

"Just wait till the sun goes down and the stephanotis and *sadap* start up."

7

FOR ELECTRA the days at Douka start early. Before Nikos or Dimi are awake, before Lina and Aja and Ariadne arrive on their scooters and moped.

With the sun still low behind the hills and the air cool from the night, she pulls on her sweats, ties the laces on her trainers, and leaves the house for her morning run. Down to Anémenos with its quayside tavernas, its one hotel, its gift shop, postcard racks, and harbour. No ferries here, just a dozen old *caïques* berthed along the quay. Blue hulls, white uppers, with slanting black eyes on the bows. And, during the season, yachts. Sleek and white. Weekend sailors from Piraeus, from Hydra, and Spetses. And flotilla squadrons, lined up in orderly ranks. Electra had come here twice with her father and sister, childhood voyages on the family yacht, setting sail from their berth in Mikrolimano below the Athens Yacht Club. A night's stay, perhaps two. Never more than three. Never thinking for one moment that one day she would have a house here. And such a house. With such a history. Had they ever sailed past Douka, she sometimes wonders? Or moored in its small cove to swim? They must have done, but she can't remember.

Not that Electra ever runs as far as the village. It is just too long a route for her now; after everything that has happened, too much of an ask. Turning back for Douka when, gratefully, she sees the single blue dome, faded gold stars, and tilting cross of Aghios Spyridon rise above the slope. Before the straggle of whitewashed houses begins, tumbling down to the harbour.

In Kolonaki, in Athens, she does the same. Every morning. Four blocks from their house on Diomexédes to the gates of the Amalia Gardens and its dusty running track. Or, if she's feeling energetic, seven blocks to the sloping paths of Lycabettus. But nothing on either of those runs compares with her route on Pelatea. The beauty of it. The peace. Down through the gardens first. Across clipped lawns still damp from the dawn sprinklers; past cool, shadowy groves of fig and olive, and walls of palliered plums and peaches, to the bordering stand of pines. Straight on, and she'll come to the beach. But it's not far enough, and it's not good running: all those troublesome pine roots and fallen cones, and the carpet of brown pine needles, soft underfoot but treacherous too. So slippery and slidey. Which is why Electra always turns to the left, past the palm and eucalyptus to the lower garden gate where her path cuts through a corner of the vineyard and joins the road to Anémenos.

According to the i-phone strapped to her upper right arm, the route is a little short of eleven kilometres and takes her a little shy of fifty minutes. But that doesn't take into account the slope on the way back, and the terrace steps to the house. By the time she reaches home her heart is pounding, and the front of her thighs scream.

For Electra it's a special time. Time alone. And on Pelatea, more alone than she ever is in Athens. No cars, no bikes, no pedestrians, no other runners. Just her. And her music. Her Bose sound buds kept in place by her headband. All the oldies she loves… The Stones, Steely Dan, Fleetwood Mac, The Doobies. And the classics, too. Mozart, Bach, Handel, Beethoven

Something for every mood.

Something to fill those dark silences that sometimes come; crowding in around her.

It is on one of these early morning runs, that second week at Douka, that the strangest thing happens. During a Bach *adagio*, near enough to Anémenos to see the onion dome of Aghios Spyridon rise above the trees, Electra becomes aware of someone running behind her; footfalls not quite matching hers. As though another jogger has caught her up, and is about to overtake. Just as they do in Amalia Gardens.

So she casts back over her shoulder.

But there is nothing. An empty road rising behind her.

And then, with every step she takes, the music softens and slowly fades, leaving her head filled with a distant white noise. Like the low crackle of static between tracks on a vinyl album. And into that empty static she can hear not just the footfalls of the unseen runner behind her, but gasps of breath, too. Tight and sharp and even. So close. In her ears. Filling her head.

And then, a total silence.

She pulls up sharply. Snatches the buds from her ears. Looks around her.

Nothing. No one. Just the rising tap and buzz of cicadas, the beating of her heart, and an icy ache in her throat.

Hands on hips, she bends over to catch her breath, works her neck, the white plastic buds swinging between her ankles.

She straightens, panting lightly, shakes out her arms and legs, and arches her back; casts around once more.

Nothing.

Works the buds back in her ears.

And the next track starts up. Another fugue.

So strange, she thinks. She was sure she'd heard something.

And then she remembers the Tropsodol, which always makes her feel a little lightheaded when she doesn't take it.

Tropsodol. Chlorsodyl. Heripsyn.

The blue, the pink, and the white.

Tropsodol for the shakes and the sweats, and the stronger Chlorsodyl to chase away the darkness when she wakes unrefreshed from the Heripsyn.

In Athens, at home, Nikos lays them out for her in a tidy line on the shelf above the bathroom sink. In case she forgets. Two blue Tropsodol capsules every morning, and the round pink Chlorsodyl. And at night, on her bedside table, the white oval Heripsyn that tastes of chalk.

The past year she's been taking them every day, as prescribed. Relying on them. Nikos, too. But she's decided they no longer serve a purpose; that she is better without them. Or, at least as good. So, a month before leaving Athens for Pelatea, she'd swept up the pills and flushed them away. The sleepers, too; but into her bedside drawer. Just in case.

A fresh start, out here on the island.

After all this time, more than a year now, she is certain she is past her moment of madness.

The madness that came to her on the fourth floor of the Lycabettus Clinic.

An early morning delivery. Their second child, a daughter, Mantó. After the freedom fighter Mantó Mavroyénous, from the rebel island of Mykonos, who was known as much for her money as she was for her bravery and beauty. According to Nikos, she had sailed with the Admiral and Laskarina Bouboulina to fight the Turk in Nafplio and Pylos.

Electra was at home, had been late to bed, when the first pain came. A searing cramp in the pit of her belly that seized her thighs and doubled her up, made her gasp and cry out. Rather than call an ambulance, they left Dimi with the nanny and Nikos drove her to the clinic.

Forty minutes later Mantó Contalidis was delivered by Caesarian section. Stillborn. An undetected looping and knotting in the umbilical cord – like a twisted shower hose – blocking blood and choking off oxygen to their little baby girl.

That's what had done for her.

And done for Electra, too.

A grey, glistening parcel. That's what she'd imagined.

Not alive, like Dimi; that bloodied squirming little bundle, arms waving, reaching for breath. But a sac of silent bulky tissue, ladled out of her like a lukewarm, greasy broth.

That's the image that filled her head, made her sweat and shake and lie awake, night after night in her private room at the Lycabettus Clinic.

Aching with the loss.

A part of her gone; ripped away.

Afterwards, back home on Diomexédes, she'd kept to her bed, shutters closed. Forgot to eat, but not to drink. Wine first, then vodka. To ease the pain. She wasn't alcoholic; she just knew that a few glasses lightened the load. And through it all Nikos was kind and understanding, stayed with her when she needed him, left her alone when she asked; when she wanted to drink.

And then, one bright summer morning, six weeks after Mantó's passing, they had taken her away; out of her room, her home, the city. To the Aetolikou at Lagonisi. A clinic for nervous disorders that Nikos's doctor had recommended.

Where the medication began.

Not Tropsodol, Chlorsodyl, or Heripsyn. Not to begin with. There were other drugs back then. Drugs she didn't know the names of, because no one bothered to tell her. Brought to her bedside four times a day, in white plastic cups. Those first few weeks just trial and error. To see what worked. Surgical strength prescriptives that took the legs from under her, put her down like a haymaker punch to the point of the jaw.

After three months they'd let her home every other weekend.

To be with Nikos and Dimi.

Then every weekend.

And it was those two men in her life who finally brought her back.

Under medication, of course.

8

ARIADNE, back from her stay on Aegina, moves silently through the house. She'd seen Electra running across the lawn a few minutes earlier, and she knows it will be the best part of an hour before she returns.

Running. Always running, running, running, that one. Some honest to goodness labour and she wouldn't have to bother, thinks Ariadne. Wouldn't have the time.

So the old housekeeper is on her own. Taking a look around; seeing what they've done to the place in her absence. The two salons, the study and library, the dining room. She had done her best in the weeks before their arrival, unpacking what she could, trying to find a place for everything, but she has to admit that it has taken Milady to bring it all together. She certainly knows how to make it work, thinks Ariadne; there's no denying that. But then, with all that money, and all that time, who couldn't?

But it's not the home that Ariadne remembers. Nothing of the old Contalidis. And not a home that she'd be comfortable in. A scatter of shamefully threadbare rugs and faded carpets that anyone in their right mind would throw on a bonfire or roll up and take to the dump at Falakiri. Persian, or Chinese, or Indian made no never-mind. Almost falling to bits by the looks of them – and the very devil to beat or vacuum. Sofas and armchairs that looked too low and angular to offer any sort of real comfort; and a struggle to get yourself out of, thinks Ariadne, once you're settled.

And ornaments everywhere, a most extraordinary collection of pointless bric-a-brac – china this, and glass that, splintered wood, and rusting metal, and peeling stone; just a nightmare to dust and clean, but there you are. Flowers, too, and houseplants – all to be watered, and sprayed, and cared for, of course. And who'd be doing that? she wonders. As for the paintings… well, it's not the kind of art she's used to seeing at Douka. Just wild, formless splashes of colour. Large canvases and small, framed and unframed, the paint slapped on in dollops as thick as her cousin's *koulourakia* dough. And, in the entrance hall, a scrawl of black neon lettering, would you believe, that looks like it spells 'home'. Just… floating against the wall. Not a wire nor plug to be seen.

Nor any of the family portraits either: the Admiral, standing proud like a swashbuckling pirate; his son, Diomedes; his grandson, Theodoros, and the rest of them. All these relegated from the main rooms to the upstairs corridor, set between each of the bedroom doors; the men on one side, wives on the other.

And not an icon to be seen anywhere.

Not a blessed saint in evidence.

Which would please the old man. Old man Petrou, that is.

And may the good Lord rest his sorry unforgiving bones, she thinks with a shudder.

Such a godless man, and no mistake.

And crossing herself, glancing around, Ariadne returns to the kitchen.

9

"TAKE IT from an architect," Nikos tells Electra their first days together in the house at Douka. "There are always things that go wrong with a rebuild. Any build. Even mine."

But nothing goes wrong. Not at first.

Not until Nikos is called back unexpectedly to Athens.

He had taken two weeks off to help get the house up and running, to settle them all in. It had sounded too good to be true. As it proves to be. On their second Tuesday, after Zephyros delivered the orchids and houseplants, there is a call from Athens. A meeting with the Philippiades brothers about their new place in Vouliagmeni. He has to be there, he tells Electra; a grim, apologetic expression, hands spread. Nothing he can do about it.

So she drives him to Navros the following morning, and watches him leave with Manolis, the two of them in the wheelhouse, ducking through the chop. He'll be back on Friday, but until then the house belongs to her and to Dimi.

Three days, two nights. The place to themselves.

Which is when the things that Nikos had warned her about begin to happen.

Small things first.

It starts in the kitchen after her drive back from Navros, probably before Nikos has even reached the mainland with Manolis.

The two village girls, Lina and Aja, are prepping vegetables at the table and Electra is brewing herself a coffee when a rattling sound starts up in the water pipes – like someone tapping on a window pane. Slow at first, but gathering momentum, as though seeking attention. A growing urgency to it. The girls stop their chopping and their peeling, and Electra frowns, puts down the coffee pot and walks to the sinks, thinking to turn on the taps to relieve what she assumes is some kind of air lock, some pressure in the pipes. But when she is only a few steps away, the rattling rises to a frantic whistling, slides into a high-pitched scream. And with a mighty crack one of the tap heads shears clean away from its mounting, and shoots across the kitchen like a bullet; smashes against the fridge door, and drops to the floor; leaving a dent, and spinning on the tiles.

Instantly water sprays from the unsecured pipe, lashing across the room like the jet from a fireman's hose, drenching the women in seconds. Yelping and screaming, the two village girls drop their knives, scoop up towels from a laundry basket and run through the spraying water to block it off, while Electra dives beneath the sinks to close the feeder valve and stop the flood.

For a moment there is silence, just the slosh and drip of water and the memory of that rising rattle, the screeching whistle and explosion of water. Wide-eyed with a shocked disbelief, they look at each other, their clothes sticking to their bodies, hair plastered to cheeks, and mascara streaked. And in that moment, quite unable to stop themselves, they start laughing; reaching for one another, heads together, the three of them, clinging on for dear life.

"Just as well no one was standing in the way of this," comes a stern voice from the kitchen doorway. It is Ariadne. She has picked up the sheared metal tap head and is holding it up; turning it in her fingers, examining it. "That could have done someone some damage," she says, looking around with a puzzled frown.

It is the water, Electra supposes, seeping away through the kitchen flagstones before they are able to properly mop up the flood, that is responsible for the electrics playing up.

That evening, after putting Dimi to bed, Electra is watching a movie in the smaller of the two salons when the lights flicker and the television blinks off. With a sigh of irritation, she mashes out the joint she's been smoking and in a weak moonlit darkness she makes her way to the kitchen in search of the torch that Nikos has put out of Dimi's reach in a cupboard above the fridge.

If he's climbed up and taken it and it's not there, or if the battery's dead, I'm going to scream, she thinks.

But it is there, and the battery isn't dead, and a bright white halogen beam sweeps across the kitchen, sending shadows scurrying across cupboards, walls, and window blinds. Back in the hallway Electra goes to the library, pushes open a section of book-spine panelling, and shines her torch into the fuse box it conceals.

Nothing amiss. Every fuse switch in the 'On' position. Everything in perfect working order.

Which is odd, she thinks. In cases of shorting or power surges, an overloaded fuse is automatically ejected. But the four rows of fuse drives for the ground floor, first floor, and basement are all closed. Not a single one open.

Something the water has done, she wonders?

Closing the fuse-box panel, Electra goes to the light switch by the library door. It's up, in the 'Off' position. She flicks it down, and the four lamps round the room snap on. The electrics are clearly working again. Yet she has done nothing more than shine a torch into the fuse box.

Leaving the library, she switches on the lights in the hall and in the kitchen. And they all work. It isn't any leaking water, she decides. Nothing drastic. Just a temporary power cut.

It isn't until she's halfway across the hall that she realises the lights and the television in the salon are still off. If there had been a power-cut, they'd have come back on after the power was restored. But they haven't. The room is in darkness save the light from the hall spilling through its open doors.

She reaches for the switch. It is up. In the 'Off' position.

She tries to remember if she had turned it off herself, testing the lights before leaving the room to check the fuses. But she can't be sure. Puzzled, she goes to the TV. The remote has been missing for days now, so it has to be switched on and off manually. But the button is flush with the screen. She frowns. Did she do the same with the TV that she did with the light switch? she wonders. Turning them on and off to check the power before leaving the room?

Again, she can't remember.

Except she must have done, because the lights and the TV are off. And if it wasn't her who'd switched them off, then someone else had to have done it. And there's only Dimi in the house with her, asleep upstairs. And she certainly didn't see anyone lean across the TV screen and meddle with the controls.

Then she looks at the low coffee table in front of the sofa.

And chuckles.

The mashed-up joint in the ashtray. An empty glass beside it.

In her state she wouldn't remember anything.

10

ELECTRA sleeps late the first morning Nikos is away. Not the Heripsyn, but the grass. Her own secret medication. When she wakes, she's alone in her bed, just the dented shape of Dimi's head on the pillow beside hers, and the sweet boy-smell of him. Thank goodness for the girls, thinks Electra; stretching, yawning, ruffling her fingers through her hair. They'll keep an eye on him for her.

And then she hears it.

Downstairs, somewhere in the hallway. A great tearing wrench, like cloth being ripped; followed by a rifle-shot crack, a second's silence, and then a shattering crash.

Electra leaps from her bed, grabs a gown and hurries from the room. She can taste the dust in the air before she reaches the stairs; sees it rising up past the landing banisters in a slow rolling cloud.

From the hallway below.

Something knocked over, she wonders, something smashed on the concrete floor? By Dimi, or one of the girls?

But she is wrong. As she comes down the stairs she sees it, just as the kitchen door swings open and Dimi and the girls appear. They have all heard it, and all come running.

Beside the door to the main salon, near the foxed mirror with its gilt frame and Dimi's bronze, a wide jagged scab of plaster more than a metre across, like a giant piece of jigsaw, has torn away from the wall. Lies in scattered shards across the concrete floor, like broken plates at a *bouzoukia* dance.

And where the plaster was, a gaping wound. Just bare, smoke-blackened stone beneath the missing slab of stucco.

Electra steps around the rubble, looks up at the wall, and breathes in the sharp, acrid smell of burning.

Ariadne calls the local builder, Minos Karoussis, in Kalypti. Tells him what has happened. He will be there in an hour, he promises. It's nothing to worry about.

Ariadne passes this on to Electra. "He says these things always happen. Damp plaster that doesn't set. Or paint put on too soon. Or maybe too much lime in the mix. Or some such…" She shrugs.

By the time Minos arrives, the women and Dimi have cleared the rubble, the broken shards of plaster; swept up the spill of stony splinters. He stands in front of the wall, looks up at the hole, pulls at his grey moustache. "Today I plaster, tomorrow I paint." And he looks at Electra, takes in her anxious expression, and smiles. “It is not as bad as it looks, Madam. A small job, and it is done.”

But Electra does worry. Every time she passes him. Coming back from her run, coming down from her room, crossing from kitchen to study. Going to lunch, coming back again. There he is. A rumpled groundsheet speckled with dried paint droppings, a bucket of smooth mortar, another of water. Watching him on his ladder, an elbow through a rung to reach out, wooden hod in one fist, trowel in the other, like an artist at his easel. Slapping dollops of pink plaster across the open wound, sweeping it left and right in arm-reach arches; a smooth sandy whisper. Floating the blade over its shiny surface, back and forth, until there’s not a line to be seen, save wet and dry.

And gradually the smell of burning is lost beneath the sweet dusty scent of setting stucco. And Electra starts to calm.

“There,” says Minos, stepping down from his ladder at last, gathering his things. “Today and tonight it dries. Tomorrow I come back and paint. As good as new, I promise.”

Yet there is worse to come.

The very next morning.

Something the builder, Minos, from Kalypti, cannot make good.

Electra returns from her morning run, stops in the kitchen for a glass of water, then goes to her room to shower. Minos is already at work, up on his ladder, groundsheet down, daubing a thick white paint onto the dried plaster scab. He greets her with a smile and a nod, and assures her that she won’t be able to see where the plaster came down when he’s finished with it. She thanks him, and can see already that when the new shiny paint he’s using has dried to a matt finish, it really won’t be noticeable.

Fifteen minutes later, wrapped in a towel, warm from the shower, she comes back into the bedroom and stops dead in her tracks. Eyes fixed on the floor. On the tiles of Mexican Honey Oak that Nikos had shipped at great expense from a specialist hardwood dealer in Texas, and at equally vast expense fashioned into thousands of interlocking spearhead-shaped blocks for the bedroom suites. Soaked in mustard oil and sanded to a silky finish, they’re as smooth as paper and glow like the honey they’re named after. Except something terrible, something… inexplicable has happened.

In the time it has taken her to shower, at least a dozen of these tiles have risen, their spear-tip points slanting up from the floor like the bristles on a dog’s back. High enough to stub a toe, to trip over. In a rising panic Electra goes down on her knees and inspects the damage more closely, running her fingers over the raised wood. Not just slanted upwards, she can see now, but curved. The wood tip of each spear-shaped tile actually curled back, as though the wood has warped.

A block of wood? Two centimetres thick?

It can’t be, surely?

And in just a matter of minutes?

And then Electra remembers the flood in the kitchen – all that water spraying everywhere… Such a mess. But that had been on the ground floor, she reasons. There couldn't have been any damage up here. Unless it's another burst pipe, she thinks; another air lock. Somewhere unseen.

If Electra had still been taking her pills, she might have reacted a little less anxiously. But she isn't taking her pills, except an occasional sleeper; and right now, without them, her heart is pumping. And then she has a thought. The other rooms? The other bedrooms laid with the same oak tiles? Guts knotting, she hurries down the corridor, pushes open the bedroom doors one after another, checking the floors. But there's nothing. Everything as it should be.

So just the tiles in their room. Which isn't so bad, she thinks.

But then again, if it's just their room, then it has to be her fault, that she's to blame; that's what Nikos will think. Who else could have done it, he'll say? But if every room had warped tiles…

As Electra knows, Nikos has a fiery temper when things upset him. In an instant his face will harden, his tan deepen, his eyes will narrow and glitter, and his jaw set. It is frightening to see; and more frightening still to be its focus. Only Dimi is immune from his rages. The boy can do no wrong.

And these raised wood tiles, Electra knows with numbing certainty, will be enough to set him off. The tiles, of all things. If Nikos had been asked what he loved most about the house, about the reconstruction process, from an architect's point of view, Electra knows that her husband will say the bedroom floors. Before the dyed concrete, before the touch-shade windows, before anything…

Down in the kitchen she asks Ariadne, the girls, and Dimi if any of them have spilled any water in her bedroom. The tiles are loose, she tells them; the floor must have got wet somehow. But they all shake their heads.

Maybe, says Ariadne, with something approaching a soothing smile, it's like the plaster in the hallway. Something wrong with the way the tiles were fitted, perhaps?

But the worst is not over.

When Electra takes them upstairs to show them what's happened, she gasps in disbelief. There are now even more tiles tilting up. As if the floor itself is rejecting them one after another. Pushing them out, one by one. Even under the rugs; tenting the fabric.

Now, for sure, Nikos is going to have a fit.

She looks at the time. A little after nine. In just a few hours she'll be picking him up from Navros, which means there is nothing she can do between now and then to put it right. So he won't know.

Which means a glass or two more of Contalidis wine with her pita and houmous lunch; something to settle her nerves, to stiffen her resolve.

But the wine doesn't help. All the way to Navros, Electra frets, trying to work out how best to break the news to Nikos.

And should he be driving, or should she? When she tells him about the tiles…

Which is when her mobile rings.

She pulls over, finds the phone, and swipes the screen. It's Nikos.

"Nothing to worry about," he tells her. "Just to let you know I'm on the ferry. Be there in twenty."

"That's great. I'm nearly there…" she says. And then, bucking up her nerve, she continues, "I'm afraid there's been a problem. The floor tiles in the bedroom… some of them seem to have risen." She decides not to mention the flood in the kitchen, or the plaster in the hallway. Minos has done such a good job that she doubts he'll notice. And the scented candles she has lit have easily covered the smell of new paint and plaster.

There is silence on the other end of the line, and Electra holds her breath, wondering if she's explained it properly; if he understands what she's told him. But he has.

"Don't worry," he replies. "Probably a reaction to the glue. It happens. If they're too badly warped I've got plenty enough spares to replace them. Otherwise I'll just re-glue them."

And that's it. A great wave of relief sweeps over her. He's not surprised. He's not angry. And he hasn't blamed her. Maybe she should have mentioned the flood in the kitchen as well, and the plaster coming off the wall. A clean sweep. But it's too late now.

"By the way," he goes on. "I've got a surprise for you."

11

WHEN ELECTRA arrives at the harbour in Navros, the ferry is backing into its berth in a swirl of milky blue water, its ramp already descending. Seagulls wheel and caw, and black smoke blooms from the ship's funnel into a sun-bleached oyster-white sky. She parks the Jeep by the Admiral's statue and walks towards the landing quay.

With a screeching grate of metal sliding on stone, the ramp clangs down onto the quayside, and out of the ferry's shadowed hold come t-shirted backpackers and revving tip-toed scooters, old market flatbeds loaded with supplies, and dusty rental 4x4s.

And there, over the heads of the local women calling out their flat roofs, and rooms, and rooms with bath, to the backpackers and tourists, Electra sees Nikos. Pink polo shirt, linen jacket over his shoulder, a hand brushing back his tumbling black hair.

And beside him, her surprise. The Stavrides, their friends from Athens. Vassi, already bulky from a contented married middle-age, and his wife, Iphy, wise beyond her years and elfin-like between her husband and Nikos; the three of them coming down the ferry's ramp, seeing her and waving.

Electra waves back, and at that moment feels both pleased and sad. Sad she won't have Nikos to herself after three days apart, but delighted that their first guests are such good and old friends. Throughout her illness Iphy was a constant, comforting presence who seemed to know when Electra wanted to see her, or needed her. She never intruded, judged, advised. Never once asked that deadening question '*How are you feeling?*' which most of her visitors relied upon to get the conversation moving. Just talked, when Electra wanted to talk; happy to remain silent and just hold her hand when that's what Electra wanted; when there were no words. A special friend. And maybe it is their presence that has tempered Nikos's response to the risen tiles, Electra thinks, hurrying towards them. She'll never know, of course, but she is grateful all the same.

"How's Dimi been?" asks Nikos, as they stow their bags in the Jeep. "Behaving himself, I hope."

"Exploring the garden, most of the time. Or down at the beach. With his new friends."

"New friends? From the village?"

"I suppose they must be. Dimi doesn't say."

Nikos gives her a *what-did-I-tell-you* look. "Have you met them? Do they have names?"

"Dio, Lavri, Karo something…" She tries to remember. "They always disappear when they see me coming."

"You're an Athenian. You'll frighten them."

"Did I frighten you?" She hands him the car keys and slides in the back beside Iphy, waving Vassi to the front with Nikos.

"Terrified me."

"I remember."

Forty minutes later they turn off the road to Anémenos and drive through Douka's gates.

"Oh my God, Niko," gasps Iphy. "You didn't say. It's… Shit, I want it. Vassi, why won't you build me something like this?"

In the front seat Vassi peers through the dusty windscreen, through the line of cypress and eucalyptus, and whistles. "Now I understand why we haven't seen so much of you."

With a flourish of spitting gravel, Nikos pulls up in front of the house.

Iphy opens her door and steps out of the Jeep. "Niko, Ella," she says, looking up at the house. "I just don't know what to say…"

"Say you'll help me with lunch, while these two do their tour of inspection. Let's just hope they're still talking when they get back."

After showing Iphy to her room Electra hurries to her own bedroom, opens the door and, stomach tightening again, looks inside.

At the floor.

And cannot believe it.

Not a single tile out of place, the floor as flat and perfect and polished as it ever was; everything as it should be. As though she'd imagined those rising, curled spear-points.

Nikos was right. Not a problem. Just one of those things.

How silly she'd been to worry so.

Maybe it's relief that the floor tiles are no longer an issue, and that Nikos appears not to notice the new plaster and paint in the hallway, but that Friday evening Electra is in high spirits. After a late lunch in the kitchen garden, they'd gone down to the beach to swim; diving from the raft, lying in the last of the sun; Nikos and Vassi taking turns to snorkel with Dimi.

Now it is dark. Dimi has been put to bed, dinner is over, and the four of them go to the terrace above the lawns for a final drink. The night is warm, the air lightly scented with jasmine and orange blossom, and when they've settled themselves at the table, Iphy asks Nikos about the house.

"Ella said it's been in your family a long time."

"More than two hundred years," he replies. "Except for a short break."

"So that would be… Petrou? Ella told me about him."

"Xandros Petrou. On Pelatea, everyone has a story to tell of Petrou."

"So what happened? How did he come to get the house?"

Nikos glances at Electra who's heard the story a hundred times. She smiles, waves him on. She knows he loves talking about the house of the Contalidis.

"Well," Nikos begins, "for us, it was the winter of 1987. I was fifteen, but I still remember it. Colder than anyone could remember; snow on Pelamotís, and rain down here. Day after day. And the sea boiled. Three, four times a week the ferry couldn't make it over here, so the fishermen couldn't get their catches to the mainland for sale and canning. The fish went bad, and villages like Anémenos and Kalypti lost money. So my father, Theo, decided that rather than depend on fair weather and the mainland cannery at Lynassós, he would build a cannery and refrigeration plant right here on Pelatea. It was a good idea. Tins are easier to keep and transport than fresh fish, and he'd decided that savings and profits would be considerable. But to carry out his plan he needed more money than the family had, so he mortgaged the house here on Douka. And he took the mortgage with Petrou, who was offering a better rate than the banks."

"So what went wrong?" asks Vassi, pouring himself more Metaxa, swirling the brandy in his glass. "As if I can't guess."

Nikos shrugs. "What usually happens. Petrou raised the rates. My father fell behind with his payments, and Petrou repossessed. I remember helping my parents pack, putting things into store, and moving to the smaller house in Navros. I remember passing Petrou's vans on the road. It killed my mother. But my father never gave up. Nothing came of the cannery at Pelépsos; he lost everything. But the old man was determined to get the house back. And he did. Eventually. With a little help." He looks across at Electra, smiles, blows a kiss to her with his fingertips.

He's getting older, thinks Electra, watching Nikos tell the story of Petrou. There are wrinkles in his cheeks, hard vertical lines where before there were dimples; and curling flashes of grey in his sideburns. Which rather suit him, she decides. Statesman-like; dashing, elegant. He is such a good-looking man. Handsome. Lean and strong.

Like the Admiral, judging by the portraits.

And someone else, too, someone… familiar. Someone she can't quite place.

When he's finished his story, Nikos offers Vassi a cigar and both men, with soft, pleasurable groaning, put their concentration into lighting them. Flames flare from the tips of the Cubans, and smoke rises into the still night air.

Electra glances at her watch. It is just before midnight.

She holds up a finger, as though feeling for a breeze.

"Listen," she says. The two men and Iphy look at her. "Just listen. See if it happens. Every time I've been out here – just about now… There! Isn't that extraordinary?"

The others frown. They don't understand; they haven't noticed.

"The insects. The crickets, and the frogs," Electra explains. "Whatever they are, they all fall silent."

And they have, as though a switch has been thrown. Their warm, lulling buzz has gone, replaced by a deep dark silence save the rustle of palm fronds like the distant crackling of a campfire. "Always the same time. Like it's suddenly their bedtime."

From somewhere in the grounds comes the bark of a dog.

"Interesting," says Nikos, rolling the cigar between his fingers, drawing in its aroma. "I'd never noticed that before."

"How so? Interesting, I mean?" Electra asks.

"Well, I'm sure it's just coincidence, but it was about this time that Douka burned down. Or rather, when the fire started. That's what they say, anyway."

Iphy shivers, gathers the shawl around her shoulders. "Well, if it's bedtime for the bugs, they've got the right idea," she says. "Because it's bedtime for me, too."

"And me," says Electra. "Once men light their cigars, our moment is gone. We've been dismissed." She pushes away from the table, goes to Nikos, bends down to kiss his head. He reaches up, pats the hand on his shoulder.

"We won't be long," she hears Vassi tell Iphy.

"Tell it to the angels," Iphy whispers.

Sometimes, when Electra brushes her teeth, she thinks of steam trains. It's the brush in her mouth that makes her think of them; the sound of the bristles against her teeth, in her cheeks, in her head. Like the old steam train she caught as a girl, from Stathmos Station, going up-country to stay with her aunt…

Choof-choof-choof, chuff-chuff-chuff…

And as she brushes, she can make the train go fast or slow. A game she plays; a game she enjoys. Memories.

She puts away the toothbrush, rinses with mouthwash and leans forward to spit it into the sink. And shivers. A rush of goosebumps racing across her back and shoulders and up into her hair, tightening the skin of her scalp. And she realises then that the taste of the mouthwash is different. Not minty and antiseptic, but sweet and creamy. Like overripe mangoes. Sticky. Cloying. Maybe it's the drugs, she thinks, sliding her tongue over her lips, across her teeth. Or rather the lack of them. Maybe not taking her medication after all this time has started to affect her sense of taste.

And then she remembers being pregnant with Mantó. For the last few weeks of her pregnancy she couldn't bear the taste of mangoes – her favourite fruit – and even now she can't quite make up her mind about them. They bring back the memory of her swollen stomach, and the weight of it, and they make her sad.

She licks her lips again, sucks at her teeth.

And, in an instant, the taste of mangoes has gone.

Minty and antiseptic, just as it should be.

From the pitch black of sleep, at a little after three in the morning, Electra and Nikos are woken by a thunderous hammering on their bedroom door.

"Niko! Ella! It's Vassi. I need help. Iphy's not well. I mean really not well. We need to call a doctor."

When they get to Vassi and Iphy's bedroom, it's clear that help is definitely needed. Iphy is on the bed, curled up on her side, arms crossed over her chest, hands gripping her shoulders. She is groaning and shaking, white as a sheet and, like the bedspread, pillows, floor and rug, she is covered in a creamy, speckled spill of vomit. Her hair, her cheeks, her arms… There are bunched towels around her which Vassi has used to clear up the mess, or as much of it as he can. Now, snatching at one of them, Iphy clamps it to her mouth as a new swell of sick surges out of her.

"I'm so sorry… So sorry," she whispers, when the hurling allows. Then she throws up again, a great liquid flood that drowns her words and spatters onto the tiled floor.

"Wrap her up," says Nikos. "It'll be quicker to drive her ourselves. Ella, call the hospital and let them know we're on the way. Vassi, I'll meet you downstairs."

And ten minutes later, Electra watches the Jeep's headlights cut through the trees as Nikos heads for the hospital with Vassi and Iphy in the back seat.

Standing in the doorway, she feels Dimi's small, hot hand slide into hers. Somewhere a dog is barking.

"Is everything alright, Mama…? Because there's a really, really bad smell upstairs."

"I thought you were dying."

"Me, too. I can't tell you… I was so frightened." Iphy is lying in bed, on the second floor of the hospital in Navros. It is Saturday morning, just a few hours later.

"And I feel so ashamed! How terrible! The mess… I am so, so sorry. Will you ever forgive me? The bed, the linen. That beautiful wood floor."

"Next time I'll put you in a tent in the garden."

"At least there's going to be a next time… I certainly don't deserve one. Even a tent."

"So what does the doctor say?"

"That there's not the slightest thing wrong with me, would you believe? Something I ate, though I can't believe it. And we all had exactly the same. But just in case, Vassi's booked me in for a check-up when we get back to Athens. We're taking the evening ferry."

"You're leaving tonight?"

Iphy sighs. "I feel so guilty…"

"But you must stay with us, until you're quite better. Surely…"

"I'd rather be home, darling Ella. You know? In my own bed. In case…" She reaches out a hand, and Electra takes it. Cold and small and bony. "I just wouldn't feel comfortable… I couldn't bear it happening again."

"I understand, of course I do. But that doesn't mean I won't miss you both horribly."

And so it is that Iphy and Vassi take the evening ferry for the mainland, Nikos calling ahead to arrange a taxi for them on the other side.

On their drive back to Douka, Dimi, in the back seat, asks, "Will the house smell for a long time?"

12

COLD TURKEY. Electra wonders if that is what it is. Coming off the medication. The Tropsodol, the Chlorsodyl, and Heripsyn. Not just taste, and the occasional lightheadedness, but other things. Little things. Surprising her. Like her memory. She'll go to pick up her pen, only to find it isn't where she could have sworn she'd left it. Same with her phone. She wants to call Nikos or a friend, and she can't find her cell; turns the place upside down looking for it, then finds it in the least likely places. Places where she can't remember putting it. The knife drawer in the kitchen, on a bookshelf in the library, under her pillow or duvet, between a pile of towels in their linen cupboard; as though it's been deliberately hidden.

And it's not just phone or pen. Sometimes it's her bag, or her cigarettes, or her lighter, or laptop, or car keys. Never where she thinks they are, where she thinks she left them. Sometimes she feels like an old woman struggling with early-stage dementia. It has to be the drugs, she decides. Coming off them. Not taking them anymore. It has to be. She isn't old. She isn't going senile. Not yet anyway. And not any time soon, she hopes.

She's not the only one forgetting where she put things. Dimi is just as bad. His Play-Station controller, his iPad charger, the TV remote, his goggles, his snorkel. And just like he is in Athens, he's always forgetting to turn off the lights when he leaves a room, or the TV when he isn't watching it. Or, more unsettling after the scare with the floor tiles, the taps in his bathroom. The only difference is that in Athens he'll take the scoldings. Accept the blame. But on Pelatea, he'll argue the toss. "I did switch it off, I did so. I promise. I promise I did."

Which irritates Electra, that he should lie to her when he is clearly in the wrong. And every time he denies it, saying it's not him, answering back – stubborn, implacable, just like his father – it always makes matters worse. The argument escalates. They both lose their tempers. Twice she's sent him to bed early, and twice he's stomped away, up the stairs, down the corridor, slamming his bedroom door.

Now there is trouble with the car.

Where, before, any problems seemed restricted to the house – the burst pipe, the electrics, the plaster, the raised tiles, and items going missing – now they centre on the Jeep.

Small things to begin with.

The starter motor is the first to play up.

One morning, when Electra turns on the ignition, the three-litre engine whinnies and whines, hiccoughing its way to a final resentful contact like an old man loosening phlegm in his throat.

When she takes it to the garage in Anémenos, the old mechanic, Sotiris, listens to what she tells him, takes the key from her, tucks a paper cloth over the front seat leathers and slides in on top of it.

Six times he switches the engine on, and six times it catches perfectly, much to Electra's astonishment and embarrassment. Getting out of the Jeep, Sotiris sweeps the paper cloth from the seat, crumples it up, and gives her a look.

She knows that look. He's thinking, *Athenian*. But his smile is kindly, and he waves away her wallet; there is nothing to pay for.

Then, in a sudden shower of rain on her way back from visiting friends in Pecravi, the wipers start to shudder and stutter across the windscreen when before they slid over the glass with an oily, satisfying hum. And the rain – a fearful insistent drumming on the Jeep's roof and bonnet – is suddenly impossible to clear, smearing the sloping, twisting road ahead.

Electra has to slow right down, peering anxiously through the noisy snorting of the wiper blades.

Then, as she pulls through Douka's gates, the shuddering stops, and the wipers behave as they should.

And the rain ceases as quickly as it started.

It is on their way to visit Theo in the hospice outside Navros, she and Dimi, that the Jeep throws its first real tantrum.

Winding up the slope towards Akronitsá the Jeep's engine seems to lose power. No matter how hard Electra presses the accelerator, the revs fail to respond. From fourth gear she drops to third and then second to maintain momentum, until finally she's pumping the clutch and grinding the gearstick into the slot for first. When they reach the pass in the hills the engine jerks wildly as though she's released the clutch too soon, and then dies with a wheezing grunt.

In the ticking silence that follows Electra grits her teeth and wonders what to do.

"Call Manolis," says Dimi. "He'll come and help us. Or Ariadne. Or Sotiris."

Rather than rely on Ariadne, or face another exchange with Sotiris, Electra phones Manolis and explains the problem. But he's out on his *caïque*, he tells her, taking tourists to Falirikón for a beach barbecue. Electra's heart drops. But Manolis promises he will call his cousin, Christos, in Calamotí, and get him to help her. No more than an hour, he promises.

So Electra and Dimi settle down to wait, lowering their windows, then opening their doors to bring in some cool air. Then they get out of the car, and Electra sits on the verge, her back against a low stone wall, in the shadow beneath a line of whispering tamarisk. As usual Dimi starts lifting stones with the toe of his sandal, looking for scorpions. Then he finds a stick and starts rustling it through the weeds; poking at holes in the wall. A lizard scuttles out, but no scorpions. Undeterred, Dimi continues with his search, moving along the side of the road. Electra watches him, smiling fondly.

Maybe she dozes there, on the roadside, closes her eyes for a moment, but in an instant she is awake. She has heard a sharp cry, and looks around for Dimi. He is nowhere to be seen.

Getting to her feet, she calls out, "Dimi! Di-miiii?"

But there is no reply, just a rising hum from a grove of wild olives further down the slope. Followed by the sound of someone running frantically through the trees towards her. And a screaming familiar voice.

"Mama! Mama! Quickly! Quick, quick!"

And there is Dimi, dashing into the road and turning uphill towards her. Running. Waving his stick and screaming for her to get into the car.

Which, of course, she doesn't do.

But then she sees something behind Dimi, a dark shadow following him out onto the road and rising over him in a heaving swirling cloud above the treetops; like starlings dancing in an evening sky.

And the hum is louder now. And angry.

Bees, thousands of them. Millions, maybe. All of them coming after Dimi in a shifting brown swarm; the hum turning to an ugly, aggressive buzz that grows louder as they gain on Dimi; his hands waving the air, slapping away the first of the bees that have caught up with him.

Electra leaps into the car, closes the windows, and looks back to see Dimi just a few metres away; tiring now, slapping more vigorously.

And then he is in the car, breathless, slamming the door shut, as the swarm surrounds the Jeep. Covering the windscreen and side windows like a moving pelt of fur, searching for a way in, clustering in corners as though their will and their weight will shatter the glass and allow them access. And revenge.

"What did you do, Dimi? What did you do?" asks Electra, remembering now the line of hives in a clearing just a few metres from the road.

"I didn't do anything, Mama. I promise."

"But you must have done something to make them so angry," she insists, certain that it's Dimi's fault.

"Nothing. I didn't go near them. But then, suddenly, I heard them start buzzing and I could see them coming out of the hives… So, I just ran... Back to the road. And they followed…"

"Are you stung?"

He shakes his head. "Just a bit scared. I thought they'd catch up with me."

"They nearly did," says Electra. "But you're safe now."

By the time Christos arrives from Calamotí, there's no sign of the bees. Not a single one. But Electra and Dimi stay in the car until he knocks on the driver's window.

Of course, once again, the car starts immediately, the engine roars into rich lubricated life, and Christos accepts Electra's apologies with a puzzled expression.

13

"HE'S BEEN troubled."

"Troubled?" asks Electra. She has left Dimi at the old Contalidis house after Lysander offered to take him fishing for octopus with his son, Kostis. The boy was still nervous from the bees, and when he clambered out of the car he'd looked around as though the swarm might have followed them down from the hills.

"Not himself," the nurse continues, glancing back at Electra as they climb the hospice stairs, their footfalls echoing emptily in the stairwell. The air is still and stale, and smells of the old. "Well, you know what I mean. Not how he usually is."

Beyond the barred landing window Electra can see a spread of flat white rooftops and the silvery glitter of the sea beyond.

"Usually, he is very easy," the nurse says, as she turns for the last flight.

"And now he's not?"

"The last few weeks. Night-time is the worst. We just can't get him to sleep. So restless. But he's had his lunch now, so you might find him a little dozy."

At the top of the stairs, the nurse turns right and leads Electra past a line of closed doors. On each door is the Christian name of the occupant – Anna, Chrisas, Stavros – written in chalk on a black tile in a metal bracket. Above each bracket is a small viewing window. They are like cells on a prison corridor, thinks Electra, except for the paintings between each door – fishing boats, an olive tree, a village street – and on a table at the end of the passage a vase of wild flowers.

Theo Contalidis's room is the last on the corridor. The nurse knocks on the door, opens it, and steps aside for Electra.

"Just push the bell beside the bed if you need anything."

Electra thanks her, and the door closes behind her with a soft click.

Because it's on a corner Theo's room has two windows, both of them barred like the landing windows. One looks out over the town's rooftops to the sea, the other onto the car park and a slope of yellowing grass. Above a line of terraced olive trees edging this parched spread of lawn Electra can see the distant ridges of the Akronitsá hills that she's just driven across from Douka. A jagged outline; a soft blue in the distance.

Two chairs have been drawn up beside the window overlooking the town and Nikos's father sits in one of them; a soft plaid blanket tucked around his legs, a blue suit jacket over a striped pyjama top. His head is tipped a little to one side, lips slightly parted. A walking stick stands against a cast-iron radiator beneath the window.

Electra sits beside him, drops her bag to the floor and reaches for his hand, strokes the skin with her fingertips. It soothes him, she knows.

"*Kalimera, Papou,*" she says. She has always called him the more familiar *Papou*, just like Nikos. The same way she addressed her own father. Using it with Theo always makes her think of him.

"I'm not sleeping," the old man says in a frail voice, and his fingers tighten around her hand. "I won't sleep. I daren't sleep."

Electra squeezes his hand back. "I know, they told me. But you really should, you know. Everyone needs their sleep." As she knows so well herself. She looks at the hand in hers, the skin smooth and puckered pink over the knuckles. From the fire at Douka. A matching strip of burned skin runs from the top of his right ear, across his cheek and into the collar of his pyjama top. The tightening scar pulls at the corner of his mouth and gives his speech a rough slur, as though he's been drinking. It also puts a slant on his right eye, its centre dark and black and curious, the eye itself loosely hammocked in a fleshy weeping red.

"They keep giving me injections…"

"To help you sleep. The nurse told me."

"But I don't want to sleep. I told you. Why don't any of you pay attention, and do what I ask?" He pulls his hand free from hers, digs it under the blanket and pulls out a handkerchief; bunches it with bent fingers, and wipes at the bad eye. His middle and index fingers are stained a vibrant nicotine yellow and there's a dull gold spot on the pad of his thumb from years of tapping the filter. There is no smoking at the hospice, and Electra wonders if he misses it. But perhaps he's forgotten about cigarettes, just as he's forgotten so much else?

The more the old man wipes his eye, the more agitated he seems to become, muttering to himself. She hadn't expected this quite so soon. Maybe now a cigarette would calm him. She reaches down and picks up her tote, pulls out a paper bag. "I brought you some figs from the garden."

"The garden?"

"At Douka. The figs are wonderful now."

At last Theo puts down the handkerchief and tips back his head, as though better to see the fruit Electra is offering.

"I love figs," he says, and sounds, suddenly, like Dimi. Like a greedy little boy.

"I know. That's why I chose them. They weren't quite ready when Niko came to see you, so he brought the peaches instead."

"Niko?"

"Niko. You know, Nikos?"

Theo nods, but she can see he doesn't recognise the name. Electra wonders for a moment if he knows who she is.

"He had to go back to Athens," she continues, splitting the fig between her fingers and handing it to him. "For work. He said to give you his love."

The old man takes the fruit, lifts it to his mouth and sucks in the pulp. When he's done, a cluster of seeds clings to the corner of his burned lip. He looks around with the emptied fig skin in his hand. Somewhere to put it. Electra reaches for a tissue, wipes away the seeds at the corner of his mouth, then takes the fig from him, wraps it in the tissue, and drops it back in the paper bag.

"I'll put the rest by your bed," she tells him, and she rises from her chair.

Which is when he grabs her arm, pulls her down towards him. Close enough for her to smell the warm, sweet scent of the fig on his breath.

"Is he there? In the house? Have you seen him?"

"No, he's in Athens. I told you. At the office, for work."

"Then he'll be back soon," he says, and lets go of her arm. "When he's finished with me. Then you'll be for it."

The old man starts to laugh.

A slow, breathless cackle, like a door creaking open.

Without humour. Cold and dry.

"He's back on Friday," Electra says, rubbing her arm as she walks to the bed. He might be old and losing it, she thinks, tipping the remaining figs into a bowl on the bedside table, but he still has some strength in him.

A real Contalidis.

Right till the end.

Three months in the Acute Burns Unit in Athens' Hygieia Clinic; a shuttered, air-conditioned room sealed from the traffic four floors below on Erythrou Stavrou Street. Two months' convalescence in the clinic at Maroussi; a garden suite this time, with a sliding glass door and a small terrace hung with purple jacaranda. And now, back on Pelatea, in his corner room at the Navros hospice.

Clean, comfortable rooms, thinks Electra as she drives back into town, and caring staff. But just rooms, and just nursing staff. Not home, and not family. After almost a lifetime at Douka, this is where the old man ends up. No wonder he feels bitter. Because that's what he is, she decides. Somewhere deep down inside him there's a dark, restless pit of bitterness and resentment. His smile thin and lopsided, cruel and sarcastic, and his laugh that nasty, humourless cackle.

And who can blame him, she thinks? Her father-in-law may eat the figs and the peaches that she and Nikos bring from the gardens at Douka, but he knows as well as they do that he will never again see the trees they grow on, the trees he once tended.

This thought gives Electra a sharp and unexpected stab of guilt. That she is the one returning to that glorious house, while Theo lies in a room no larger than their linen store.

Maybe it's just as well his memory is fading, his mind going. Nodding with fatigue when she leaves him, still carrying on about how much trouble she's going to be in when Nikos returns; that there's nothing she can do about it, she'll just have to face it.

Whatever he means by that.

It had been different with her own father. A flick of the fingers and he was gone, at his birthday lunch; brought down in seconds when his heart gave out. Raising his glass one minute, the next face down in a smashed soup plate. Right there, at the table; a chilled *avgolomeno* soaking into his beard and dripping into his lap. A dozen or more people, frozen; looking in astonishment at the balding, freckled circle on the top of his head and the curiously slumped shoulders; his last breaths bubbling through the spilled soup.

Electra tries to remember who moved first. Her mother, she seems to recall, at the other end of the table. Taking a deep breath, before pushing back her chair to go to him, as if what she'd been fearing for so long had finally happened. No need to hurry. No need to take a pulse, or call emergency services.

The great Mikis Stamatos. Dead. No question.

The funeral at Apostólikou; his coffin in the family crypt.

Where would Theo end up, she wonders?

At Douka, is what he's told them a hundred times.

"*When I'm done with you all, and I'm just a stack of bones, build me into a wall among the olives. From there I'll be able to see the house and the sea. And I will be a happy ghost.*"

14

DIMI IS still out on the harbour breakwater with Lysander and Kostis when Electra calls at their house to pick him up. Lysander's mother, Alexandra, ushers her in, bustles ahead across stone-flagged floors; says they won't be long, that Lysander promised he'd be back with the boys by four. Another twenty minutes. Would Madam like some coffee? She has just brewed some.

It is the first time Electra has been alone with Alexandra, and out of politeness she accepts, takes the seat she is shown to. At a round metal table on a balcony overlooking a cobbled courtyard that smells of cut wood, varnish, and shavings, its high wood doors bolted shut, its stone skirtings painted with a light blue border in the island style.

Once the Admiral's carriage had clattered into this yard, his horses stabled in the low building on the right, which the carpenter, Lysander, has turned into his workshop. Electra knows about the stables. She has read the Admiral's diaries. As well as his horses, he kept his treasures there: an octant, telescope, and charts, sails and rope and canvas, grappling hooks, powder and cannon. A sea-going storeroom. Everything he would need on his voyages. She looks down at the courtyard through a trellis of jasmine, tries to imagine him there, in his flowing crimson topcoat and knee-high boots; his red beard, his sashed waistband, and *vraka* breeches.

"And how is dear Theo?" asks Alexandra, putting two white china cups on the table. Steam rising from the coffee, its surface glistening with a cluster of coppery bubbles. Without waiting for an answer, she goes back into the kitchen and returns with two glasses of water.

Electra sips the coffee, tastes its sweetness, chews the grounds in her teeth. "He is… comfortable," she replies, reaching for the water. "But he is old…"

Alexandra nods and sips, puts the cup back on the table. Takes some water, too. "He was a good man. He always wanted the best for everyone. A real Contalidis. Trying to build that cannery, just to make life easier for us all back then." She shakes her head. "And that Petrou. Taking the house. It broke the man's heart, it did. Killed his wife."

"Did you know Petrou?" asks Electra, for something to say. She has heard all there is to hear about the man; from Nikos, from Theo. But, like the journalist she once was, she asks out of habit, and curiosity, as well as politeness. There is always more to learn if you search for it.

Alexandra grunts, glances around as though Petrou himself might be listening. Then she looks at Electra.

"Everyone knew Petrou. Looked like all the other old men, you know? Dirty old shirt, dark suit. A good-looking man when he was young, like they all are; but the last few years gone to seed, fat as a puffer fish," she says, lowering her chin and blowing out her cheeks to show what she means. "And stooped at the end, with dark little eyes that squinted at you, took your measure. And loose hands; oh, you wouldn't believe. A goat, he was." Alexandra gives a brisk *tsk-tsk* of disapproval. "And a drunk, too. A sot." The old lady purses her lips, straightens her cuffs. Eyes to the table, eyebrows up. "He'd been drinking, so they say, the night he died. The Contalidis wine. They say he drank it like water. All those harvests, and the joke was he polished most of it off by himself. Drowned himself in it, you'll hear some people say," and she chuckles, as though she agrees with them; one of their number. "Lost his balance, he did. Took a fall, and that was that. Though there's some," she continues, working a finger under her collar, "who'll tell you he didn't do it all by himself."

But before Electra has a chance to find out more about Alexandra's suggestion, the front door bangs open and Dimi is running down the hallway to the kitchen balcony, the bees forgotten.

"Mama, Mama," he yells. "Look, look… I caught an octopus." He slaps a plastic bag on the table, rattling the cups, and the handles fall open. And Electra sees the same bundle of mottled grey flesh she'd imagined in that clinic in Lycabettus.

The sun is low when they get back to Douka, the limestone walls of the house glowing gold in the late afternoon light. Sun glinting off windows and copper downpipes, the sea above the treetops a restless amber quilt. The air is warm and scented, and the garden trills with the drilling hiss of insects.

"Can we cook it for supper?" asks Dimi, swinging the carrier bag as they walk towards the house. "Kostis told me how. Can we light the barbecue? That's the best way to do it. That's what Kostis said."

"Of course, you can. Grilled octopus… yummy," says a distracted Electra. She had tried to persuade Dimi to leave the bag and its contents with Lysander and Kostis, but the boy would not be moved. So it has come home with them, on Dimi's lap, strapped in with him, wobbling on every turn. And as he tells her for the hundredth time how he'd caught the beast, hauling it from its home among the harbour pilings, all Electra can do is gulp back the gagging that rises in her throat. That rounded bulge in the plastic bag. Its rank, rotting, seabed smell.

But the barbecue won't light. There is gas enough, and the previous evening it had worked just fine. But not tonight.

"We could build a fire," Dimi suggests.

"Why don't you grill it in the kitchen. Just the tentacles."

Dimi thinks about this, frowns. "Will you chop them off for me?" he asks.

Electra shudders. “Didn’t Lysander or Kostis tell you how to do it? It can’t be that difficult. And *Baba* will be very proud when he hears about it. Catching and cooking your very own octopus. A real Contalidis.”

So Dimi slices off the eight suckered arms with the sharpest knife he can find, and lays them out under the grill; goes on tiptoe to watch the withered tentacles wave, spit, and shrivel.

Standing by the open kitchen door, Electra lights a cigarette to cover the smell of burning flesh; swallows another mouthful of wine to settle herself.

“Shall I throw the rest of it away?” asks Dimi, holding up the bag.

“Outside, in the bin,” Electra manages. “And tie a knot in the bag.”

15

THE FOLLOWING day Electra's mother arrives on the island by helicopter. It is the only option if she is to visit Douka. Gina Stamatos cannot bear to be near water. Stand her in a puddle, Electra and her sister Yianna always joke, and she'd probably be seasick. So the family firm, Stamatos Stone, has chartered the flight for her. Delivery to a patch of level waste ground outside Pelépsos where Theo's cannery was meant to stand, and pick-up from the same spot three days later. Which suits Electra. Pelépsos is closer to Douka than Navros, and the place suitably discreet – she hates to think what the islanders might say at such a conspicuous display of wealth when the country is so deeply troubled. The chopper sets down in a cloud of dust shortly before midday, but only when the rotors are turning at idle and the dust has settled does her mother appear. The cabin door slides open, a small set of steps are lowered, and she climbs down; sees Electra and Dimi, and waves.

"Go on then," says Electra, now that the rotor blades have almost stopped, and pushes Dimi forward (she's been terrified of helicopters since she heard the story of the man who gets out of one, drops to a knee to hug his five year-old son, and then hoists the boy high into the air, forgetting the spinning blades).

Dimi is off like a shot, running to his grandmother, hugging her waist, and then offering to carry her bag. Such a little gentleman, thinks Electra, but it'll be heavier than he thinks. A three-day stay means at least nine changes of clothes for her mother, which means a case too heavy for a ten-year old to manage. Instead, a member of the crew brings it to the car and tips it into the boot.

Gina loves the house, says how clever Nikos is, and is enchanted by everything she sees, everything Electra shows her. For the next three days, she is the most wonderful company. She plays patiently with Dimi, goes searching with him for lizards and scorpions, and doesn't once ask Electra how she's feeling; avoiding any direct mention of the recent breakdown. It's done, it's gone, now let's get on with things is the way Gina thinks. But she doesn't say that either.

It is only at lunch on the last day that that she speaks her mind.

"It's a beautiful house to be sure, but a sad house too," she says, fitting a cigarette into a silver holder, flicking her lighter. "Don't you feel it?"

Electra is surprised. "Not at all. What do you mean, sad?"

"It's what your grandmother would have called a house of spirits; too many of them."

"There's a lot of history here, Mama. If there are spirits, it's just echoes."

Gina shrugs in a *suit-yourself* manner, waves a jewelled hand, blows out a plume of smoke. "Beautiful, as I say, no question. But…" she shakes her head. "But I don't think I would want to live here." And then, leaning closer to Electra, she says, "Do you know, last night, I got out of bed to go to the bathroom and it was as if… as if I could almost feel those tiny wood tiles actually moving under my feet. Shifting. Like water. Would you believe it?" she says. "Lucky I wasn't seasick."

16

THE NIGHT-DUTY nurse is at her station, shoes off, stockinged feet on a chair, and is playing backgammon on her cell phone. It is a few minutes before three in the morning, and dark in the hospice hallway, the only lights a dim caged bulb outside the front entrance and the Anglepoise on her desk, pointed to one side so that she can better see the screen of her mobile and the roll of the dice. She is playing against the computer, and decides that the computer and her husband have the same kind of luck – always those handy doubles when the counters are gathered in columns on their home board. One double after another, just like her husband, and only three of her counters taken off. Still a dozen to go – a chance to catch up – but she knows the computer will beat her easily. Her dice are thrown for her, rolling across the screen – a three and a one – but there's no time to make her move.

From somewhere above comes a low, metallic, clattering sound that steadily grows in volume, carried like a strident echo along empty water pipes, amplified and overlapping by the time it reaches the three radiators in the reception hall.

For a moment she can't think what it is. And then she knows. Old man Contalidis again, dragging his stick across the ribs of his radiator. A dozen or more times so far this week, but somehow louder now. More urgent. If she doesn't get up there quickly, he'll have the whole place awake and groaning. If the racket hasn't roused them already. Why he never presses his bell, she'll never know…

Putting aside her phone, she goes to the medicine cabinet and removes a phial of Anavalium from the top shelf; strips the sterile wraps from a syringe and hypodermic and, fixing the two components together, pierces the phial's plastic cover with the needle. This fast-acting anaesthetic is only prescribed for use in those cases where patients need to be sedated quickly, for their own safety. And this, the nurse decides, is one of those occasions – regardless of her patient's safety. Suitably armed, she slips on her shoes, comes around the desk and makes for the stairs. She'll get him back in bed, slide in the needle, and he'll quieten in an instant. Sixty seconds and he'll be out for the count.

By the time she reaches the second floor landing the rattling is thunderous, echoing from every pipe and radiator the length of the corridor. Yet not a single light has come on in any of the rooms she passes; no sounds of complaint from any of her other patients. It is as if they still sleep, undisturbed by this ungodly clamour, louder and more insistent than the hospice fire alarm.

At the end of the corridor, she pushes open the old man's door, and reaches for the light switch.

And in the instant the light comes on, the rattling from the radiators stops.

Silence, a deep echoing silence.

So deep a silence that she can almost hear the beats of her heart. And certainly feel them.

And then she sees something that makes her frown; something that tightens the skin on her scalp; something that sends an icy puzzling shiver down her spine.

The old fellow's walking stick hangs from the wardrobe door handle, just as they leave it every night when they settle him down.

And its owner is in his bed. Just his head and shoulders showing above the sheet. Just as they'd left him. Securely tucked in.

But his face…

Now the nurse gasps.

The old eyes of Theo Contalidis are wide open. Wide, wide open. So wide that the nurse can see the globed roundness of the eyeballs. As though the eyes have somehow been pushed from their sockets, drawn out of his head. Staring up at the light she's just switched on.

And his mouth…

Thin red lips bared over clenched yellow teeth, bubbling white spittle sliding a silvery course down his chin, the breath hissing out of him.

17

"A STROKE, Niko. A bad one. That's what they say."

A low sigh. Resignation. Something expected, but still unwanted.

"I'll come home."

"There's no point, my darling. And you've got too much going on. They moved him from the hospice to the general hospital this morning, and I went with him to make sure he was properly settled. He'll be in good hands there."

On the end of the line Electra can hear the sound of traffic, the beeping of car horns. Her husband is out on the street. In Athens. Kolonaki? Diomexédes? At his office in Pangrati? And she feels a sudden pang, a desire to be there with him. Not here, on this island, alone with Dimi.

"If you're sure," he says. "Can you last until tomorrow? I'll get Manolis to pick me up early."

"Of course I can. And there's really nothing you can do." And then, "Apparently he's had these strokes before, did you know that?" The Contalidis family doctor, Fotis Paradoxis, had explained everything to Electra that morning, after the transfer.

For that is what it is. A massive haemorrhagic incident that has pretty much buckled the old man's brain. That is the word the doctor used. Buckled. The seventh incident he is aware of, though none of them as critical as this one.

"Paradoxis told me," says Nikos. "Four or five, after the old man moved back to the house. They think it's how the fire started."

"But you never noticed, did you?"

"No one did. Sometimes he was just a little slow on the uptake, or he slurred a bit, as though he'd been drinking. Which he liked to do, if you remember?"

"Well, Dr Paradoxis says this one is far worse. Although his eyes are open, it's impossible to tell if he's taking anything in. He doesn't even blink. Just looks right through you. And not a word. No apparent ability, or even desire, to communicate. He's just… sealed away, and they don't know if he'll ever come back." And then, softly, "I'm so sorry, my darling."

So it is that Nikos comes home early that Friday, calling in at the hospital after Electra picks him up from the harbour. She tells Nikos she'll stay in the car, that he should go in by himself, that she's brought along a book to read. But she manages only a few pages before she looks up and sees Nikos coming down the hospital steps, heading in her direction.

"You were right," he says, leaning against her door. "He didn't know who I was. I don't think he even saw me." Nikos clears his throat, wipes an eye.

"And I so wanted him to visit the house, you know? Now that it's finished; to see what I've done to it. I should have got him out there sooner. But he never seemed to want to. Always saying he wasn't up to it. A touch of flu, dizziness, a tricky ankle. I'll come out next time, he'd say. But of course he never did. And now?"

"You did all you could. You couldn't have tried harder."

Nikos takes a breath, casts a look around the parking lot. "You want me to drive?" he asks.

"I'm fine. Unless you want to?"

"No. Just get me home."

It is a quiet evening. A light supper, the News on TV – demonstrations against austerity cuts, against Brussels, crowds and flares and police lines in Syntagma; Electra suddenly glad she is here – and then Nikos goes to bed.

Left on her own Electra pours herself a final drink, a splash of Cointreau cracking the ice, and curls up on a sofa in the library; picks up her book, finds her place. A history of the siege of Nafplio. A dry read that has so far made no mention of the Admiral. After just a few pages she puts the book down in her lap and thinks of the old sea dog. Coming back to the family home, planting his garden, living out his last years here on the headland of Douka. In his nineties when he died. A long, long life.

She thinks, then, of all the other Contalidis; the ones who followed him. Boys, always boys: his son Diomedes, and his grandson Theodoros, named after the freedom fighter Theodoros Kolokotronis; followed by Giorgios, the two brothers, Leonidas and Dimitrios, Theo, and Nikos. Their portraits, with the exception of Nikos, lining the corridor upstairs. The Admiral himself – the largest of the paintings – in his tasselled jacket, hand on the jewelled hilt of a curved scimitar, with the sloping battlements of Palamidi smoking behind him; his son, Diomedes, with his father's thick walrus moustache, at the helm of a ship; a booted Theodoros, windswept hair, in the saddle of a rearing horse; Giorgios, as a naval officer; a youthful Leonidas, clutching a handful of order papers, speaking in the Senate; Dimitrios, as an old man, in a winged white collar and pinned cravat, sitting at the Admiral's desk, some document in his hand; and Theo, bright-eyed and smiling, in open-necked shirt and belted trousers, his hand on a globe, a world to conquer. This old house their home, where they all grew up, where they lived; and where, except for Leonidas who died in Athens – and Theo – they spent their last days.

And their wives, of course. Smaller portraits, in oval gilt frames. All islanders, all the best families, facing their husbands across the corridor: the Admiral's fearsome wife, Eleni Dimitriou, with a musket across her lap; Despina Papandreas, black berry eyes, chubby-armed, pink-cheeked, in a cream crocheted shawl; Athina Ellinaki, with swaddled baby Giorgios in her arms; Angeliki Tsakiri, a tortoiseshell comb holding back a tumble of lustrous ruby-hued hair; Panagiota Stavroula, in lace collar, stern and unsmiling; the elegantly coiffed Anthoula Kavarnou, in a ball gown, with a fan in her hand, pearls at her throat and wrist; and Theo's wife, the young and glamorous Kalliopi Efstathiou, in a striped gardener's apron, sitting on the terrace at Douka, with a trug of flowers at her feet, the only wife who didn't die here.

Her mother was right, thinks Electra, finishing her drink. It is indeed a house of spirits, generations of departed Contalidis; and she feels them around her, feels their warmth. Imagines them moving through these ancient rooms, the soft whispered sounds of their passing; crinolines and boots; the distant echo of their voices, young and old.

Everyone who ever lived here, within these stone walls.

Except Petrou, and Petrou's nephew.

Of the late Petrou, Electra has no image. Nothing. All she knows of the man, she has learned from Theo and Nikos – his lechery and treachery, his envy and his greed. And the only physical description she has is from Lysander's mother, Alexandra. Fat as a puffer fish, she'd said. And Electra sees straining buttons and double chins; and eyes, black and beady; a stooping figure…

The book falls from Electra's lap and she wakes with a start.

She is cold and she shivers, rubs her arms as she gets to her feet. She looks at her watch. A little after eleven. She can't have been asleep for long.

Somewhere out in the grounds a dog barks.

She switches out the lights in the library and hallway, and climbs the stairs to bed.

18

ELECTRA hears him, first.

Somewhere to her left, among the olives. A dry, insistent chip chipping of stone. She's just finished her morning run to Anémenos, and is on her way home. She's decided to walk the last kilometre and has taken out her ear buds, letting them swing against her thigh as she walks. The morning is clear and warm and silent save her footsteps. No insect buzz, no bird song. All hers. That's when she hears him.

Electra stops, and looks up the slope. The olive trees are low and thin limbed but their sheer number and thick foliage are enough to limit any view. So she comes off the road, scrambles up the bank, and looks again, peering through the twisting branches, past the silvery leaves. That chip-chip sound is up ahead, just out of sight. For a moment she thinks of turning back. Dimi will be up and looking for breakfast. She doesn't have time to waste. But she carries on, just a couple more trees, a few more metres. And as she climbs away from the road, the sound grows louder, the chip-chipping now replaced by a series of stony *thunks*, and the chatter of falling grit and earth. She knows she's close.

And then she sees him. On his knees, shirtless. A section of walled terracing has collapsed, and he is working the stones back into the rooty earth of the slope. Chipping the stones to shape, patching them into the wall.

She pauses then, watches. His tanned back wide and strong, muscles sliding beneath the brown skin as he reaches forward, forcing a fallen stone into the crumbling soil. Then sitting back on his heels, dusting off his hands. Which is when he senses he is not alone, that someone is there, behind him, and he swings round, sees her; deep brown eyes latching on to hers, a curl of black hair flopping across his brow.

If he hadn't turned and seen her, Electra would have left him to it, heading back down the slope as silently as she had come. That's what she'd decided to do, the moment she discovered what the chip-chip sound was. But now that he is looking at her, she'll have to say something. It's her olive grove, after all.

"*Kalimera*. I heard the chipping," she begins, thumbing over her shoulder to the road below them. "Thought I'd see what it was."

She is suddenly aware of her appearance. Her blonde hair knotted and awry. A dark line of sweat down the front of her grey t-shirt, between her breasts. The revealing gap between the hem of her t-shirt and the waistband of her sweatpants. The way the sweatpants have caught and ridden up and now cling stickily between her thighs, from the run and the climb through the olives. As far as she can tell, he hasn't taken his eyes from hers. But still… She feels strangely exposed, vulnerable.

He swings up off his heels and faces her, pushing back the curl of hair from his brow. In his late twenties or early thirties, she guesses. The boots, the thick cotton work trousers, a black leather belt cinching them at the waist. And bare-chested. Beautifully bare-chested, with a smear of creamy stone dust across the shiny brown ridges of his stomach where he must have wiped a hand. She tries hard not to let her own eyes stray.

He smiles, shrugs, but says nothing.

So she carries on, to fill the silence, to cover her embarrassment. "Are you from the village? From Anémenos?"

"No. Over there," he replies, pointing past her towards the house, presumably to the small settlement of Kalypti beyond the Douka headland. His voice is warm and friendly, a man who is sure and certain of himself. He gestures back to the wall. "It needs doing. The roots should be covered."

"Of course… So, thank you." She makes to turn, gives him a friendly smile, and raises a hand to wave. "I'd better be getting back," she says. And then, looking at the broken wall; just a hammer, chisel, a wood-handled trowel. "Do you have something to drink, to eat? Out here?" She realises she hasn't seen a van or a car parked anywhere. "It's getting hot already."

"It is fine, thank you. I am all right."

"I'll send one of the girls over with something," (Lina, the plain one, she thinks.) "Some water, some coffee…"

She waves again and starts to turn. Which is when the tip of an olive branch strokes across her cheek and into her hair. Catches it, snags it, and holds it tight.

"Ouch, dammit…" How stupid she is, like a teenager. She can't believe it. And as she struggles to untangle her hair and free herself, she sees him come towards her.

"Excuse, please," he says, and putting his hands on her waist he steps in behind her, between her and the tree trunk. Raising the hands to tease the branch tip from her hair; those large, dusty hands that had been chipping at stone not five minutes before now brushing softly against the back of her head, his fingers in her hair, a forearm resting gently against her shoulder blade. That close. Close enough for her to smell him. A warm citrus scent, earthy.

And then he has her free.

"*Ecce*, it is done," he tells her, and he steps away, almost respectfully, holding out a hand to bring her clear.

She takes the hand, hard and calloused, and feels him draw her towards him.

"There," he says, and lets go of her hand. A nod, a gentle smile.

"*Eph'aristo poli*," she manages, pulling her hair tight around her head, smoothing it down. "Thank you so much. How silly of me." And dry-mouthed and breathless, she turns and makes her way back to the road.

As she clambers down the bank, she looks back, listens, and hears the chip-chip sound start up again. And wonders, again, if he'd noticed that line of sweat down the front of her t-shirt?

Wonders, too, if he had been able to smell her – as she had him?

And had he watched her walk away, looked at her body?

She shakes her head – what is she thinking? – and sets off for the house.

Dimi will be wondering where she is.

19

WHEN ELECTRA comes in to the kitchen from her run, the two girls from the village are giggling amongst themselves and Ariadne's expression is somewhere between a frown of disapproval and a rare, almost grandmotherly, smile.

"Did I miss something?" asks Electra, pouring herself a glass of water from the tap, looking at the two girls and then at Ariadne.

The old housekeeper shakes her head. "Nothing, Madam. It was just…" She gives an apologetic shrug. "Lina asked Master Dimi if he'd like some yoghurt and honey and he said–"

"I said I don't like bees, and I don't…" starts Dimi.

"Or, more accurately, you said you don't like bee spit. Is that it?"

There is a gurgle of suppressed laughter from the girls, but they can't hold it in. It doesn't take more than a few seconds for Electra and then Ariadne to join them. Dimi looks at them, perplexed.

"What?" he says, pouring another load of Coco-Nuts into a bowl while no one is watching, and reaching for the milk, "What?"

When they recover, Electra tells Lina about the young man working in the olive grove; that something should be sent out to him from the house and could she take it? Behind her back, Ariadne frowns.

"The olive grove, you say?" asks the housekeeper.

"That's right. Just inside the estate. On the Douka slope."

"And a wall was down?"

Electra nods, feels suddenly hot. A little breathless. Wonders if Ariadne notices? "He was fixing it."

"Someone from Anémenos, was it?"

"No, he said he was from Kalypti. Anyway," she says, turning back to Lina. "Could you be a darling and take him something?"

"Of course, milady."

After her shower Electra stays in her room, in her bed, pillows propped up behind her, working on her notes. But she finds it hard to concentrate. Sometimes she has to read the same page twice. Finds herself back in the olive grove. Caught in that branch, and his hands in her hair, his body against hers. The smell of him. When she catches herself thinking of him, she shakes her head and, with a *tsk-tsk*, tries to get on with her work. Really, Ella. Really!

It isn't until a little after midday that she closes her laptop and comes down for lunch in the kitchen garden with Nikos and Dimi. Aja has made the boy his favourite *spanakoppita*, the only way Electra knows to get her son to eat spinach, the thin green leaves concealed amongst layers of feta cheese and crispy, buttery filo pastry. Taking their plates to the table, feeling the welcome shade of the sailcloth above them, Electra sees Lina and Aja pulling on helmets, clambering onto their scooters for the ride back to Anémenos. Their work done.

"Did you find him, Lina?" she calls out.

The girl frowns.

"The man working in the olive grove, rebuilding the wall?" Electra reminds her.

Lina shakes her head. "I went out there while you were working. I took some bread and water and sausage, like you asked, but I couldn't find him. He wasn't there. No one was there."

Maybe he'd started early, finished the job and gone home, thinks Electra, stacking their lunch plates in the dishwasher. Or gone on somewhere else, to another job.

And yet…

There had still been so much for him to do. Such a large stack of stones piled on the ground beside him to fit back into the wall. He couldn't have finished the job that quickly, and left no sign of his being there. Electra had asked Lina about this, and she'd been quite certain. "No stones, Madam. I couldn't find anything."

And for no apparent reason Electra feels a flutter of unease. A sensation she can't quite explain. A coolness over her skin. The slightest puckering shiver. Because he had been there. Just where she'd told Lina. She is certain of it. No more than thirty metres from the path, near the lower gate to the house.

Had the girl misunderstood, and gone somewhere else?

Electra sighs, tries to catch her breath. She might be getting her taste back, and her sense of smell – the scent of the *sadap malam* and stephanotis growing stronger day by day – but maybe coming off the medication is causing other less familiar, less comforting side effects. The coolness, the sudden shivering, the occasional breathlessness. She should never have stopped taking the pills, she decides. She'll have a word with Paradoxis. Perhaps the time has come to review the medication, maybe lower the dosage. Start again.

And as she slots the last plate into its rack she senses someone behind her, spins round.

It is Nikos. "Sorry, Ella. I didn't mean to startle you. I'm going down to the beach. Dimi wants to ski. You want to join us?"

She shakes her head. "No, you two go ahead. I think I'll have a rest. I feel tired."

"Well, if you change your mind you know where to find us."

She leans up and kisses him lightly on the cheek. "Don't go out too far. And don't go too fast, you hear? He's only little."

"He's a Contalidis," he tells her, picking an apple from the fruit bowl and biting into it. "We're tougher than you think."

Upstairs, undressing, she hears their voices down in the garden; father and son, the pair of them heading for the beach. She goes to the window, and as she closes the shutters she sees them disappearing into the pines.

With the shutters closed, the bedroom is softened to a grey shade. Shifting, silent, timeless. The sheets on her bed cool and smooth, the pillows soft and giving. Outside she hears the distant drilling buzz of insects and, far beyond, the sound of a speedboat carving trails in the bay. Electra closes her eyes, a hand cupping her cheek; the way she likes to sleep.

She has taken no Heripsyn, but she dreams. The first time in a long time without the drug's help. Two separate dreams. Neither of which she is aware of dreaming. Just their formless memory when she wakes.

First of all her father coming to the room, crossing the spear-tip tiles. The soft slap of the jute soles of his espadrilles. The give of the mattress as he lowers himself down beside her. The soft weight and warmth of his hand on her arm, the smoothness of his palm, and his whispered words: "Take care, my princess; take care."

The second dream comes more slowly.

Another presence, not her father's. Someone else in her room. Someone in her bed, not sitting on its side. And then a weight on her chest, a rising heat between her legs. The need to move her hips, to buck and squirm. Yet, also, an unwillingness to engage. A holding back, not wanting to proceed. But, try as she might, there is no fighting it. No cooling the heat. An urge too strong to resist. And she feels the brush of stubble against her breasts, and a gentle coaxing hand between her thighs, easing their softness and smoothness and warmth aside. And slowly she lets them part, gives herself to it; wanting it now, not wanting it to stop; a rough plunging urgency that grows and grows until she gasps; a beading sweat on her lip, her brow. A head of tumbling black curls above her, arms locked tight, a firm muscled body held above hers; deep brown eyes cast down to look at their slapping, shuddering bellies. Smooth, sun-browned skin and broad shoulders, tightening sinews and catching breath. And all around her the scent of oranges, and earth, and dusty sweat.

And then, "*Ecce*, it is done," a voice tells her, and she feels him slide out of her, and away, and the weight is gone.

And she is awake.

And the bedroom door opens.

It is Nikos.

"Still sleeping?" he asks. "I didn't think you'd still be here."

He comes to the bed, puts a hand to her forehead. “You’re hot,” he says and sees the flushed cheeks and the trembling. “Are you okay?”

“I’m fine, just fine,” she replies, her throat thick with sleep, and smiles up at him. A guilty, close-call smile, as though she’d been doing something she shouldn’t have but getting away with it; relieved that he hadn’t come to their room any earlier.

To catch them.

Catch her…

Whatever it was.

Just a hot, sexy dream. Of that young man in the olive grove.

Oh, Ella, she thinks, whatever next?

It is only later that she remembers her father being there too, sitting on the edge of the bed, saying something to her, his lips moving.

But try as she might to remember, the words remain unheard.

20

AFTER a restless night's sleep – Dimi on one side, all elbows and knees, and Nikos on the other, snoring gently, the dead weight of his arm across her shoulder – Electra starts her day with the Tropsodol. She doesn't have the shakes or the sweats, but she knows the drug's seductively deadening effect. A little like being stoned, which isn't that bad. And just the one capsule to begin with, she decides. Not two. To see what happens.

And she feels good. By lunchtime she's taken her run, driven Nikos to Navros for the early ferry, and returned home to make a first-draft start on the final chapters of her manuscript. The Admiral's last days at Douka. She's jumping ahead a bit, but she needs to set it down. To give herself a destination; something to aim for. And to help her picture that distant time, she has Eleni's journal. The Admiral's wife. The woman with the musket on her lap. The old lady's writing is oddly uneven, thin and faded, the ink sometimes smudged, making the pages hard to read. Pages crisp and stiff, as though they might crack and split not bend or crease with the turning. The journal had been found in a secret drawer in the Admiral's desk, Nikos tells her, and he's made her promise that she'll treat the book with care.

1848. November 10th. Ioannis keeps to his bed. His eyes are closed, and his breathing steady. But he is weak. It will not be long.

November 14th. Diomedes comes today, looking old and grey. With his shaking hands and rheumy eyes. With Despina. I swear the woman gets larger every time I see her. Always eating. One day she must burst, surely. And such homespun clothes. She looks like a peasant not a Papandreas. But she is kind. Kisses the old man. She, too, knows the time is close... I think we all do. They are staying. I have put them in Dio's old room at the end of the corridor.

November 15th. I have sent out no word, but there must be some knowing sense that the end is drawing near. In the morning, Theodoros rides over from Kalypti, hurrying through the hall as though he may be too late, his black boots ringing out on the floor stones, straight into the salon to see his grandfather.

Just before lunch, Athina arrives with Giorgios. The boy has come over from the mainland, from the academy on

Loudovikos. *He is in his cadet's uniform. A tight blue jacket and black wool trousers with a red stripe. The brass buttons gleam. When he is brought to Ioannis, my dear husband smiles and tears come to his eyes. He has recognised none of us, but he seems to know Giorgios. He takes the boy's hand, and draws him closer. Whispers something in his ear. The boy seems uncertain, but says, "Yes, sir."*

A few minutes later (here the words are smudged; tears, wonders Electra?) *Ioannis tries to rise from his bed, as though to join the company that has gathered there, coughs, attempts to draw a breath, and then falls back.*

We are all there when he goes, as he would want it: Diomedes and Despina, Theodoros and Athina, and Giorgios. And me, sitting on the bed beside him, holding his hand, so sad to see this brave, good man, my husband, slide away.

Later that day, I ask Giorgios what Ioannis whispered to him. The boy frowns. "Great-grandfather asked if the sails were full," he tells me. "I didn't know what to say, I didn't understand, so I said, 'Yes'."

But I understand.

When she finishes reading, Electra puts the journal aside. And realises she's… jealous. Jealous of her husband for having such an extraordinary family; merchant-traders, admirals, freedom fighters, senators, landowners. The Stamatos may have a great deal more money, she thinks, but they don't have this… this remarkable, this wonderful history. Why, before her grandfather bought his first quarry at Pentalidis the Stamatos were nothing more than herdsmen and farm labourers. And on her mother's side, there was nothing really special; Gina's mother a teacher, her father a country doctor. Neither branch of the family with such an illustrious past, stretching back centuries.

Nothing like the Contalidis.

But now, of course, she is one of them.

21

THE FOLLOWING week Electra and Dimi drive to Navros. They are going to meet the photographic team from *Arki-Tek*, an Athenian design and architecture magazine that wants to feature Douka for a story on historic Greek homes. The Contalidis house is one of three that will appear in its New Year edition, and the last to be visited by the team.

Nikos had planned to be there for their arrival, but he calls to say he's been held up in Athens. He will return before they leave, he promises, but for now Electra must handle it herself; briefing her on what she must do and say. She feels cross that he should imagine she might let him down, but she says nothing. Instead she reassures him that everything will go splendidly, and that he is not to worry; he can trust her. And in her heart she forgives him. He is nervous, that's all. He wants the house to look its best. And it's as important for her as it is for him. It has already been agreed with the magazine's editor that Electra's biography of the Admiral will be mentioned in the text, with details of its forthcoming publication at the end of the story.

There are three people on the shoot. The photographer, a writer, and the photographer's assistant. They have come across on the ferry in a rental Hyundai SUV packed with their cases and equipment. Electra introduces herself, and Dimi, and there are smiles and handshakes.

Gert, the photographer, is German. He is tall with rounded shoulders, an easy smile, and a wispy black beard that he plucks with spindly fingers as creamy white as alabaster. He wears baggy cargo shorts, dusty desert boots, and a multi-pocketed canvas waistcoat over a black t-shirt. Electra notices how his grey eyes are never still, looking everywhere at once. At her, when they shake hands; and then at the boats, the quayside houses, the tavernas, and *kafeneion*. Taking it all in, like an eager tourist. She guesses he is somewhere in his early forties and she likes him immediately – just the looseness of him, the slim elegance, the unruly thatch of black hair. So un-German.

The writer is younger, somewhere in that indeterminate zone that stretches from the late twenties to the early thirties, with a bright red bandanna holding back a mass of soft auburn curls. She is a little taller than Electra and wears a knotted Hawaiian shirt, pleated cotton slacks, and espadrilles. Her name is Costanza – Cossie, she tells Electra to call her – and she works as an editor in the magazine's Athens office. She is here, she explains, as writer first and stylist second – on hand to help with the shoot. Her face has a smooth, fresh look, sprinkled with freckles. Not a lick of make-up. A face that is bright and excited, Electra decides. An expectant, confident look. She seems ordered and efficient, if a little flustered, and strangely ill at ease. A first meeting, Electra decides; the pressure of a new assignment; a new owner to deal with; a team to organise and a deadline to meet. Electra knows how she feels.

Last to be introduced is Gert's assistant, Franz. Twenty-something, ragged blonde hair tied in a ponytail, his wrists bound in a tangle of silver bracelets and grimy ribbons, two silver studs in each ear lobe. He's not as tall as Gert, but what he lacks in height he makes up for in build. A broad chest stretching a blue t-shirt that's nicely faded, with the word 'CREW' printed on the back, and wide shoulders that remind her of the man in the olive grove, which makes her flush when she thinks it.

Introductions done with, Dimi tugs at her arm and asks if he can drive back to the house with Gert and Franz? With a nod from Gert, and a 'sure thing' from Franz, he climbs into the Hyundai, and Electra invites Cossie to join her in the Jeep.

"You look like you've come for a month," says Electra, as they drive away from the port with the Hyundai following behind.

"In this game it doesn't pay to travel light," Cossie replies. "The one thing you leave behind, you can bet the farm you'll need it the first day out."

Thirty minutes later, having established that Gert is gay, that his assistant isn't, and that Cossie is single, Electra says, "Well, here we are," as she pulls through the gates, dropping down through the stands of spindly, peeling eucalyptus. "Home, sweet home."

After a tour of the house and a get-to-know-each-other lunch in the rear courtyard, Electra makes her excuses and retreats to her study. She doesn't want to get in their way, she tells them, and knows that they will be better served having the time and the place to themselves. Even if Dimi insists on going with them. "I can show you everything you need to see," he tells them.

That evening they meet up again for supper on the topmost terrace, beside the opened cistern. Lina and Aja had prepared their meal that morning: a rich bean soup *fasolada* to start, with a bubbling creamy *moussaka* to follow. All Electra has to do is warm up the dishes, and dress the salad. She could have asked the girls to stay, and serve at table, and they would happily have done so – given the handsome Franz – but Electra was worried that Ariadne might choose to stay on with them.

"It was my husband's idea to open up the cistern," she explains, when Cossie asks how they'd managed to build the pond they sit beside, its mossy banks and lily pads lit by filigreed lamps that she and Nikos had found in Marrakech. Moths dart around them, and from the dark water comes the rhythmic, gulping bleat of frogs. "He had to take up two metres of topsoil to uncover it, and then cut off the metal roof. It was a terrible job, you can't imagine. I couldn't see what he was trying to do. It seemed so… pointless.

But now… Well, I think it's my favourite place in the gardens. Especially at night, like this."

As soon as she says it, she flushes; worries that it all sounds somehow rehearsed; a little too practiced and throw-away. The kind of comment that might find its way into the article. She doesn't want Cossie to think her shallow. Or in any way manipulative. A journalist knowing how other journalists work.

"And you can swim in it, too," pipes up Dimi, who, like Aja and Lina, has taken a shine to Franz, insisting they sit side by side. They'd also fired up and manned the bread oven together, to warm the *fasolada* and *moussaka*. "But it's deep. You can't touch the bottom. So *Baba* put a ladder in, like rungs up the side over there, so you can climb out."

"But what about the house?" Cossie asks. "Where does your water come from without the cistern?"

"We have our own water supply from a bore hole in the basement, so this water here is only used for irrigation now. It's fed by three springs up in the slopes above the house, and they never go dry. Which is why the estate is so…"

"*So grün*. Verdant," says Gert, pulling the cork from a second bottle of Contalidis red. "I have never seen so green on Greece islands like this." His voice is sharp and cracked, as though uncertain about the words he uses.

Electra smiles. In deference to Gert and Franz who have no more than tourist Greek – '*para kalor*', '*kalimera*', '*eph'aristo poli*' – they have agreed to speak in English. But even their English is rocky.

"We have plums and figs and peaches and vines, lemon and orange trees too," says Dimi. "Like, you could never go hungry in this garden."

Gert nods, then puts a hand to his ear. "And what do you call them? Those things… In German, we say *frösche…*"

"Frogs," says Cossie.

"Enough for a banquet, no?"

"I've eaten frogs," announces Dimi proudly. "In France. They were yuck."

"And is the house haunted?" asks Franz, as though he is asking nothing more than for someone to pass him the cheese. "I mean, it's really old."

Dimi's eyes widen. "Have you ever been in a haunted house? Have you ever seen a ghost?"

"Well, I guess that gives answer to your question very clearly," says Gert, turning to Franz with a grin. "I mean, if Dimi hasn't seen one…"

And the grown-ups laugh.

"But have you?" Dimi persists, tugging at Franz's sleeve. "Have you ever seen a ghost?"

Franz looks at Cossie. To help him out, or to seek her approval to continue, Electra can't tell. Then Cossie turns to her, with a questioning glance at Dimi.

"It's okay. It's okay," Electra says. "Dimi loves all that stuff. Though he'll probably have more bad dreams and come to Mummy's room. Or maybe I'll be the one to get bad dreams, and go to his."

So Cossie takes up where Franz left off. "Well, there was one place we worked, the three of us. In Germany."

"*Ja, ja.* In Germany. With the model, Heidi. Don't forget Heidi," says Gert, scooping up the last of his *moussaka.* "The yoghurt girl… She is in all those ads on TV… You know the tune…?" He hums it. Electra doesn't recognise it, but smiles as though she does.

"It was my first foreign assignment," Cossie continues. "And we were doing this shoot in an old castle just outside Munich. Really, a gothic place. Just a jewel, you know? Like you wouldn't believe. So we were there the first day and everything was fine. But that night, in our hotel, our model Heidi became very frightened."

"In the hotel?" asks Dimi, a little disappointed.

Cossie laughs. "I know. Can you imagine? If anywhere was going to be haunted it had to be that castle, right? But in actual fact it was the hotel, one of those old Tyrolean chalet-type places. Lots of timber, you know what I mean?"

"But what happened?" Dimi can hardly contain himself. Electra reaches out a hand and ruffles his hair. He pays her no attention. He is almost breathless with excitement.

"Well, at a little after midnight Heidi comes to my room and asks if she can share my bed. She can't spend another minute in her own room, she tells me."

"But why? Why?" asks Dimi.

"Shush, shush, *agapi mou.* Let Cossie tell her story, and then maybe we'll find out."

Their supper finished, Cossie reaches for her cigarettes, offers the pack to Electra who takes one. By the time they have them lit, Dimi is almost hopping up and down in his seat. "So, anyway," says Cossie, blowing out a plume of smoke into the night, "I ask her what is the problem, and she tells me. First off her room is really cold, she says, even with the radiators on. But it's a strange kind of cold, which gives her the goosebumps…" She turns to Gert and Franz. "In German, it's *gänsehaut.* When the skin on your scalp and arms tightens and prickles, you know?"

The two men nod. "*Ja, ja…*"

"Anyway, she thinks she will get into bed as quick as she can and warm up. And it is good. The bed is warm. There is electric blanket. But when she switches off the bedside light, she suddenly gets this feeling that she is not alone; that there is someone in the room with her. At first, of course, she thinks it is Gert…"

"*Ich? Mir? Nein*!" exclaims Gert, with a bellow of indignant laughter. "Heidi? The yoghurt lady? It's not true. You don't tell me she says that."

"I was joking. I was joking, okay? ...But let me finish the story. So, this feeling of Heidi's doesn't go away; this sense that she is not alone. She can't see anything and she can't hear anything, but she is sure that there is someone there. And she is right. When she reaches out to switch the light back on, these ice-cold arms come round her, pulling her back into the bed... And she feels hands go round her throat, icy fingers squeezing tight, until she can't breathe. She is almost blacking out, she tells me, thrashing around in the bed, not being able to take a breath. And then the hands are gone. Just like that. It is over, and she comes running to my room. There."

Dimi's eyes are wide, mouth open.

"But what was it?" asks Electra, reaching for the ashtray. "Did you ever find out? Did someone in the hotel confirm the place was haunted?"

"At breakfast, the couple who owned it said they didn't know anything about any ghosts. They had bought the chalet just the previous year, and no one had ever mentioned anything to them, or complained about any... incidents."

"I'm thinking it's not the kind of thing you advertise when you sell a property," said Gert, with a grin, "or if you have a hotel to run."

"It was only later that we found out what had happened," Cossie continues. "From the owner of the castle, who offered to put us up when he heard about it. Which was just as well. There was only the one hotel, and no way Heidi was going to spend another night there."

"He knew about it?" Dimi asks.

"Yes, he did. But like the owners of the hotel, he hadn't heard about any hauntings either. It was only when Heidi described what had happened, the hands around her throat, that he told us about this murder, back in the war. Apparently, a soldier had come home on leave to that very house and found his wife..." – Cossie sees Dimi watching her intently – "...He found out that his wife had been... stealing. With his brother. The two of them..."

"Stealing? You mean they were having an affair?" prompts Dimi, knowledgeably.

Franz and Gert chuckle. Electra smiles, sees a flush of embarrassment creep into Cossie's cheeks.

"Well, okay, yes, you're right," Cossie replies, glancing at Electra. "I suppose that is true... Anyway, the story goes that in a terrible rage and jealousy this soldier strangled his wife. In their bed." Cossie takes a last pull on her cigarette and stubs it out. "The thing is there was no way Heidi could have known about it, or described it the way she did. It had to have been a supernatural event... Ghosts. Spirits. Call them what you will."

"Wow," says Dimi. "That is spooky."

"But what was really spooky," Cossie continues in a softer voice, "were the marks around her neck."

"*Ja, ja*, that's true. I remember. Like a necklace of bruises from fingertips. We had to cover with make-up."

Electra shivers, draws her shawl from the chair back, wraps it round her shoulders, and says, "Why do you suppose we only ever tell ghost stories at night?"

Cossie shrugs, as though the answer is obvious. "Because it's always scarier at night, isn't it?"

And then, "Hey, you hear that?" says Franz, holding up a hand. "All the frogs. The insects. They've stopped singing. Like they're listening."

And he is right, of course. The night is silent. A deep pure silence. Nothing in the shadows, in the reeds.

Electra looks at her watch, smiles. "Every time I am out here, at this time of night, it is always the same. According to my husband, it was about now that the fire started, the fire that burned down the house. It's like all the insects know."

And then, moments later, as though bidden, they start up again. The frogs and the insects. More of them than before, it sounds like. An unseen audience. Noisier, more excited. As though they, too, have enjoyed Cossie's story. And are showing their appreciation.

"So," says Gert, smacking his palms onto the table and making everyone jump. "It is being an early start in the morning, so maybe I am going now to bed. But first we help you clear the table, make everything *tipp-topp. Alles in bester ordnung*." He cocks his head. "How you say? Ship-shape? Isn't that how it should be for an Admiral's house?"

22

AN EARLY start.

Gert is as good as his word.

Electra wakes to hear him calling out to Franz in the driveway; a car door sliding shut. It is a little after five o'clock, half an hour before her alarm goes off, and the sky has only just started to lighten; stars still twinkling over Kalypti and the sea. He is speaking German and she strains to understand. "*Beeilt euch ein bisschen…*" is all she catches. Something about getting a move on…

Sitting up in bed, Electra listens to their voices as they cross the terrace and start down the steps; heading for the bottom lawn, by the sound of it, and the line of beach pines. Electra is impressed. She knows from her runs that this particular spot will give them the very best full-face view of the house; and any time now its noble stonework will glow like gold when the sun comes up over Anémenos. And Gert has found it. After such a short time at Douka.

Finally, in the silence that follows, she gets up from her bed and goes to her bathroom; resisting the impulse to take a peep through the window; remembering Niko's strict instructions about not getting in the way of a shot; as if she needed reminding. Pulling on her running sweats, she takes a single Tropsodol, and an hour later is sitting at the kitchen table, watching the TV morning news, when Cossie knocks on the door and comes in.

"Hi. So sorry if we woke you," she says. She is wearing belted khaki shorts and a man's white shirt, tied like the Hawaiian one she'd worn the day before. Between shirt and belt buckle Electra can see her tummy button, like a tiny opening on a hard flat surface. A knot in a piece of wood.

Electra waves away the apology. "Would you like some coffee? Breakfast? Have you eaten yet?"

Cossie shakes her head. "Another hour or so, maybe. Would that be okay? We'd like to take advantage of the light up on the top terrace. The pool there looks lovely."

"Any time you like. The girls will be up from the village at seven, but if you need anything before then just help yourselves."

It is two hours before the team return. They sit themselves down at the kitchen table, and Aja and Lina take their orders. Electra, back from her run, notes once again the girls' interest in Franz – she can hardly blame them – and is not surprised to see his yoghurt, honey and muesli delivered in record time. Aja with the bowl of yoghurt and a spoon, Lina with the muesli and honey, the pair of them almost jostling for position. She wonders what Lina would have made of the man in the olive groves if she'd found him, if he'd still been there. He makes Franz look very young, very… unformed, thinks Electra.

Forty minutes later they are back at work, down by the swimming pool, before setting up outside one of the storehouses that Nikos converted into his studio. Electra has decided to put aside work and watch how they do things, standing behind Gert as Cossie and Franz move an urn overflowing with bright pink pelargonia – an inch here, an inch there – until Gert is satisfied. When he sees her behind him, he steps back, invites her to look through the viewfinder. The angle he has chosen is extraordinary, and Electra sees the storehouse as if for the first time: the white stone walls, the window shutters painted in a blue wash, the pelargonia tumbling just so.

"Magic," she says.

Gert considers this, tugs at his beard. "Magic. *Ja, ja.* And this perhaps, too," he says, pointing two fingers to his eyes.

Electra isn't sure if she's said the right thing, hopes that she hasn't upset him; but Cossie saves the day. "Magic, for sure. And eyes, too. Magic eyes, maybe. But Franz and I to make it all happen," she says with a grin, dusting off her hands.

It is the sun almost directly overhead that finally brings their morning's work to an end, and they join Electra and Dimi for lunch in the kitchen garden. But not before Gert has taken a dozen or more shots of the table. Laid with a blue linen cloth, it is set with dishes of olives and pepper strips, *tzatziki* and *taramosalata*, a bowl of shelled eggs, a tomato salad scattered with crumbs of *feta* cheese, a basket of toasted *pitas*, icy jugs of water, a bottle of Contalidis red, and a bunch of blue anemones in a cream pottery jug. With the camera turned this way and that, Gert circles the table, gesturing to Cossie to move this bowl of olives there, that basket of *pitas* "more closer, *bitte*," and for the vase of flowers or the ladder-backed chairs to be minutely adjusted. And Franz beside him, holding up a hi-power lamp, directing its beam at the table – to eliminate shadows, Cossie explains to Electra.

After their lunch the increasing glare and heat make outside work a problem, so they start inside the house, with set-ups in the library and in the study. The two rooms are snug and cosy and Electra is pleased and relieved to see that the shots come easy, that everyone is happy. Now they move to the hallway. The first set-up that Gert wants to do is from the opened front doors, looking across the hall to the curving staircase. Once again, Cossie and Franz are on hand to do his bidding. When he is satisfied and ready to start, Cossie joins Electra out-of-shot in the dining room.

"He looks like he's a good photographer."

"Very good," replies Cossie. "One of the very best."

"A nice guy, too. But why are they always gay, will you tell me?"

"Don't ask. I could write a book… Hang on, that's what *you* do, isn't it?"

The two women laugh, and it seems to Electra that Cossie is becoming friendlier, a little warmer. But she is still a little uncertain. She was a journalist herself; she knows the score. The way you play your subject, cosying up to them. Gaining their confidence. Getting what you need. Is that what Cossie is doing? She must tread carefully, that's what Nikos would say. Trust no one.

"But for all the niceness, he has his moments," Cossie continues. "There is some temper there, I can tell you. A nightmare, believe me, if anything goes wrong. For Gert, everything has to be perfect. Or else."

If proof were needed of Gert's dark side, it is provided on the very next set-up. Electra and Cossie are still in the dining room when there is a bellow of rage from the hallway.

"They're not here?" It is Gert, speaking in German. Rough and rasping.

The two women glance at each other; Cossie with a sigh, and a *see-what-I-mean* look. As though it had only been a matter of time.

In the hallway Franz is on his knees, scrabbling his way through his camera bags, searching for something. Electra and Cossie arrive in time to see Gert stoop down to take a swipe at Franz. The slap is hard enough to knock his assistant's head sideways, like a punchball in a boxing gym, but Franz continues with his search, obviously used to this kind of treatment and paying it no heed. Dodging out of the way when Gert tries to deliver a second swipe.

"They were here this morning," says Franz, his voice level. "I knew you'd want them."

"Well, they're not here now, are they?"

Electra is almost paralysed with a shocked embarrassment – the bad temper, the raised voice, the casual aggression – and a rising panic; can't think what to say or do. And it was all going so well…

But Cossie seems unconcerned, takes it in her stride. "What's the problem?" she asks.

"The damn filters. To cut the glare and reflections on that table-top," snaps Gert, pointing past them to the dining room. "We're supposed to have three of them. But it appears our good friend here has left them in the studio. Or in our hotel in Athens. Or on the plane even. Wherever they are, they are not where they're meant to be – which is here, *verdammt*! Where they *need* to be." This last is directed at Franz, sitting back on his heels. An apologetic shrug, a puzzled shake of the head.

"Why don't we spray it?" Cossie suggests. "The Philoxy will take off the shine. I've done it loads of times. Here." She goes to her tote, pulls out an aerosol can, and offers it to Gert.

Electra sees him snatch it from her, and tip back his head to read the small print on the label. Then brings the can closer, squints. "And it works, you say?"

"Like you wouldn't believe."

Gert turns to Electra. "It's okay with you we use this spray?" His usually gentle grey eyes are small and hard.

"If it's okay with Cossie, it's okay with me. Go ahead," says Electra, not sure she'd dare say anything else.

He turns back to Cossie. "And there is no damage, you say?"

"None at all. Just spray it on, leave it twenty minutes to set, and when you're finished you just wipe it off with a damp cloth."

"So, we give it a try, yes?" says Gert, and lopes off into the dining room.

23

COSSIE'S spray may have saved the day, and spared Franz further injury, but the loss of the filters has clearly put Gert in a fractious mood. Plain rude and boorish, Electra decides. Like a spoilt child.

At dinner that evening, taken in the kitchen, the air scented with thyme and rosemary and marjoram from the open kitchen door, he grumbles on about the filters – how much they cost, how long he's had them, how he hopes the insurance company will cover their loss, and complaining about Franz's inefficiency. Ignoring everyone else, he heaps his dinner plate with the food the girls have prepared for them, and then proceeds to play with it, pushing it around with a fork as though what he'd piled so high on his plate he now has little appetite for.

Such a nice man in so many ways, and hugely talented, thinks Electra, kissing Dimi goodnight, smoothing back his waves of hair, but so ridiculously childish. Cossie is right. A nightmare. Throwing a tantrum because he can't find his favourite toy.

It is with a certain relief, therefore, that the party breaks up early. This time Gert makes no offer to help with the table clearing; giving them only the briefest of nods before heading off for his bed; leaving Franz and Cossie to help Electra with the chores.

When they are done, Electra takes a bottle of wine from the fridge and offers the pair of them a nightcap.

Franz declines – "It's scaffolding day tomorrow, so I better check everything out" – but Cossie accepts.

Out on the terrace Cossie takes a seat at the table, apologising for Gert's behaviour, but Electra remains standing, takes a breath, "If you promise not to write about it in your article…" she begins, and then pauses, shoots Cossie a conspiratorial look.

Cossie frowns.

"I mean, I don't know if you smoke…?"

Cossie's frown disappears, replaced by a look of delighted surprise. She clearly understands what Electra is suggesting. "You mean… a joint? Hey, what a great idea." She beams. "And definitely off the record. I promise."

With a sly grin Electra leaves the terrace, puts on some music in the salon, and returns a few moments later with her box of tricks. Nikos would not approve, she thinks. But then he is in Athens, and she's here. She knows, too, it is the right thing to do. She and Cossie… Just the two of them… Two girls together.

Thirty minutes later, they have moved from the table and are sitting out on the top flight of terrace steps, their wine glasses set down beside them. From the salon comes a low Beethoven sonata.

"This just has to be about the best place in the world to get stoned."

"Isn't anywhere good?" asks Electra, and they both chuckle.

Somewhere out in the darkness a dog barks.

"How many do you have?" asks Cossie. "The dogs, I mean."

Electra shakes her head. "You mean for security? Well, none."

Cossie considers this. "Didn't sound like it yesterday."

"How do you mean?"

"Well, there's certainly one around. I heard it outside my room, when we went for a rest after lunch. I thought it had to be a guard dog, and you hadn't mentioned it. Sounded big. Like a mastiff or something. A chew-your-arm-off kind of dog. No way I was going to open the door and give it a biscuit, I can tell you that."

"How odd," says Electra. "It must have come up from the village, looking for something to eat."

"Yeah. Me."

And then it happens. So suddenly that afterwards, recovering from the shock, neither Electra nor Cossie are able to say for certain, or agree, what did actually happen.

Or, more precisely, in what order.

Was it the volume on the Beethoven suddenly turned to maximum, and blasting across the terrace loudly enough to be heard in Anémenos that came first?

Or the shadow that raced across the lawn just a few feet below them?

Or the sudden snarling bark of a dog somewhere very close by?

Or their wine glasses sent spinning away, smashing on the steps?

Whatever it was, however it started, it sets their hearts racing, a scream catching in both their throats.

Back in the house, tipping the remains of their broken wine glasses in to the waste bin, Cossie looks at Electra with a questioning tilt of the head.

"We might have been stoned," she says, "but what I don't understand is how come the glasses went flying when we were holding on to each other so tight. Did you kick yours over? I can't remember if I did or not."

Electra thinks about it. Decides they must have done.

How else could they have smashed?

24

"YOU DIDN'T hear the music?" Electra asks the following morning, when she returns from her run.

"Not a thing," says Gert. "Cossie already asks me the same thing."

The team have been down on the beach, they tell her, working on shots of the Balinese pavilion, and they are tucking into their breakfast, dusty and tired and hungry. This time Gert does not play with his food – scrambled eggs and bacon, toast and honey – and wolfs it down, as though his bad behaviour the previous afternoon and evening has given him an appetite. He even ruffles Franz's hair, in a show of affection. Like Electra, with Dimi.

"Deaf as stones the pair of them," says Cossie, sitting back with her coffee mug clasped in her lap. "How they didn't hear it, I'll never understand."

"It didn't wake Dimi either," says Electra. "Out for the count."

And so it goes, plates of food delivered to the table by Aja and Lina, and then cleared away when they finish.

"So," says Gert. "We are inside again. On the top floor if that is okay? The bedrooms? And also with the scaffolding. For some elevation."

Electra says that it is fine, that they are free to go and do whatever they wish. If they need her for anything, they will find her in the study.

She takes a late lunch alone, at her desk, and has just finished the last of her wine when her mobile rings. It is Nikos, calling to say that he's at Tsania and will be taking the next ferry. The news thrills her, and she hurries upstairs, praying the team will have finished with their bedroom so that she can get herself ready. Her prayers are answered, and an hour later, showered and changed, she is on her way to Navros.

The ferry is twenty minutes late, and when Electra sees Nikos stride down the ramp and give her just the briefest wave, she knows he is in a bad humour. Is it because the ferry was late, or something at work, she wonders? Or simple irritation that he's been forced to miss the last two days with the magazine crew photographing his family home? He'd been so looking forward to it.

His embrace is as brisk and business-like as his wave, and she knows immediately that he wants to drive. Taking the passenger seat, buckling on her safety belt, she prepares herself for a hair-raising trip back to the house. At least Dimi isn't with them, thinks Electra, as they speed away from the quay and turn onto the seashore road. It would take a crowbar to separate Dimi from Franz.

"So how's it been?" asks Nikos, his mood seeming to settle now that he's behind the wheel and heading for home.

"Hectic. They never stop. It's exhausting."

"But it's been fun, too?"

Electra is tempted to tell Nikos about the lost lenses and Gert's tantrum, but decides to keep that to herself. Instead she says, "They're nice. Gert and his assistant, Franz, work well together, and Cossie really knows her stuff. You know that music stand? She moved it into the corner for one of the salon shots, and it looked so good I'm going to leave it there. She's got a brilliant eye."

And so it goes, Electra bringing Nikos up to speed – what they'd photographed, what they'd said, what *she'd* said; Nikos taking the corners with just the palm of one hand on the wheel; Electra holding the strap of her safety belt, swaying with the turns through Avrómelou and Akronitsá, and praying at every one that goats don't stray onto the road.

Nikos and Gert hit it off immediately, and Electra notices the way that Cossie shakes his hand, almost coyly, rather taken aback when he leans forward to kiss her cheeks. And the way Nikos smiles at her, the Contalidis smile. Such a terrible flirt, she thinks.

Since it's their last night together, Nikos has suggested that they go to Anémenos for dinner. Not to one of its harbour-side tavernas but to an *ouzeri* he knows, where the food, he tells them, will be far more memorable.

So it is that they drive down to Anémenos. Gert, Nikos, and Electra in the Jeep; Cossie, Franz, and Dimi following behind in the Hyundai. To be welcomed into the *ouzeri*'s dimly-lit interior a few blocks back from the port, its high ceiling supported by twisting tree-trunk timbers, its floor just shiny hard-packed earth, and its walls lined with stacked barrels. As always the place smells like a cellar, an underground airless bunker of mushrooms and dampness, draped in dusty forgotten cobwebs.

Wrinkling her nose, but covering it with a smile, Electra greets their hosts, the Kariakis *ménage*, shakes hands that feel crusty and stiff with labour, and manages to conceal the slide of resentment she feels that Nikos should have brought them all here. What was he thinking? Of all the places they could have gone. After she's spent the last few days laying on the very best that Douka has to offer; making sure her guests have everything they need, and doing it all for Nikos. Even one of the touristy Anémenos tavernas on the quayside would have been cheerier than this. And though she knows the food will be good, in a rough peasant-y sort of way, and that Nikos loves it here, she prepares herself for the hard plastic chairs that always scratch the backs of her legs, the chipped china they must eat from, and the sharp, scalding taste of the *ouzo*. It's cold, too, thanks to the earthen floor, and she shivers as she takes her seat; the table set with a worn plastic cloth that has seen better days; the owner's wife, in a stained housecoat of a similar vintage, summoned to bring forth a selection of *mezédes*.

As Nikos promised it's a memorable meal, and when, finally, they return to the house – Electra with a thankful sense of relief to be home again – the rest of the party appear warm and cheery from the food. And, save Dimi, just a little unsteady from the wine and *ouzo*.

Which makes what happens next so shocking. So unexpected and upsetting.

Electra has just put Dimi to bed – warm and tousle-haired, his breath sweet, his little hand slipping from hers as he falls asleep – and is walking along the corridor from his room when she hears a soft chuckling. Like someone drawing in breath and letting it out; a jerky, almost asthmatic sound. And right in her ear, as though someone has crept up on her. She spins round, but the corridor is clear; just the brass lamps shining pools of light onto each of the family portraits.

That's when Electra hears the singing.

A raucous, grating sound, echoing up from the main salon.

Loud, tuneless, drunken. But unmistakeable.

"*Deutschland, Deutschland über alles,*
Über alles in der Welt,
Wenn es stets zu Shutze und Trutze
Dum-di-dum, di-dum, di-dah…"

As she comes down the stairs she sees Franz and Cossie hurrying across the hallway to the salon, followed by Nikos.

"He said he was going to bed," says Nikos, when she joins him. "He's drunker than we thought."

But not just drunk. It's worse than that.

"Shit," says Nikos, when they reach Cossie at the salon door.

"My flowers," gasps Electra.

Somehow Gert has managed to clamber up on the scaffolding beside Electra's pyramid slope of orchids. Stamping his feet on the platform as though marching along to the song, he has opened his flies and is urinating on the flowers. Hips thrust forward, a long golden arc descending onto the blooms, making their stalks and budded branches bend and flutter as the pattering stream hits them, spraying over every shelf, splashing down onto the polished concrete floor.

And while he stamps and pees, Franz tries desperately to catch hold of him, grabbing at his trouser legs, to stop him. But he cannot manage it. Finally, with a grunt, like a man hauling himself from a swimming pool, Franz hoists himself up onto the platform and gets his arms round Gert.

But the singing continues. The words slurred, but remembered:

"*Blüh'im Glanze dieses Glückes,*

Blühe, deutsches Vaterland...!"

For a moment the two men seem to dance on the platform. Franz, from behind, clasping his arms round Gert's waist, Gert now shooting out his right hand in a stiff-armed salute.

"*Sieg Heil,*" he screams, "*Sieg Heil...*" as they spin around on the platform, Gert's long dripping penis swinging to and fro from his open flies.

It cannot last like this, and it doesn't.

Staggering backwards Gert stamps down on Franz's foot, Franz rears back, and the two of them topple from the scaffolding, crash down into the orchids; wooden shelves shattering, the pots flung up in a showering spray of soil; broken blooms sent skitter-scattering across the floor.

And standing there in the doorway – eyes wide, scandalized, horrified at what she has witnessed – Electra hears the chuckling sound she'd heard upstairs. Low and throaty and losing power, as though there is no longer breath enough to drive it.

It is not Nikos, it is not Cossie or Franz, so it must be Gert, she reasons. Still giggling at his performance, rolling around on the floor in a tangle with Franz.

What did he think he was doing, she wonders?

Behaving like that. Drunk or not, it is inexcusable.

Simply... outrageous.

But the giggling soon stops, and now Gert is moaning, groaning loudly like a cow that's lost its calf.

25

“**SOMEONE** told him to do it. That’s what he says.”

It is Friday morning and Cossie is back from the hospital in Navros where Gert has had his broken arm set and plastered, and the cut on his forehead, from the edge of a splintered shelf, stitched, daubed in iodine island-style, and bandaged. She stands by the fridge, just a few steps into the kitchen. “There’s a slight concussion, too, which is why they’ve kept him in,” Cossie tells Nikos and Electra. “But he remembers enough to send his most sincere apologies to you both.” And then, in an attempt at his defence, she says, “I have never seen anyone so ashamed.”

Nikos pulls out a chair from the kitchen table and sits down beside Electra. Somewhere in the house comes the sound of a vacuum cleaner. He shakes his head, sets his lips tight. It is clearly not Cossie’s fault, but Electra knows that her husband is in no mood for apologies. Or any defence. And she is right.

“Someone told him to do it? Really? And he expects us to believe that? And forgive his appalling behaviour?” He gives Cossie a look as if she, too, is as much to blame. “My grandfather was shot by the Germans, here at Douka, with nineteen other men herded up from the villages. Did you know that? Did *he*?”

Cossie shakes her head, lost for words. “I don’t know what to say,” she manages. “I just…”

Despite herself, Electra feels for the younger woman. She knows what it’s like to face Nikos when he’s in this kind of mood. She’d like to speak up for the poor girl, but Nikos hasn’t finished.

“Well, it had better be the best goddam story you’ve ever written,” says Nikos, softening a little, as though he realises he’s taken it too far. “And the magazine better make Douka the feature’s lead property. And the cover!”

“Of course, I’m sure that won’t be a problem,” Cossie replies, desperate to make up lost ground. “Your house is beautiful. The perfect lead. And I’m sure a cover…”

But she is interrupted.

“I regret there may be problem with that,” says Franz. He has appeared behind Cossie, and stands in the kitchen doorway. He looks as crestfallen as her. He, too, had been at the hospital the night before with Gert and Cossie. He’d broken two fingers in the fall from the scaffolding, and they are splinted together with white gauze and pink plasters.

“Problem? What problem?” Nikos glares at him across the kitchen table.

Electra can feel the temperature rising again.

"There are…" The young man spreads his hands, looks at Cossie as though for help, for support. But he knows he is on his own. He is the one who must break the news. "There are no pictures…" he says at last.

Cossie frowns, looks at him with a puzzled expression, as though she can't quite understand what he's said.

"No pictures? What do you mean, 'no pictures'?"

"The hard drives are blank. Three cameras, three drives. But there's nothing… I have searched all over."

Cossie seems to wilt, reaches out a hand to the side of the fridge, as though for support. "Nothing? But we had dozens of set-ups, hundreds of shots."

"Not anymore," says Franz. "Not even Polaroids."

"And there's no back-up? No memory…?" Cossie's face has turned white, pale with shock. For a moment it seems possible she might faint. She turns to Electra, to Nikos. She has no words. Then she looks back at Franz. Helpless. Disbelieving. Desperate to find a solution. "But how can that happen?"

Franz sighs, shakes his head. "Last night, at the hospital, Gert tells me he wiped them before our trip to the *ouzeri*. Tells me he has no choice. It has to be done. And like the dancing, the singing, he says, too, that somebody tells him to do it. So I think he is still a little drunk, maybe? I mean he acts strangely the last few days. Odd, you know? Not himself. Anyway, when I get back here this morning, I check the cameras." He starts nodding. "And he has. That's what he's done. Everything's gone."

"You're telling us there are no pictures?" asks Nikos in a low voice.

Electra knows that voice. She puts out a hand, rests it on his arm, as though to calm him.

But he won't be placated. "After three days? Nothing?"

Franz shakes his head.

Nikos turns to Cossie.

"So where does that leave us?"

"I don't know what to say," she stammers. "This is… It's never happened before."

"Well, it's happened now, so what are you going to do about it?"

"There's no time to reschedule. This was the last shoot. We'll have to go with what we've got. Just the two houses…"

"And Douka?"

"I'll talk to the editor. We'll sort something out," says Cossie.

There is a moment's silence, and Electra senses that Nikos's temper is easing. But it is not her hand on his arm that has done it. It is something else. He has seen an advantage. A bigger feature. No sharing with two other properties. And if he gets his way, a cover too. She knows her husband. Once an islander, always an islander. The Contalidis would be proud of him.

"I know you will do what's necessary," he says, his tone more gentle now, conciliatory, and he smiles. "And please, don't worry. It's clearly not your fault. Or yours," he continues, turning to Franz. "Just so long as when you do return, our friend with the singing voice and broken arm is not behind the camera."

An hour later there's a tentative knock at the study door. Electra looks up from her screen, and sees Cossie standing in the doorway.

"We're loaded up. It's time to say goodbye."

"Are you sure you won't stay for lunch?" asks Electra, getting up from the desk and walking over to her.

"I think we should go, don't you?"

The two women embrace. "Just so long as you promise to come back soon. I shall miss you."

"And I shall miss you. And Dimi. And your lovely home. I'm just so sorry everything went so wrong."

Electra walks with Cossie to the Hyundai. Franz is showing Dimi how to do some complicated handshakes involving fists and fingers and various slaps.

"Hey, I got it," Dimi shouts, after a fault-less round, and beams with delight.

Nikos comes up the path from his studio and Cossie goes to him, shakes his hands, and guiltily accepts the kiss he gives her on both cheeks. Electra notes it. That old Contalidis charm. He's still thinking about a lead feature and cover.

There's a cough behind Electra. She turns. It is Franz.

"I am so sorry it ends like this. And sorry not to be coming back. Maybe one day?"

"Dimi would never forgive you if you didn't."

"He is a good boy. I like him, too."

Electra reaches up to kiss him. "Take care, Franz, and maybe find yourself another photographer to assist."

Franz nods. "That is good advice, I think. And a photographer who does not slap my head." He makes a face and rubs the side of his head where Gert had hit him. "But there is another thing I must ask. It isn't just those filters I am losing. There are two lenses, also. I have searched everywhere, but I cannot find them. If they turn up, please can you let me know?" He gives her a piece of paper with his name and telephone number on it. "I will send courier to pick them up."

"Why don't you come and pick them up yourself? It would be lovely to see you again."

And that is that. Five minutes later, with a wave from Cossie and a beep-beep from Franz, the Hyundai heads up the drive.

26

LATE THAT night Electra is in bed. She is lying on her side, reading Dinos Stivounaki's acclaimed account of the siege of Nafplio. She's more than half way through the book, but despite numerous references to Mantó Mavroyénous there has been no mention yet of the Admiral.

Behind her she hears the bathroom door close and a moment later Nikos climbs into bed, settles himself, and then draws up close behind her. She can smell his warm clean body, and feels him hardening against her; knows what he wants.

And now, just two pages from the end of her chapter, the Admiral suddenly appears.

> "*He was a tall man,*" writes Stivounaki, "*with a handsome black moustache and hard, calculating eyes. He came to the meeting at Argoliki with the widow Mavroyénous, and sat beside her, whispering in her ear. It is clear from other accounts that the two of them were close, that this Contalidis was a trusted aide, maybe more...*"

Electra wants to read on, but knows she cannot. Must not. They haven't made love since Navros and their first night here at Douka, and she knows she can't deny him. Shouldn't. And doesn't want to. At once pleased, and relieved, after all she has been through, that he still wants her, loves her, needs her. Just as it always was, before the Lycabettus, the Aetolikou; as though nothing had happened, nothing had changed.

And so, bending down the corner of the page, she closes her book, and drops it to the floor.

"Switch off the light," he whispers. "But don't turn around. Stay right there, like that."

She does as she is told, and closing her eyes she charts the passage of her husband's hands. A soft, enquiring approach this time; a gentle exploration. Nothing rough or hurried. The pattern of it so familiar, so... comforting. One hand reaching down for the lacy hem of her nightdress, drawing it up, the silk sliding over her skin. The other hand guiding himself towards her.

And she plays her part, does what she knows he likes; shifts her hips, pushes herself against him; and he finds her, slides into her.

And it begins.

It is having him behind her, so close, that suddenly makes Electra think of the young man in the olive grove; the man in the belted trousers, bare-chested, with that creamy smear of dirt across his belly; the man with that sweet earthy scent who'd stepped behind her, put his hands on her waist and freed her hair from a branch. And as she raises her leg to draw Nikos deeper, breaking step, which makes him catch his breath, Electra finds herself thinking what she might do to that young man; out there in the olive grove, with the sun on their bodies, amid the hot humming buzz of insects. And what she'd like him to do to her; the rough bark of an olive tree against her back, her arms resting on its branches, raising herself up for him…

Afterwards, in the darkness, as Nikos turns and settles himself for sleep, Electra remembers something. Something she'd meant to ask him.

"You didn't tell me your grandfather was shot at Douka."

"He wasn't," says Nikos, his voice muffled by the pillow.

"He wasn't? But you told Cossie…"

"I wanted to make a point," he replies. "And it worked. If you really want to know, it was Petrou's father who was shot."

"Petrou's father? By the Germans?"

"Not exactly."

"Then by whom?"

Nikos sighs; soft, sleepy, satisfied. "The partisans. After the war. He was an informer."

"But shot here? At the house?"

"Do you really want to know?"

Electra thinks about this. Does she, or doesn't she?

Will the knowing somehow taint the house?

Wherever it was; wherever it happened.

Out in the grounds, she supposes.

On the terrace? In the kitchen garden? The rear courtyard? Outside the guest cottages, or Niko's studio?

She imagines a firing squad. A stake. A wall. A blindfold. A line of men; rifles shouldered, aimed, fired.

Or maybe it was just a pistol to the head? A single bullet. No wasteful formality for the partisans. Just a rough and ready kind of justice.

And she wonders, then, what happened to the body?

Did they cart it off, or bury it somewhere close by?

Somewhere in the grounds? An unmarked traitor's grave?

And then, did Petrou know? That his father had been shot at Douka.

How old would he have been? she wonders. In his teens, his twenties?

So, of course he'd have known. How could he not?

But it hadn't stopped him wanting the house.

So why should it bother her?

"Yes," she says at last; quietly, keen now to know. "Tell me."

But Nikos gives that familiar little sigh, clears his throat, and she knows he is asleep. There will be no answer now.

She lies there, thinking of Petrou's father being shot here at Douka, listening to Nikos's breath come slow and deep, then turns back to her bedside table.

She switches on the light with a soft click and reaches to the floor for Stivounaki; finds her place and starts to read.

27

FOR SOMEONE who had made his fortune in the quarrying business – limestone, and its various subsidiary products – Mikis Stamatos possessed the most beautiful hands. Delicately turned wrists, pale plump palms, bronzed thinly-boned top parts, and long elegant fingers finished with perfectly formed nails. And never a line of dirt in the tips or cuticles. These were not a merchant's hands, unless the merchandise happened to be paper or silk. But at no time was Electra aware that her father took any special care of them. No moisturiser, no manicure. They were the hands of a poet, a pianist, she always thought. Unlike her own hands. She had inherited those from her mother. Broad, stumpy and short-fingered. A workman's hands. It was her sister, Yianna, who had her father's hands. A model's hands. An artist's hands.

It is those hands that Electra watches now, on the screen of her laptop, as her elder sister pulls back her tumbling brown hair to wind into a knot. The long fingers, the pointed painted nails, working the handfuls of hair into a tight bunch then sliding a paintbrush through it, like a spear through straw. And over her sister's shoulder Electra sees the loft apartment in Manhattan where Yianna lives. An early morning sun streaking through dusty windows. Steel girders, wood beams, brick walls. And a large canvas, unframed, standing proud on an easel behind her. A giant magnolia, with curving cream petals and a scarlet heart. For the last two months it has stood there with just the back of it showing. A blank stretchered canvas. This is the first time that Electra has seen the other side.

"You finished it," she says.

Yianna turns her head, looks at the painting. "I put it there so that you could see it. Do you like it?" There is the slightest disconnect between her voice and the movements of her lips, like a soundtrack just a few beats behind the action.

"It's marvellous. Like the magnolias at Apostólikou. I can almost smell it. I want it."

Yianna laughs. "Too late, Sis. It's sold. Off to a collector this very afternoon."

"Tell him you've changed your mind. He can have his money back."

"Already spent, hon. And anyway, haven't you got enough of my stuff?"

And so the two sisters talk, as they do at least once a month. Electra on Pelatea; Yianna in Manhattan. They may not have the same hands, but they've ended up in the same kind of place. Two Athenians, living on islands.

First they talk of their families. Nikos and Dimi, and Yianna's daughter, Maya, and her husband, Miles Franklin, a neurologist at Bellevue. All the news. New York. The house on Douka. Then they talk of themselves, what they've been doing, exchanging gossip, telling stories – books they've read, films they've seen. Just touching base, staying close.

As usual Yianna leaves the important questions for last.

"And how are you?" she asks, quietly. "Are you feeling any better?"

"Good days and bad days, you know," says Electra, with a sigh. "But the good ones seem to come more often than the bad." She's not sure if that's true or not, but she says it anyway. For her sister.

"Well, that's something, I suppose. But you're still looking pale, Ella, and too thin. You should eat more. Please. For me?"

"I never seem to feel hungry," she replies. Just thirsty, she thinks.

"That's the medication. You might not be hungry, but that doesn't mean to say you're not. Breakfast, lunch and dinner. Three meals a day. And more than a mouthful of this, or a lick of that. Promise me?"

"I promise."

And then, leaning to the side, looking past Electra, Yianna says, "Hey, you've got company. You should have said. I'll let you go." And with a kiss blown from those gorgeous fingertips, the screen goes blank and the connection is broken.

Electra frowns. Turns.

Company?

She's in her bedroom. Alone. Dimi's down in the pool, and she can hear Lina and Aja beating a rug on the terrace.

Electra sighs. Just like her sister. Always in a rush, in a hurry. Talk done. Time to go. Any excuse.

Electra thinks nothing of it, though she feels a strange coolness in the room, and a sudden stillness, and shivers. She looks at her watch. Time for lunch. Time to do what her sister made her promise to do. She might not feel like eating anything, but she'll try. For Yianna.

And afterwards, another drive to Navros; to pick up her agent.

28

"SO THIS IS where it all happens. This is where he's hidden you away."

Just like Iphy and Cossie before her, Chrysta Hadsopoulous stands in front of the house at Douka and whistles. "Some fucking bolt-hole, Ella."

Chrysta is taller than Electra, but neither as slim nor as elegant, and a dozen years older. In Athens she was a friend of a friend, and it was through this friend that Electra sent Chrysta a proposal for her biography of the Admiral; a one-page synopsis and the first four chapters. Just two days later Chrysta telephoned to say that she loved the idea, and wanted Electra's approval to pitch the book to Massalia Press, one of the city's most prestigious publishers. A week later, Electra and Chrysta signed a contract with Massalia, and celebrated the deal and their new friendship over a bottle of Kalambaki and bowls of *giouvetsi* on the terrace at Targa.

"Is it haunted?" asks Chrysta, as Electra shows her to her room; Iphy's bedroom, where a new mattress, re-waxed floor and a dozen scented candles from Jo Malone in Kolonaki have done their work. "Does the Admiral ever make an appearance?"

Electra starts. It is the second time in a week that someone has asked about ghosts.

"Well if he does, he never makes himself known," she replies; and smiles at Chrysta, who smiles back in a strange way.

"Two hundred years is a long time," she says, unzipping her case. "Maybe he's just getting to know his new guests before he introduces himself. Taking your measure."

"Maybe he is. And making sure I don't write anything bad about him. Or else..."

"Make him as fucking bad and bloodthirsty as you like. Bad and bloodthirsty sell."

"But only if it's true, surely?"

Chrysta gives her another look, arches an eyebrow.

Electra feels a little naïve. Her agent seems so much more capable, so much more worldly-wise. And despite their new friendship, still a little intimidating. Like her language... The two of them may have got on well in Athens, in a business surrounding, but Electra wonders how it will be out here on the island. The two of them alone. Chrysta is Athenian, after all. But then, so is she. Why shouldn't it work?

"You know the great thing about the dead?" says Chrysta, folding a pair of jeans into a drawer. "They can't sue. And Massalia may be a highly-respected publishing house, but believe me they'll be expecting some fucking colour. So it might be a good idea to give it to them, before they start asking.

Anyway, didn't you tell me once that the Admiral had some Turkish general hung from the ramparts of Nafplio by his testicles?"

Electra gives it some thought. "I'm not sure that I did. And I'm not altogether sure that it's physically possible. Is it?"

Chrysta chuckles. She goes to the bathroom, sets out her toiletries, calls over her shoulder, "You're the writer. You decide. Me, I just sell the book. And make you and me some fucking money. Which, for a first book, is starting to add up," she continues, coming back into the bedroom. "In fact, I might just have sold serialisation rights to *I Kathimerini*. Didn't you write for them back in the day?"

"As a freelance. Just a few stories. Most of them spiked."

"Well, not this time, honey. I showed their literary editor your first few chapters and he wants to see more."

As they make their way down the stairs, Chrysta asks, "Any creepy-crawlies I need to look out for?"

"You don't have them in Athens?"

"Only hanging around Bar Safridi, and they're easily dealt with."

The two women laugh.

"So, my esteemed client, let the fun begin," says Chrysta in her growly voice, sliding her arm into Electra's. "I'm owed some down time and it seems to me that this is the perfect fucking place to take it."

What Chrysta means by 'down time' looks suspiciously like work to Electra. While she prepares dinner that first evening, Chrysta takes a wedge of Electra's manuscript onto the terrace and settles down to read. Ominously, she has a red Biro tucked behind her ear.

It seems an age before she reappears. Electra is setting the table in the herb garden when Chrysta comes out from the kitchen, waving the pages in her hand.

"It's very good, Electra. I mean, very fucking good."

"You like it?" Electra is suddenly paralysed with delight. She cannot believe it. Chrysta is the first to read the manuscript, and she's been on tenterhooks since her agent took it to the terrace.

"There's bits and pieces need tidying up, which I'm sure you know about," says Chrysta. "But you've caught the Admiral brilliantly. He's just so real. So unlike the usual dry, cardboard historical character. And fucking sexy, too. That bit where he meets Eleni Dimitriou. Up in the hills… Is that true? Did she really take a shot at him?"

"That's what Nikos says. Family history. She thought Ioannis was a Turk, in his pasha pantaloons, so she took aim with her musket and brought him down. An arm wound, though she didn't know it at the time. Reckoned she'd killed him. But when she went to check the body, he leapt up and pinned her down. There was a fight. He won. Just. And the rest, as they say, is history."

"Well, bring it fucking on. More of that, please."

That night, after Dimi goes to bed, the two women sit on the terrace where just a week before she and Cossie had scared themselves half to death. It's the same kind of starlit night but a crescent moon, thin as a nail clipping, now shows above the pine and palms. Chrysta has worked on the Contalidis wine, and Electra knows she isn't far behind.

"So when can I have it?" asks Chrysta. "The final draft."

"Another month. Maybe two. I'm working on the last chapters right now, but I want time to polish."

"End of August? September?"

"Make it September, when I'm back in Athens. Just to be safe."

"Promise me?"

"Promise you."

29

WHEN ELECTRA returns from her run the following morning, Chrysta is in the kitchen. She is wearing striped blue and green pyjamas, has a cup of coffee in one hand, and her mobile in the other. But she's not on the phone to a client. She is playing *Temple Run 2* with Dimi.

"He's good. Furthest I've got is six thousand metres, but he's way ahead."

"She can't slide," says Dimi. "She jumps too soon, and she hits the tree trunks every time."

"Story of my life," says Chrysta. "I don't slide, I jump too soon, and I can't avoid fallen trees. So what's the plan, historian?"

"Well, a bit of history as a matter of fact."

Two hours later Electra, Chrysta, and Dimi are in the Jeep with a packed lunch prepared by Lina and Aja. They take the road to Navros, but after just a few kilometres Electra turns left at a fork and skirts around the back of the Douka headland before dropping down to Kalypti and the coast.

"They won't be the greatest ruins you've ever seen," says Electra. "But there's something about the place. Most of the tourists head out to Messinos for the ampitheatre, or Pecravi and the temple of Diana, so the Sanctuary of Epione at Kalypti has stayed off the radar."

"So what's there?"

"All the usual things, just not so many of them. And nothing standing. But it's the sense of, well… peace, tranquillity, that makes it so special."

"So Epione lives up to her name?" says Chrysta.

"You mean 'Soothing'? Yes, absolutely. Somehow the place refreshes you. You leave feeling better than when you arrived."

"And it's got the biggest scorpions you've ever seen," says Dimi from the backseat.

"Nice," says Chrysta, with a mock shiver. "Sounds just my kind of place."

Driving through Kalypti, its straggle of whitewashed houses built right down to the edge of a shingle beach, its fishing fleet of seven *caïques* drawn up on its sloping shore, Electra keeps an eye out for the man in the olive grove. But there's no sign of him.

On the other side of the village she turns away from the sea and winds up into the hills across parched slopes of low scrub. At the top of a rise, the road suddenly dips down and the landscape changes – stands of eucalyptus and tamarisk, a dusty green against the bare stone headland of distant Douka.

When they reach the sanctuary, Electra parks in the shade and they pull out their hamper, blankets, and Dimi's collecting jars from the boot.

"We can walk, or take those," says Electra, pointing to a rope of tethered mules, ears flicking, tails swishing.

"Mules, mules," says Dimi, hurrying ahead.

"Is it far?"

"Maybe a kilometre. That's all."

After a moment or two's consideration, Chrysta elects to walk with Electra while Dimi, the hamper, blankets, and collecting jars are loaded onto two of the mules.

"There's no kiosk," says Chrysta, looking round. "Don't we have to pay? Get tickets?"

"At Messinos and Pecravi, but not here," says Electra. "Just an undertaking to leave the place as you find it. And maybe some coins in the collection box over there."

It doesn't take long for the two mules, Dimi, and the boy who leads them to draw ahead, leaving Electra and Chrysta to walk the path alone. A warm sunshine slants down through the branches, the soft green foliage rustles and whispers, and the air is fresh and resinous. Somewhere, unseen, there are goats, their bells clinking, and close to, the desperate ringing of cicadas. A thick electric buzz.

"The site dates back to the third century BC, maybe earlier," says Electra, finding it difficult not to drop into historian mode. "And, as I said, the temple is dedicated to Epione. Not many people have heard of her, but she was married to Asclepius, god of medicine, and the mother of Panacea and Hygieia."

"So healing runs in the family…"

"You could say. There's not much left of the temple but you can still see part of an inscription mentioning her."

"So what did they do here? Why this sanctuary thing?"

"It was considered a place of peace and healing. People came from all over the island, and from the mainland, too. Many died here – of old age, of battle wounds – but they died peacefully and, so legend has it, painlessly."

Up ahead the trees part and the path opens onto a sun-bleached pitch of land surrounded on all sides by trees. And above the furthest trees the slopes of Douka loom over them, suddenly closer, higher than they were before. The ground is stony, dusty, and scattered amongst the weeds are sections of fallen columns, toppled plinths, and, rising no more than a low course of stones, the ancient foundations of buildings and pathways, polished to a sliding gleam.

And nobody to be seen. The Sanctuary of Epione is completely deserted.

Twenty metres away, with a stick in one hand and a collecting jar in the other, Dimi is already off in search of scorpions. The mule boy has unpacked their hamper and blankets and has put them in the shade of a tamarisk. When he sees Electra he points to his watch. Electra holds up three fingers and thanks him for his help. He nods, gathers up the reins of his mules and leads them back to the path.

"It's extraordinary," says Chrysta, looking around. "Such a magical place, and there's no one here."

"Maybe two hundred visitors a year. Something like that. I've been here many times and never had to share it with more than three or four people. Often, it's just me and Dimi. Like I said, the tour groups just don't come here."

"I'm feeling better already," says Chrysta, and jamming on a forage hat she steps out into the full glare of the sunshine. "Like my own little classical play-pen. So, you going to give me the tour?"

While Dimi works his way across the site, using his stick to push aside stones and agitate any clumps of weed, Electra shows Chrysta the inscription to Epione on a fallen pilaster and explains how the sanctuary would have worked. The temples to Panacea and Hygieia and Asclepius where offerings would have been made; the long rows of single-cell dormitories; the stony foundations of a walled garden where medicinal herbs were grown; and, on the far side of the site, through a thin stand of tamarisk, Electra leads Chrysta to the caves of Douka.

"Once these caves were filled with bones," she explains. "Ossuaries. But they've been cleared. Now, as you can see, there's just a series of underground chambers." Her voice sounds hollow and it echoes as they step out of the sunshine, passing beneath a rock overhang into the cool shade of the first cave.

But what Electra hasn't told Chrysta, she doesn't need to. As always, the Sanctuary of Epione works in its own mysterious way.

"Wow," says Chrysta, almost reverentially. "No bones, maybe, but there's this sense of… I don't know… Peace? Just like you said." She pulls off her hat and wipes a wrist across her forehead.

"I better check on Dimi," says Electra. "Let him know where we are. Just give me a couple of minutes."

"Is it okay if I go on by myself?"

Electra smiles. It's what she's been expecting; what everyone she brings to Epione asks. "Of course. It's the best way. Why don't I wait for you outside?"

"Will I need a torch?"

"Wherever you go, there will always be light."

"If I'm not back in an hour…"

"I'll send in the marines…"

"Just the one will do. Or maybe two," replies Chrysta with a grin.

Outside, Electra walks through the trees back into the sunshine and onto the sloping field of fallen stone. At first, in the glare, she can't see Dimi and her heart starts to race. Where is he? Where has he gone? But then he stands up from behind a low bush and holds up one of his collecting jars.

“It’s the biggest one yet,” he calls out to her. “You won’t believe it. Come see…”

By the time Electra has taken a half-dozen steps, Dimi has covered the distance between them; brandishing the jar, breathless with excitement. “Look at it. It’s a monster.”

Electra takes the jar and studies the scorpion that Dimi has captured. It is certainly big. A dark coppery body, legs stiffly spread for purchase on the smooth glass, its segmented tail arched, its pincers waving.

“Just make sure you don’t get stung,” says Electra, wishing he’d wear the gloves she can see stuffed into his pocket. “And keep your hat on,” she adds. “If you need me, I’m at the caves with Chrysta.”

30

BACK AT the caves, Electra has company. Sitting on a log of chiselled stone, one of a pair that once stood at the entrance to the Epione catacombs, is an old man click-clicking his way through the black beads of his *kombolói*. He wears sunglasses – plastic, old and cheap – a dark suit, and crumpled white shirt buttoned to the collar. His shoes are wrinkled and black, leather and unlaced, dusty and scuffed, and his hair and beard are a thick silvery white. A black dog is curled up at his feet, and starts to growl softly as she approaches. His owner looks up, thumbs and fingers working the beads, nods to her and taps the dog with his foot. The dog quietens, but Electra can see a beady black eye kept on her, hackles slightly raised. She wonders where they have come from, this man and his dog, to appear so unexpectedly when the site had seemed so empty.

"It is a fine day, *Papou*," she says, using the honorific of 'grandfather' for all men over seventy. Which he clearly is, even closer to eighty she reckons.

"Always a fine day with Epione," he replies. His voice is low and raspy, and he clears his throat before he speaks again. "Always a fine day. And a fine place to be."

She sits on the same fallen column and turns towards him. "Have you come far?" she asks.

The old man waves a hand towards Kalypti, and the beads swing between his fingers. "And you?" he asks in return.

"From Douka. The Contalidis house on the road to Anémenos."

He nods, considers the information, as she knows he will. Everyone knows Douka. But he offers no comment. Click-click go the beads. Click-click. Another soft growl from the dog. "Pólu, Pólu," says the man. "Quiet, old girl."

Electra looks towards the entrance to the caves, but there's no sign of Chrysta. She is not surprised. In those cool chambers it is easy to lose track of time. One vaulting chamber leading to the next…

"I know that house," the old man says at last, and she turns back to him. "The house that burned."

"That's right. A terrible accident." And as she says the words, she can almost smell the smoke; a soft sinuous scent of burning wood and hot stone.

The old man nods in agreement. Terrible. Terrible, yes indeed. "And before the fire, old Petrou's house."

"That is so. For a while," she says. "Did you know Petrou?"

A lizard scuttles out from under the column they sit on, and scampers past the old man's shoes. The dog, Pólu, watches its progress; a run in fits and starts, as lizards do; pausing, panting, craning its wattled neck to left and right as though checking for passing traffic. Electra watches, too. And wonders if the dog will go for it. The lizard is long and thick-bodied, with a blue flash on its scaly chest and tiny black diamonds down its spine. Dimi would be after it in an instant, but the dog stays where it is. Just the tiniest movement of its snout on its paws, to better follow the lizard's journey.

Her companion is also watching the reptile, when he speaks. "He was not a bad man," he says. "Not as black as they paint him."

Now it is Electra's turn to make no comment. Perhaps there is a relationship between the two men; a family connection, some distant friendship. It would not do to offend him, so she remains silent.

"You have seen the caves?" he asks now, as though to change the subject.

"Many times."

"And your friend?"

Electra is surprised that he should know about Chrysta. Had he seen them among the ruins, without their seeing him?

"Her first time. I thought it would be nice for her to explore on her own."

"They say that is the best way. She is not frightened to be by herself?"

"In the Sanctuary of Epione?"

"I suppose," the man says, as though, for a moment, he's forgotten where he is. Or maybe, thinks Electra, that such confidence can sometimes be misplaced, the world being the kind of place it is. She cannot decide. But there is something in his tone that makes her get to her feet.

"Maybe I'd better go and make sure."

The old man shrugs. "As you say, I am sure she is perfectly happy. Perfectly safe." And he chuckles, as though remembering now where he is; that Electra's friend could not be anything else but happy and safe.

And she is.

Electra meets Chrysta in the fourth chamber, making her way back to the entrance.

"You're right. It's just… magical. Maybe with all those bones it might have been spookier, but I felt… so relaxed. And the air… so fresh and cool and clean." She takes a deep breath, and casts around.

"Hungry?" asks Electra.

Chrysta frowns, thinks about it. "Fucking starving," she says, and taking Electra's arm, they walk back to the entrance.

Electra can't have been gone for more than a few minutes, but when she and Chrysta step out of the caves the old man and his dog are nowhere to be seen. She peers through the trees, but there is no sign of them. Nor can she see them anywhere on the sloping pitch of ruins, as she and Chrysta gather up Dimi and his collecting jars, and head towards the tamarisk trees where their hamper and blankets are waiting for them.

"Looking for someone?" asks Chrysta, kicking away pine cones before snapping open a blanket and laying it on the ground.

"There was an old man at the caves," says Electra, scanning the treeline, the ruins. "We were talking. But he's disappeared."

"Like he'd never been here," says Chrysta, unscrewing the top of a plastic water bottle and handing it to Dimi. "Maybe he's one of Epione's spirits?"

"He was old, but not that old," replies Electra, settling herself on the blankets and reaching for the hamper. And as she draws out foil wraps and plastic tubs and neatly-folded napkin parcels – hard-boiled eggs and *taramosalata*, some *tzatziki*, a dozen slabs of crusty village bread, slices of smoked island pork, a fresh young goat's cheese, peaches and grapes – she recalls their conversation. About Petrou. *Not as black as they paint him*, the old boy had said. As far as Electra can recall, it is the first kind thing that anyone has ever said about Petrou.

"You want a beer?" asks Chrysta, levering the caps off two bottles she's found in the ice box, and handing one to Electra.

They tip the necks of the bottles together with a glassy chink, and a cold bubbling foam flows over their fingers.

"*Yassas*," says Chrysta.

"*Yassas*," says Electra.

"What about me?" asks Dimi, looking at the beer.

"Just a sip," says Chrysta, "but don't tell your mother."

31

THE DAY is almost done when they arrive back at the house. They are tired and dusty and sun-worn, and after unloading the Jeep they head off in separate directions: Dimi, to add his finds from the Sanctuary of Epione to the growing menagerie of lizards, snakes, and scorpions he keeps behind Nikos's studio; Chrysta, to the top terrace for a dip in the cistern pool – "I'm too sweaty and too filthy for the swimming pool," she says; while Electra, with a strong reminder to Dimi to wear his gloves when he's emptying his jars, opts for a shower and a short siesta. If she's not up by six, she tells them, they must come and wake her. They're grilling a goat's leg for supper, and need to get the barbecue up and running.

But Electra has no time for sleep. As she comes out of the bathroom, naked, towelling her hair dry, she hears Dimi screaming for her.

A long, distant scream. "Ma-ma! Maaah-Maaah!!"

From somewhere behind the house.

Those damn scorpions, and those damn gloves, she thinks; and hopping to pull on jeans and struggling into a t-shirt, Electra runs from the bedroom.

Outside she hears Dimi call again, but from the top terrace... So no scorpions. Instead, she finds Chrysta shivering by the edge of the pool. And sobbing. Legs pulled up to her chest. Arms clasped around them. The sun has gone from this side of the house and the water in the pool is black and still. Chrysta is wearing just her bra and pants, her shorts and t-shirt and trainers in a pile beside her. She is dripping wet, her teeth chattering, her dyed blonde hair slicked against pale cheeks.

"She was drowning," says Dimi, anxious to explain, in case Electra is cross. "She was under the water."

"If he hadn't shown up like he did..." says Chrysta, with a weak smile; reaching for Dimi's hand and drawing him to her.

"But whatever happened?"

"I wanted to show her Hydra..." says Dimi, pointing to one of his collecting jars on the ground beside Chrysta's clothes. A small brown snake is curled up in it, peering through the glass, tongue flicking out, eyes beady and black. "But when I got here, I couldn't see her anywhere. And then I did... Under the water... Not moving..."

"It was like a cramp," Chrysta explains. "Too much sun, maybe. Or the cold of the water. I jumped in, went under... and I just couldn't get back up to the surface. Couldn't move my legs or my arms. Like they were clamped together."

Electra turns to Dimi. "And you went in after her?"

The boy shrugs, uncertain; still not sure if he's going to be told off. "I called for you, but there was no time. I knew I had to do something. She was down there too long. And no bubbles, or anything."

"So you jumped in?"

"It wasn't difficult, Mama. I just dived down and got her, pulled her to the steps. She was all cold and stiff…"

"I think I need a drink," says Chrysta, reaching out a hand.

"I think we all do," says Electra, taking the hand, and pulling Chrysta to her feet. The woman is still cowed and shaking, so Electra stoops down for her t-shirt, wraps it round her shoulders. "Let's get you down in the sun where it's warmer," she says. Then, turning to Dimi, "And what a brave boy you are," she says to him. "I'm so proud of you…"

And as she says it, she hears a chuckling sound in her ear. Close and throaty. Unmistakeable. And with a chill shiver that scatters pin-prick goosebumps over her shoulders and scalp, Electra recognises the sound; knows she's heard it before: the night Gert performed on the salon scaffolding; and just a few hours earlier, at the Sanctuary of Epione. That old man with the dog had just the same dry, catching chuckle.

But it's not a chuckle, she realises. It's a breeze that's come from nowhere; rustling through the grass stalks at the edge of the pool; rippling across the surface. She can see how the sound matches the progress of the breeze.

Later, after putting Dimi to bed, Electra goes to the study where Chrysta holed up after supper to read what's left of Electra's manuscript; tilted back in Electra's chair, crossed ankles on her desk. It's colder than usual, a chill in the air, so Electra lights a fire. The sound of pages turning. The striking of a match. The snap and crackle of vine cuttings and kindling. As the first flames flicker round the room, Electra settles herself in her corner chair and tries to work out how many more pages Chrysta has to read; wonders what she'll think of them, what she'll say? She watches, sees her agent frown, turn the pages back; re-reading. For Electra it is silent torture.

Finally, Chrysta puts aside the manuscript and sighs deeply.

"Is it that bad? When it started out so well?" asks Electra. She tries to make her tone light and breezy, but she can feel her heart hammering with anxiety.

"It's not the writing. It's not the subject. It's just…" Chrysta shakes her head. "It's just I can't fucking seem to concentrate. Nothing to do with the book; it's just my mind's not on it. I think my little ducking in the pool frightened me more than I was prepared to say. In front of Dimi, I mean."

Electra frowns. "I don't understand."

"Well, see, it wasn't just believing that I was going to drown. There was something else… It was like…" Chrysta pauses. "It was as if something was actually holding me under." She shakes her head again, as though she can't find the words to properly explain what she means. "Not a cramp. Nothing like that…"

A log in the grate shifts on the settling vine clippings and firefly sparks shoot up into the chimney.

"It felt… it felt as though I was being held there," Chrysta continues. "As if someone was down there, waiting for me. And when I jumped in they caught hold of me, fucking wrapped themselves around me. I remember trying to scream… but of course I couldn't. All I did was lose most of whatever air I had in my lungs. Which made it all worse. Made me fucking panic. And the more I panicked, the tighter the hold on me…" Chrysta looks at Electra. "You'll think I'm fucking mad, I know. But that's how it felt. As though I was being held under. By something. Someone."

Electra smiles. "It was the sun. The beer. And then that cold water. The shock of it. It couldn't be anything else."

Chrysta doesn't look convinced. "I suppose… It's possible. I just can't shake the feeling that there was someone down there with me. Someone who wanted to do me damage. And look," she says, peeling up the sleeves of her shirt. "Look at these."

There are pale red marks on the top of Chrysta's arms, just above the elbows. Pressure marks, by the look of them. The kind made by tightening fingers.

"Well, I know what those are," says Electra.

"You do?"

"Don't you remember? Sitting on the edge of the pool, and coming back to the house, you had your arms clasped tight. To stop the shivering. They're the marks of your own fingers."

Chrysta shakes her head. "Maybe. Maybe you're right." She frowns, but Electra can see she's not convinced. "I hadn't thought of that."

It is only later, as she prepares for bed, that Electra remembers the fingertip bruises around the neck of the girl that Cossie had spoken of. The yoghurt girl. Heidi. She smiles at the coincidence, but thinks no more about it.

There are clouds the morning Chrysta leaves for Navros, and the ferry to Tsania. A long grey bank rolling up behind the Douka headland like a breaking wave, throwing a stiff northerly breeze ahead of it to gust through the tree tops and rattle the palm fronds.

"No wonder it was so chilly last night," says Chrysta, loading her bag into the Jeep. "*Meltemi.* A summer storm. Sorry to leave you with the bad weather."

"I'll survive," says Electra, and watches as Chrysta gives Dimi a big farewell hug.

"My hero," she says.

"Don't go swimming if I'm not around," says Dimi, whose friends from the village are coming up to the house to play. Electra has already asked Aja and Lina to keep an eye on them.

"No chance, and I promise I'll put in some practice on *Temple Run*."

Dimi looks serious. "You'll have to."

The drive to Navros is spent in companionable conversation. Some suggestions for Electra's book. Their agreed September deadline. Talk of a tour to promote the book that Massalia Press have suggested. TV and radio. It seems to Electra that a good night's sleep seems to have eased Chrysta's concerns about the incident at the pool, the feeling of being held down, and her friend makes no mention of it.

As they crest the pass in the hills above Avrólemou, the bank of cloud thickens and darkens and a wind starts to buffet the Jeep. Down on the coast they can see white-tops in the channel between island and mainland. In the harbour the blue hull and white flanks of the island ferry are clearly visible beyond the town's rooftops. A plume of black streams from its smoke stack, whipped away like a silk scarf in the wind.

"Do you think the ferry will leave?" asks Chrysta, suddenly restless, as though the thought of having to stay on the island a moment longer is more than she can bear.

"It has to be worse than this for the ferries to cancel. It'll be fine, you'll see."

And it is. When Electra pulls up on the quay, the ferry's ramp is down and cars and trucks are rolling on, foot-passengers with cases and backpacks keeping to the sides, showing tickets.

"Thank you," says Chrysta, as they embrace. "You have a lovely home, and I really enjoyed myself. Next time a little more of Epione please, and a little less of that fucking cistern pool."

They kiss a final time, and Electra watches her friend join the queue of passengers.

Chrysta turns and waves. "September, remember? You promised."

"September," Electra calls back.

32

AFTER WATCHING the ferry pull out, and waving one last time to Chrysta at the stern rail, Electra decides to kill two birds with one stone. While she is in town she will call on her father-in-law.

Theo Contalidis is back from the general hospital and sits in a day room at the hospice. A nurse in a bulging blue cotton pantsuit waddles ahead, shows her the way; arms swinging, fast and efficient as though there's no weight to contend with. How fat people always walk, thinks Electra. At the door, the nurse points Electra to an armchair pulled up to a set of open terrace doors, with a view of the garden beyond.

Electra knows that the visit is more for her, and by extension Nikos, than it is for the old man. As Doctor Paradoxis warned them, the stroke has done irreparable damage. The last time she visited, Theo never once looked at her, nor said a word. It was as if he didn't see her. Just the distant, blinkless stare of a dead animal, and a drooping bottom lip revealing four narrow teeth set fast and yellow in his lower jaw. So Electra is expecting nothing more from this visit. A short one, she decides, as she crosses the day room; maybe a quarter of an hour; maybe more if he responds in some way.

At least she'll have been there, tried.

Which will please Nikos, make it easier for him.

She sees the top of Theo's head first, a pale scalp scabbed from some knock, wisps of grey hair standing awry, as though the old man has pushed his fingers through it without patting it down afterwards. She reaches for a chair, straight-backed with a rush seat, and draws it over, setting it beside the old man.

Now she can see him properly. The pink, scarred cheek, the skin-puckered right hand resting in his lap, its fingers held loosely in his left hand. He is wearing a white shirt, its cuffs unbuttoned, and brown trousers that bunch up around his waist as though they're so big he has to be seated to hold them up. Either he has pushed his slippers aside, or they have simply fallen off. His feet are bare, and white and faintly veined, the toenails as yellow as his smoker's fingers and teeth. As Electra draws close she can smell soap. Someone has bathed him, and shaved him. But there are still patches of white stubble on his chin and throat, just the scar of burned skin free of it.

"*Yassou, Papou,*" she says, sitting down, making herself comfortable. She reaches out a hand and rests it on his arm. Firmly enough to feel the narrow columns of stiffened sinew and bone.

Immediately he turns to her, fixes her with a cold black stare, his right eye couched in its sling of red. The movement startles her, and for a moment she finds it difficult to assemble a smile of greeting. But she manages it.

"And how are you today?" she asks, knowing from her own experience what a trite question this is; but she says it anyway. "You're looking well. Are they taking care of you?"

It is then that his eyes switch from hers to a point just behind her right shoulder. He holds the look, watching, peering. And thinking that a nurse has come over to check on them, that this is what has caught his eye, Electra turns. But there is no one there. She looks back at the old man, and slowly, almost anxiously, his eyes return to her. Then they swivel back once more to the same point just behind her. It makes her shiver. As if he can see something that she cannot. She looks again. Again, nothing.

"Nikos says hello. I spoke to him this morning. He's in Athens. Working hard. He told me to tell you that Douka looks wonderful, and that you must come and see it soon."

Nikos has said no such thing. Indeed, he hasn't phoned for the last two days. But Electra says it, because it sounds caring and comforting. Because, if Theo understands what she is saying, he will be pleased that they are thinking of him. That Douka is waiting for him, and that everything is right with the world. Light and breezy chatter. As if nothing is wrong. The way you might speak to a child of a certain age.

Slowly the old man shakes his head.

Electra is surprised by the response. Not only has he looked at her, he appears to have responded to the suggestion that he must visit them at Douka. Even if he clearly doesn't want to. It's all that shake of the head can mean.

"It would do you the world of good," Electra continues, persuasive; knowing it will never happen. "And the gardens are looking lovely."

Once more the old man's eyes dart behind her, over her left shoulder this time. As though whoever is there has moved; someone standing there, listening in.

This time Electra doesn't bother to turn. Instead, she looks out through the terrace window, to the slope of garden beyond. A border of trees. Paths around lawns, benches and wheelchairs; other old men and women, sitting and walking. And nurses, too. Watching them, helping them, talking to them. The sky is dark, and a cool breeze shivers through the twisting limbs of jacaranda that frame the doors. Soon, she thinks, it will rain, and all the people she can see will be brought inside like washing from a line.

When Electra turns back to Theo, his grey eyebrows have knitted together and his eyes continue to dart between her and whatever it is he thinks he can see behind her. Left side, then right side. Backwards, and forwards. Almost fearfully, it seems to Electra.

Then his mouth opens and he starts to say something. A gargle of strained words that Electra can make no sense of. He repeats the same sounds again. And then again. And again, until a line of spittle slides unhindered from the side of his drooping lip.

Electra finds a handkerchief in her pocket and leans forward to wipe the drool away. And as she sits back, bunches up the hankie and slides it back in her pocket, she suddenly understands what it is that Theo is trying to say.

"You have brought him with you… You have brought him with you… You have brought him with you…"

Electra smiles and shakes her head. Does the old man think Nikos is there with them?

"No, I told you," she says. "Nikos is in Athens. He'll be back on Friday. I'm sure he'll pop in to say hello. Tell you all the news. About Athens, and work, and Douka."

The old man's frown deepens, and a shivering breath rises out of his chest. He looks suddenly… frightened; fretful, thinks Electra. He seems to shrink away from her, fold himself up in the chair. Even raises his arms, as though to protect himself.

It is time to go, Electra decides. She glances at the clock on the wall. She has been there a little more than ten minutes. But it is enough. For him, and for her.

More sounds gurgle out of the old man's chest as she stands, pushes back her chair, and leans forward to kiss him. And as her lips touch the top of his head, the sounds he is making become a whisper, as though the old man doesn't want anyone to hear what he is saying.

"Take him way… Take him away… Take him away…"

"You're right, *Papou*. It's time to go." Electra straightens up, looks across the day room and catches the eye of a nurse. The woman gets the message, comes over to them. She slides between them, and straightens Theo in his chair.

"There we are," she says. "More comfortable now? And wasn't that a nice visit? Did you have a good chat? And wasn't it lovely to see your daughter. But you're looking tired, Mr Contalidis. I think, maybe, it's time for your afternoon rest."

And that is how it ends.

With a blown kiss from Electra, that the old man doesn't seem to register.

The nurse taking Electra's place.

The moment to turn and leave.

33

OUT IN THE hospice car park, dancing wind devils spin up the dust. There is no blue sky to be seen, the cloud cover low and ponderous, like a lid screwed tightly down. Electra narrows her eyes against the flying grit, lowers her head, and hurries to the car. Soon it will rain, and the whirling dust will be gone. When she reaches the Jeep there's already a fine creamy skin on the windscreen.

In the driver's seat she pulls on her belt, buckles it, but before starting the engine she digs into her tote for her cigarettes. The packet is empty, and she swears softly. Then she remembers the glove compartment. Sometimes there's a packet there. Stretching the seat-belt, she reaches across to it.

But it's not a cigarette packet that Electra finds.

Something quite different. Unfamiliar. An odd shape. Out of place.

For a moment Electra can't understand what it is that she holds in her hand.

Black, tubular, lighter than it looks; its surface rubbery and dimpled and scattered with tiny red and white figures.

Then she sees the name. On the cap. Six letters. In white. *Nikkor.*

And suddenly it registers, and she remembers. Knows what she has found.

One of the lenses that Franz had lost during the photo shoot.

She puts it on the passenger seat, and delves back into the glove box.

Another lens, longer than the first. Just a little heavier. And two smaller circular containers. She unscrews the lid of one and, bedded down in grey foam, she sees a round tinted lens filter. The loss of which had marked the moment that Gert turned into a monster.

How on earth did they get in the car, she wonders? Did Franz put them in the glove compartment for safe-keeping? Did they borrow the Jeep without telling her? Maybe when they were doing those long shots from the upper olive groves across the Anémenos road? They must have done. And Franz just forgot.

And then the rain comes, making spots in the dust on the windscreen; growing heavier, cutting rivers through it. She starts up the engine, gives a couple of swipes with the wiper blades, and turns out of the hospice.

Back at the house, Electra finds Cossie's business card and phones her mobile number. There is no reply, so she leaves a message, then tries the girl's work number. Whoever she speaks to at the magazine's editorial offices in Athens tells Electra that Cossie is away until the following morning, but that she will let her know about the lenses and filters. She takes Electra's number, and that is that.

Ten minutes later, sorting through her notes for the final chapter, Electra suddenly remembers the scrap of paper that Franz gave her. His cell phone number, should she find the lost equipment. And she knows exactly where that scrap of paper is. When he gave it to her, she'd put it into her shirt pocket, then transferred it to the pin board in the kitchen. And that's where she finds it.

This time her call is answered, but it's a girl on the end of the line, not Franz.

"Hang on a moment, I'll get him for you," the girl tells her. An American accent.

Electra hears the mouthpiece being covered and the muffled sound of his name. *Franz, Franz, Franz.* A few seconds later he is on the line.

"Hi, Franz, it's Electra. I'm just calling to let you know that I've found your lenses, and those filter things."

There is a long pause, as though Franz doesn't quite know who it is, or what is being said. What lenses? What filters? And then he has it.

"Electra. It is good of you to call, to let me know," he begins, uncertainly.

"You sound tired," says Electra.

"I was in bed, sleeping. It's... early, here. I'm in the States. San Francisco. On another shoot."

"I'm so sorry, I didn't realise."

"That's okay. No problem."

Electra can hear a rapid whispering in the background. A girlfriend? Wondering who the woman is who's calling her lover so early in the morning?

"So what should I do with them? The lenses, and things? Do you want me to send them to you? To Gert?" Saying the name makes Electra feel a little uncomfortable.

"You had better send them to me."

"So not Gert?" Electra is relieved. She starts looking for a pen and paper to write down Franz's address.

There is another pause on the end of the line before Franz replies.

"You didn't hear? Cossie didn't tell you?"

"Tell me what?"

"Gert is dead. In Munich, just after he got back. He hanged himself in his studio."

Since Franz had quit as Gert's assistant to work with another photographer there hadn't been much more he'd been able to tell her, save the fact that Gert had been horrified by his behaviour at Douka. "He couldn't explain it," said Franz. "Kept repeating that he wasn't drunk... that someone, some impulse, had made him do it..."

And that's all Electra had been able to establish on the call to San Francisco.

It is Nikos, at the weekend, who gives her the full story. From Cossie, who hasn't yet returned her calls.

That Friday evening they sit on the terrace after Dimi has gone to bed.

"Cossie says Gert had money trouble," Nikos tells her. "Apparently he gambled. And it looks like it all got too much for him. A couple of days after getting back he tied some wrapping twine to a beam, and stepped off a camera case."

"So you've seen Cossie?"

Nikos smiles. "And got what we wanted, my darling. A solo spread in *Arki-Tek*. For the Summer issue. A cover, too. I made her promise."

"I phoned her about the lenses, left a message, but she didn't call back."

Nikos spreads his hands. "She's a busy girl. Deadlines. Trips. But I'm sure she'll ring. Maybe she's a bit embarrassed… after what happened."

That night he is tired, looks tired, goes to bed before her. And when, finally, she follows him he is sound asleep.

She goes into the bathroom, takes a Heripsyn, and only after she has swallowed it does she think about Gert. As she slides silently into bed, she hopes she doesn't dream about him.

The studio beam, the wrapping twine, the camera case.

34

ON SATURDAY morning, back from her run, leaning against a kitchen counter, Electra knocks over her coffee mug. It skitters across the counter then plunges to the floor, shattering on the stone tiles. She had reached for it without looking, thinking she knew where she'd put it down. Yet somehow she'd misjudged the distance; her fingers brushing against it, not getting a proper grip, tipping it over.

An accident, so silly. But Electra suddenly realises why. The time of the month. Except, now, for Electra, there are no times of the month. Any month. She will never again conceive; she will never have children. That's what the doctor had told her at Lycabettus, after Mantó. Softly, with a gentle, understanding smile, a consoling hand on her wrist, and just the smallest shake of the head.

Yet still, without warning, Electra feels those first initial stirrings, as though the time is coming. Like an amputee might sense the presence of a lost limb. And this is one of those times. The first indication of what is to come.

Because it's not just the phantom physical aspects that present themselves – the gentle cramping, the spreading flush. It's her mood, too. Always a little listless, fatigued, in the days leading up to the moment, the moment that never comes; a little irritable, impatient. And clumsy.

Sitting at the kitchen table, Ariadne looks up as the splintering shards of her cup scatter across the tiles. She catches Electra's eye, and Electra recognizes the look. The old woman doesn't miss a trick, she thinks, although on this occasion the old biddy is wrong in her assumption. That Electra has her period. That she is not pregnant. That she will be upset. Because women like Ariadne always imagine that other, younger women want to be pregnant. For whatever reason. And they don't call it the curse because it may hurt, or be messy, but because it's the curse of not falling pregnant. Of not giving a husband what he wants. That's how Ariadne sees it.

And whether Ariadne is sad for her, or disapproves of her as a woman and a wife, or is secretly pleased that she's letting her poor husband down, it's this unwanted familiarity, the unsought intimacy of that look, that so galls Electra. That Ariadne knows these things. How Ariadne can *see*. Or thinks she can. As though she were an intimate member of the family, rather than just the housekeeper.

If there is one good thing about this phantom menstruation, however – indeed, something that Electra knew about before Lycabettus and Mantó – it is that its approach always precedes a very creative, productive time for her. When she was a journalist, she could knock the features out, like a bowler taking down tenpins. And it'll be no different now, writing this book about the Admiral.

For the next couple of weeks, she will be on a roll.

And for the first time since agreeing to it with Chrysta, Electra knows for certain that she will hit their deadline.

It is lunchtime when she sees Nikos and Dimi. After a quick shower, Electra had gone to her study and closed the door, always the sign that she should not be disturbed. And despite a passing footfall, and a whispered conversation somewhere close by, she has been left alone; nearly four hours hammering away at the keyboard. The last days of the Admiral.

She'd been expecting lunch in the kitchen. A *meltemi* could last days, and given the blustery conditions on her morning run she'd assumed that that's what they'd do. But she's wrong. Warm sunshine streams through the kitchen window, and a large hamper stands on the table.

"I told Dimi we could take out the boat. Find somewhere for lunch," says Nikos, latching the hamper closed. "If you've finished, that is? We didn't want to disturb you..." He nods around the kitchen. "I let the girls go early."

Girls, thinks Electra? Ariadne, a *girl*?

Before she can say anything, before she can think, the kitchen door bursts open. It is Dimi.

"Did *Baba* tell you? We're going out on the boat. We're going out on the boat."

Right through the week, after Aja, Lina, and Ariadne leave for the day, Electra always resists her son's pleas to be taken out on the boat. "*Dad won't mind*," he tells her hopefully. "*Dad said it would be okay*." But she never has. She just doesn't feel confident enough. The boat isn't new, but it still cost them a substantial sum. And, along with the house, it is Nikos's pride and joy. So she knows how furious he would be if anything went wrong; if she damaged it somehow, scraped it, or did something to the engine. Given her record with the Jeep, she feels justified in saying no. But now that Nikos is here, he can do the honours. And she can't bear the idea of letting Dimi down. He is beaming with delight. He knows she has no argument. She has to agree.

So she does, just a moment more to gather her thoughts; still somewhere back in the winter of 1848.

"Give me time to grab a swimsuit," she says, "and I'm all yours, my darlings."

An hour later Nikos backs the Riva out of the pagoda boathouse. It is a beautiful craft. Swooping black hull. Sleek wood trim. Sparkling varnish and brass fittings. And plump cream upholstery. As comfortable as a salon sofa. Nikos, barefoot, legs spread, stands at the wheel; Dimi beside him, peering over the side, calls out instructions. “Loads of room here, *Baba*. Go on, go on… You’re fine.”

Out in the cove, Nikos keeps the revs low until they reach the rocky nose of the Douka headland. Once past it, father and son brace themselves, and Nikos pushes forward on the throttle. With a roar of power, the bows of the Riva rise up and the stern settles into a boiling trail of white water.

They drop anchor ten minutes west of Kalypti, in a small bay far enough away for the headland of Douka to be no more than a distant slope of brown rock only marginally higher than the land on either side of it. Before lunch they swim, diving off the bows into cobalt depths, Electra hauling herself up on the stern platform to watch Nikos and Dimi swimming beneath her. Two brown eels, one longer than the other. Small orange shorts, and a larger black pair.

They take their lunch under the canopy that Nikos has devised for the Riva, and set up over the rear deck like the sail shades at the beach pavilion and in the herb garden at Douka. It is not sturdy enough to put up when the Riva is moving, but when she’s at anchor this creamy stretch of canvas provides easily enough shade.

It’s not long after their lunch that Dimi asks if he can swim. There’s a rule about not swimming for thirty minutes after a meal, but the boy is growing impatient. Electra and Nikos may be content to lounge on the cushions, talk, finish their wine, but Dimi wants something more.

Electra looks at Nikos, who consults his watch.

“Another ten minutes,” he says.

The boy’s face drops.

“Oh, let him go,” says Electra. “He’ll be fine.”

Which she thinks about later. Giving in to the boy like that.

If I’d kept him on board for another five or ten minutes, like Nikos wanted, maybe the danger would have passed beneath us. Unseen, undisturbed.

But it is not to be.

Nikos and Electra watch their son snatch up fins, mask and snorkel, and clamber up on the bows. He sits with his legs over the side, pulls on the fins, then stands to work mask and snorkel over his head. Pushes the mouthpiece between his lips, and jumps from the boat.

The Riva rocks a little, and their empty wine bottle clinks against the ice in the bucket.

There’s a splash.

Nikos shakes his head, tight-lipped. But Electra smiles.

And, seconds later, comes the scream. As Dimi breaks the surface.

A shocking, terrifying screech of pain.

Repeated. And repeated. And repeated.

A howl with every breath.

Nikos and Electra leap from the table and climb up onto the bow.

Dimi is below them, thrashing at the water, screaming.

"Jellyfish," says Nikos, with a grimace, and dives into the water, grabs Dimi's arm and drags him back towards the stern platform. Electra follows them along the side of the boat, clambers down onto the ledge and holds out her hands. Together, they hoist the boy aboard. He is shivering and screaming, and Electra can see, as the water streams off him, that his lean brown body is scattered with tiny red marks – on his arms, shoulders, chest, and legs. Pinprick spots that will swell into trailing red welts that Electra knows must sting horribly.

The first thing Electra does is dry him with a towel, patting his skin as he writhes around on the seat where just minutes before they'd been having lunch. And as she does so, with soothing whispers, his screams reduce to a breathless sobbing. Meanwhile, Nikos fires up the Riva, hauls in the anchor and heads straight for the beach. When he gets there, he leaps ashore with the ice bucket, loads it up with handfuls of sand, and climbs back aboard.

"Here, cool damp sand. An old Contalidis trick," he says, and starts rubbing it onto Dimi's skin. This rasping application of the sand soon starts to quieten Dimi. His breathing steadies, and the sobs subside.

But their day is over.

While Electra continues to rub the rising trail of red spots with the sand, Nikos backs the Riva away from the beach, spins the wheel, and pushes the throttles forward. Soon they are bumping their way across the chop, Dimi curled up on the seat, his head in Electra's lap.

At the wheel, heading for Douka, Nikos glances back at them. No smile, just a frown on his face. And Electra wonders if it's concern for the Riva's cream upholstery – all that wet sand – or anxiety for his son that makes him do it. But what a dreadful thing to think, she reprimands herself, and feels a hot flush of shame. Wasn't he the one to dive in, when they heard Dimi screaming; to drag the boy back to the boat, despite the stings that he, too, received? What is she thinking?

And then, at last, they're back at Douka, and Nikos hurries ahead, carrying Dimi up to the house. The boy is quiet now, but he still sobs; and flinches when Electra applies Anoxin from the medicine chest in the kitchen, her fingertips tracing the cooling pink cream over the trailing red ropes of stings.

"All those scorpions and snakes," says Electra, later, to Nikos. "And he gets stung by jellyfish."

35

THAT SUNDAY they stay at home. Just the three of them. No Aja, Lina, or Ariadne. A quiet day. The house their own.

The scarring on Dimi's body has already faded, though it is still possible to see a jagged tracing of red welts across the top of his arms, which he can't stop scratching.

"Don't scratch; it will make it worse," Electra tells him.

"I'm not."

She gives him a look.

The day is bright and cloudless, a whisper of breeze rippling the surface of the pool where they stretch out after lunch on shaded loungers. Dimi, forbidden to swim, stays inside watching TV.

Nikos dozes, just an occasional, gentle snore to mark the passage of his dreams. Beside him, Electra reads a biography of another Greek admiral, Andreas 'Miaoulis' Vokos, a wealthy corn-merchant from Hydra who sailed with Ioannis Contalidis against the Turk off Cape Matapan, at Suda and Pylos, and to the beseiged city of Missolonghi.

Maybe, like Nikos, their lunch and the day's sultry warmth have tired her more than she imagines. Or the account of the Greek fleet's manoeuvres in the Argolic Gulf is too heavy and lifeless to hold her attention. Whichever it is, she puts aside the book and, after staring idly at the shifting surface of the pool, she reaches for her glass of wine.

She has taken just a sip when she is aware that she and Nikos are not alone. She can hear footsteps coming along the kitchen path and onto the terrace. The scuff of rope-soled slippers; the tap of polished boots. But no shapes, no shadows – just this sound of movement, and a growing sense of some close and stifling presence.

Putting down her glass, not daring to look behind her, Electra reaches for Nikos, puts her fingers on his shoulder and shakes him, to alert him. But there is no response beyond a raised hand swatting her fingers aside, and a grunting turn on the lounger, now showing his back to her.

"Niko, Niko," she whispers, urgently. Then she stops. A coldness has fallen across her, as though a cloud has passed in front of the sun, and her skin dances with a series of shivery fits. On her arms, across her shoulders, into her scalp, and down her back.

Now the footsteps are closer, louder too – the scuffing and the tapping – until she can actually feel the draught from people walking past her, one after another; the air fluttering with unseen movement, filled with the sinuous, sickly smell of old clothes and sweat and fear.

Suddenly there is silence, and a stillness. No further sound, no movement.

Electra sits up on her lounger, and rubbing the shivers from her shoulders she looks around. The shimmering surface of the pool, the creamy limestone tiles that surround it, the house rising up behind her. All as it should be.

And yet…

From nowhere, behind her now, between their loungers and the house, come other sounds. Voices, this time. Two kinds. The first low, and murmuring. The second clipped, and certain. But for the life of her, she cannot make out a word.

And then…

In the very next instant, one single jerking sound brings everything into focus. A loud, mechanical ratcheting which she recognises immediately. The unmistakeable sound of bolt-action rifles being loaded, rounds chambered.

And, in her fevered imagination, the guns being raised, and…

…A voice, a man's voice, whispering in her ear, close enough for her to feel the breath against her skin.

"He wants you to die. He's going to kill you."

But the words are lost to the sudden, scattered staccato sound of gunfire shattering the sunlit peace of the afternoon; echoing off the lofty walls of Douka, ringing out in harsh clattering notes that sweep down over the terraces to the distant line of pines and the beach beyond.

Electra springs up from her lounger, eyes wide, heart pounding; a choking scream catching in her throat, then bellowed out as she comes awake.

"My darling, my darling, *agapi mou…*" It is Nikos, kneeling beside her lounger, reaching for her, drawing her into his arms. "Are you all right? You were dreaming, a nightmare… You scared me half to death."

And coming out onto the terrace, there is Dimi.

"Mama? Mama? Are you okay? What was that scream?"

And trembling, shivering with an icy chill, Electra calls out to him, trying to laugh it off, trying to make light of it. "Just a dream, my darling. Just the most horrible dream."

36

FOTIS PARADOXIS, the Contalidis family doctor, arrives forty minutes late and is effusive in his apologies. His Tuesday morning surgery in Navros had gone on longer than expected, he explains, and he hopes he hasn't inconvenienced Electra. He is in his late sixties, a small bird-like man with a beaky nose, thin black hair, lush black eyebrows, darting black eyes and a thick black stubble that looks like it needs a couple of shaves a day to control. His lips are thin and pink amidst the black bristles, and his teeth a sparkling white. He wears a cream linen suit with a black waistcoat, a looping gold watch chain strung across it, and he sports a Paisley bow-tie in a worn white collar. A panama hat completes the picture, and a big black bag proclaims his profession; he could be nothing other than a doctor on a house call. As he steps through the door, he drops the bag on a chair and sets his hat on the Admiral's desk.

After shaking his hand and ushering him in, Electra assures him that there is no inconvenience, that she is pleased to see him, and that it is kind of him to come so far. Such a long drive, she says, when he must be so busy; she would have been only too happy to visit his surgery, she tells him.

But he waves a hand. A pleasure, Madam. No trouble at all. Such a lovely day, such beautiful countryside. And the drive over to Douka has done him the world of good, he tells her, taking in a deep breath and letting it out with a smile; as though he has hiked there, as though the air is more rarefied on this side of the island.

She offers him coffee, some water, some wine? He asks for water and a coffee, so she leads him to the kitchen.

Of course, Electra knows why the good doctor suggested a house call. He wants to see the house; wants to see what they've done to the place. So, when he has finished his coffee and the small talk is over, she asks how long it has been since he last visited Douka?

"Three, maybe four years now," he replies, looking around the kitchen. "When old Mr Contalidis came back, of course. And after the fire."

"Did you visit while Petrou was here?"

Fotis Paradoxis shakes his head. "Oh no, not Petrou. Cigars and brandy were his preferred medicines. And they seemed to do the job. In his eighties when he died, and just a handful of consultations."

"With you?"

"Not with me, no. On no account. With Grigoriou, in Messinos. We shared our notes, of course. With just six doctors on the island, it is important to stay in touch."

There is a moment's silence. Paradoxis puts down his cup, and looks around the kitchen.

"A little different from when I was last here," he says. "Though I see you have kept the old stone sinks."

"Nikos insisted they stay. 'Generations of Contalidis dishes have been washed in them', he said. 'They're part of the family now'."

Paradoxis chuckles. "And he is right, of course. And about the only things that survived the fire. I remember washing my hands in them many times. When Nikos was sick, or his mother... No running water upstairs in those days unless you carried it up in jugs..."

"So, can I give you the tour? If you have the time?"

He pulls out his pocket-watch, flips open the lid, and then slides it back in its snug. "Why, I would love to see what you have done. The last time I was here, after the fire, it was just a shell. Everything gone. Only the walls..."

And so Electra shows him around the house: the two salons facing the terraces and gardens; the dining room with its half-timbered walls; and the library and study at the back of the house, cool and shaded, looking out onto the walled courtyard and the rising sun-blanched slopes of Douka.

"Remarkable," he says, time and time again, as they move from room to room. "I remember there were wide plank floorboards everywhere..."

"According to Theo, they were made up from decking. From the Admiral's ships."

Paradoxis nods. "And it was probably the varnish on them and the tarring that contributed to the blaze... Such a conflagration. You could see the glow in Navros, you know? Such a tragedy. Although the blue concrete floors are more than I expected."

"So cool in the summer. And in winter, they are heated."

"Heated? My, my. And so smooth. Like glass."

Upstairs, Paradoxis admires the bedrooms, the bathrooms, the spear-tip tiling, pausing between rooms at each family portrait. Nods at each one, as though greeting old friends; crossing the corridor from the Contalidis men to their wives.

"An extraordinary family, Madam. A grand dynasty. And back where they belong. But how did they survive the fire?"

"The month before, would you believe, Nikos had them sent to Athens for cleaning and re-framing. If he hadn't..." She spreads her hands. "And the Admiral's desk, downstairs? Dragged from the flames by two of the firemen. A miracle."

After the tour is over, Electra shows Paradoxis into the main salon and they sit across from each other.

"Now, Madam, how can I be of assistance?" He sits forward, clasps his hands, and smiles. "If it's about your father-in-law I regret to say that there is little improvement; and none, I fear, that can be realistically hoped for."

"No, no," says Electra. "It's nothing to do with Theo. It's about my medication. The pills..."

Paradoxis tips his head like a bird on a branch. "Which are?"

"Tropsodol, Chlorsodyl, and Heripsyn."

The good doctor purses his lips. "Prescribed for you by...?"

"Doctor Fastiliades, at the Aetolikou Clinic."

"This would be following your... upset? A breakdown, I believe?"

Electra takes a breath. "Losing my baby, yes."

"Well, they are certainly strong prescriptives, Madam. A considerable... cocktail. And each relying on the other, as I'm sure you've discovered. Which is why they are so often prescribed together. The Heripsyn to help you sleep, the Chlorsodyl to... refresh you, and the Tropsodol for... balance. As I say, Madam, strong medicine. And the dosage?"

Electra tells him, and he nods. "A high dose, indeed."

"But I've stopped taking them..."

"You've stopped?"

"I felt I didn't need them anymore."

"So you stopped taking them. Just like that." Paradoxis frowns.

"Sometimes, the Heripsyn. Occasionally the Tropsodol. Or the Chlorsodyl... But otherwise..."

"Self-medication is never to be advised, Madam. As I'm sure you know. And you haven't spoken about this to Doctor Fastiliades?"

Electra admits she has not. She doesn't like Fastiliades, she tells the doctor, and she knows he would never agree to any changes in the dosage. "They're just too strong. I feel... controlled. Almost... deadened. And I don't want to feel like that anymore."

"Does your husband know? Have you told him?"

Electra shakes her head. "When he's here at the weekend, he still sets them out for me. The Heripsyn at night, the others lined up in the bathroom every morning. In case I forget. He'd be cross if he knew, and I don't want to worry him. You won't say anything, will you?"

"Perhaps you might tell him yourself, when you feel the time is right."

"Thank you."

"So, tell me. Have you noticed any side effects since you stopped the medication?"

Relieved by the doctor's promise of discretion, Electra reels off the things she's noticed. Her increased, or reborn, sense of smell, taste, hearing. The occasional dizziness, and breathlessness, and the way her hands sometimes shake; and how she can't seem to stop the shaking. "I sit on them," she says with an awkward smile. "Or put them in my pockets. Until it stops."

Paradoxis nods. "Coming down so swiftly from such strong medication will have all sorts of effects, of course. And for every patient these effects can differ greatly. Smell, taste, hearing all sound rather good to me..." he chuckles, as though he should be so lucky. "But apart from the shaking and dizziness, which I would expect, has there been anything else that you've noticed?"

"Sometimes, I lose things, and can't remember where I put them," she manages. "And dreams. I have the strangest dreams." But she does not say just how disturbing, and real, these dreams can be. Indeed, sometimes she wonders if they really are dreams. She feels so awake when they happen. Like Sunday's experience on the terrace.

"Ah," says Paradoxis, nodding. "That will be the Heripsyn. But otherwise, has there been any… stress – over small things? Maybe some mental or physical discomfort? Even paranoia, perhaps? A sense that the world is against you? That you can't do anything right?"

Electra tries to think. "No, not really. Although, I suppose, sometimes I can be a little short-tempered, easily irritated. Which didn't seem to happen before… If Dimi's being naughty, you know, that kind of thing? And any sort of untidiness, around the house – clothes lying around, lights left on, taps dripping. As if it's been done deliberately, to annoy me. Ridiculous, I know, but…"

"And do you drink? Take other drugs?"

Electra shakes her head, and the doctor nods approvingly. "Never a good idea," he says, but she is not certain he believes her. Didn't she offer him a glass of wine when he arrived?

"So," Paradoxis continues. "I would say that you really should resume the medication as directed by Doctor Fastiliades. But perhaps we could reduce the dosage by a half, and see how things go? The Tropsodol comes in capsule form so take just the one rather than two. As for the Chlorsodyl and Heripsyn, just half a tablet. There is a dividing line on each; you just bite it, like so."

37

THERE ARE four men from Anémenos and Kalypti employed at Douka to keep the gardens in order. They work on a Tuesday, Thursday, and Friday. Which is why Electra is surprised to see one of them weeding a border on the lower lawn that Wednesday afternoon.

Electra is alone in the house. Dimi is out with Lysander and Kostis learning to sail at Vanti Bay, and will be dropped back at the house that evening. Which means she has the whole day to herself, undisturbed, to work on the book.

She stays in her study until she hears a deep silence settle on the house – when Ariadne and the girls have left for the day. She looks at her watch. A little before one. She'll finish the sequence she's on – the last meeting between the Admiral and Mantó Mavroyénous at Suda – and then fix herself some lunch.

An hour later, she pushes away the laptop, stands and stretches. Her fingers sing from the keys and the muscles in her lower back take some gentle rolls and switches to settle back in place. Writing, she decides, is a hazardous occupation.

In the kitchen she makes some pita fills, pours herself some wine, and carries her lunch tray to the terrace. It is then, settling the tray on the table, that she sees the man on the bottom lawn. He has his back to her, bent over the border he's working on, so she can't see his face; whether it is Lina's father, Elias, or her brother, Dilos, or Joannou, or the one whose name she can never remember, the one with the moustache, she can't tell. But there is something familiar in the way this man moves. The rhythm of his body, the reach and draw back of his arms, the bunching of his shoulders under his blue work shirt.

Back in the kitchen Electra slots her plate and glass and cutlery in the dishwasher, then remembers the gardener. Even though he's in the shadow of the pines above the beach, it will still be hot out there. Usually this is the time the Douka gardeners take a break, retreating to the cool of the tool sheds. But this man has carried on working.

Taking a bottle of water from the fridge, Electra pulls on a straw hat and leaves the house, crossing the top-most terrace and going down the first flight of steps. On the top lawn, her view of the lowest terrace is restricted and she loses sight of the man. But reaching the next set of steps, she sees him again, standing now, walking along the border as though admiring his work. She calls out to him, but he seems not to hear her. Once again she loses sight of him as she crosses the second lawn, but when she reaches the final flight of steps there is no sign of him.

She stops on the bottom step, and looks around. For a moment she wonders if he has gone into the trees to relieve himself – which might be embarrassing if he comes out to find her there, so close – but she can see no sign of a blue shirt in the shadows of the pines. Nor can she see him further along the line of trees as they rise up towards the vines, or to the right, the land sloping down to Kalypti.

And, she notices now, there is no sign of work on the borders: no pulled weeds, no freshly turned earth, no cuttings. She looks around, trying to decide where he might have gone: to the beach for a swim, which she knows the gardeners sometimes do? Or to the tool sheds to rest up?

The beach is closest so she goes there first; down through the pines, negotiating the roots and fallen cones. But the crescent of sand is deserted. No swimmer here, no idle sunbather. Retracing her steps Electra makes for the sheds, a line of lime-washed storehouses that separates the pines from the first of the vines. Again there is no sign of the man, no one answering her call; so she leaves the bottle of water on the shed doorstep and heads back to the house; taking the longer path beside the vines rather than going back to the lawns and climbing the terrace steps.

The path is narrow, a studded mix of polished stone and dirt that has lain here for centuries; leading up to the guest cottages, and from there, along a paved path lined with oleander, to the house. She is coming round the side of the end guest house, the one where Cossie stayed, when she hears a low growl. She stops, listens. Beyond the guest cottages, unseen, the palm fronds rattle as a breeze shifts through them, and she notes that the steady hum of insects has faded as though it's too hot for them to perform. Carefully, quietly, listening out for another growl, preparing to come face to face with the dog that had frightened Cossie, she peers around the side of the guest house, keeping close to the stone wall.

And there it is, its coat a dull, dusty black. But no monster this. Lying on a fat, balding belly, a greying snout between its paws, its familiar black eyes hold hers, and its lips, twitching for a snarl, show more gum than teeth. And sitting beside the dog, on the step of an old mounting stone, in the shadow of the guest-house eaves, is the old man from Kalypti and the Sanctuary of Epione. Black homburg pushed back on his head. Hands clasped on the top of his stick, as though he has just settled there for a moment to catch his breath. The same black suit and white buttoned shirt, the same leather shoes. No laces, dusty and creased. The only things missing are the *komboloi*, and the cheap plastic sunglasses.

He touches the side of the dog with a foot. "Pólu, Pólu, shush now. Shush," he *says*, seeing Electra come round the corner; looks up at her as though he has been expecting her, as if he knows that this is the way she will come; gives her a nod of greeting. His eyes, through the wrinkles, are bright and black, like the polished beads of his *komboloi*.

"I hope you don't mind," he says. "I was just passing by, and it was hot."

"It is good to see you again, *Papou*," she says, wondering how this could be when he is several hundred metres from the road to Anémenos. Perhaps, she thinks, he is on his way to Kalypti, and has taken a short cut across the Douka property. But it's still a long hike, and if he is heading for Kalypti, then he's chosen the wrong time of day for such a journey. It is an hour or more past midday, and the heat is intense now, dry and dusty, almost stifling. No wonder he's decided to take a rest.

She stands in front of him. He looks small and hunched and tired, and she wishes she had kept the bottle of water rather than leave it at the tool sheds. If the guest-house doors had been unlocked, she'd have fetched a glass of water from the nearest bathroom. As it is, she says, "Please, come up to the house. Rest there a while, and I can get you something to drink. For your dog, too."

The old man goes through the traditional village ritual of a nod and shake of the head – not quite a 'yes', not quite a 'no' – followed by a small shrug, as though, at the very least, the offer is worth considering. Then he opens his hands on the top of his stick to accept her invitation.

Another language, thinks Electra; and not a word spoken.

It is fifty metres from the guest cottages to the edge of the terracing, and a further twenty metres to the herb garden beyond. But there is no shade worth speaking of on the way there, and though the path is not steep enough to warrant steps, there's still enough of a slope to slow the old man down. When the path opens up at the top terrace so they can walk side by side, Electra offers her arm. But he waves it off with his stick, as though he has no need of help. "*Ochi, ochi*," he says, a shortened breath for each word.

Then, finally, the ground levels and they walk between the raised herb beds to the kitchen door where he comes to a sudden halt, as though he cannot go further. The dog, Pólu, pushes itself against the old man's legs as though urging him on. Electra makes the decision for him, steps forward, opens the door and stands aside. "Please come in, *Papou*," says Electra.

The old man eyes her uncertainly. And then, "Stay," he says to the dog, and pushes him with his stick to a line of shade beneath the kitchen windows. The dog does as he's told, finds a spot, circles it a few times then flops to the ground, panting. And as her guest passes her, Electra can smell garlic and woodsmoke on him, and, somewhere beneath it, a softer sweet old-fashioned scent, the scent of ancient barber shops. Coming in after him, she goes to the table, pulls out a chair and beckons him to it. As he settles himself, taking off his hat, looking around the kitchen, Electra finds a glass, and fills it at the fridge.

"I'm Electra," she says, putting down the water in front of him. "I quite forgot to introduce myself." When he has taken a few sips, she holds out her hand. "Electra Contalidis."

He puts down his glass and, almost reluctantly, takes her hand in his, gives it a limp once-up-and-down shake. The hand is icy cold from the glass.

"And you are? You haven't told me your name."

"Alexandros," the old man replies.

Electra cannot decide if he's given her his surname or Christian name. Or maybe both: Alex Andros.

The old man senses her uncertainty. "Everyone calls me Aleckos."

"So, Aleckos. It is a long walk to Kalypti."

"At my age every walk is a long walk."

"Can I offer you a lift home when you are ready?"

"That would be very kind. But what I would like best is to see this house. Now that I am here again. It has changed so much."

Electra is taken aback. "You know it? You have been here before?"

The old man chuckles. "My mother worked here as a young woman. My father, too. Many years ago. For the Contalidis. I came with her many times when I was a boy."

Finishing his water he gets up from the chair, reaches for his hat and stick. There is, it seems to Electra, a new vigour in him. A sudden sprightliness she hadn't noticed before. He is clearly ready for the tour, so Electra leads him from the kitchen and shows him what they have done to the house. He nods, or frowns, at everything he sees. As though he remembers, or can't remember. Or maybe because he isn't sure, Electra thinks, what he makes of how they have decorated the house – her sister's paintings, the *objets*, the TV and computers, the furnishings. Not to mention the concrete floors dyed blue. She offers to show him the rooms upstairs, but he shakes his head. The stairs, he tells her. Instead, he puts on his hat and, leaning on his stick, he walks out onto the terrace.

"I should get you home," she says, glancing at her watch.

"Please not to bother. I shall walk. From here it is not so far," he replies, adjusting the brim of his hat and nodding to the bottom lawn. "I will be home before you can drive me there," he says.

"Are you sure? It's really no bother."

In answer, he gives a sharp little whistle; and a moment later his dog lopes around the corner and out onto the terrace.

"We forgot to give him water," says Electra.

"He'll have it when we get home. He will be fine." And with that the old man starts down the terrace steps, his dog at his heels.

Electra watches him across the lawns, wondering if he will turn so that she can wave.

But he doesn't look back. And then, on the lowest level, Aleckos and his dog simply disappear.

There one minute, gone the next.

Blending into the shadows, or blocked from view by the trees or the terracing, Electra can't say.

38

THE FOLLOWING day, after Ariadne and the girls have left, Minos Karoussis, the builder from Kalypti, calls by to check on his plastering and painting. He stands in the hallway with Electra, and looks at the wall.

"What did I tell you, Madam? It is perfect. You can hardly see where the work was done." He turns to Electra and gives her a sly grin. "Did Mr Contalidis notice anything?"

"Not a thing, Mr Karoussis. You were right."

Remembering he's from Kalypti, she offers him a coffee, which he accepts; and when they're sitting at the kitchen table she asks about the old man she met at Epione, the old man in whose chair Minos now sits.

"There are many old men in Kalypti, Madam. Fishermen, old builders like me. The young ones, they don't stay too long these days." He takes a sip of coffee, the cup held with surprising delicacy in his bulky builder's hand, and follows it with a mouthful of water. "Do you have a name?"

And though she knows the old man had told her his name, she simply can't remember it.

"Silvery white hair and beard," says Electra, trying to picture him; surprised she can't provide more detail.

Minos thinks about it, frowns, then shakes his head. "Maybe he comes from further down the coast? Did he say he was from Kalypti?"

And Electra is not sure. Did he say he was, or not? All she can recall is that wave of the hand, in the direction of Kalypti. Like the young man in the olive groves; he'd done the same thing, used the same gesture.

"It would be a long way to come from anywhere else on his own," she says.

"You'd be surprised how far some of those old boys can wander," Minos replies.

After Minos leaves, Electra returns to the study and works on her book until it's time to pick up Dimi from Pelamotís; a birthday party for the Lountzis boy, Andreas. His parents, Iakavos and Marika, are old friends of Nikos, but Electra has little time for them. Iakavos is a football and politics bore, and Marika has a tight, disdainful haughtiness about her. The raised Ariadne eyebrow and, more often than not, a look of simmering disapproval. Small-minded. Island-minded. Electra always makes an effort, of course – for Nikos – but it's never easy. When she'd driven Dimi to their house that morning, she'd dropped him at the gates, watched him join the other kids, and then driven off with just the briefest wave and smile to Marika. Have fun…

But as she pulls out of Douka's drive for the return journey, Electra knows it won't be so easy this time round. And it's not. The usual scramble of tiresome mothers, chattering like sparrows; Marika and Iakavos thanking everyone for their son's birthday presents; offering plates of cake and glasses of wine to toast the birthday boy – which Electra takes advantage of, to swallow down a Tropsodol – until finally, thankfully, she is able to scoop up Dimi, make her excuses and leave, shushing his pleas to stay just a little bit longer.

Enough is enough, she thinks. She's done her duty.

Later, after she's managed to get a sugar-rush Dimi to sleep, Electra rolls herself a joint and sprawls out in front of the television with a bottle of Contalidis white. Watches *Out of Africa*, cries at the end, just as she cries every time she watches it, and then struggles off the sofa. To find, unsurprisingly, that she's just a little unsteady on her feet, which makes her giggle. But not so unsteady that she has too much difficulty locking the doors and switching out lights. She is crossing the hallway for the stairs, still a little light-headed, with a gentle sway to her walk, when she hears the low, single buzz of her mobile. A message.

This time her mobile is where she left it. On the hall table beside her sister's bronze of Dimi. She picks it up. An unknown caller. She swipes to the message.

Phone this number. Ask for Nikos.

She doesn't know the number, but thinking it may be important she calls as instructed.

"Thanos, good evening," comes an oily voice.

She recognises the voice, tries to place it. And the name. Thanos, she thinks. Thanos? Thanos? And then she has it. Of course. A small quayside restaurant on the road to Vouliagmeni. Chic and expensive. But absolutely not her kind of place. Too brash, too commercial, too… touristy.

"Restaurant Thanos…" the voice says again.

"Is a Mr Contalidis there?" Electra asks.

"Mr Contalidis? Let me see…"

Electra remembers the voice now, the *maitre d'*; round and squat with a ridiculously thin moustache set too high above the top lip. The way he ran his finger down the reservations book on that old timber lectern when Nikos took her there. Before they were married. It was a very romantic spot. Trust Nikos to know it. Tables set out on a jetty, tablecloths as pink as the evening sky, candle stubs in knobbly red glass jars; the gentle suck of the sea against stone pilings.

And then the *maître d'* with the thin moustache is back on the line. "Yes, here we are. Would you like me to…?"

"No, no. It doesn't matter," she interrupts. "I don't want to disturb him."

She breaks the connection, but there are suddenly so many things she wants to know. Who sent her the message, and how does this person know Nikos is at Thanos? And why should he or she message her to tell her where her husband is? Heart unaccountably thumping, she goes to 'Recents' and finds 'Nikos'. Presses the name, makes the call.

Nikos answers on the sixth ring. "Hello, my darling. Is everything okay?" He sounds concerned.

"No, no, everything's fine," she manages, realising she's not really in the best state to talk to Nikos, but covering it well. "I was on my way to bed. I just thought I'd call to… to… let you know I miss you."

"And I miss you, too, *agapi mou*. But I'm back tomorrow. If I can manage it, I'll catch the early ferry."

"Call me and let me know."

"Yes, I'll do that."

"So what are you up to?" she asks.

"Finishing up. It's been a busy day. The Philippiades moving in."

"You're at the office, or at home?"

"Heading home now," he replies.

"Well, take care, Niko, and I'll see you tomorrow."

"I'll phone you about the ferry."

When the call is over, Electra chides herself. She should have been bolder. Should have asked about the restaurant – directly. Instead, Nikos has phrased his answers in such a way that he has not incriminated himself.

But had he done it deliberately, or not? Did he have something to hide? Thanos was not what you might call a restaurant for business meetings. Not with that jetty, and pink cloths, and candles guttering in their red jars.

But maybe, with the Philippiades so close…?

All Electra can say for sure is that Nikos was at Thanos.

Whoever had sent her the message knew it, and the restaurant had confirmed it.

And if she had called him when he was 'heading home', then he must have left Thanos within seconds of her speaking to the *maître d'*. He'd have hardly had time to start the car.

If Nikos is having an affair, Electra knows that it isn't the first time he has been unfaithful. In the twelve years they've been together, Electra is aware of three liaisons. She didn't know the women, and didn't want to know them. She'd simply read the signs. Put two and two together. The first time had been the hardest to bear, not two years after their marriage, and just months into her first pregnancy. But it hadn't lasted, and nor had the other two.

And she had done nothing about it. Followed her mother's example and kept her suspicions to herself. And it worked. And, she believed, their marriage was the stronger for it. She'd seen off three interlopers, three contenders – maybe more, who knows? – but Nikos was still her husband. Would always be her husband.

Anyway, that's how men were. That's what her mother had said; that's why her mother had excused her own husband's several indiscretions. And Nikos was certainly no exception. Such a flirt. It was no surprise that other women fell for his charm. But these affairs had never lasted; never would.

Electra had girlfriends who'd raised the roof when they'd discovered their husbands' trangressions; and those marriages that didn't end in divorce still suffered for the confrontations. No, she'd decided early on. She would cause no stir, make no waves. She would let it pass. Let him play. He had so much to lose after all.

And he does love her. She knows that for certain. Would never let her go. Cares deeply for her, and for Dimi. He had shown that quite clearly after Mantó. No one could have been more loving. More understanding. And she loves him for it. Will never stop loving him.

And that, she decides, as she slides into bed, is why she will say nothing. Because it is not important.

But what is important, and intriguing, she suddenly thinks, is who sent her the message?

Someone who knows Nikos. And her.

Someone who has her mobile number.

She looks at the time. It is late. But not too late to call. To find out who it is.

Reaching to the bedside table she picks up her mobile, swipes to open, and taps for 'Messages'.

But there is no listing.

No message, no unknown caller.

Had she deleted it, she wonders? She can't remember. But she must have done. How else could it have disappeared?

How stupid, she chides herself.

But she is relieved, too.

Now she doesn't have to call. Can't call.

That is what Electra thinks as she puts her phone back on the bedside table and switches out the light.

And with just half a Heripsyn she falls asleep, her cheek cupped in her hand, and dreams of Nikos.

The man she loves.

Mayhem

(Πανδαιμόνιο)

39

HE WAS everything she had ever wanted, ever hoped for, in a man.

From the very first moment there had never been a second's doubt. Indeed, she couldn't quite believe her good fortune.

She had met him in her editor's office in Athens. He was wearing an open-necked white shirt, black linen jacket and jeans, and was barefoot in black buckled loafers. When she came through the door he sprang to his feet, reached for her hand and shook it – a dry, strong clasp. And a smile... oh, that smile. Lips creasing into his cheeks, denting them with tiny dimples; teeth as white and even as a toothpaste ad; eyes brown as honey and sparkling, like warm pools dancing with sunlight; hair a tumbling wave of black that he pushed back with spread careless fingers – hair not long enough to reach the shoulders, but full and glossy, wild and wilful, hair that refused to be put back in place. He'd pulled out a chair for her, waited till she was seated, and then sat back down himself, turning in his seat to include her; crossing his legs, hitching the knee of his jeans.

Which was when she'd noticed his shoes – no socks, bare feet. Smooth brown skin, and just a wisp of dark black hair at his trouser hem. It was oddly intimate, to see those tanned, well-turned ankles, and she had felt a strange... discomfort wasn't quite the right word, but she was... well, she was aware of it. His body... Lean, tall, broad shouldered, energetic. The open-necked shirt, only the top button undone; the white cuffs with amber studs as brown as his eyes; and his hands. Strong, but elegant hands. Almost an artist's hands...

She knew the name, of course. Nikos Contalidis. A joint partner in ConStav, one of the city's most exciting architectural design practises. Had seen his work featured in newspapers and the trade press: a restaurant make-over in the old meat-packing district of Psiri; an art gallery in Gazi; a German banker's villa extension in Filothei; a school sports stadium in Vironas; a shopping mall in Peristeri. All of them small to medium projects, but each commission completed on time, within budget, and with a minimum of fuss or fanfare. There was no need for any of that. The work spoke for itself. A new classical form, with occasional Bauhaus and modernist accents: bright and light, clean and spacious; all sheer glass and dressed limestone and smooth polished concrete. As far as she had been able to tell it was Nikos who had the artistic vision, his older partner, Vassilios Stavrides, the one who put that vision into construction. But they worked together well, sharing the same aesthetic; a new kind of dream team. Which was how *I Kathimerini* had described them in their feature on the banker and his extended Filothei villa.

But none of the pictures that accompanied the Filothei article or the other press stories about ConStav – the new commissions, the ongoing projects, the various awards-nominations that had started to mount up – quite did justice to the man who sat at her editor's desk. That soft, cajoling voice, and those twinkling honey-brown eyes taking her in. But it wasn't just the colour of his eyes, or the way they settled on her, that she particularly noticed. It was their steadiness. Their gentleness. Like his voice. And not once did he look at her in any way that wasn't friendly, enthusiastic, professional. Exactly how he'd have behaved if she had been a man.

Which intrigued her.

And slightly annoyed her.

Three hours after that first meeting, Nikos Contalidis had phoned her; told her how pleased he was that they would be working together; wondered whether she would join him for lunch the following day?

If he had suggested dinner, she would have said no.

That he should suggest lunch was a different matter.

A point in his favour.

Not that he needed any more points.

From the moment Costanza Theofilou set eyes on Nikos Contalidis she knew that they would become lovers.

His wedding ring meant nothing.

Just a hoop of gold.

Cossie had noticed the wedding ring within minutes of meeting him; when he brushed his fingers through his hair. A glint of gold, loose against the brown knuckle of his left index finger. It was the first thing she looked for in a man who caught her attention. Taken, or not. Up until now, it had always made a difference. Married men were not an option. There had been offers, of course; advances made. But there had always been enough single men to fill her time.

Nikos Contalidis was different.

The morning of their lunch, in her studio apartment in Thiseio, Cossie decided against her usual office uniform of jeans, trainers and Hawaiian-print cotton shirts in favour of a more formal outfit. A tailored tweed jacket, a pale brown suede skirt that reached to just above her knees, and a pair of red Chrisos Trisakis stilettos. When she looked in the mirror she nodded approval. The jacket highlighted her narrow waist, the crisp white shirt with the top two buttons undone provided a certain emphasis to what lay beneath, and as she turned on her heel she saw, over her shoulder, how the Trisakis stilettos gave a long, tightening definition to her calves. Formal, but not too formal; business-like, but stylish. The very picture of a modern, professional woman. It might draw a comment or two from some of the boys in *Arki-Tek*'s Art department who were more used to Cossie's pared-down office look, but not enough to arouse undue interest or fuel any speculation. She was booked for a business lunch, after all.

With a final glance at the mirror, bending forward, lifting her chin, and seeing just the shadowy suspicion of cleavage, Cossie left her apartment and went to work.

She was late for their lunch.

Deliberately.

Closer to one than the agreed twelve-thirty.

He was sitting on a bar stool at Acteon, a popular brasserie on Alexandrou in Metaxourgeio. Dark blue jeans, light blue polo shirt, and a brown Timberland blouson. And his trademark barefoot loafers. He had ordered a bottle of Amyntaion which stood in a bucket on the bar. When he saw her come though the entrance, he'd asked the barman to fill her glass, and crossed the room to greet her. A handshake, a tentative kiss on her cheek. Friendly, informal. Not weighted in any way.

For the next hour or so they had talked business; the kind of off-the-record interview-style chat that Cossie was so good at. Drawing out her subject, engaging him, the full blast of her attention on him: how he'd met his partner, Vassilios Stavrides; the early days of ConStav; how they'd dealt with the financial crisis, the bad times, the good – the usual drift that *Arki-Tek* preferred for their lighter, front-of-book features; on this occasion the half-page story that Cossie was writing for the August issue about ConStav's latest project, a small-businesses unit in Piraeus.

"We work best when we work together," he told her, a real passion in his eyes, even if it did sound like an oft-repeated sound-bite. "And that doesn't just mean colleagues, the people we work with. It also means where we work, how we work. And for that to happen, our environment is crucial – space, light, freedom, comfort…"

So it went, a gentle jousting until, over their coffees, they spoke about other things – books, films, places they loved. Lightweight stuff, getting a brief personal resumé after the business had been dealt with.

Then, after finishing his coffee and calling for the bill, Nikos had leaned across the table towards her, a hand reaching out to hold her arm, draw her nearer.

"I want to fuck you," he'd whispered in her ear.

Just like that.

She wasn't surprised. She'd been expecting it. But maybe more gently put – in which case she might have declined. The sudden roughness of his words, however, and the touch of his breath in her ear, the soft brush of his stubble against her cheek, the warm salty scent of him, as though he'd just stepped ashore from his boat, and the tightening pressure of those fingers on her arm, persuaded her otherwise.

"Fucking's the easy part," she whispered back, and as he drew away from her she saw the frown she'd hoped for, fighting with that warm lazy smile.

She took control from the start.

When they left the brasserie she hailed a cab and told the driver to take them to the King George Hotel on Syntagma, where she'd called to reserve a room an hour after getting to work. Just in case. And he didn't question her, didn't ask what was going on; just gave her that smile of his and sat back in his seat, happy to be led wherever she suggested.

At the hotel, with the bedroom shutters latched, an early summer sun slanting through the slats, she had put him through his paces. Gently but insistently, continuing to take control; telling him softly what she wanted, and how, and where, and when. And he had complied, as though content to do her bidding. Afterwards, as he lay back on his pillow, hands clasped behind his head, she'd slipped from the bed and showered, leaving the bathroom door open so he could see every move. And when she came back to the room, drying herself, she knew that he was waiting for her to return to the bed, or be invited to. Instead, she reached for her underwear, and began to dress.

"You're going?"

"Yes." She pulled on her shirt and started to button it. "Editorial meeting at four-thirty – the October issue. Can't be missed." She zipped up her suede skirt, tucked in the shirt, and reached for her jacket and tote.

"I'll call you," he said, as she leant across the bed to kiss him goodbye.

"No," she said, tracing a fingertip down to the tip of his nose and onto his lips. "I'll call you."

40

FOR THE first few weeks of their affair Cossie didn't ask about the wide gold band on Nikos's left index finger. And made no reference to his wife, or the domestic side of his life, as though she – and it – didn't exist. And if they did, well, Cossie simply wasn't interested. Whatever-her-name was, she was not a part of their game.

It was Nikos who mentioned her first, strolling along Iraklidon, arm in arm, on their way back to her apartment on Efestiou Street. They had met for a drink after work, and Cossie had noted he was not in his usual high spirits. The smiles were few and far between.

"My wife is not well," he had said softly, when Cossie asked what was troubling him.

Ah, she thought, so this is it. The end of the road. The glowing review she'd written on ConStav's latest project in Piraeus had been handed in, and now she was getting her marching orders. He would see her to the door of her block, and that would be that.

And married or not, she had to admit she'd be sad to see him go. She'd grown very fond of him. His gentleness, his caring, his thoughtfulness. She admired his work, too. His very considerable talent. Their time together had been fun. Special.

"I'm sorry to hear that," was all she said, not breaking step. Not really wanting to know more, but knowing there was more to come. Let's cut to the chase, she thought. It was always me, me, me with men, and she didn't have time for lame excuses.

They walked on in silence for another block. The street was busy and the bars were full.

"She had a breakdown. We lost a… She suffered a stillbirth." He took a deep breath, gave a grim smile. "At first it was… okay, I suppose. But she hasn't recovered. A few weeks ago she was taken to a clinic in Lagonisi. It's been hard on our son."

"You have a son…?"

"Dimi; nine, nearly ten."

Cossie nodded, and they turned into Efestiou.

"You've helped a lot," he said, as they reached the door to her apartment building. "I want you to know that."

But the time has come to call it quits, she could hear him say. *It's been fun, but I have other responsibilities*. Like the 'working together' sound-bite, it probably wasn't the first time he had said those words; and it probably wouldn't be the last. Maybe she shouldn't have been quite so undemanding, she thought, reaching into the tote for her key. Maybe she should have been more interested, more caring… She knew she was going to miss him. Really miss him.

"I don't know what I'd have done without you," he said, as she slid the key into the lock. She opened the door, and turned towards him. "I know I should have told you about all this earlier, but it didn't seem right. I didn't want you to feel sorry for me…"

"I don't sleep with men because I feel sorry for them," she'd replied, briskly, but with a smile. She leaned forward and kissed his cheek, stepped into the tiled hallway, and turned to close the door on him.

She was surprised by the look on his face. As if she had been the one who'd delivered the *coup de grâce*. A mixture of astonishment and despair.

"You're not going to invite me up?"

"I'm not a carer, Nikos."

"I don't want a carer, Cossie. I want you. All of you. You must have realised that?"

No. Cossie had never realised that. His wanting her. For those first few weeks it had been an affair, nothing more. An affair with a married man that would, inevitably, come to an end.

The name of the game. Much as she might hate it.

Because it had been fun; and she'd loved it. More than she could have imagined. The frantic, headlong, thrilling rush of it. The texts, the calls, the assignations; so many glorious stolen moments. The heat and passion of it all. But at no time had she ever thought to press him about his intentions; or ask anything that might suggest an interest in where their affair was headed. It was enough just to be with him, for however long it might last; no matter what the future might hold. That was the nature of affairs. That was the game they were playing. She knew it; everyone knew it. No rules, no expectations. Just the now.

But, suddenly, in that doorway on Efestiou, everything changed.

The way he looked at her. The words he spoke. His eyes, his voice.

The moment she stood back, opened that door to him. Let him in.

The next step.

When the game became something more.

Of course, she was interested in his other life. How could she not be? And, increasingly, once the game had changed, she wanted to know more about it. But without asking directly.

Which was why, one lunchtime, Cossie left *Arki-Tek*'s offices on Panagiotis, caught the metro to Kolonaki, and walked past the Contalidis house on Diomexédes. It was a corner property, with the thick green crown of a fig tree showing above a high white wall. The house was narrow but had four floors, sheathed in ConStav's signature shaded glass and smooth limestone; the top-most level with a roof garden, the lower level with a ramp dropping down off the street to a basement garage. It was in an exclusive part of town, and surprised her. Clearly there was money in the family – either the wife's, or his – because ConStav, successful as the practice was, would not yet be providing the kind of salary needed to cover the cost of a property like this one.

It was on her second pass of the house, on the other side of the street, that the front door opened and a young woman stepped out. Just a girl, really. The nanny, she supposed. Blue jeans, ripped at the knee, and a pink angora top too short to cover the t-shirt beneath. And coming out with her the boy. Dimi. There was no doubt about it. Just a smaller version of his father… The same fall of black hair, the same good looks. Taking the nanny's hand, and heading down the street with her.

Following at a distance, Cossie watched them as far as Patriarchou where they took a pavement table at a burger restaurant.

Back home on Efestiou, Cossie thought about the house, thought about Nikos, and wondered what would happen to them.

41

WHATEVER freedom she and Nikos enjoyed through the following summer and autumn – with his wife confined at the Aetolikou, and Dimi at school, or at home with his nanny, or on sleepovers with friends – it all came to an abrupt end when Electra returned home for good. After her initial three-month confinement at the clinic, she had come back to Athens every other weekend; and then every weekend. Until, finally, she stayed; her time in treatment at an end.

Which meant that Nikos was not so… available.

And then there was the house on the island. Douka. That was also starting to make demands on his time. He had told her about it, the old family home on Pelatea. It had been badly damaged in a fire and Nikos was rebuilding it; a modern take on an old Admiral's house (perhaps the money was his?) with all the ConStav flourishes. One evening he brought the plans with him to Efestiou, and a stack of photos. The house was still pretty much a building site, but Cossie could see its potential; that it would become a very impressive property.

"Maybe you should run a feature on it," he said, rolling up the plans and snapping a rubber band round them.

"Maybe we should," she said. "If you like, I'll see what the editor says."

Yet despite these obstacles their relationship continued to flourish. She was a part of his life, an increasingly important part; and he was rapidly becoming a part of hers. There was just a wife and a child to accommodate. A wife, she was learning fast, who was becoming a burdensome strain on Nikos. Her moods, her neediness, her drinking… Sometimes when they met, there would be a tiredness in his eyes, as though he hadn't slept. But he never complained, and she never asked for details.

It was enough that he was with her; that he wanted to be with her.

And that she was with him.

And she made sure that she provided everything he needed.

Christmas was not a good time. Just a few stolen phone-calls in nine days. Electra's mother had come in from the country and was staying for the holiday. There was no way he could manage an easy getaway. And Cossie understood. But understanding didn't make the separation any easier. Rather than stay in the city by herself, she joined her brother and parents on a ski-trip to Austria.

"I missed you," was the first thing he said, when he saw her again. At the apartment on Efestiou.

"I missed you, too."

"Missed you more."

"Not possible." A dismissive, teasing tone.

"It is when you love someone."

Which, though she tried hard not to show it, took her breath away. The word had never been spoken.

"You're a married man, remember?" was all she could manage.

"Absence makes the heart grow fonder," he said, with a sad smile. "And the mind clearer."

She gave him a long steady look, screwed up her mouth as though she was working out her next move. And then, "Come with me," she said, taking his hand. "Your Christmas present's waiting for you."

Afterwards, he was quiet. "I have time for dinner."

"Next time. You should be getting home."

"You don't mind?"

She paused. "Of course, I mind. I don't want you to go, but you have to. We both know that." She said it softly, without rancour, and it was as close as she had ever come to saying how she felt.

When he was dressed, Cossie wrapped a throw around herself and followed him to the apartment door.

"When the house is finished," he said, "Electra's agreed to spend the summer there. With Dimi. It will be good for her. And for us."

"And when she comes home again?"

"Let's wait and see what happens."

"I'm a popular girl…"

"Not too popular, I hope."

"Let's wait and see what happens," she replied, and pushed him out of the door.

Rested her back against it, and breathed out deeply.

Of course, the editor loved Cossie's idea for a feature on renovated historic houses. Three properties that had been transformed; three owners who were interesting and newsworthy. Two on the mainland, and the third on Pelatea.

"I think you should write it," the editor told her, a week after Cossie had suggested it at an editorial meeting. "Come up with a list of photographers. I want a different team for each property."

Sitting at the editor's desk, Cossie had been stunned. Never, not for a single moment, had she imagined that she would be asked to write the piece. The feature was a big one, four thousand words; the lead story slated for the Christmas issue. And there were many more senior staffers – not to mention a brigade of more experienced freelancers – who could have been tapped for the job. But she was the one commissioned. The rest of the day she spent worrying about what Nikos would have to say about it. He wouldn't like it, she was certain.

But he did.

"Congratulations. I'm so proud of you. Not just front of book anymore, and those smaller features, but up there with the best. Your editor must think a lot of you."

"But it will mean going to Pelatea…"

"Of course, and why not? You'll love it. So who else am I sharing space with?"

And that was that, as far as Nikos was concerned.

But for Cossie, the prospect of going to Pelatea, and meeting Electra, her lover's wife, was a deeply unsettling one. She was even going to stay at the house with them. How horrible that would be. The deceit alone made her shiver.

But Nikos had insisted. Simply a practical consideration, he'd told her. The nearest reasonable hotel was too far away, and was sure to be fully booked for the season. It simply wouldn't work.

And though she made her objections clear, Nikos would have none of it.

The first house selected for the feature was an ancient monastery in the hills above Larissa, restored by an English writer and his wife and opened as a small boutique hotel. The second property was in Thessaloniki, an old mill house that a retired lawyer had spent a fortune restoring. Cossie had spent three days at each, with one photographer who was a delight to work with, and another who was difficult.

And then it was the house on Pelatea.

Douka. Nikos's home.

The evening before her departure, Nikos rang her doorbell.

"I thought you were on the island," Cossie said, panicking.

"I missed you. I wanted to see you. And…" He paused. "I thought it might be better if I wasn't around. That it would make it more difficult for you. And for me, of course. I wouldn't have been able to keep my hands off you."

At which point he reached out for her, and as the sun slipped through a milky summer haze over the city he led her to the bedroom.

42

SHE LOOKS so fragile. That's what Cossie thinks when she meets Electra the first day. So tiny, so… old; her head, improbably large for her body. Standing on the quay at Navros, waiting for their ferry, with a shawl drawn tightly around her shoulders. She could have been an island woman waiting to entice tourist back-packers with a good rate on a spare room. Except the shawl is an exquisite silk Paisley, the cream blouse and blue slacks the finest silk too, and the court shoes shiny, low heeled, gold buckled. She wears big round sunglasses with gold frames, which she slips back up into a mass of artfully streaked blonde curls the better to see the crowds disembarking. She looked like a reed; slim, tall, elegant… but yes, fragile; frail and wistful, too. Nervy, agitated, like a thoroughbred under starter's orders. And beside her the little boy, Dimi, whom Cossie had seen with his nanny, now bronzed from the sun.

Electra doesn't see them at first, coming off the ferry ramp in a line of cars. So Cossie buzzes down the window and waves. It could only be her. And Electra waves back, tentatively; loses a grip on the shawl which the breeze snatches from her shoulders and sends spinning out like a flag unfurled. Gathering it back, she waits for them to pull out of the traffic and park; comes towards them, almost forcing a smile of welcome as though she's had to draw it from somewhere deep inside her. A twitching, uncertain movement in the lips. Like a light bulb catching only an intermittent charge; flickering on and off.

"Welcome to Pelatea," says Electra, in a thin, brittle voice, reaching out to shake their hands. Cossie first, then the photographer Gert, and his assistant Franz. Electra's hand is cold and bony, like holding a bag of twigs. Once again Cossie is aware of an intense fragility, something fractured like her voice. A pure-bred Athenian, from a wealthy family, but out of her element here on the island; and obviously still scarred by her breakdown, the loss of a child. For just a moment, Cossie thinks how cruel it is for Nikos to bring her here, and leave her. But after all this time, perhaps he's decided that she's fit enough to be here, to live on the island with Dimi. That it will be good for her, somewhere without distractions, to get her back to her writing. To occupy her time.

And then, as Gert snaps off a couple of frames of the Admiral's statue that the boy, Dimi, has pointed out to him, Cossie sees Electra's faltering smile turn to a look of horror as a seagull lands on the Admiral's greening head, settles its wings, shakes its tail feathers and proceeds to squirt a long messy streak of white down the Admiral's cheek, and onto his shoulder.

The incredulity. The despair. The powerlessness.

Of all the things that could have happened… And Gert taking pictures.

If Electra could have strangled the bird, or snatched away the camera and thrown it in the harbour, Cossie suspects she would have done so without a thought to the consequences.

"Don't worry," she says, with an easy laugh, feeling a sudden burst of sympathy for the poor woman. "If we use the shot, we can always photoshop it out, or come back another day."

The relief and gratitude that floods Electra's face is extraordinary… Like a weight lifted.

As if such a thing can be helped…

Electra, it seems, is even more nervous than Cossie. Which serves to bolster Cossie's resolve. She can do this, she thinks. She can be with this woman, stay in her house. She can handle it. And for the first time, she realises that she's glad Nikos isn't around. He'd been right; it would have been a great deal more difficult if he'd been there with Electra. At least now she has the time to sort herself out, and settle into the job without any distraction.

But that time is shorter than she might have hoped for.

Cossie had assumed that they would follow Electra and Dimi to the house, but it isn't to be. Dimi asks if he can go in the rented Hyundai with the two men, who promptly say that would not be a problem; all the boys together. Leaving Cossie alone with the woman whose husband she is sleeping with… Indeed, has left only a few hours earlier.

"Is the house far?" asks Cossie, as the coast road opens up ahead.

"About thirty minutes. To the end of the beach, and then up into the hills. We're on the other side of the island." Electra glances at her, and smiles, then looks back to the road as though she can't risk taking her eyes off it for a moment.

It is clear to Cossie that Electra is not the most confident of drivers. She sits forward as though she has trouble seeing over the bonnet of the car, and she keeps both hands firmly gripped on the wheel, her knuckles white and pointed. It is as if the car is too big for her, too brutish to control, and needs all her attention. When they reach a fall of rocks at the end of the coast road and it is time to turn inland, she shifts the wheel through her hands as though it were too hot to touch, when most people would have casually swung it with one hand, or at the very least crossed arms to complete the movement. When the road straightens, Electra lets the wheel spin back through her fingers and the Jeep gives a little shimmy before straightening.

As they wind their way up into the hills – Electra even more preoccupied with managing the twists and turns, her back as stiff as timber, chin raised as high as it will go – Cossie fills the time with easy chatter about the dangers and delights of photo shoots; of lost lenses, and temperamental photographers, and inefficient assistants; about sudden power cuts, and terrible weather.

"Have you worked with Gert and Franz before?" asks Electra, starting to work the brake as the road tips down to the south of the island, and checking the rear-view mirror for the Hyundai.

"Once before, in Germany. They're a very good team," she replies, going on to explain that Gert is gay, and Franz straight.

"Very good-looking," says Electra, taking a chance to glance across at Cossie.

"Franz? Very, but a little young for me." And as she says it, she feels a flush of heat rise up into her cheeks. But Electra doesn't see it. Instead, she slows the Jeep, checks again that Dimi and the two men are still behind her, before flipping the indicator and turning through pillared gates into the drive.

Cossie swallows, her pulse rises.

Nikos's house.

She is here, at last, and in control.

So far.

43

THE HOUSE is magnificent, simply takes Cossie's breath away. A broad, noble façade, proud and fine, facing the sea. Upright, solid, its massive limestone blocks whitened by the midday sun, its sloping barrelled roof tiles bleached a soft rose pink, and its terraced stepped lawns edged with shading stands of palm and cypress and eucalyptus. And behind the house, the tree-dotted stony slopes and blank inscrutable heights of Douka.

"Wow," is all Cossie can manage, climbing out of the Jeep. "It's… it's beautiful. I had no idea…"

For the first time since meeting them on the quay, Electra seems to relax.

"Oh, I'm so pleased you like it," she says, rubbing the fingertips of one hand against the palm of the other, as though working in moisturiser. "We… love it, too. My husband's family home."

Behind them, car doors slam and Gert strides past them. Looking at the house, taking everything in, and whistling at what he sees. He turns to Electra. "May I?" he asks, gesturing with his camera, maybe aware that his snapping the seagull and statue had unnerved his hostess; that permission should be sought.

"Of course," says Electra. "Go wherever you want…"

And off he marches, with Franz hurrying after him, tugging the strap of a camera bag over his shoulder, followed by Dimi who's been entrusted with a tripod.

"Don't get in their way, *agapi mou*," Electra calls after him; but the boy pays no heed. She turns to Cossie. "Do you need to go with them, or shall I show you around?"

"Lead the way," Cossie replies.

If the outside of the house, undamaged by the fire, retains its original proportions, the interiors are sleekly modernist. ConStav in almost every regard, Cossie thinks. From its polished blue concrete floors to its mighty limewashed beams Douka's cool, lofty airiness is almost museum-like in its feeling of light and space; its soaring stuccoed walls set here and there with vast colour-daubed abstracts, crossed muskets and corsair blades with scarlet braided tassels, a brass-studded ship's wheel and, in the hallway, a swirling tangle of purple neon by Bisconti.

Yet comfortably intimate too, she decides. Snug and warm and welcoming, with cushioned window seats, plump, tapestried ottomans, and deep, scroll-winged armchairs set around a brick-lined hearth in one salon; a nest of low-slung Neuhausen chrome-and-leather sofas, Gatti bean bags, and padded Eames recliners in another.

And everywhere a most extraordinary and eclectic mix of decorations and *objets*: faded Indian rugs and Persian prayer mats, tall Chinese vases, sneering Indonesian masks, painted Santos figurines from the Philippines, a copper-bowled charcoal burner, and various chipped busts and muscled statuary displayed on delicately lacquered Japanese table tops and fluted marble plinths. All of which fill Cossie with a strange and unsettling sense of envy, even jealousy; these mementoes of a past that Nikos and Electra have shared together; the travelling they must have done.

And plants and flowers in abundance: moss-covered trunks of drooping fern, braided bushes of silvery spear-tip ficus, and spikey, succulent stands of extravagantly flowering cacti; in dented copper urns, or flaking pottery tubs, or roughly-hewn stone troughs. And orchids; every shade, every shape, all lapping green tongues and delicately-turned petals, filling the rooms with a soft creamy scent. And in the corner of one of the salons a forest of white blooms and browning stems built up like a snowy slope... Cossie may have seen the plans that Nikos had shown her, but there was no preparing her for the finished article. The house, she decides, is simply sensational.

"As you probably know," Electra is saying, leading her from one room to the next like a proud curator, "the interior was pretty much gutted by the fire. Hardly a wall or partition left standing. A furious, hungry blaze by all accounts... All the old timbers destroyed – floorboards, beams, most of the panelling and painted ceilings. Such a terrible loss. But the original floorplan remains the same: these two salons, the dining room, the hallway, the library and study, the kitchen, the bedrooms upstairs. But what Nikos has done is... I don't know... he's somehow started afresh, without losing anything. I mean, here," she says, gesturing with a thin, bony hand, bracelets perilously loose on her wrist, "this is the room where the Admiral died, on a day bed, over there by the window, surrounded by his family. And though he wouldn't recognise it now, I do like to think he would find it... familiar. And be pleased with what Nikos has done."

She turns to Cossie, smiles uncertainly; seems suddenly flustered.

"But listen to me. I must sound like an estate agent. It's just... It's just so special here. He's done such an extraordinary job, and I can't help feeling so proud of the house. And Nikos."

"I understand you're writing a biography of Admiral Contalidis," says Cossie. "It must be wonderful to write the book here, where he lived."

"Oh, it is. Of course, it is. I'm so very fortunate. But I'm going to have to knuckle down, now that we're settled. No more... excuses." She gives a sharp, brittle chuckle. "Time for a little self-discipline," she continues, and another tenuous smile flutters across her lips.

By 'excuses', Cossie is in no doubt that Electra is referring to her breakdown, following the stillbirth of their second child. With the throwaway suggestion that it is somehow of no consequence. All in the past.

It is the short little laugh that accompanies this dismissal that persuades Cossie that Electra is far from over it.

44

BY THE TIME Electra and Cossie finish their tour, the two girls who work at Douka have prepared a lunch which they serve in the rear courtyard between the study and library, its rough stone walls covered in thick branching foliage and weighty blooms. The table is an oval slab of dressed limestone set on a sculpted Doric base, and the girls lay it with wooden platters of cheese and bread, faïence dishes loaded with *tiropittes* and *dolmadakia*, tubs of *taramosalata* with shelled boiled eggs and, in the centre of the table, a wide blue glass dish filled with a tangle of wild salad leaves. After they have taken their places, Electra offers wine, a chill dry white.

"It is our own wine," Electra explains. "The vineyard was planted by the Admiral."

"It is good," says Gert, tilting his glass to the light to catch the colour of the wine. "Like a Riesling, you know, but not so sharp or sweet. What do you think, Cossie?"

With a complimentary nod and smile, she agrees that it is, indeed, a fine wine. But fails to mention that this is not the first time she has tasted it. On two or three occasions, Nikos has brought bottles of the same wine to her apartment on Efestiou; for lunch, for dinner, and afterwards in her bedroom. It is a secret that makes her feel guilty, yet excited, in equal measure.

After their lunch, Electra excuses herself. She wants to get back to her work, she says, but tells Cossie and Gert that they are free to go wherever they want; to make themselves at home.

And so, with Dimi in tow, they walk around the grounds, down to the beach, and return through the orchard, stopping at various points to look up at the house.

"He is a talented man, this Contalidis," says Gert, as Dimi and Franz chase after a lizard.

Cossie feels a spark of pride, and love. A strange and surprising sense of… ownership, possession, that she has not felt before. "Yes, he is, isn't he?"

"The house is magnificent, don't you think? So full of history… but ideas, too. It is such a place I would like to live in. To retire to. Such a feeling of peace, don't you think?" He sighs fondly, scratches his wisp of a beard with thin pale fingers. "You have known him long, this man Contalidis?"

"My editor introduced us, for a story we did last year on a project of his in Piraeus."

Gert nods approvingly. "It is a good choice you have made. The pictures will be great. Fabulous. But for now, I think it is rest time. A couple of hours to refresh. Too hot for anything, and the light… too strong, don't you think?"

He looks at his watch. "Let's meet up at five, back here. The first set-up, yes?"

Rest does not come easy for Cossie.

Alone in her room, in one of the guest suites beyond the kitchen herb garden, she sits on her bed and texts Nikos: *Have arrived safely. House stunning. Miss you.* When it's clear that no reply is forthcoming, she lights up a cigarette, lies back and listens to the distant click and buzz of insects. It has been like the first day of any shoot. The meeting, the greeting, the arrival on set, the anticipation of work about to begin.

And yet…

Electra.

For Cossie, it is all about Electra.

Not the house, not the team, not the assignment. Not yet.

Just this woman, Nikos's wife. The woman who shares his bed, his life; the mother of his child. Wistfully beautiful, carelessly elegant, wealthy by birthright. But a broken doll. A flickering shadow now. Restless and nervous, like a small bird fluttering weakly behind a pane of glass.

Another woman, a stronger woman, a woman less pampered, less entitled, might have survived the tragedy of a stillbirth. But that woman is not Electra.

Cossie tries to imagine the two of them together. Nikos and Electra. Here on Pelatea, and in their Athens townhouse on Diomexédes. At lunch parties and dinners, receptions, with friends and family. And alone together, watching TV, laughing, talking. Just as she and Nikos do on Efestiou. She can see them, but she can't quite… pair them. Islander and mainlander. Country boy and city girl. Twelve years together, yet now somehow… separate. Different people. Different lives.

Once, of course, they had been a couple. In the library and the study, following after Electra, Cossie had seen the photos on the walls, on the desk. Holiday snaps. Studio shots. Colour, black and white. The two of them, younger, on a beach together. In ski suits, at a mountain restaurant. In Rome, and Paris. At their wedding. With Dimi: in a christening gown with Mama; in a toy car being pushed by Nikos; the pair of them swinging him over the waves.

As she lies there Cossie thinks, too, of the bedroom Electra showed her on the tour of the house. Their bedroom. A large airy space over the main hallway, with a floor of stunning spear-shaped wooden tiles. Intricately interlocked and patterned, smooth as silk and lightly grained; warm from the sun slanting through four narrow windows and sliding terrace doors that overlook the gardens and distant sea. Furnished with a suite of blonde Shaker furniture: a curving sofa, a low dressing table and stool, a pair of matching chests of drawers. And their bed, of course. The size of her kitchen in Thiseio. A carved and painted headboard. A long, scalloped footboard. Draped in shifting drifts of the finest muslin. Facing the windows and terrace.

This is where they sleep together.

Where they make love.

Cossie tries to imagine Electra doing to Nikos what she does to him in Thiseio. No, she thinks. No. Electra is just too… submissive. Too… ethereal, intellectual. Too dislocated. She is not, Cossie decides, a sexual creature.

But then who can say? Who knows what happens when the bedroom door closes?

It's just… It's just that they seem so unlikely a match. Electra, fragile, fractured, old before her time; Nikos, full of life and youth and vigour. It's not difficult to understand what Electra sees in him – the man he is, his talent; their child, their life together. But she can't quite get a handle on what Nikos sees in her? Once maybe, but now?

Surprisingly Cossie feels no guilt about her affair with Nikos. Surprising, because she had thought that she would; in the days leading up to the trip; leaving Tsania on the ferry; when she saw Electra waiting for them on the quay. And though there was discomfort in those first few hours, being with the wife of a man she is sleeping with, the man she is in love with, that feeling has almost gone.

And it makes Cossie glad.

But then, from nowhere, as she stubs out her cigarette, Cossie sees the hard, lined face of the housekeeper. Ariadne. Standing in a corner of the kitchen. Stern and disapproving. A widow's black dress. Low hem, high collar; belted and buckled. Thick black stockings. Laced black shoes. Grey hair, streaked with a few strands of black, tied back tight as a ballerina's bun. Hands clasped in front of her.

And small dark eyes.

Watching everything. Seeing everything.

A brief little nod when they are introduced. But no smile. Not like the two girls preparing food at the kitchen table. Lina and Aja. Excited by the visit. People from a magazine.

If anything is going to make Cossie feel uncomfortable, she decides, it is this old woman. And if Nikos had been there, she realises now, it would have been so much worse. This woman, she is certain, would have seen straight through her; in an instant. Would have known…

How on earth, Cossie wonders, can Electra bear that spectral, disapproving presence? She didn't ask, of course, but Electra had volunteered the information as she showed Cossie the guest cottages. An old family retainer, she'd said. She comes with the house. Mornings only. As though Electra had sensed Cossie's response to the woman, her unease.

Yet while she may not feel any guilt, Cossie does feels a certain sadness for Electra; a kind of sympathy. Alone here on the island, with that old crow in attendance, and just those two girls for company. Caught in the middle. Too young for Ariadne, too old for the girls.

Which is the moment Cossie stiffens on her bed.

45

THERE IS something outside her room.

Passing her door. But coming back.

It's not Franz, and it's not Gert. She'd heard their doors close a while ago. Not a sound from either of them since then. What she can hear now is a soft padding. An animal of some sort. Four legs, not two.

For a minute or so there is silence. As though the animal has moved on. A guard dog, Cossie wonders?

And then, as she starts to relax, the padding sound returns, stops outside her door, and she can hear the creature panting, as though it has returned from a long run. Huh, huh, huh. She can almost see the tongue lolling, like a pink version of those orchid leaves in the salon.

And then – bump! Its weight pressed suddenly against her door, making it creak. Which makes her start.

Another bump, harder this time, more determined; as though the animal is trying to butt its way in. And now there is scratching; claws scrabbling frantically at the gap beneath the door; the door beginning to shake.

And a hungry snuffling, as though the dog has scented something.

Quietly, bravely, to settle her nerves, Cossie gets up from her bed, tiptoes to the window and peers through the shutters. Better to see the beast, she reasons, than imagine it. But the slats are set at the wrong angle to afford any direct view of the doorway, so she raises a hand to readjust them. Which is when the snuffling changes to a low, menacing growl, as though the dog knows she is there.

A shiver races up Cossie's spine, and she hurries back to her bed, scrambles onto it and draws her knees to her chest.

The growl continues, just short of a bark. There is more scratching, too, more scraping and, most unnerving, a further series of hefty bumps strong enough to rattle the doorlatch.

And then, just as she thinks the door cannot hold a moment more… finally, there is silence.

Two hours later Cossie wakes to a soft tapping at her door.

"Rise and shine," says Franz. "Gert says ten minutes, in the far orchard by the road."

"Sounds good. On my way," Cossie calls out, surprised that she should have fallen asleep; looks at her watch. A little after five. Twelve hours earlier she had woken to a kiss on her shoulder from Nikos, and his fingers seeking her out. And she misses him; she'd like to…

But then, the very next instant, she remembers the dog; how frightened she'd been. And as she packs her tote – cigarettes, lighter, pen, notebook, a small bottle of water, sunscreen – she wonders what might have happened if, for some reason, she'd opened the door, or not latched it properly? What would she have done if she and that animal had come face to face? Or rather, what might the dog have done? It has to be a guard dog, she decides; surprised that Electra hadn't said anything, hadn't warned them.

On her way to the orchard, Cossie looks around for signs of the animal. But there is nothing. No kennel, no food or water bowls to be seen. By the time she reaches the orchard where Franz has set up a tripod, she puts the dog out of mind and turns to see what Gert has seen. Above the sloping tops of the trees the house stands proud on its stepped terraces, now spilled with lengthening shadows, its limestone walls splashed with a golden evening sunlight. The earlier brightness has softened, the sky is a richer, deeper blue, and the lawns a lush green pooled with shadows. It looks, thinks Cossie, like some hazy eighteenth-century landscape painting. For a story on historic houses, it is the perfect shot. Taken at the perfect time. Almost a cover.

When Gert finally steps away from the tripod and Franz hurries forward to move the camera for the next set-up, Gert gives her a look and nods his head, smiles. It is good. They have started. And if he is happy, she should be too.

"You found just the right spot," says Cossie. "Just perfect."

"And more to come," says Gert. "We will make good pictures here, don't you think?"

46

THERE ARE three more set-ups among the trees before they call it a day and head back to their rooms. Electra is waiting for them. They come round the corner and there she is, dressed in cream slacks, a pale pink silk blouse, with a soft Cashmere jumper over her shoulders. She is gripping the ends of the jumper sleeves as though she needs them for balance, to steer with, like sails or a rudder. For a moment she looks as though she has been caught snooping, but then she gathers herself.

"I saw you up in the orchard, but didn't want to disturb you. In case I got in your shot or something, and messed things up. So I kept out of sight, crept down from the kitchen." She pauses, looks at each of them as if for approval, understanding.

Cossie can feel her discomfort, and thanks her for being so considerate. Getting in the way of a shot is such an easy mistake to make.

"I only kill you if you ruin a set-up is all," says Gert, and everyone laughs, Electra a second or two behind them.

"It's just," Electra continues, "I came to ask if you would like supper on the upper terrace? With Dimi and me. It's lovely up there in the evening. If that's okay for everyone?"

They all agree it sounds a very good idea.

Electra glances at her watch, without releasing the sleeve of her jumper. "Say… Say in an hour? Does that give you enough time?"

The top terrace is an easy walk from their guest cottages, along a stony path that winds up between bulging banks of rhododendron. They have all three showered and changed out of their working clothes, and there is a light spring in their steps after such a good start to the shoot.

Electra and Dimi are waiting for them, Electra sitting by the cistern pool and Dimi working the bread oven where their supper, prepared by Aja and Lina, is warming up.

The meal is fun, relaxed and easy, and Cossie notices that Electra appears more comfortable, a little more at ease. She still eats like a bird, picking at her food, but she listens to their stories, joins in the laughter; and after they have cleared the table and carried everything down to the kitchen, they wish each other good night and go to their rooms.

It is, Cossie decides as she prepares for bed, a very encouraging start to the shoot. And if they can keep up the good work she is certain that Douka will be the lead house in *Arki-Tek*'s story.

It is what she wants, for Nikos more than herself.

47

IF THE EVENING shots from Douka's orchards had been good, the sets the next morning look even better.

Like every shoot, the day starts early. Cossie has always been an early bird, and she glories in the limpid morning light and shifting sprinkler rainbows as they tramp down to the lower lawn for the first set-up. It is chill in the shadows of the beach pines, but the house above them is washed in a luminous creamy glow; framed with leaning palm and spindly cypress, its windows a soft grey-blue from the sky.

"The place looks better every time I'm seeing it," says Gert, waving the first of his Polaroids to develop the print. He studies it intently, hands it to Franz, then minutely adjusts the tripod; looks through the viewfinder for one final check. He stands aside to let Cossie see what he has seen.

What Cossie sees is another glorious view of the house, closer now than the previous evening's orchard shots; the terraces providing a rising sense of perspective that gives the house a certain height and haughty nobility.

She is about to take her eye from the viewfinder when she notices a shadowy figure, standing at one of the bedroom windows; Electra, half-hidden by a shutter. And Cossie knows at once that she is watching them. Which surprises her, after Electra had made so much effort the previous afternoon to keep out of sight when they were shooting from the orchard; and had made a point of telling them so.

And yet…

Cossie squints through the viewfinder, minutely adjusts the focus. There's certainly someone there, but she's no longer quite so certain that it's Electra… While it's difficult to make out actual features from this distance, it seems to Cossie that the figure in the window is taller than Electra, possibly due to the angle of the shot; and, if anything, a little more weighty, substantial… Almost a different set to the head and shoulders. And, somehow, older? It's impossible to say for certain… Just a feeling… But then, it can only be her.

Cossie draws back, wipes her eyes, and then looks through the viewfinder again. Blinks, squints again, and…

There is nothing there.

Just the edge of a muslin drape shifting in the breeze from the open window. Which sends an icy race of goosebumps up her arms and into her scalp.

"If you have finished playing with my focus," says Gert, "maybe I can take my shot now?"

After Gert has completed four separate sets from the lower lawn, they pack the gear and head up to the cistern pool where they'd had dinner the night before. As they pass the house, Cossie excuses herself for a moment and knocks at the kitchen door. Electra is sitting at the table with a glass of water and a dreamy look on her face. She is dressed in running kit, and watching the TV news.

"*Kalimera*," says Cossie, "I hope we didn't wake you?"

"Not at all," Electra replies. "I'm usually the first up, but you beat me to it. The girls aren't here yet, but would you like some coffee, some breakfast?"

Cossie is touched by Electra's concern, but tells her not to worry; they are going to do some work on the upper terrace and then come down for more set-ups around the house. Maybe they could have their breakfast then?

By the time Cossie, Franz and Gert finish at the cistern – another set of gorgeous photos filled with obliging dragonflies that dart around the pool in shimmering squadrons – Electra has returned from her run, and Aja and Lina are ready with their breakfast. As the two girls fuss over Franz, Electra catches Cossie's eye and smiles at her, a conspiratorial smile that makes Cossie feel oddly uncomfortable. It seems somehow wrong to share such intimate exchanges with a woman whose husband you are sleeping with, whose touch you can still feel on your skin, and whom you've spoken to that very morning – the first time he's phoned since she's been at Douka; stepping away from Gert and Franz at the cistern to take his call.

After breakfast, they set up by the swimming pool where Cossie asks Dimi if he'd like to help by stirring the water with his hand; sending ripples across its surface to turn the house's reflection into a shifting Impressionist mirage. Cossie only does it to please the young boy, to make him feel a part of the team. But the invitation, and his enthusiasm in being included, so delights Electra that Cossie feels even more unsettled. It is as though she is somehow encouraging a friendship that can only be doomed to betrayal, and she resolves to keep a distance between them.

But it is not to be.

After the pool shots, they go to the line of old storehouses which Nikos has turned into his studio, with Electra and Dimi tagging along.

"I hope we're not in the way," says Electra, as she and Franz struggle with a pot of pelargonia; positioning it just so, for Gert.

"Not at all," Cossie replies, a little breathless; feeling the lie but knowing there is nothing else she can say. And for a moment – just a moment – she is cross with Nikos. Putting her in this position.

What on earth was he thinking, she wonders, deliberately encouraging her to spend time in such close quarters with his wife?

Is it some kind of test? Does he want to see how the two of them get on? Or does he want her to see the kind of woman he is married to? The hardship he suffers? So that she can better understand the difficulties that face him? To better understand the kind of man he is? To love him more?

Is he playing some game with her? With them?

Matters get worse at lunch, when Gert insists on photographing the table in the kitchen herb garden before they sit down to eat; shooting on a hand-held Leica from every conceivable angle. Repositioning all the prettily-painted stoneware bowls and mouthwatering dishes, but taking so much time about it that a swarm of flies descends. One or two at first, and then, from nowhere, a buzzing black cloud of flashing iridescence that reminds Cossie of a scene in a second-rate horror film. Flies as fat as nail heads settling on the food. Which sends Electra into a frantic dance of napkin-swatting and hand-waving. Like the seagull on the Admiral's statue; something beyond her control.

Cossie doesn't know how to respond. Should she feel sorry for Electra, or should she be quietly amused at her obvious discomfort?

48

AFTER LUNCH, it is back to work with some interiors; starting in the study and library. The set ups are straightforward, just a couple of angles for each room, and everything is going well until some lenses can't be found and Gert loses his temper.

"*Die filterlinsen sind nicht hier*?" Cossie hears him bellow, and the afternoon's calm is suddenly shattered. Apologising to Electra who's been chattering on about her father's Murano table, she hurries from the dining room to find out what is happening; relieved to put some distance between herself and Electra. Job first, hostess second, even at the cost of Gert's temper tantrum. How it has to be; how she wants it to be. For obvious reasons.

Out in the hallway, stomping around the camera cases, Gert explains that he is concerned about glare from the dining-room table-top and needs a softening filter which his "*verdammter assistent*" appears to have lost. Cossie breathes a sigh of relief, goes to her tote for a can of Philoxy, and hands it to Gert, telling him they can spray the surface of the table to soften any reflections. Job done. Thank the Lord.

But if the problem with the missing filters has been solved – even if Franz's puzzled frown remains – it's immediately clear that Gert's mood has soured. No matter how much Cossie tries to placate him, he won't let it rest, and the dining-room shoot that follows is a torture of clipped commands and bristling irritation.

Their kitchen supper that evening isn't much better, a mournful, uncomfortable affair that only improves when Gert excuses himself early and stalks off to his room. But not before telling Franz, in no uncertain manner, to make quite sure that their gear is in proper order for the following day – two camera cases for the morning beach shoot, and the scaffolding unloaded from their car for the afternoon interiors.

"*Ist das klar*?" he snaps.

It is to make amends for Gert's behaviour that Cossie accepts Electra's invitation to share a last drink on the terrace. If he had not acted up in such a spoilt, bad-tempered manner she would have declined the invitation, blaming their early start. But now she feels she cannot.

"I'm so sorry for the way Gert behaved," she says, following Electra to the terrace. "There's really no excuse… I'm sure he'll be better after a good night's sleep. It is always so stressful – equipment, weather… you know? Until the last shot is taken, there is always so much that can go wrong."

"Please don't worry," says Electra. "Let's just put it down to the artistic temperament. When deadlines loom Nikos can be just the same. So tense, wanting everything to be right. To be perfect."

This unexpected confidence takes Cossie by surprise. Not just that Electra should say it, but because it's a side of Nikos that she has not seen. And she wonders why Electra, who has been so careful in her dealings with the team, should share such a thing with a stranger. So personal, so unguarded. And with a journalist, to boot. Someone writing about the house, and the family, with particular reference to ConStav. Letting down her guard like this seems so out-of-character.

Or is it deliberate, Cossie wonders, taking a seat at the terrace table?

And then, with a sudden chill, Cossie wonders if maybe Electra knows something about Nikos and her? Does she suspect anything? Is this increasing closeness deliberate? Is there more to it than just Electra, the house owner, and Cossie, the journalist, whose magazine is featuring the property?

Standing beside her, Electra puts down a bottle of wine and two glasses she's brought along. The glasses clink together, and the bottle lands heavily. She seems to sway slightly, and Cossie realises she's a little drunk. She tries to remember how much her hostess has been drinking, but it doesn't seem enough to account for that unsteadiness and the slight slur to her voice.

But there is no chance to consider it further. There is another surprise in store.

Electra has remained standing and, putting a hand on Cossie's shoulder – to steady herself, Cossie thinks? – she asks if Cossie would like a joint; a little smoke before bedtime, so long as it stays a secret between them?

It is the last thing that Cossie had expected, and she realises immediately that to say 'no' would appear unfriendly, censorious even.

"What a great idea," she says, despite her misgivings. "And definitely off the record. I promise."

Later, back in her guest cottage, Cossie locks her door, and closes the shutters; latches them tight. Listens for a moment to see if the dog returns. The one that snarled at them on the terrace, and the one that bumped against her door. Or are they one and the same?

But there's nothing.

Just the low, drilling trill of insects.

And then, as she turns from the door, she sees the glow of her mobile on the bedside table.

A missed call. Nikos's number.

She'd love to hear his voice, to speak to him. And she's about to call him back, when she realises that she's in no condition to do so. Because she knows she's still hopelessly stoned, and that Nikos would not approve. Not at Douka; and not on a story.

She doesn't even risk an answering text, in case he calls her back.

So she switches off the phone and, a little unsteadily, heads for the bathroom.

49

ANOTHER early start, down on the beach.

The Balinese pavilion, on a bank of emerald tamarisk, looks magical in the soft dawn light. Gert, a different Gert from the day before, is full of energy and enthusiasm without, it seems, any recollection of his bad behaviour the previous evening; or any understanding that an apology – to anyone – might be in order.

Typical bloody photographer, thinks Cossie; but she lets it pass, as she knows she must. They have this last day for shooting, and she cannot allow anything to get in the way. When the final photo is taken she can do what she wants, give him a piece of her mind. Until then, it's keep Gert happy and get the story in the can. So she cheers him on when he discovers that if he sets up his tripod on a low scatter of rocks at the far end of the cove, he will have not only the beach house but Douka as well, looming above a background line of pines.

On their way back to the house Cossie drops behind Gert and Franz and phones Nikos, to make up for not calling him back the night before. But there's no response, so she leaves a message telling him that they have nearly finished the shoot and that she cannot wait to see him. Then she texts him. *Dinner when I get back?* She presses 'Send', waits a moment or two, but there is no reply. She isn't surprised. She suspects he is playing safe; he might call at an inappropriate moment, or leave a message that Electra might see. Best not to risk it.

In the kitchen Aja and Lina have prepared breakfast. Scrambled eggs and ham, toast and conserves, yoghurt, honey and muesli. They are half way through the feast when Electra returns from her run.

"I'm so sorry about last night," she says to Gert and Franz, pouring herself a glass of water at the stone sink. "I hope the music didn't wake you."

"We never hear a thing," Gert replies. "Cossie already asks us…" He shrugs, and smears a knife-blade loaded with fig jam onto his toast.

"How they didn't hear it, I'll never understand," says Cossie. "Deaf as stones the pair of them."

"It didn't wake Dimi either," says Electra, looking puzzled. "Out for the count." And then, "I hope you won't think me unsociable, but I'd like to get on with some work this morning. Is it okay if I use the study? Have you finished with it?"

"The study is fine, of course. It is all yours," says Gert. "It is just the upper floor we will be working in. And I will make sure no one make any noise, *ja*?"

And that is how they spend the day, setting up scaffolding and lights, taking photo after photo, with Electra tucked away in her study. For which Cossie is extremely grateful. Now she can concentrate on the shoot without having to play best friends with her hostess – and her lover's wife. It is only later that Electra makes an appearance, coming into the kitchen where they've been taking some small detail shots – the old stone sinks, a vase of flowers, a bowl of fruit.

"How's it all going?" she asks, breezily. There is something light and excited about her, Cossie thinks. Her eyes sparkle and her smile is wide, and Cossie notices the make-up, the freshly-washed hair, and a soft trail of perfume – cool and flowery. She has also ditched the daytime jeans, white t-shirt and espadrilles in favour of Capri pants and a pale blue silk blouse, much the same outfit she wore when she came to meet them at the ferry.

The very next moment Cossie understands why.

"I'm going in to Navros," Electra continues, picking up her car keys and heading for the garden door. "Nikos is coming in on the ferry and, since this is your last night with us, he has asked if you will join us both for dinner? Not here, at the house. A place he knows, in Anémenos."

Before Cossie can think of anything to say – or indeed get any kind of grip on this unexpected development, not to mention that hateful '*us both*' – Gert tells Electra how nice that will be, and yes, they would all love to meet and have dinner with Nikos. Wherever he chooses. And, if she wants, why not leave Dimi with them, so they can all look for scorpions together? Another five minutes, and they'll be done for the day.

"So long as you don't get in the way, or get stung," she says to Dimi, wagging a playful finger at him. And then, with another sunbeam smile and nervous little wave, she is out of the door and gone.

If the news of Nikos's impending arrival has put a spring in Electra's step, it hits Cossie like a bombshell. He had made it quite clear before the shoot that he would stay away and leave Cossie to it. Which, at the time, was both comforting and sad. Comforting, that she wouldn't have to deal with having him around; and sad, that she wouldn't see him until her return to the city.

Now, caught on the hop, she doesn't know how she feels. Excited, yes, like Electra. But also filled with a nervous, thrilling kind of dread. How on earth will she manage with him here, so close? And how will he behave, in the same house with the two women he's sleeping with? The only blessing is that the housekeeper, Ariadne, has gone home.

What a way to finish the shoot.

Cossie hears the Jeep return as she steps from the shower; two car doors slamming. As she dries herself she feels a tightness in her chest. How will she handle this? How will he handle it? The very least he could have done, she thinks, was call her, text her, tell her he's coming; to prepare her. But he hadn't – for whatever reason – and somehow she'll just have to make the best of it.

And the tightness in her chest gives way to a kind of soft irritation. She is cross with him again, for making her feel so vulnerable. But then she remembers the missed call the night before, and her decision not to reply. And the crossness cools. He was going to tell her; he tried to warn her; to explain. It is not his fault. But then, she thinks, he could have texted.

Deciding not to compete with Electra, Cossie dresses simply. The floral print frock she wore on their first evening at Douka which Nikos hasn't seen, the black lace-up espadrilles, and her favourite blue scarf tied in her hair, the knot just an inch above, and to the side of the wave in her hairline. She looks in the mirror, leans forward to apply the tiniest lick of lipstick, which could easily pass for lip salve, and the merest stroke of eye shadow. As for perfume, she decides that the scent of the shower gel will be quite enough. Fresh and fruity.

She stands back to see what he will see; what Electra will see. Nothing out of the ordinary, nothing that suggests anything more than a certain professional smartness.

And there is a formality to be observed, after all.

It is their last night at Douka, and they are going out to dinner with its owners.

But she acknowledges, too, that she has dressed for more than that.

And then she remembers the bracelet. The one Nikos gave her the day after she told him she'd be doing the story on Douka. A knotted gold band from Zafroudi's in Kolonaki. Thin, but heavy. The oily, clunky way it slides on her wrist. And as she leaves her cottage, checking the clasp, she knows that, for all the simplicity, she will outshine Electra. And that the bracelet says more than anything about her place in Nikos's affections.

Cossie is pleased to see that she is the last to make an appearance on the terrace, coming up the side steps from the herb garden. The evening is warm and silky, the sky a deepening blue, the sun still strong enough to cast long fingers of shadow.

Nikos is the first to see her, as though he's been waiting just for her. He is talking to Gert, but breaks off when she steps from the shadows into the last of the sunlight. He strides across the terrace, takes her hand, plants a chaste kiss on her cheek.

"Ah, Costanza, how lovely to see you again. I hope you have had a successful time here at Douka." Then he takes a step back and, far enough away from anyone to overhear, he whispers, "You look lovely, my darling."

Which sends a wild blooming blush into her cheeks, as he leads her back to the party.

And so the evening begins.

50

THEY TAKE two cars to Anémenos, driving past busy quayside tavernas and up through a tangle of cobbled back streets that make the tyres thrum. Parking in front of a nondescript village house, no different to its neighbours save a set of high wooden doors with a Judas gate, they gather round Nikos.

"You will wonder where I have brought you," he says. "But I can promise you that the *Ouzeri* Kariakis will feed you better than any of the tavernas down by the harbour."

At which point, as if on cue, the Judas gate opens and an old lady leans out to beckon them in, smiling and nodding at each of them as they step past her into a vault-like room lit by a single bare light bulb.

Cossie loves the *ouzeri* on sight, and feels a shiver of hungry anticipation. The simplicity. The authenticity. Trust Nikos, she thinks, to know such a wonderful place, and have the confidence to bring them here. Knowing they'll love it, just as he does. The lofty, shadowed ceiling, the floor a shiny hard-packed earth, and the walls lined with massive barrels raised up on pallets, steel hoops rusted, wood stained a greeny black at the seams. It might not be an *Arki-Tek* destination, she knows, but it's no less memorable for that. And the homely informality of it all, as though they've been invited to spend the evening with an island family who count their years of hospitality in generations. It couldn't be better. As far as she's concerned it's the perfect way to end their stay on Pelatea after the refined pleasures of Douka: rickety plastic tables pushed together to accommodate their party, a plastic table cloth whose original pattern has been lost to years of wiping down, and a half-dozen plastic chairs that stand at odd angles thanks to the uneven floor they are set on.

They take their places without any direction, simply choosing a chair and sitting. When they are settled, the crew on one side, their hosts on the other, Cossie finds herself directly opposite Nikos.

"It is Niko's favourite place on the island," says Electra to Gert, as a pair of thick tallow candles are lit and placed on the table. She says it, Cossie notices, in a way that suggests she cannot understand how such a small and apparently dismal space could hold such a special attraction for her husband. Beyond her understanding, Electra's words imply, *but there you are...*

Yet Gert, Cossie can see, is as entranced as she is; watching with a hungry, wide-eyed pleasure as the meal begins. No menu here. No ordering. Just sit and wait for whatever is brought from the kitchen, somewhere in the shadowy depths beyond the barrels. Baskets of roughly-chopped crusty bread and chipped bowls of wrinkled olives, followed by thick white china plates loaded with hot and cold *mezés* that mother and daughter Kariakis slide onto the table: the usual speckled *tzatziki* and a browny pink *taramosalata* with quartered hard-boiled eggs; dishes of char-grilled octopus tentacles and golden sliced calamari; lightly-battered sardines the size of a stiffened little finger; grilled Halloumi and Saganaki cheeses; vine leaves stuffed with rice and chicken; and bowls of goat *souvlaki*, beef *stifado* and rabbit *yuvarlakia* served with steaming pitas. Plate after plate, one after another, pushed around the table to sample and share island-style, the dampness of the room soon overtaken with the warming scents of mint and oregano.

And the *ouzo*, of course. Drawn from one of the barrels by old man Kariakis and served in traditional copper flasks. An *ouzo* with which Nikos is clearly familiar.

"The Kariakis brand is without equal," he tells them, raising his glass and turning it in the candlight. "Mainland or island, it is the best. Double-distilled in the back-yard," he thumbs over his shoulder, "and stored in here where it is cool and dark. Of course, the family will never tell you what they use to flavour the brew, but if you taste it carefully, without the addition of water or ice, like this, you might just notice a hint of cardamon. Or maybe cloves." He turns to mother Kariakis who is taking away cleared dishes for her daughter to replace with new ones. "Am I right, Mama Kariakis? Cardamon? Or cloves?"

The lady of the house, in her headscarf and apron, shrugs, and laughs, as though she does not understand the question; as though Nikos is speaking in a different language and she does not want to appear impolite. And in the corner, sitting on a stool, the old lady who beckoned them in, cackles with glee.

"But whether you drink it plain, or with water or ice, be warned," Nikos continues. "It may not strike you as the strongest drink when you take your first sip, but it works on you gradually, building up in your system before releasing itself like a hurricane. Which is why you should always eat these *ouzomezédhes* as you drink it."

It is on the word 'hurricane' that Cossie feels something touch her ankle. Before she can think rat, she realises that it's a bare foot. Nikos's foot. Now sliding up between her knees. Which she clamps tight, trapping the foot. Instinctively, not teasingly. He cannot be doing this, she thinks, sitting there next to his son, pouring his wife another glass of *ouzo*, while his toes wriggle against her skin; as though pleading to be released so they can stray further. Which, after a moment's indecision, Cossie does, drawing her chair closer to the table, readjusting the edge of the plastic cloth, and resettling herself to spread her thighs so the foot can reach her. Which, tantalisingly, making her breath shorten, it does.

For long minutes, as the food is passed around and the *ouzo* drunk, Nikos continues with his footwork, chatting away as he does so. Asking everyone if they're enjoying the meal? Have they tried the *tyropita*, a Kariakis speciality?

Or the *horta* salad whose emerald leaves are picked on the slopes above the town? Or the Lagana flatbread scorched from the grill? And when he speaks to her, he speaks in a low voice, with a softly complicit smile, as his toes gently stroke and tease her, making her own voice catch and quicken when she replies.

If the rest of the party is gently tipsy when they bid farewell to their hosts and stumble through the Judas gate onto the pavement, Cossie is simply flushed. Brought so close, yet thankfully denied. How she would have managed at the table in such a condition she cannot imagine? Now all she wants is to be back at Douka, in her cottage, waiting for Nikos. For she is sure that he will find some excuse to leave Electra and come to her; to finish what he has begun. And she wants him to, more than she has ever wanted anything in her life. The thrill of it…

Since she has drunk less than the others, Cossie offers to drive the Jeep, with Franz behind the wheel of the Hyundai. To her surprise, she is joined by Electra and Dimi, with Nikos electing to go with Gert and Franz.

"You look a little… unsettled," says Electra, as they set off down the street. "Though I notice you didn't drink too much of the Kariakis brew. I hope it wasn't something you ate?"

"I've never been a great fan of *ouzo*," Cossie manages, her voice still a little uncertain; wondering with a rising panic if, somehow, Electra knew what Nikos was doing under the table. But it's not possible; she couldn't have. Or could she? "It's that taste of aniseed," she continues, clearing her throat. "I suppose you could say I'm a wine and beer sort of girl. And just a little bit tired, too," she adds. "It's always the same at the end of a shoot. It takes it out of you." And as she drives along the quay, following Electra's directions for the road to Douka, she feels again those pressing toes, and cannot help a short sigh slip between her lips.

Without taking her eyes off the road she senses Electra turn in her seat and look at her. "Or perhaps it's the chill in there," Electra continues. "I always find it so cold… and damp. Like a cellar. And everything just… primitive. But Nikos does love it so."

Back at the house, Electra excuses herself and takes Dimi upstairs to bed, saying she will be down shortly; while Nikos pulls the cork on a final bottle of label-less *ouzo* given to him on their departure by old man Kariakis himself. He pours a shot for Franz, and for himself, and offers the bottle to Cossie who shakes her head, and to Gert who waves his hand and makes his excuses. It was a fine evening, he says, and a grand meal, and now it is time for his bed. But first, he tells them, his voice slurring a little, just one last check on the scaffolding for the final shots tomorrow morning.

When Franz offers to do it for him, Gert gives another dismissive wave. "No, no. I do it. Is okay…", and weaves his way out of the kitchen.

It seems only moments later, Cossie and Franz and Nikos settled at the kitchen table, talking of the food at the Kariakis *ouzerí*, that they hear singing. Or rather a kind of loud uncertain humming. Distant, yet somehow familiar, deep and resonant. At first Cossie thinks that either Gert or Electra must have put on some music. But then she hears the voice. And the language. It is Gert.

The three of them look at each other in puzzlement; Franz and Nikos putting down their glasses.

"Is that Gert?" asks Nikos, pushing back his chair and getting to his feet.

Cossie and Franz do the same, and follow Nikos from the kitchen, out into the hallway, hurrying past him and heading for the salon as Electra comes down the stairs.

By now the voice is loud, and the song instantly, if grotesquely familiar; its slurred lyrics accompanied by a heavy stamping.

"Oh God," says Cossie, stopping in the doorway, her hand rising to her mouth.

Oh God, oh God, oh God…

51

COSSIE'S hands are tight on the wheel as she swings the Hyundai out of Douka's driveway, headlights sweeping through the olive groves before straightening out onto the road. Her lips are as tight as her hands, and her heart thumps with a righteous, disbelieving anger. She is still stunned by what happened in the salon. Hugely embarrassed. Mortified.

"How could you?" she says. "What were you thinking?" Gert is lying in the back seat of the Hyundai, his arm in a make-do dishcloth sling, head lolling, every swaying turn of the car and pothole drawing short painful groans from him. "What possessed you?"

"He said someone told him to do it," said Franz, quietly, sitting beside her, his injured hand in his lap. As though the word 'possessed' had prompted him to pass on Gert's excuse. "When I was getting him into the car, he says there was this voice in his ear. Said it would be fun. So that's what he did."

"Jesus," Cossie says, gritting her teeth, wanting to shake the very breath out of her injured backseat passenger. "Really?" But she shivers nonetheless, as she races through a sleeping Akronitsá and brakes for the first of the hairpins down through Avrómelou; seeing above the trees and beyond the spread of headlights, across the darkened slopes, the wavering pinprick lights of Navros.

Soon the twists and turns are behind them, and they are passing fields of maize and olive, turning onto the beach road; dry stone walls and bamboo stands flashing past on one side, a rise and fall of grass-topped dunes and the shifting blackness of an unseen sea on their left.

What will they think, Cossie wonders? What will they do, Nikos and Electra?

How can she ever face them again?

But face them she must. To pack up their things, and to apologise once again for Gert's… just unbelievable, unforgiveable behaviour.

And there she was, thinking that Nikos would come to her cottage to finish what he had begun at the *ouzerí*. Some chance now.

She wonders too, more importantly, whether Gert's outrageous performance will have any impact on the course of her affair with Nikos? Will it give him pause for thought? Draw him closer to his wife? Will he use it as a means to bring their relationship to an end, when they next meet up in the city? Or maybe it'll just be a phone call, a brief apologetic conversation… The end of the road. Now that the Douka story is in the bag. Now that she's done all she can for him.

Surely not, she tells herself. He's not like that.
And it isn't her fault. She hasn't done anything wrong.
But only time will tell.

The Navros hospital, when Cossie finds it, is quiet. A long, two-floor block overlooking an empty parking lot at the back of the town. Just a neon-lit panel above the doors – *Hippokrateio Pelatea* – and lights beyond in an empty hallway.

While Franz helps Gert from the back seat, Cossie goes ahead, finds the reception desk and rings for attention. When a nurse appears, Cossie explains the situation – two casualties, a broken arm, broken fingers, maybe a concussion – and a doctor is called. While Gert and Franz are taken away for examination and X-rays, Cossie fills in the various forms – names, addresses, telephone numbers, the magazine's insurance details – then steps outside for a cigarette, checking her mobile to see if Nikos has messaged her. Not a thing.

She finds a bench, sits down and lights up, stares across the rooftops at distant stars, and thanks the Lord that the shoot is over... Just those last orchid shots to take – no longer an option – but everything else in the bag.

So look on the bright side, she thinks. After three days at Douka they have more than enough for the story. At least, there's that.

Thank God, thank God, thank God...

52

IT IS LIGHT when Cossie and Franz leave the hospital. Gert, with his arm in a plaster cast and a confirmed concussion, has been kept in for further observation. All being well, the doctor tells her, in the corridor outside Gert's room, he should be ready for discharge that afternoon. He asks if she would like to see her friend, but she shakes her head. She can see him through the window in the door. That is enough. Otherwise, she's not sure she can trust herself not to inflict further injuries. And if he is concussed, then what would be the point? Let him suffer alone. Let him stew, she thinks.

Franz, his two fingers splinted, waits until they start out on the coast road before he says anything.

"Time to wrap?"

Cossie nods, reaches across and squeezes his good hand. "It's not going to be fun."

"Happy to be leaving all that to you."

"Thanks," she replies, and smiles ruefully.

By the time they reach Douka, it is like every other morning. As though nothing has happened. Nothing out of place. The sun on the lawns, sprinklers tapping; the darker shadows of the cypress, the lighter ones of eucalyptus; the occasional rattle of palm fronds in a warm breeze.

While Franz heads off to the cottages to pack up their gear, Cossie makes for the herb garden and kitchen. Whatever lies in store, she knows she can't avoid it. Might as well face the music now as later. And as she knocks on the door and opens it she hears the distant sound of a hoover, a gritty, clattering kind of sound that suggests gravel being reluctantly sucked up. The salon, she realises; the remains of the night before.

Electra, in her running gear, is sitting at the kitchen table with a coffee cup and a bottle of water. When she sees Cossie she smiles, with more feeling than Cossie had expected, and asks how she is? She must be exhausted. Would she like some coffee? Some breakfast? Standing at an ironing board, Ariadne takes one disapproving look at her, disconnects the iron and snaps the board back into its concealed storage space. Gathering up a basket of folded linen, the housekeeper heads for the kitchen door just as Nikos appears. Across the room Cossie can see the old lady's raised eyebrow and tight lips as she passes him. The look she gives him is eloquent. *What kind of people are these to come to our home, to behave the way they have, and cause such damage*? is what that look says. Then the door closes and, thankfully, she is gone.

Like Electra, Nikos gives her a smile, but it is lean and swift. Business-like. He pulls out a chair next to Electra, and sits down.

"I really don't know how to begin to say how sorry I am for last night..." Cossie begins. "And how sorry Gert is. He was... He was just so drunk. More than we thought. And he is so ashamed," she continues, though she has no idea whether he is or isn't. She casts around, not certain whether she's said enough; how to continue. "He said someone told him to do it, that's what he says," is all she can muster. In his defence. In her defence.

It's clearly not enough, and what follows leaves her numbed, lost for words. Everything so much worse than she had imagined. Nikos's grandfather shot by the Nazis, here at Douka. Oh God, oh God... she had no idea. How could she have? She feels suddenly light-headed, almost faint.

Yet, at this moment of utter dejection and desperation, there is still worse to come.

Someone has come up behind her, and she turns to see Franz. His face is flushed, his features slack and haunted. He spreads his hands, shakes his head, seems to be searching for words.

But finally he finds them, and what remains of Cossie's world comes crashing down.

If Gert's behaviour the previous night had seemed outrageous – almost too much to bear – the news of what he has done to the hard drives, destroying all their work, is even further beyond Cossie's comprehension. Beyond catastrophe. Not a single picture. Not even the working Polaroids. Franz has checked everything, he tells her. Double-checked. Three cameras, three drives. Blank. Dozens of set-ups, hundreds of shots. No back-up that he can find. No memory. No Cloud. Nothing.

"He's done what?" says *Arki-Tek*'s editor, when Cossie calls the office from her cottage, explains what has happened. Starting with the previous evening's drunken display, and finishing with the wiped drives. "You are joking. Please tell me you're joking."

Tears are streaming down Cossie's cheeks. She dare not speak. She shakes her head as though she's in her editor's office, across the desk from her. But she is not. She has to answer. She takes a breath and says, "No joke. It's a disaster. Not one single set-up. Everything's gone."

Her very first major commission. A car crash.

What will she do? What can she do?

What she won't do is tell her editor what Gert had apparently told Franz at the hospital. That somebody had told him to do it. Like the singing and the stamping. Maybe later, but not now.

There's a moment's pause. Cossie can hear a fingernail tapping on a glass desk top. When her editor comes back on the line, the older woman's voice is softer.

"And how are you, my dear? You sound..."

Fresh tears well up in Cossie eyes, and her throat tightens. Too tight to dare to speak. But she has to. She sniffs, clears her throat.

"Been better," she manages.

"I can imagine. Not fun. But leave everything with me. Just get back here as soon as you can, you hear? And leave that bloody man there if you want to. And don't worry. This has nothing to do with you. Okay?"

"Okay."

A little after four o'clock that afternoon, Cossie stands at a stern guardrail on the island ferry and looks back over a churning wake at the sun-bleached huddle of Navros, and the hills and ridges of Pelatea. Gert has been discharged from the hospital and is sitting inside with Franz, but Cossie cannot bear to be anywhere near him. His snivelling apologies, his refusal to acknowledge his actions. When they reach the mainland it will take an hour or more to make the city, and she cannot imagine how she will last that time in his company. So she stands alone on the promenade deck, looking back at the distant spine of dwindling blue hills and thinking of the house that lies behind them.

And the man who lives there; the man who smiled, and kissed her when she came to say goodbye and, before drawing back, whispered in her ear, "Monday evening? Acteon?"

53

THE FIRST time they met, Nikos knew she was the one for him.

As simple as that.

An almost immediate response.

Bright and whip smart. Independent, free-thinking. He had read her stories before he met her. Learned to look out for her by-line. Short pieces. Witty. Sharp and informed. They made him laugh, they made him think. And then he met her, in her editor's office. They were considering a short piece on him for their Style section, if he was interested?

Of course, he was interested. It was early days. He needed to put ConStav on the map. He needed to get the name around. Make his mark. And he knew that she could do it for him. A half-page, thousand-word profile, with her by-line, would make all the difference.

That she was as beautiful as she was witty and well-informed was something he hadn't been expecting. Tall and lean and elegant. He'd never met her, never seen a photo. That meeting in her editor's office was the first time he'd laid eyes on her.

She was late for that first meeting, bustling into her editor's office amidst a flurry of apologies. Shaking his hand, taking the chair beside him, settling herself; tote on the floor, scarf unwound, her legs crossing; a warm, sinuous scent pulsing off her. Black suede ankle boots with a brass zip on the heel and pointed toes, slim-fit blue jeans that made her legs look impossibly long and slender, and a pale blue cashmere cardigan unbuttoned over a man's blue and white striped shirt. Cuffs and links. A strand of pearls at her throat. A chunky gold nugget of a signet ring on her left little finger. An old Omega on a leather strap, as carelessly loose on her wrist as a bracelet. Tiny blue studs in her ears. Sapphires.

Everything blue and tanned and young and healthy.

But as effortlessly chic and stylish as she was, it was her looks that caught the eye, commanded attention. Curling gold blonde hair falling across her shoulders, tucked back behind an ear; high cheekbones and a tanned, flawless complexion; lustrous red lips, even white teeth, and wide brown eyes that sparkled.

All that. And rich. Very rich.

Electra Theia Stamatos.

Not ship-owner or ship-builder rich, perhaps – no Niarchos, no Onassis – but her family's wealth was still considerable. Not a wall was built or plastered, not a road laid down, nor a tube of toothpaste, or tin of paint, or sack of soil conditioner produced in Greece without limestone from Stamatos

Stone, quarried from Stamatos land, transported by Stamatos Haulage. ConStav contractors used no one else. In truth, there *was* no one else.

Two hours after their first meeting, Nikos Contalidis picked up the phone, called the newspaper's editorial department and asked Electra if she would care to have lunch with him.

She thanked him, but said no.

54

NIKOS CONTALIDIS was used to hearing no. And when he did, he knew why. His family may have been older and more celebrated than the Stamatos clan, but he was an islander and the Stamatos were Athenian. Just second generation, but still… He should know his place. Pirates and patricians. A country boy in the big city. It wasn't the first time he'd come up against similar prejudice. And he knew it wouldn't be the last.

When Electra's story finally appeared in the Style section of *I Kathimerini,* he called their offices once again and asked the switchboard to put him through to Electra Stamatos. But that was as far as he got. Miss Stamatos was a freelance contributor, had no desk, and was not a staffer, the switchboard operator informed him, adding that she was unable to provide him with any means of contact. Which was odd, since he'd been put through before. Had she been sacked? Had she resigned? He asked to speak to the editor, but was told she was otherwise engaged. Would he care to leave a message?

A simple 'thank you' was the message he left with the operator; for the editor, and for Electra. But after a week there had still been no response.

Three months later – after any number of unsuccessful attempts by Nikos to contact Electra – he literally bumped into her. At an architectural awards dinner in the ballroom of the Athens Hilton on Vassilissis Sofias. He had taken his girlfriend, a willowy redhead who worked for a marketing company in Kolonaki, and he was on his way to the Men's Room when someone called his name. He turned, saw a friend, waved… and the next instant, turning a corner, still waving, Electra Stamatos was in his arms. And he in hers. All elbows and knees and hands. Embarrassed confusion. The breath knocked out of them. Her clutch falling to the floor; the pair of them reaching for it and bumping foreheads. Which was the moment they recognised each other.

"Electra. What an unexpected pleasure."

She had smiled, with the slightest frown. He might know her name, but he could see, in that quizzical, breathless look, that she couldn't remember his. Or, maybe, pretended not to.

"Nikos, Nikos Contalidis," he offered. "ConStav. You wrote a lovely piece for *I Kathimerini*. I tried to call you, to thank you…"

"Of course, Mr Contalidis. How nice to see you."

Mister, not Nikos.

She put out her hand. He took it. Cool and smooth. And he held it a beat longer than she might have expected.

"So, are you up for an award?" she'd asked, reclaiming her hand.

"Not this time. Next year perhaps."

She'd nodded; gave it some thought. "That's the spirit," she said; and then she'd straightened, as though to give him the opportunity to move out of her way and let her pass. Instead, he'd stepped forward.

"I owe you a lunch," he said. "And this time I won't take no for an answer."

"How kind. Lunch. But isn't lunch for losers?"

"Call it a business lunch."

"That's what I mean."

"Dinner seemed… forward."

"You don't get awards for being timid, Mr Contalidis." And with another of her sparkling smiles, she'd stepped past him and the moment was gone.

Or, not quite.

Twenty minutes later, having established where she was sitting in the vast Athens Hilton ballroom, he'd walked over to her table, and put his business card in front of her. She looked up, surprised. Her companion, an over-tanned fifty-something in slim white tuxedo, gave him the once over, frowned, and was about to lean forward, say something, when Nikos turned the card over for her. Tapped the message, smiled at her companion, and wished her a good evening. On the back of the card he'd written *O Krittikos. Wednesday. 9pm.*

Shortly before ten the following Wednesday evening, Nikos had finally given up on Electra Stamatos. Had asked for the bill for the bottle of wine he'd ordered and nearly finished, when he saw her across the pavement tables, chaining a bike to a lamppost. Trainers, sweats, and a zip-up black Puffa jacket.

Not what you wore at O Krittikos.

Unless, it appeared, your name was Stamatos.

Welcomed by the owner himself; handshakes, effusions.

And a wave from her when she spotted him, pointing him out to the owner, who promptly escorted her to his table. In an instant, it seemed to Nikos, this acknowledgement from Electra Stamatos, this most basic association with a city name, had elevated him in the owner's eyes from a man sitting alone, brooding over a bottle of wine, to a welcome, respected and much-loved guest. There'd be no kitchen-door table for him the next time he visited O Krittikos.

There was still another surprise to come. Having made all the running with Electra, Nikos now found himself overtaken in the first-date stakes. Two hours later, in her penthouse apartment in Plaka, Electra unzipped her Puffa, peeled off her sweats and, in no uncertain terms, told Nikos exactly what she wanted from him. It was not what Nikos had expected – so soon, so uncomplicated – but he was only too delighted to oblige.

55

THEY WERE together a year before he met Electra's parents. An uncle's sixtieth birthday on the terrace of the Athens Yacht Club, on a headland above Mikrolimano. Her mother, Gina, was Electra thirty years on – the same sparkling brown eyes, but creased with age, patched with laugh lines; the same gold hair, but silvered now and tightly bound in a perfectly coiffed French pleat; as tall as Electra but thinner, dressed in a pale yellow Chanel suit; skirt tight, buttonless jacket trimmed in white; buckled black court shoes.

"So you're the mystery man. A Contalidis, I understand. You should feel at home," she said, waving a dented silver cigarette holder at the portraits around the main salon. "Admirals, all."

Electra's father, Mikis, with tightly-clipped grey beard, bushy grey eyebrows and hard flinty eyes, was not so easy or welcoming.

"ConStav, you say? Never heard of it. Construction?"

"Architectural design. We use your limestone."

The old man nodded. "Good choice."

And that was that. A tap on Mikis's shoulder. Someone wanting a few minutes of his time. His back turned on Nikos. Dismissed.

He was hardly more welcoming when, a year later, Nikos asked his permission to marry Electra.

"How's that business of yours?" he had asked. Eyes just as flinty. Suspicious. Once an islander, always an islander.

"Good."

Mikis considered this. "Prospects?"

"Better still."

"You did that office block in Pattission, yes?"

"Yes."

"But didn't use my limestone." Mikis Stamatos had clearly been keeping an eye on him.

"I found something better."

"You mean cheaper."

"Both, as it happens."

"Won't last, you know. Too soft. Couple of hard summers and some wet winters and it'll stain. Mark my words."

If old man Stamatos had been talking about married life with Electra he was wrong. Just as he was wrong about the limestone in Pattission. The marriage lasted. One year, two; and then Dimi. And the islander, grudgingly, was accepted into the family. Electra's elder sister, Yianna, had produced a granddaughter, but a grandson was a whole new ball game.

"Business looking good," said Mikis, one Sunday lunch at the family's country house on the road to Livadia; watching his grandchildren play on the lawn. "You need any help, you know where to come."

"I want to buy a house," Nikos told him. Which took the old boy by surprise.

"If I'm not mistaken, you already have a house. On Diomexédes."

"This is my family's home. On Pelatea. It is on the market. I want to buy it back. For Electra. For Dimi."

He could have said, more honestly, that he wanted it back for his father; for the honour of the Contalidis. But he knew that wouldn't work. There was only one way into the Stamatos wallet.

"On one condition," said Mikis. "Electra holds the deeds." No room for manoeuvre; the Stamatos behave-yourself clause.

"As you wish."

Exactly what he'd said a year later when Electra's father bailed out ConStav after a client reneged on completion terms and left the firm vulnerable. A thirty per cent holding, in Electra's name, to tide them over. Non-negotiable.

And so the Contalidis home on Douka was his. Or rather, Electra's, who agreed that Nikos's father, Theo, could take up residence again, moving from his cramped accommodation in Lysander's house. The old boy may have lost his home, but now, twenty years later, he could have it back.

Electra had had reservations, of course.

"Don't you think he's too old for a place like that? All on his own. Rattling around."

"He has the housekeeper, Ariadne Papadavrou; she'll keep an eye on him," Nikos had countered. "She'll make sure he has everything he needs. The house will be in good hands, believe me."

And so it had been. Three contented years. Until a chilly winter night when Theo dozed off and dropped a cigarette into his armchair; or a candle fell from its holder; or a log on the fire broke apart, scattering glowing splinters onto a rug – it was never confirmed what had caused the conflagration. The house of the Contalidis burned to the ground. Theo dragged from the flames. By the widow Papadavrou herself.

What Nikos hadn't expected was how deeply Electra fell in love with Douka.

The first time he took her to Pelatea, and drove her over the hills to Douka, a weekend with his father shortly after he'd moved back in, she'd been quiet. Bored at the prospect of a weekend out of the city; away from her friends, away from the action.

And then she had seen the house.

Petrou may have let the estate slide during his residency – a slide his nephew had tried to contain – but Electra had seen right through the poor state of the property; the weed-strewn terraces, the untended groves, the gloomy high-ceilinged rooms. And loved it at first sight.

But there was more, something Nikos hadn't anticipated.

When Theo showed Electra around, she'd paused at the family portraits. Frowned, as though for the first time she had understood that Nikos wasn't just an islander. And he knew it, could see it in her expression; knew what she was thinking. For the very first time. He was a Contalidis. There was history here. A provenance. Something the Stamatos clan, for all its wealth and power and position, lacked. And thanks to her father, and her husband, all this was now hers.

On the ferry back to the mainland, she'd gripped his arm at the stern rail.

"What would you say if I told you I wanted to write about the family? Your family. Douka. The Contalidis. The Admiral, his exploits, and all the sons who came after him. I think it would make a wonderful story."

"I would say that you are the very best person to make it happen. I can't think of anyone better qualified."

56

WITH HINDSIGHT, looking back over their time together, Nikos acknowledged that he had never really, never actually… loved Electra. He had wanted her, of course – the cool, sophisticated Athenian. Young, fresh, beautiful, clever. She was good for him, good for ConStav, too. And more than a notch up from the willowy redhead in marketing. And all the others like her.

But wanting, he soon discovered, wasn't loving.

And nor was wanting strong enough to keep them together when the going got tough.

When it all came tumbling down.

In the house on Diomexédes, Nikos was working late in his basement studio when he heard what sounded like a distant cry from the upper floors. Followed soon after by the hurried footsteps of Dimi's nanny coming down the stairs; his door flying open.

"It's Madame Contalidis," she said, breathless, pale. "There's something wrong."

The drive to the Lycabettus Clinic was short, but fraught. Nikos swerving left and right, blaring his horn, taking the traffic lights with a heart-stopping disregard; Electra curled up on the back seat groaning, crying out. And with every desperate cry, the harder Nikos hit the horn and pressed down on the accelerator.

The staff were waiting when they arrived at the clinic, alerted by their nanny; Nikos pulling in between two ambulances. A gurney was trundled out, the back door opened, and Electra scooped out; Nikos watching with a rising dread as his wife disappeared through a set of swing doors. He'd been shown to a waiting area. Someone would be down to speak to him as soon as they knew what was happening, he was told.

It was a little after three in the morning before a doctor in blue scrubs brought the news. There had been complications; the pregnancy had been compromised and their second child was lost. He was sorry, his sincerest condolences, but there was nothing they had been able to do. But he could see her now, the doctor said, and he was taken to her room, left with her. But there were no words, nothing he could say. Nothing he could do to stop her silent tears. He stayed with her until she slept, and then he went home.

The days that followed were hard. Sitting by her bed, holding her hand, smoothing back her hair. Whispering words of comfort, support, encouragement. Her father visiting, her mother, her sister. Friends, like Iphy. But no real reaction from Electra. Just a deadness about her; no spark, no liveliness, none of that confident Stamatos toughness. It was as if something other than the foetus had been dragged out of her, and lost. Some vital organ, without which she seemed unable to function.

But reaching through his own grief, after those first few days, there had grown in Nikos, slowly and steadily, an icy resentment. That she should succumb so completely, and not fight back. That she should allow this setback to stop her in her tracks, and put their lives on miserable, destructive hold. Not to mention the attention she received. From family, friends, assorted well-wishers. Because she wasn't the only one who suffered. His child had been lost, too. His daughter. Bundled up, and disposed of somewhere.

Yet no one seemed to take account of him.

There was only Electra to comfort.

Only Electra…

Other women managed, he thought to himself. Other mothers pulled themselves together; these things happened all the time. Tragic, of course, but… Sometimes, sitting at her bedside, he wanted to reach out and shake her. Come on, come on… Snap out of it. Life goes on. It's time to leave all this behind. I have, now you must.

A week later he had brought Electra home. A nurse engaged to care for her those first few weeks, to bathe and dress her, to supervise the medication, to sit with her and watch her. Nikos camping out in a guest room, comforting Dimi; coming in each morning to their bedroom to kiss her goodbye. Returning from work each evening with a slice of her favourite honey and almond *baklava* from Heronitsis, figs from the tree in their garden or the market on Spetsilides Street, an armful of magazines and newspapers.

And gradually Electra began to rally. Sitting up in bed, not lying back staring at the ceiling. Her appetite returning. Watching television, albeit blankly, as though she couldn't quite connect with whichever programme she'd selected. But always the blinds closed, the room in shadow.

It was guilt, that's what everyone told him. This… distance. The loss of a child. A sense of failure in the mother; that it was her fault. Could only be her fault. But she would get over it, they all said. Give her time.

Which Nikos did.

Of course.

He had no choice.

When her nurse was finally let go, it seemed to Nikos that Electra really had started to recover. Each morning she would get out of bed, shower, dress and come downstairs. Sometimes a smile, a careless, dismissive wave when he asked how she was, how she'd slept, until he knew to stop asking. She would kiss him goodbye, see Dimi off to school with the nanny…

And then, alone in the house, she would drink.

Carefully, secretly. Vodka. Bought in the local supermarket when he was at work, or the nanny on the school run.

Empty bottles wrapped in newspaper and hidden in the trash so the glass wouldn't clink. The full ones hidden under the bed. In her underwear drawer. Poured into plastic water bottles for her bedside table. No mixers, no ice. The screw cap off, and the bottle tipped back. Swigged like lemonade.

And with the drink there followed a rapid decline in her mental state. A slurring, an unsteadiness; always reaching for something to hold onto as she made her way round the kitchen, the salon, down the stairs.

And then she started to lose her temper.

With Nikos, with Dimi, with the nanny.

Anything could set her off. The grating of cutlery on a plate, or a dirty saucepan left in the sink. The dripping of a tap, or the barking of a neighbour's dog. A door slamming. The volume of the television or radio too high, or too low.

Within weeks of the nurse being discharged, Electra was back in her room, blinds down, and Nikos was at his wit's end.

What's wrong with Mummy? Dimi would ask.

And Nikos would comfort the boy, and wonder the same thing.

Wonder what the hell was happening, and what was he going to do?

The breakdown that followed was deemed too serious for home confinement. A ranting, raving whirlwind of foul language and drunken destruction one Sunday morning that had Dimi and his nanny hiding in his room, and Nikos calling the family doctor for help. Dodging the glasses and plates hurled at him. The punching, the pushing, the spiteful words spat out at him. By the time the doctor arrived, Electra was back in her bed, unconscious, a tiny cut in the middle of a swollen lower lip.

"She fell," said Nikos, as the doctor examined the injury. "Slipped on the floor and hit the side of the table. Knocked herself out."

Thirty minutes later a private ambulance drew up on Diomexédes, and a sedated Electra was strapped to a gurney for immediate transfer to the Aetolikou Clinic at Lagonisi.

The first month no visits were allowed, just weekly reports.

The second and third month, no more than an hour-long visit once a week, with a nurse in attendance. Wheeled around the gardens of Aetolikou.

And then, finally, she was home again.

But not the Electra he knew.

She was different somehow. No longer the woman he remembered.

Nothing like her.

Stick thin, the appetite of a bird.

The voice a quaver, as brittle as an icicle.
The rare smiles a drugged rictus.
Brown eyes hollow and distant.
Nothing really registering.
Even Dimi noticed, only because he could twist her round his little finger. Chocolate. Fizzy drinks. It was as if she'd forgotten how to say no.
But by then it didn't matter.
Everything had changed.
He had met Cossie.

57

ACTEON is always quiet on a Monday evening. Lunchtime is busy, but by late afternoon the brasserie is empty and just a few people on their way home from work drop in for their first evening drink. If there are reservations for dinner they will have been made for later, locals mostly; maybe a few tables out on the terrace, when the sun has slipped away and the August heat is just a slow simmer.

Nikos, nursing the last of a beer, watches Cossie from the back of the brasserie. Coming off the street, across the terrace, stepping out of the sunlight and casting around for him in the gloom. He waves, and she sees him; waves back. She is wearing a white t-shirt and Levi jacket, a short black pleated skirt that swirls as she walks, and laced black espadrilles. Her legs are long and tanned, and her hair loose to her shoulders. She is breathless when she reaches the table and, he can see, a little uncertain, even nervous after the catastrophe at Douka.

Nikos stands, reaches for her arm, draws her to him and kisses her cheek.

"I missed you," he says, and it seems to reassure her.

"I missed you, too. And I'm so, so sorry…"

They take their seats, and he holds up a hand. "Nothing to be sorry about. These things happen. And it wasn't your fault."

"I just don't know what got into him. To behave like that, with the singing, and then wipe all the shots. Everything gone." She raises her hands to her head, as though holding a crown, then drops them to her sides. There are still no words.

A waiter appears and they order a bottle of wine, some house *mezédes*.

"How was the trip back?"

"He made it in one piece. I didn't kill him. But I wanted to. Every time he started to say sorry, to try and explain what he'd done, I just told him to shut up. I didn't want to hear a word out of him."

"And how was your editor?"

"Furious with Gert. Says he's finished. Called his agent and read the riot act. But very kind to me, so understanding."

"What happens now?"

"Since Gert was only involved in the Douka shoot, it's been decided to run with the two other houses, as a smaller lead. And re-do Douka for the Summer issue. A stand-alone. And cover." She looks at him, and he knows what she is thinking. *Is it enough? Will he forgive me?*

"So everything works out in the end," he says, and then, "And you get to do the shoot, write the story?"

"I hope so. I think so. If I've still got my job."

"I'll make sure of it," he says.

"If I am on the shoot, it'll be strange going back to Douka."

"You mean, Electra? Seeing her again?"

His question seems to catch her by surprise. It isn't quite what she meant, about seeing Electra again, but now she has to answer.

"It wasn't easy, Nikos. I mean, she is your wife. And you and I…"

"I wanted you to see what she's like. How it is. To understand."

Cossie frowns.

"What I'm trying to say…"

The waiter reappears with their wine, opens the bottle, pours, then returns with three small saucers which he slides between their glasses – some grilled octopus, strips of pepper and *feta* squares, *tzatziki* with fingers of toasted pita.

When they are alone again, Nikos continues. "She can be difficult. I mean, she is so much better than she was, but…" He shakes his head, reaches for a toothpick and spears a piece of *feta*. He doesn't know what else to say.

"Do you love her?"

Nikos gives Cossie a long, long look. He knows how much it will have taken for her to ask him this, and knows what it means; that their relationship is moving up a gear, more than it was. She holds his look, waiting for his answer.

And he is honest; he tells her the truth no matter what the cost.

"I'm not sure I ever really loved her, Cossie. Not like… not like I should have done. I just got carried along, I suppose. She was beautiful, she was sexy…" He shrugs. "And I was flattered by her interest, loved that she loved me…"

"And does she? Does she love you?"

"I think so. I don't know. It's different somehow. And she's changed. Nothing like she used to be. The breakdown…"

"So what do you want to do?"

Nikos sighs, smiles. "I want you to take me back to Thiseio. I want to be where I love to be. And to make up for what I've missed."

Afterwards, beneath the streetlight shadows of Cossie's bedroom, the fan turning slowly above them, she asks, "If Gert hadn't done what he did, would you have come to my room that last night? After the *ouzeri*?"

"It might have been difficult," he chuckles. "I'm sure I would have thought about it. And if I could have… If it was possible…" Instead he remembers the night after Cossie and Franz left Douka; making love to Electra, but thinking all the time of Cossie. Yes, he thinks, if Gert hadn't decided to entertain them, then he would have. For sure. He would have crept down to her cottage, knocked on her door and…

"I wanted you so much that night. I don't know how I managed at the table."

Nikos frowns in the shadows. “I don’t understand.”

“You know,” she nudges him playfully in the side. “Your foot. Under the table.”

“My foot?”

“What you did to me. With your toes.”

Nikos tries to work out what Cossie is talking about, but he is suddenly tired. He wants to sleep. “I’m not sure I follow…”

“Nikos!” Cossie raises herself on an elbow, looks down at him. “You know exactly what I’m talking about.”

“I remember I reached out and touched your foot. Just to let you know I was thinking of you. That I was there. That I wanted you. And you looked so… gorgeous…” His voice trails off.

“And the rest,” she says, snuggling up to him. “Sitting there at the table, I nearly choked; don’t know how I held myself back. Another minute…”

But Nikos doesn’t hear. His eyes have closed and he sleeps.

58

MUCH AS Nikos loves Douka, he loves the city too. His work. The excitement of a new commission – plans to be drawn up for a shopping arcade around the corner from Acteon; managing a difficult construction out in Kollathea; negotiating with suppliers; bidding for new business, and courting the press.

And Cossie, of course.

From Monday until Friday, the city is theirs, though of course they must take care. The Stamatos family is well known, as, increasingly, is he; not just Electra's husband, but the new big thing in architectural design. He has a name, a growing reputation, and people recognise him; people he doesn't even know.

So he and Cossie are careful when they are out together; no hand-holding, no kissing, nothing that could be misinterpreted. If they are spotted, if some old friend of his, or Electra's, comes up to their table or bumps into them in the street, there must be nothing to give them away. And if introductions are called for, which they would be, why, she is Costanza Theofilou, an editor at *Arki-Tek*. She is writing a story on Douka, on ConStav, for the Summer issue; and yes, she has been over to Pelatea, seen the house, met Electra… Isn't it brilliant? What a story it will make.

But it doesn't happen. There are no tricky moments. No need for introductions, nor explanations.

That first week back in Athens goes quickly for both of them. Site visits for Nikos, a touch-and-go loan-extension meeting at their bank with Vassi, while Cossie is busy working on her historic houses copy, or finishing off some pressing Diary pieces for the November issue. After Monday's meeting at Acteon and their night in Thiseio, they meet up for lunch on Wednesday at a neighbourhood bar near the ConStav office, and on Thursday evening they're back at Acteon. The following day Nikos is off to Pelatea for the weekend, and is desperate to spend what little time he has left with Cossie.

When he gets to Acteon he's an hour late. Breathless, not wanting to miss a minute of her; sitting in his taxi and wishing it through the evening snarl-ups. For a green light, or for a slow car in front of them to turn off. But he's texted her, warned her of the delay, apologised.

She's sitting at the bar, as pale as paper, when he finally arrives.

"I got a call from Franz," is the first thing she says, as he draws back from a kiss and hoists himself onto a stool, asking how she is. "It's terrible, just terrible. Gert's dead. A few days back in Munich, and he hangs himself. I'm just…" She shakes her head, takes a breath.

Nikos hears the words, but it takes him a moment to absorb them; to make any kind of sense of them.

"He's dead?"

"They found him in his studio. No note, nothing. According to Franz, he had money worries. He gambled apparently. But it had never been a real problem. Sometimes Gert would complain about costs – the studio rent, printing expenses and fees, of course. You weren't there, but at Douka he got in a real sulk over some missing lenses. How much it was going to cost him, yadda-yadda. I mean, way out of line. Took a swipe or two at Franz for losing them." Cossie takes a breath. "But like Franz said, it never lasted; the temper, or the money worries. He might not have been a first-rank photographer – not fashion, you know – but he was good, had a reputation; pulled in good commissions from good titles. Easily enough money, but…"

"But?"

"But Franz says it wasn't money this time. It was Douka. He just couldn't get over what had happened there. Just… couldn't deal with it. What he'd done. Kept telling Franz it wasn't his fault, that someone had told him to do it…"

"The *ouzo* talking," Nikos says, grimly; shaking his head, reaching for her hand.

"It's just so… upsetting, you know? Such a shock. And I was so hard on him, so unforgiving. Just couldn't bear to talk to him. I mean, this time last week…" She pauses, looks forlorn.

Nikos glances at his watch, nods. "That's right. This time last week we were heading down to the Kariakis for dinner. But it's not your fault. You did nothing wrong."

Tonight in Thiseio, there is no lovemaking, just a gentle comforting.

"Please, just hold me," says Cossie, curling up on her side, her back to him, drawing his arms around her, squirming herself into the warm spooning shape of his body. The squirming makes him hard but he lets her be, content to do as she wishes. To hug her, to hold her tight, with no expectation. In a strange sort of way he finds it curiously satisfying. That she can trust him; that he can trust himself.

No demands.

But as he drifts off to sleep, Nikos knows that there's always the morning.

59

WHEN THERE are two women in a man's life, a wife and a mistress, it is easy, almost unavoidable, to make comparisons. Nikos is painfully aware of this, from the moment Electra picks him up that Friday afternoon, off the ferry from Tsania.

There is a nerviness about her, which is starting to irritate him. This burdensome neediness which she tries so hard to conceal, and which he tries so hard to ignore. Pretending everything is fine, normal, when for both of them it's abundantly clear that the opposite is true.

And the way she looks. More make-up than is called for, as though she is making a special effort; the blusher too strong, the eyeshadow too extravagant, the eyebrows too arched and overstated, those thin lips just too, too red. The whole effect serving only to emphasise the narrowness of her face, the hardness of it. The way it's suddenly aged.

Of course, it makes him think immediately of Cossie, her effortless youth and beauty. How she'd looked, on the shoot, coming out onto the terrace his first evening at Douka. The simple shining clarity of her complexion; the natural unadorned architecture of cheekbone, chin, nose and forehead. Not to mention, as he well knew, the firm, full, yearning tightness of her body. Not ten years between the two women, Nikos estimates, but a lifetime of wear and tear carved into his wife's gaunt features, with nothing to replace what's been lost.

To make matters worse that Friday afternoon, Electra has dressed in the kind of outfit that might look fine for lunch in Kolonaki, but fails here on the Navros quay. Garish swirls of colour on a sleeveless summer frock showing bone-thin arms that would be better covered, and too much wrinkled knee; the way the *meltemi* wind presses it against her bony frame. It puts Nikos in a fractious, petulant mood. Like a little boy who's unwrapped a Christmas present to find the wrong toy; not the one he wanted. It may be his mood, the end of a busy week, but it's just the way he sees Electra now. His wife. The wrong plaything. Yet he knows he must try to make the best of it.

As he drives them back to Douka and listens to the chronicle of her week – the visit from Chrysta, her agent's enthusiastic response to the manuscript, the September deadline they've agreed on, the episode with Dimi at the cistern, and her visit with Theo – Nikos acknowledges that this is no longer the woman who took him back to her apartment in Plaka and told him what she wanted him to do. Just a shadow now, twelve years on. And he wonders how he would feel if Cossie wasn't in his life, if he hadn't been unfaithful? Would he simply accept Electra for what she is, what she's gone through, what she's become, and make the best of it? Would he try to make her better, help her find her old self? Or would he be planning an escape? Wondering how to extricate himself from a situation that he finds ever more stifling.

What was it Cossie had said, that first lunch of theirs, before she took him to the King George? *Fucking's the easy part…*

How right she was, and, he has to admit, how like Electra she is. Or rather, how Electra used to be. Taking control from the very start. A strong and independent woman.

But however he plays it through in his head, Nikos cannot settle on a picture of what the future holds. All he knows with any certainty is that he can never leave Electra. Never divorce her. And with equal certainty, and a deep fatherly affection, he also knows that a few kilometres away, there is Dimi waiting for him. And he cannot wait to see his son.

Of course, Cossie isn't the first time he's strayed. There have been others before her. And he thinks of them now as he and Electra fall silent, negotiating their way through the twists and turns out of Avrómelou, heading up to the pass. He knows that she likes him to pay attention on this stretch of road; that she won't mind the silence, thinking of it as caution, and he welcomes the space.

In his experience, married women were always the least complicated, less likely to cause a scene. Usually they'd be in their mid- or late thirties. Bored with their husbands, or feeling unwanted; taken for granted after the first flush of marriage, their lives all too rapidly revolving around children, home, and shopping. Easy prey. Just a bit of fun, afternoon delight; his various partners usually as keen as he to keep it discreet. The excitement was all. The thrill of it. The secrecy. And desire, of course; that tantalising, lustful hunger. Another man's wife. Taking what wasn't his to take. The pirate in him.

And when the time came to move on, he always liked to keep it friendly, which worked with a married woman. As though they had done nothing more than share a coffee, a glass of wine. Guilt, fondness, call it what you will. A phone call now and then, just to say hi, just to make the point that their time together had meant something; that he wasn't just a heartless shit. Remembering a birthday, a simple text message. And sometimes the occasional replay, if, or when, the opportunity presented itself. No arguments. No harsh words. No expectation, or recrimination.

Just one never-to-be-breached proviso; never the wife of a client.

It wasn't quite so straightforward with single girls, however. If they had a boyfriend, they were usually off-pitch. Investing all they had in the possibility of a relationship going somewhere; a future they weren't prepared to jeopardise with a careless fling. Those that remained were on the look-out. For some of these, married men were an immediate no-no. They'd heard the stories, more downside than up, and behaved accordingly. But there were still the others; the ones who didn't listen, didn't care. Who didn't seem to mind the gold band on his finger; who made their wanting plain. A fuck was a fuck. Better than sleeping alone. And he had simply obliged. Leaving them to make the play, which made it easier for him when the time came to move on. Once, or maybe twice. A week, maximum. Three times or more, and the ice started creaking underfoot.

When the original fuck was not enough.

Fucking's the easy part…

And like an expert tracker, Nikos recognised the signs, knew when to make the break without risking too much fuss.

What constantly astonished him was how easily and convincingly he could lie. To the women he slept with, of course. But more importantly, to Electra.

As they spin down from Akronitsá, Nikos wonders if she ever knew, or ever suspected anything? Certainly, she'd never confronted him, never given any sign of displeasure. No cooling. No sense of distance between them. None of the usual signs one might associate with a wife's suspicion of a husband's adultery. Which seemed to suggest that if she had known about his indiscretions, then she had no problem with them, tolerated them because she knew they were not important. Like so many wives. Just so long as he played by the rules. But somehow Nikos is not convinced. He really does believe he's had a clear run. That she's never found out. Doesn't suspect a thing.

But what happens now, thinks Nikos, as he pulls through Douka's gateway and beeps the *Star Wars* theme to alert Dimi of their arrival?

What happens now…?

With the woman he's left back in Athens.

With Cossie.

60

LIKE EVERY weekend at Douka, it is Dimi who provides Nikos with all he needs to recharge his batteries, and, consequently, to limit his time with Electra. Since she spends the week with the boy, she's usually only too happy to let Nikos take over while she works on her book. It is no sacrifice, for either of them. Better still, Dimi clearly loves Douka, just as Nikos did when he was growing up; utterly content and entranced by it. And most weekends the two of them spend hours together; pottering around the estate, playing in the pool, or driving down to Anémenos to fish from the quay.

But for once the weekend in Douka fails to provide Nikos with the escape he needs. By the time he slides his key into the front door of their house on Diomexédes, he is exhausted.

Glad to be away from it all.

Sympathy, he decides, has a shelf-life.

"You look like you had fun," says Cossie when they meet up at her flat the following evening.

"I've had better times," says Nikos. He flings himself down on the sofa, accepts the drink she's prepared, and runs her through the weekend. Electra getting far too thin, the jellyfish incident, and Sunday afternoon's nightmare, in both senses, with Electra nearly screaming the house down out on the terrace.

"She was white as a sheet, shaking. Scared the living daylights out of me, and Dimi."

"It'll take time," says Cossie, joining him on the sofa, a glass in one hand, the other sliding into his jacket. She reaches up and kisses him. "You'll have to be patient with her. You have no choice."

Once again, Nikos marvels at Cossie's understanding. At no time has she ever had a bad word to say about Electra, even though she's had ample opportunity – either listening to his stories, or having been at Douka for the shoot. Which, Nikos knows, wouldn't have been easy for Cossie, with Electra hovering around, the way she does.

"Were you stung badly?" Cossie asks, as though to change the subject. She puts down her glass and reaches up to undo his shirt buttons. "Why don't you show me?"

In the months that they have been together, Nikos has fallen into the habit of testing out his tastes and opinions on Cossie – whether it's politics (which always bore Electra), or films, or books, or music. Or taking her to places he associates with Electra. He knows why he does this. He likes to see how different the response is. On one occasion, when he'd shown Electra his favourite piece of sculpture at the National Archaeological Museum – a life-sized bronze torso of an ancient warrior wearing an open leather jerkin – she had squeezed his arm and whispered, suggestively, "I wish we could see the rest of him."

When he showed the same piece to Cossie, she'd looked at it with a kind of wonder. "It's so beautiful," was all she said, in a soft, astonished voice. "So vibrant, so alive." And he knew that she wanted to reach out a hand and touch it, to feel the smooth polished metal beneath her fingers. Just how he'd responded when he first saw it. But not reach for what wasn't there, as Electra had done with such flagrant suggestion.

Restaurants and bars are another favourite testing ground. O Krittikos, Vrasidia, Acteon. None more so than Thanos, on a stone jetty near Vouliagmeni, where he'd taken Electra years ago to celebrate a new commission. For whatever reason, she'd taken against the place, employing her iciest city hauteur and refusing to be impressed by either the seashore setting or the food. Both of which Nikos loved. Which had disappointed him, taken the shine off the evening and dulled the celebration. Making him feel like an islander again; a trick, he suspected, that Electra liked to use to discomfort him, when she felt he was getting above himself. It was a trait of hers that he detested, and it could put him in a bad mood for days. Or until she relented; said or did something to appease him.

Cossie, on the other hand, had delighted in Thanos, declaring it her favourite ever restaurant, wondering how she had never heard of it before; its discovery a delectable treat, its secrecy an even greater thrill. The week following the jellyfish incident at Douka, Nikos takes her there for a second visit, the pair of them shown to the table at the very end of the jetty where he'd sat that time with Electra, before they were married; pink-clothed, red candle-lit, a restless sea slapping and sucking the stones beneath them.

Two hours later, he is helping Cossie into her coat when his mobile buzzes. It is Electra, the first time she has called when he's with Cossie, and he feels a strange excitement; his wife and his mistress overlapping.

He looks at Cossie and smiles sadly, mouths *Electra*, enjoying the honesty; a complicit, binding kind of honesty. Pushing open the restaurant door for her, following her out onto the pavement.

The conversation is brief, a *just-called-to say-hi* kind of call. But there is a tone to the voice that grates. Without actually saying it, he can tell that Electra wants to know what he is doing, where he is, who he's with. A checking-up call. Quietly resentful. Not liking it that she's not with him; the Athenian stuck on the island, while the islander enjoys the city. And, no surprise, she's been drinking. He can hear it in her laboured drawl.

"I'm sorry," says Nikos when the call ends; slipping the mobile into his pocket, buzzing open the locks on his car.

"It's not a problem," Cossie reassures him. "Is everything okay? Dimi?"

Nikos is tugging on his seat-belt, but he pauses. The manner in which Cossie says his son's name, the name itself on her lips, and the genuine look of concern that accompanies it, is comforting in a way he can't quite explain. Without a thought, he reaches across, draws her to him and kisses her. A long, lingering kiss; the only way he can think of to properly express his gratitude, stroking her cheek as they part, eyes locked on hers.

Which is maybe why he doesn't pay any undue attention to a car coming towards them, slowing down; its headlights splashing them in passing light, then speeding off.

61

ON PELATEA that Saturday, Nikos knocks on his father's door at the Navros hospice and enters. The shutters are closed and the angled slats spill thin strips of sunlight across the red-tiled floor. It is warm in the room, the air still and muggy, smelling of rumpled bed linen and old man. It's two weeks since Nikos last called at the hospice, and he's sad, if not altogether surprised, to find his father with the same wide-eyed blankness.

Nikos sees a bowl of figs on the bedside table; a bruised, punctured purple, fat and dusty. He knows they're from Douka, brought in by Electra earlier that week. At first Nikos had felt guilty, the way she visited so much more often than he did. But now, with the stroke, he doesn't feel so bad about it. The old man probably can't tell one of them from the other, or what they're doing at his bedside; or even, who the hell are these people?

But he goes through the drill, the dutiful son, pulling up a chair beside his father's; chatting away, a little louder than he might normally; telling Theo about his life in the city – the deals, the people – and his life at Douka: the olive groves, the vineyard, his adventures with Dimi.

And all the while Theo stares blankly at the hands in his lap, or at Nikos, or, fearfully it seems, at a point over his son's shoulder.

Twenty minutes later Nikos bids his father farewell, with a kiss on his smooth scarred cheek and a pat on the shoulder, promising to come back soon. He has turned for the door and is reaching for the handle when he hears a voice.

"Kill her. You can kill her."

He spins round, but his father hasn't moved. The same blank-eyed look, directed now at the cast-iron radiator below the window.

It's a long time since he's heard his father speak, just the occasional slurred ramblings. But as he crosses the parking lot he can't be sure that the voice he'd just heard belonged to his father. Something in the tone – its briskness – and the precision of the words were so at odds with the old man's blank stare. As for the message, there's no way really to explain what the words – or what his father – meant. Were they directed at him? They had to be; there was no one else in the room. He pulls out of the parking lot with a frown on his face, and heads down through Navros to the quay. In twenty minutes the ferry from Tsania will arrive, bringing with it two friends from Athens and their ten-year-old daughter.

Ilias and Ana Doukakis have known Electra a great deal longer than Nikos. All three are Athenians, born to wealthy families; Ilias an eldest son, Ana and Electra both younger sisters. The two girls had been privately educated at

Moraitis in Psychiko, studied history together at Kapodistrian in Zografou, and both had dropped out in their senior years. Electra because she was bored, Ana because she'd met Ilias, a thirty-year-old investment analyst with a Goldman Sachs subsidiary. Tapped for a transfer to the New York office the pin-striped executive had popped the question at the start of Ana's final year, and had left for his new posting six months later as a married man.

Nikos has never felt entirely comfortable with either Ilias or Ana. Ilias is a few years older, more than a few kilos heavier and has a well-fed, humourless manner; never happier than pontificating on the debt-crisis debate and the wrong-footed fiscal failings of government finance ministers like Yanis Varoufakis and Euclid Tsakalotos. At a dinner in Athens earlier that year, Nikos had overheard Ilias calling them 'yokels'. For a man employed by a company that had significantly mishandled their country's negotiations with the European Union, Nikos finds Ilias's pompous declarations on government finances and national belt-tightening nothing less than odious. Coming as they do from a man who, it was rumoured, channeled his various and substantial earnings through off-shore shell companies to avoid tax; a man who liked nothing more than spending large amounts of money on expensive Swiss watches and Savile Row suits, of which he seemed to have an inexhaustible supply; and buying top of the line motor cars, driving them a month or two, before casting them aside for a better model.

On this occasion, on their first visit to Pelatea, Ilias manoeuvres his latest purchase – a gleaming black Jaguar F-Type convertible – off the Tsania ferry with much impatient revving of the engine. When, finally, he makes the ramp and comes down onto the quay, a little faster than he should, the Jaguar's low clearance – abetted by his own considerable weight – brings forth a wincing shriek of metal against stone. Watching from the sidelines Nikos hides a smile, and has no doubt that this will be the Jaguar's last outing.

If Ilias is ponderously overweight his wife, Ana, is the exact opposite. Not quite as thin as Electra, and not quite as tall, she is well-maintained and well-upholstered – thanks to various surgical procedures, Nikos suspects – with a cap of bobbed black hair, piercing blue eyes that have to be lenses, and a sharp tongue that Electra always likes to describe, and excuse, as wit not rudeness. If there is any common ground with her husband, it is her frighteningly ostentatious way with money.

Judging by their uncomfortable smiles as Ilias brings the Jaguar up to him, Nikos suspects they feel the same affection for him as he does for them.

"Ilias, Ana. Welcome to Pelatea. How lovely to see you both. And Mina. What a treat."

"Won't it get dreadfully dusty?" asks Ilias, scuffing the leather sole of a Ferragamo loafer on the dyed concrete floors at Douka. He has been in the house approximately two hours and has yet to deliver anything approaching a compliment on Nikos's painstaking restoration of such a fine old house. As for Ana, she has remarked only on the spread of orchids that have recently been sent over by Zephyros in Kolonaki to replace the ones that Gert had desecrated. If anything this new display is even more extravagant, and Ana is ecstatic in her response. Not for the house, thinks Nikos, just the bloody orchids. The only good thing about his guests that weekend – just the one night, thankfully – is their tomboy daughter, Mina, a school-chum of Dimi's, who'd shot off with him the moment they arrived, as though intent on putting as much distance as she could between her and her parents.

That evening, after Dimi and Mina have excused themselves from the dinner table, Nikos, Electra, Ilias and Ana make themselves comfortable on the terrace and the conversation settles into its usual Doukakis pattern.

"The way property's going," Ilias is saying, "now's the time to buy. You wouldn't believe what's out there." He sounds, Nikos thinks, like a vulture passing on details of a particularly luscious corpse not too far distant that is begging to be picked clean.

"We're thinking of buying somewhere outside the city," Ana adds, an excited twinkle in her eye. "A small estate, a vineyard maybe; that sort of thing. The kind of place where we can get back to our roots, but somewhere we can reach in an hour or two from the city. Country, but close. As a matter of fact, we saw one just the other day," she continues, turning razor-blue eyes on Nikos. "Out past Vouliagmeni. The loveliest place… You know it, don't you, Nikos? Vouliagmeni?"

Nikos feels a chill. He doesn't know why, just that his skin skitters. His scalp prickles.

"The Philippiades," says Electra. "Niko's been doing a lot of work for them there."

"Yes," manages Nikos.

Ana still hasn't taken her eyes off him; cool and steady. As if she hasn't heard what Electra said. Something amused, yet malicious in her steely glacier gaze.

"Actually, we were looking for a place to eat," says Ilias; a long, low, fat drawl. "Didn't you tell us about something out there, Ella? Some restaurant…?"

"Thanos," says Electra. "Niko and I went there once. Years ago." And then she turns to Nikos. "Is that horrible little *maître d'* still there?"

"The one with the moustache? Yes, he is," says Nikos.

"I never really… liked it," Electra continues, thinking of her unknown caller. "But I know Niko drops by every now and again. Don't you, darling?"

"Myron Philippiades can't get enough of the place," Nikos replies. "We go quite often. I think he likes not being recognised. It's that sort of place. Discreet. Out of town."

Across the table, Ana smiles at him; raises a questioning eyebrow, and he shivers again.

Then, from nowhere, sharpening the shiver, Nikos remembers that slowing splay of headlights on the road outside Thanos.

And he knows.

With an icy chill.

He and Cossie have been seen.

62

IT IS A quiet Sunday evening. Nikos and Electra and Dimi have waved Ilias, Ana and Mina goodbye, and retreat to their various haunts: Electra, begging Nikos's indulgence and heading for the study; Dimi disappearing to play *Temple Run* or facetime Mina; and Nikos setting to in the kitchen to clear up after their extended Sunday lunch.

As he stacks the plates in the dishwasher all he can hear is a little voice in his head saying, '*She knows... She knows... She knows*', and, '*She saw you... She saw you... She saw you.*'

And they had been so careful, he and Cossie. Never any public displays of affection. Nothing untoward. Yet the one time he let his guard slip, in the front seat of his BMW, in the darkness, the occupants of a passing car had seen that kiss, his hand smoothing Cossie's cheek... Ana and Ilias. He is certain of it.

Nikos also remembers the way Ilias came in on the conversation, saying how they were looking for somewhere for dinner. Had he seen them, too? Or has Ana told him? Or maybe she'd pointed them out, saying *'Why, isn't that Ella's husband, Nikos?'* And the pair of them slowing as their headlights washed across the BMW, their eyes widening.

The real question is, has Ana told Electra?

Slotting cutlery into the basket, Nikos decides that it's unlikely. Ella might know that he still goes to Thanos, even called him just minutes after he and Cossie had left the restaurant – coincidence, surely – but that's as far as it goes. So probably it's just Ana stringing him along; teasing him, he thinks. Enjoying the moment. Knowing she has something on him.

The chilling Athenian superiority of it – so utterly galling.

But how, more importantly, will Ana play it? he wonders. What might she do with that knowledge? He can't, for a moment, see Ilias being interested enough to say anything – he's probably already forgotten. But Miss Chitter-Chatter Doukakis is a different matter entirely. She'll never let it go.

So if she hasn't told Electra, will she? That's the next question. *Will* she? At some point in the future. On the phone, at a party, at one of their girly lunches in Kolonaki when summer's over and Electra returns to the city. Will she deliberately mention it over their white-only omelettes and green salads, just for the hell of it? She's certainly up to it. Or, just as likely, will Ana say something without thinking? A slip of the tongue?

At least, he thinks, Ana doesn't know how serious it is, how much he cares for the woman they saw him kissing. It could be just a fling.

Nikos has finished in the kitchen and is back on the terrace, nursing a brandy soda, when he suddenly wonders what Electra would do if she did find out? He shakes his head. If it hadn't been Cossie, he'd probably get away with it; someone Electra didn't know, someone inconsequential. But Cossie? If she found out it was Cossie? The woman she'd welcomed and entertained in her own home… That would be it. Game over.

And then, from nowhere, Nikos hears again the words that he had heard the previous day in his father's room.

A soft whisper: '*Kill her. You can kill her.*'

Tipping back a mouthful of his brandy, he chuckles to himself.

"But which one, Papa? Which one would I kill? Ana, or Ella?"

63

NIKOS DOESN'T tell Cossie about Vouliagmeni. About Ilias and Ana seeing them in the car. Those headlights. He's thought it through and decided that nothing can be gained by telling her. It would only worry her, upset her. And he doesn't want that to happen. But for the first few days back in town, he keeps his distance. They might talk on the phone, text each other, and meet up at her apartment in Thiseio, but there is nothing in between. No bars, no restaurants. No outings of any sort in public.

The nightmare would be the pair of them actually bumping into Ana. In a bar, a restaurant, on the street. Where introductions would have to be made. It wouldn't happen, of course; the odds against it sky-high. But then, he realises, it has already happened. Outside Thanos.

And suddenly his line about Cossie doing a feature on Douka for *Arki-Tek*'s Summer issue seems very flimsy indeed.

By the end of the week, however, Nikos's sense of impending doom has calmed significantly.

He has worked out his strategy, if and when the unthinkable happens. Forewarned is forearmed, he has persuaded himself, and he can play it to his advantage.

As he sits at his drawing board in Pangrati he whispers the lines to himself, like a playwright crafting dialogue; the only real solution, as far as he can see, a simple but robust denial.

Quite ridiculous, he'll protest. Ana has made a mistake. You may have known her since your schooldays, Nikos can hear himself say, and believe what she tells you because you trust her beyond trust itself. But when she says that she saw me kissing a woman in my car outside Thanos, then she is most categorically wrong. Completely mistaken.

As if he would do such a thing? After all they've been through together.

And what on earth is Ana up to, he'll go on to say, making such ludicrous accusations in the first place? Without a single shred of evidence. Passing on these dreadful, hurtful things about him as though it's some kind of holy duty of friendship?

And his last words? The fact is she's wrong, my darling. Wrong. Plain and simple.

Because, when push comes to shove, there is no evidence. None. Nothing at all. Certainly nothing strong enough to persuade Electra that Ana, or anyone else for that matter, is right. That he is having an affair.

So, if he can just manage to keep a low-profile with Cossie, or keep his wits about him if he is ever confronted on it by Electra, then everything will work out fine.

No need for anyone to be killed.

64

ELECTRA is always reporting things going wrong at Douka, various glitches. She seems to enjoy bringing these problems to Nikos's attention: the electrics, the plumbing, the floor tiles rising in their bedroom. Delivered in that bored, distanced, but loaded Athenian manner, *'Would you just believe it?'*

But Nikos is pleased with the rebuild. Nearly three months in, he has no serious concerns about the house. There might be some re-pointing to do on one of the studio walls, another coat of limewash on some of the salon beams where the resin is starting to show through, but that is it.

So it's with a certain sense of satisfaction that he starts locking up the following Saturday night, securing the doors and windows, turning off lights, before crossing the hall to the stairs. Where he suddenly stops, brought up short by something. Turns around, frowning. Nothing to see, but... But he can smell something. Getting stronger. Far more noticeable now. And instantly familiar.

Smoke.

He snaps alert, looks around. He can't see any, but he can certainly smell it. Unmistakeable. All around him. The kind of smoke smell you get when you throw water on hot blackened timber, its corrugated quilted surface hissing with anger and throwing up that bitter, acrid, cauterizing scent. That's what Nikos can smell now, standing there in the hallway, on his way to bed.

That strong. That insistent.

Switching the lights back on, he checks the kitchen, Electra's study – it wouldn't be the first time she'd left a carelessly stubbed cigarette burning in her ashtray – the library, the two salons, dining room, but finds no evidence of any fire. Much to his relief. Except the smell is still there, unaccountable.

Puzzled, he returns to the hallway where he first smelled it; smooths his hand over the bare plaster, a patch of it near the foxed mirror with the gilt frame and Dimi's bronze; almost warm to the touch, as though something burns beneath it. Impossible, of course. There are no hot water pipes there, no possibility of overheating cables. And then, hand on the wall, he realises what's happened. Just another of those glitches, like all the others that Electra complains about. It's the resin. The resin sprayed on all the walls prior to plastering and painting. For whatever reason it's not doing its job.

He goes to bed, working out what he will need to do if the smell of smoke, of burning, persists. Because if he can smell it, so will Electra. The plaster will have to come off, of course; the bared stonework sprayed again, with a stronger solution this time; and then the walls replastered. Since the smell seems limited to the hallway, he hopes that any work will be localised and minimal.

When he wakes up the next morning, he wakes to the smell of freshly baked bread.

At the bottom of the stairs he goes to the wall by the mirror, places his hand on the plaster. Cool to the touch.

Puts his nose to it and sniffs deeply. Nothing. No smell.

No smell beyond the baking bread.

65

DESPITE the close call with Ana, and the threat she still poses, Nikos has no intention whatsoever of ending his affair with Cossie. There is so much more to come, and he is determined that nothing will stop him enjoying their time together. A little more cautious perhaps, but otherwise it's business as usual.

Because, truth be told, he knows he couldn't bear to lose her.

To be without Cossie would be... well, he can't quite explain how deeply attached he has become to this wild and spirited girl who fills his life with such vibrancy, such excitement... And hope. And how surprised he is that such a thing should have happened.

What he knows he hasn't yet confronted is what, exactly, he is going to do about it.

For now, though, it is enough just to wait and see where the affair takes them.

And enjoy it.

Their precious time together.

Since Electra and Dimi took up residence at Douka, Nikos hasn't missed a single weekend. He leaves Athens on a Friday, as soon after lunch as he can manage if Cossie isn't around for a final tryst, drives down to Tsania and takes the ferry to Pelatea. And on Sunday evening or Monday morning – on the ferry, or with Manolis, or taking the Riva – he returns to the mainland.

But this week, nearly three months after they made the move to Douka, he decides to change the timetable.

"I'm so sorry, my darling," he tells Electra, calling from the office on Thursday evening. "I don't think I can make this weekend. I have to go to Corinth. And with Vassi and Iphy on holiday for another week, I'm going to have to follow it up."

"Of course, you must. And don't worry about us. That lovely Swiss couple we met at Trisobbio just turned up on Wednesday, completely out of the blue. You remember, Joe and Bea, and that hotel near Milan? Well, they've got their son with them and they've rented a villa on Pelatea, the old Miannargas house..."

"Miannyiargos," he says with a chuckle, softly correcting her Athenian pronunciation.

"Anyway," continues Electra, lapsing into an island drawl, just to shame him. "I've invited them over for dinner on Saturday, to stay over, then spend Sunday with them at their thingummy villa. Dimi is beside himself. You'll be missed, of course, my darling, but you are not to worry about us. We'll be fine."

And so it is that Cossie sits up in bed that Friday morning, and gives Nikos a look of puzzled enquiry. It's still early. Cossie's alarm has yet to go off but he had woken her an hour earlier, deciding to start the weekend as he intends it to continue.

"We're doing what? But Douka?"

He looks at her with a smile, at the tousled unruly hair framing a frowning face, roughly swollen lips left just slightly apart, elbow planted on her pillow. The point of her shoulder reaches into her hair, and the sheet slides off a taut, tanned breast.

"I'm taking you to an island," he says, running the backs of his fingers across the bared nipple. "The Peloponnese."

She looks at the knuckles, and raises an eyebrow. Cossie's *And-what-d'you- think-you're-doing?* look.

"For your information," she tells him, in a bored voice, "the Peloponnese is a peninsula not an island."

"If the definition of an island is land surrounded by water then, thanks to the Corinth Canal, the Peloponnese is officially an island. And that's where we are going."

"I might be busy."

"Then I'll just have to take someone else."

"You take someone else," she says, less bored now, reaching quickly under the sheet, "and believe me, you'll be travelling without these."

Two hours later, after Cossie has called in sick, Nikos stows her overnight bag in the BMW, and they are on their way.

"You haven't even told me where we're going?" says Cossie, as Nikos threads a path through Kallithea and Moschato, looking to pick up the motorway beyond Piraeus. "I mean, where in the Peloponnese? It's a big place."

"A place called Moniakos, in the hills above Sofiko. There is something I want you to see."

"I've seen it already, haven't I? Just a couple of hours ago, if I recall?"

Nikos frowns… And then… Sometimes she is so… off the wall… that he just has to laugh. Can't stop himself, and starts giggling.

"What? What?" she grins, knowing.

"You just… I mean, it's a *place*… I'm going to show you somewhere… No, no, no," Nikos holds up a warning hand. "No, don't say it. I know you want to, but don't… you hear? Not a word."

And so it goes, car windows opened too soon, a warm breeze still lightly scented from the refineries they've just passed; Nikos feeling a lightness he hasn't felt for… well, he can't remember how long, can't think; can't be bothered to think.

He has booked a room in a small hotel on the beach at Cato Mirastós. There's a line of sunbeds and tilting, striped parasols on the pebble beach in front of it; a hotch-potch of limewashed cottages two hundred metres away facing a single stone jetty; and just three of four fishing *caïques* drawn up on the shore, leaning over on their planked sides as if exhausted by their efforts.

Just as Nikos had hoped, Cato Mirastós is exactly how he remembers it, and as they are shown to their room he feels pleased he's got it so right. Just the perfect place. A belle-époque mansion with polished mahogany floors, painted wood ceilings, and bevelled panelling. There are just three balconied suites, all on the first floor: one above the front door, looking straight out over the bay; the other two on the sides of the building. The one on the right has a view of the beach and village, and the one on the left faces a wooded hillside and distant headland. Nikos and Cossie have the headland view. Not a roof, not a road, not a patch of cultivated land to be seen through their opened terrace doors; just a rising line of pine and oak and distant blue sky. If that wasn't enough, their suite has a muslin-draped four-poster bed which they put to immediate use, and a giant cast-iron bath with all the trimmings where they adjourn afterwards.

That evening, they leave the hotel and walk along the beach until they reach the settlement's single taverna. The clipped tablecloths are a worn and faded plastic, the chairs painted blue and rush-seated, and the day's menu chalked on a board beneath a lopsided neon tube. They sit at one of four tables outside, theirs set against the wall, and Nikos asks the proprietor's wife to bring them whatever they have. "But for two only," Nikos calls out, making the old girl laugh. "And some wine, please; a white?"

For Nikos this is a first. The first time he's spent any real time with Cossie. The first time he hasn't had to keep an eye out for any familiar faces. The first weekend he hasn't been with Electra and Dimi; at Douka, or on Diomexédes.

And, he is certain, the very first time he has been in love.

In love. He has no doubt about it.

There's Electra and Douka, of course… but then there's Cossie and Cato Mirastós, or wherever else they choose to be. But this first weekend with the woman he loves, Nikos has no time for Pelatea beyond the two or three compulsory calls he makes to Electra and Dimi. Just keeping in touch, to make sure everything's fine. Hoping they're having fun with Joe and Bea, and so on. And yes, he's fine, too, and meeting the client tomorrow… And so it goes. And all the while, he can't wait to put down the phone and take Cossie in his arms.

Suddenly he has no time for Pelatea, because he has Cossie.

Everything else pales beside this wonderful woman. No room for anything else. To watch her dress (almost as wonderful as watching her undress), to watch her brush out her hair, to see her walk across a room, to see her smile, to hear her voice, her laugh…

And even when he's not with her, he still finds himself thinking of her at the most extraordinary moments: in a credit-line meeting with the bank, on the phone to his sub-contractors, talking to clients, visiting sites for renovation… her fingers lacing through his; how she likes to rest her head on his shoulder as they walk; the way she turns down her lips and sticks the bottom one out when she thinks he's being cruel or teasing her; her long curving eyelashes, her sinuous, searching tongue, the lobe of an ear; the most extraordinary lobe, that he likes to take in his mouth and suckle…

If love is a swaddling hug of warmth and contentment, a stunning and irresistible sexual adventure coupled with a deep satisfaction in being so close to someone – so compatible, so at one, so at ease – then that is what this is. That's what he feels. Love. And he… loves it. He wants to spend the rest of his life feeling like this; to be with this woman, to grow old with her.

And he knows, indeed he is certain, that what happened with Electra will not happen with Cossie.

He has been given a second chance.

And he must take it.

66

THE NEXT morning, Nikos and Cossie laze in bed until late, take a light lunch on the hotel terrace, and spend the afternoon at the beach. There are just two other couples in residence: an English husband and wife, and two German walkers. Striped regimental tie, pearls, cardigan, and a *Daily Telegraph*. Thick socks, boots, and hiking sticks. With three different languages, nothing really goes any further than a nod and a smile when they pass each others' tables, or meet in the hall, or on the stairs. And since neither couple use the beach, Nikos and Cossie have it to themselves.

Cossie is wearing a one-piece swimsuit. Red and tight and silky; high on the hips, two thin straps. When she takes off her robe and sits astride his sunbed, pulls down her straps, draws up her hair and asks him to oil her back, Nikos is transfixed. Electra always wears a bikini. Once she'd looked great in these scanty two-piece outfits, filled them perfectly. But now is not that time. Her shrunken breasts, dimpled buttocks and skinny legs, so abundantly and carelessly revealed, do her no favours. But Cossie... Well, Cossie is a quite different creature. Everything does her a favour.

"So when are you showing me what we've come here to see?" she asks later, swimming up to him and lacing her arms round his neck.

"Tomorrow, early. Sunday is the best time."

"What should I wear?"

He is tempted so say what she is wearing right now, its top peeled down to her waist, her breasts shifting in the water, shimmering beneath the surface. "Comfortable shoes," he says instead, reaching down and drawing her legs around his waist.

"I thought I might come like this..." She leans in and kisses his neck, brushes her breasts against him.

Nikos smiles. They even think the same.

The comfortable shoes are the city trainers she arrived in.

"Will these do?"

"They look just right."

"Is it a long walk?"

"Twenty minutes. But worth it."

An hour later, Nikos pulls off the main road at Agios Vlassos and follows the signs for Kiourkati. Three or four kilometres further on he turns up a narrow, stony track and stops in the shade.

"My father brought me here when I was boy, maybe ten or eleven," he tells Cossie, swinging happily from his hand as they set off along the path, through a stand of sweetly scented pine. "We were staying in Epidavros, visiting the theatre there. One morning, he drove me out here; said he had something to show me."

They walk on, the path narrowing and steepening; Nikos ahead, Cossie following. Nikos glancing back to make sure she is okay, pausing to help her up over any rough patch of rock or slope. And then the path flattens and straightens and they step out onto a gently sloping meadow of parched brown grass that rings with crickets.

"It's just up there," Nikos says, pointing across the meadow to the next line of trees. "Not far now."

Five minutes later they step into a wooded glade in the centre of which stands an ancient basilica. Its weathered whitewashed walls and single dome are mottled with patches of pink and grey, the door thickly planked, with blackened spear-tip hinges.

"The Church of Christor Pantokritor," Nikos tells her. "Byzantine, maybe eleventh century, maybe even earlier. One of my favourite places in the world." He tries the handle, but the door is locked.

"It's so beautiful," whispers Cossie. "I don't care if we can't get in, this is enough for me."

Don't tell me we've come all this way, and we can't get in, is what Electra, who has never been here, would have said.

"Oh, we can get in, don't you worry," says Nikos, pushing aside a slab of stone close to the door to reveal a space below. He reaches down, and pulls out a key that looks as old as the church. "After you," he says, turning the lock, pushing open the door, and standing aside.

After the heat of the sun and their climb, it is spring-water cool in the church, and dark, though it lightens as their eyes get used to being out of the sun. The air is still and dusty, smells faintly of damp stone and candle-wax. The floor is flagged with shiny time-polished slabs of marble, the walls patched with faded frescoes, and the ribbed dome a distant echo-y hollow above their heads. Their whispered voices seem to float about the space as though other people are talking.

"Oh, Nikos, it's… it's just magical." Cossie walks around the walls, putting out a hand as though to touch the frescoes, but stopping short. The heads of saints, long-faced, fingers curled in benediction, robes draped, the gold of their haloes softened to darkened yellow discs.

"So simple, so pure," says Nikos, looking around. "A perfect square, a perfect circle, a perfect dome, a perfect hemisphere. And every line exact. The length of the floor from apse to door is the height of the dome; the circumference of the dome the same as this ring of stone at our feet; the apse exactly half the diameter of the dome. And all this, back when they had only the most basic instruments to provide such accuracy. I like to think they did it all by eye. Impossible, of course, but… And, do you see? No windows."

"So what are those?" asks Cossie in a whisper, pointing to the windows either side of them.

Nikos chuckles. "Alabaster, would you believe? Not glass, at all. The thinnest sheets of alabaster, thin enough to let in light, to know when it is night. And still here a thousand years later. Wars, earthquakes…"

There is a rusting metal-work candle stand. Nikos slips some coins into an equally rusty tin box and removes a candle, fits it into the holder and lights it. Then he slots in more coins and brings out a second candle, for Cossie; lights it from the first, fits it next to his own, and watches the two flames flicker and strengthen. Which is when he turns to see that Cossie is no longer in the church.

He finds her sitting on the steps, her head in her hands, weeping quietly.

He kneels beside her; wraps an arm round her, draws her to him.

"There, there," he says, stunned that the basilica could have had this effect on her. But thrilled by it, too. So not what he's used to.

But it is not the basilica.

Cossie snuffles, draws a handkerchief from her pocket, blows her nose; and he realises she is pale, as pale as the alabaster windows.

"Are you okay? Is there anything I can do?"

"It must have been the walk up here," says Cossie, fanning her face with her hand.

"And the tears?"

She takes a deep breath, pats the stone beside her, and he sits.

She looks at him, looks away; looks back at him, pushes her hair from her eyes. She shakes her head, sadly, as though she can't find the words. And then, clearing her throat, "So, well, what I'm about to say may cause you some distress. For which I'm sorry. In advance. I understand how difficult it will be for you."

Nikos freezes. He knows, somehow, what is coming. This visit to the basilica, to this special place, a special place for him, has brought Cossie to her senses. It is too much for her; he shouldn't have done it. Too much, too soon.

Now this wonderful girl he loves without bounds can see the future. And she has had enough. Their affair is over. It is time for them to move on with their lives. It's been fun, but…

He couldn't be more wrong.

Beside him, Cossie reaches for his hand and takes it in hers. "It's just…" she pauses, then takes another deep breath, holds it. "It's just… I'm going to have a baby."

Madness

(Τρέλα)

67

ALONE IN her bedroom one morning Electra sits at the Shaker dressing table with its oval bevelled mirror. Like the mirror in the hallway, there's a patch of lichen-like grey foxing in one corner, and the four sculpted clasps that hold it to its wood back are browned with time. Despite its age, or maybe because of it, it is a good mirror, a flattering mirror; something in the thickness of the glass, perhaps, or the depth of the silver base.

Fresh from the shower, hair slicked back and held in a blue velvet band, Electra turns her head to left and right, raises her chin, lowers it, keeps her eyes on the face that looks back at her. The same face, but different somehow. The high Stamatos cheekbones are as fine and as elevated as they have ever been, the chin as square and stubborn, and the lips… perhaps a little thinner. It was just… her eyes. No bags, no real wrinkles yet, only the thin web of laugh lines from a different time. But now there is a darkness to the eyes that hadn't been there before. Something behind that level steady gaze. Something lost and empty. She tries a smile. Her lips and cheeks carry it as they always did – the dimples in her cheeks, the tightening of the laugh lines – but the eyes do not. A honey brown iris, a dark black pupil. Steady, but lacking any corresponding sparkle. Cold, humourless eyes. Eyes that have seen too much.

But there's no time to give it more thought. In the mirror, she sees a figure pass behind her; her new friend is back.

Electra is getting used to having Petrou around.

In just a very short space of time.

There's something familiar and warm and comforting about his presence.

And he's hers. All hers.

At first it had just been shadows. Or a movement in the corner of her eye. Or sometimes unexplained sounds – like the creaking of footsteps on floorboards when there is only dyed concrete and oak tiles. Or sometimes a murmur, a whisper; always close, just beside or behind her; enough for her to turn and look. Always followed by what sounded suspiciously like a chuckle, or a clearing of the throat. As though someone was teasing her; about to pop out from behind something and surprise her.

And always, to accompany these sounds, these shadows and movements, the unmistakeable smell of a barber's shop; of shaving soap and lotion and hot towels.

Yet none of it made any sense.

It had to be the new dosage, Electra told herself. The single blue Tropsodol, and just the half Chlorsodyl that Doctor Paradoxis had recommended; to be taken with a new pill called Phaladrin that he said would wean her off the first two, and help with the shaking, the breathlessness, and any bouts of dizziness.

But it didn't take long to realise that what was happening to her had nothing to do with her medication.

This was something else entirely.

The first time Electra actually saw Petrou he was in her study, a few days after Dr Paradoxis came to visit. She was working on her book, looked up from her laptop, and there he was. Sitting in the reading chair by the bookshelves. A kindly looking old man. With thin grey hair, a long, mournful face, and deeply-scored creases running down his stubbled cheeks. His sudden appearance made her start. But he smiled, waved his hand as though to dismiss any qualm she might have. And for some unaccountable reason she immediately felt better, calmed. As though she knew who he was; had been expecting him; was not surprised to find him there. Instead of asking herself how anyone could have opened the door, come into her study, and crossed the room to sit in that chair without her noticing.

And then, the next moment she looked, he wasn't there anymore.

The reading chair empty.

It had made her shake her head, and giggle. Too much imagination, she decided. Or, maybe, too much to drink at lunchtime. Pills and alcohol did not go well together, as Doctor Paradoxis had warned her.

Which was what she had always rather liked about her medication.

Electra drank too much; she knew that.

Or rather, not too much; just enough.

And why not, for goodness sake?

It relaxed her; made her feel confident, happy.

And the ritual of it, too. The squeezing of fresh oranges for her lunchtime vodkas after Aja, Lina, and Ariadne had left for the day, a drop or two of Cassis to sweeten and darken the juice, and that comforting crackle and snap of the ice cubes as the vodka splashed over them; or the reluctant, squeaking pull of a cork from a bottle of Contalidis white, and that first icy glug into the glass, frosting its sides; or the last Cointreau, or two, on the rocks, after Dimi went to bed. With a joint, out on the terrace – the two went so well together.

And she knew it helped her writing; and that Chrysta would approve.

So long as Nikos never found out.

The second time she saw Petrou, a few days later, she was in the cellar. There was no wine in the kitchen fridge or cooler cabinet so she'd gone to the basement door under the hallway staircase; unlocked it, switched on the lights and negotiated the worn stone steps down into the brick-vaulted space below the house. The workrooms, storerooms, log store, and the vast wine cellar where generations of Contalidis had kept their wine; floored with gravel, lined with whitewashed bins and rusting racks. Row upon row, floor to ceiling; bottles dusty, dark and cobwebbed; no labels here, just a chalked vintage year on each section. And from these Electra took her wine; always bottles from the bottom of a rack, so the empty slots wouldn't be noticed. After three months at Douka, there were few bottles left at this lowest level.

She was working the first of her bottles from its metal nest when she noticed a strange citrus smell. She wasn't alone. There was someone there, in the cellar with her. The old man from her study. Watching her. Smiling. And pointing to a bottle in the middle of a rack of reds. She preferred the Contalidis whites, but she felt a strange compulsion to please him; to do as he wanted. So she came up beside him and slid the bottle out. And the one beside it, and the one beside that; one in each hand, cradling the other under her arm as she climbed the steps back to the hallway.

For a moment, locking the basement door, she wondered if he'd be alright, down there by himself? And then she'd shrugged. Of course he would; whoever he was.

Back then, in the early days, Electra didn't know he was Petrou. Just this old man in baggy trousers, crumpled jacket, and white shirt. Everything black and white, or grey – clothes and skin and hair alike. And he never said a word. Just a smile, a friendly nod of greeting, that reassuring '*don't-mind-me*' wave of the hand. In the reading chair in the study. In the basement. On the edge of her bed. At the kitchen table. Wherever he appeared. And he never stayed long. Just a minute or two, to start with. The time it took her to finish a sentence, or light a cigarette, or sip her coffee, or swallow her wine. And then she'd look up, blink, and he wasn't there anymore. As though he was trying to get her used to his sudden and unexpected appearances.

And as the days passed, she did get used to them, and him; even started looking forward to the next time he made an appearance. Intrigued by him; who he was, why he was there.

But at no time did he frighten, or unsettle her. There was no fear.

It all just seemed so… funny, so entertaining.

Her own little secret.

Something that belonged to her alone.

Usually after a drink or two.

Maybe a week after his first appearance, he finally spoke to her. He was in the reading chair again, in the study; legs crossed, hands clasped loosely in his lap.

"You seem so absorbed when you write. Do you enjoy your work?" A soft, friendly, interested voice.

And she'd answered his question as if this was a normal conversation – though she knew it couldn't be – and she told him that yes, it was absorbing; and yes, she did love it. Going back into the past, she explained; getting to know her subjects, imagining the lives they'd led in generations past: what they were thinking, what they saw; the sound of their voices, how they dressed, the way they moved. Making history live.

"Would you read me some?" he'd asked.

So she'd turned back to her laptop, scrolled back to the start of the chapter she was working on, and began to read. After just a few sentences, knowing the lines, she'd glanced up to see his reaction…

And he was gone.

Which, after a moment or two, had made her chuckle.

Some story she was writing, she thought; enough to send a ghost packing.

Chrysta would not be impressed.

Electra knows she probably shouldn't be, but more than anything she finds herself reassured by Petrou's presence. Finds herself looking forward to that perfumed barber-shop prelude that always heralds his arrival; an appearance.

And he is never less than charming. How well she is looking, when truth be told she's horribly hung over; how prettily she's arranged her hair, when she's done no such thing; and what beautiful hands she has, when she knows for certain she does not.

But she accepts the compliments, is warmed by them.

And by his unconditional attention.

Somehow it doesn't seem odd at all that she should be sitting here with a dead man, talking to a dead man. A ghost. A spirit. For that is what he is; there can be no question about it. Even she knows that – the pills and the booze go just so far. But maybe, she decides, just far enough to put her in the right frame of mind to accept and accommodate these visits. As though she's sending out a signal without realising it. It is a house of spirits after all, as her mother had said. If only her visitor was the Admiral, she sometimes thinks; now wouldn't that be something?

"I thought ghosts only came at night," she says to him, one afternoon, as he walks around the library, trailing a finger along the spines of the books.

"What would be the point of coming to visit when you're asleep?"

Which seems, to Electra, to make an odd kind of sense.

"But aren't ghosts supposed to be frightening?" she asks, remembering Cossie's story.

"Why?"

"I don't know. It's just they always are."

"Really? Are you frightened?"

"No, I don't think so."

"Well, there you are, then. You have learnt something."

He gives her a crooked sort of look that she can't quite fathom.
And fades away.

68

THE NEXT time her friend appears, Electra asks his name; astonished that she hasn't thought to do so before.

And when he tells her, the name means nothing.

But then, strangely unsurprised, she remembers.

"You lived here, didn't you? This was your house."

He nods, waves a hand; proprietorial, as though to indicate that it still is.

"Yes," he says, with a smile. A pleasant smile. Nice teeth, too. White and even. False, of course. Sometimes she hears them clatter when he speaks. For a ghost he seems strangely embarrassed at these sounds; covering his mouth with a hand as though stifling a cough, and working his jaw to reset the dentures. Yet oddly, for a ghost, he appears unable to do anything about it.

What does surprise her, now that she knows who he is, is how little Petrou fits the descriptions she has of him. Like the historian that she is, she wonders to herself how people could have got him so wrong? How their memories are so far-removed from the reality. There's history for you, she thinks.

Fat. That's what Lysander's mother had called him; '*like a puffer fish*,' she'd said.

But he is no such thing. A little bit of a tummy, perhaps, but nothing more. Lanky would be a more precise description.

And his eyes aren't anywhere near as black or forbidding as Alexandra had suggested.

In fact, he's rather a good-looking, elegant man, Electra decides. Not a man of wealth and standing, perhaps, but distinguished all the same; dignified, gentle. Not at all unpleasant. Nothing scrooge-like or evil or manipulative about him… And no sense of the dirty old goat she'd been given to understand. He doesn't seem like that at all.

Old, of course; but kindly, friendly even.

And as she gets to know him, oddly familiar.

"Have we met before?" she asks, swinging her legs in the swimming pool one afternoon. He is sitting behind her, on one of the loungers; legs crossed, shoulders hunched, hands clasped around a knee. "I mean, I didn't know you back when… when you lived here… But have we met before, like this?"

"You can't remember?"

She shakes her head. He seems familiar, but not so familiar that she can actually place him.

So he places himself for her.

"In the olive grove. Your hair was caught in a branch."

Electra gives the smallest gasp, swings round to look at him.

"That was you? But he was so much…" She was going to say younger, but stops herself. It would sound so rude.

But he'd known what she was going to say.

"Not me, my father. Karolos. Karo. He used to work here at Douka. A handy-man. This and that."

Electra frowns; the name is familiar, but she cannot place it. And then, suddenly, she feels a wave of heat rush past her throat and up into her cheeks, as she remembers that same young man coming to her bed… A dream maybe, but all the same. And then… Or maybe not a dream, given what's happening right now – with her, and this old man. Whatever, she blushes furiously.

"And you've met my grandfather, too," old Petrou continues; with a smile, as though he knows what she's thinking. "Doesn't look anything like me, but it doesn't always work like that."

"Your grandfather?"

"The old man at the sanctuary. At Epione. And here at the house. Aleckos. With his horrible dog. Pólu. Always barking." He pauses. "That's when I knew I could make myself known to you; that you wouldn't be frightened. The way you responded to them. How you treated them." And he gave her a look that made her blush again. "Of course, you weren't to know who they were, what they were, but still… The way they just appeared, and then disappeared? As if they had never been there? Maybe you should have guessed." Another gentle wave of the hand, a tip of the head, another kindly smile. "And all the time I was here, in the house; waiting for the right moment. Right from the beginning, from the day you moved in. But you never knew, never sensed me, did you? All those little things I did to announce my presence…"

And he launches into a list of the tiny mischiefs that had so puzzled or irritated her since they'd first arrived at Douka – lights left on, phone or keys or cigarettes mislaid, the tap in the kitchen, the Jeep acting up, the tiles in the bedroom, those glasses smashing on the terrace steps… even Franz's lenses and filters. One thing after another.

"That was *you*?" She wants to be angry, but finds herself smiling.

Old Petrou chuckles, waves his hand again, that easy dismissive gesture; and in an instant he is gone.

We're like old friends, she thinks, looking at the empty lounger.

How lovely it is.

Right now old Petrou is slumped back in her reading chair, where she first saw him. Elbows on the arms of the chair, knees apart, hands just hanging there in his lap.

"Your father was shot by the partisans, wasn't he?" she asks, pushing the laptop away from her. "The man in the olive grove. Karolos. Karo."

A man who was shot before she was born… Untangling her hair, being in her bed… What an extraordinary thought. Just history, really.

"Not by the partisans. By the Germans," Petrou replies. "The partisans shot traitors, the Germans shot heroes."

"Why? How did it happen?" she asks, knowing that if the man had been shot by the Germans the reason could only be reprisals. And she is right.

"There had been an allied supply drop near Messinos," Petrou tells her. "For the resistance fighters here on Pelatea. A German patrol happened to be in the area, just four of them, and there was a fight. The Germans were killed. So…" He shrugs.

"I'm so sorry."

"Five for one, that's how they did it. Twenty men, in a line. On the terrace, here at Douka. Five from Kalypti, seven from Anémenos, and the rest from Avrómelou and Akronitsá."

Electra wants to know more. But how much more is there to know? They were rounded up, and shot. That's all there is to it. Why should she bother this old man with her questions? It would surely be insensitive to pursue it, she decides. His father had been one of them, one of twenty who had died here. She cannot imagine how he must feel.

Which is when she remembers the dream, the nightmare; out there on the terrace.

Now she doesn't need to ask.

She knows.

The following lunchtime, she and Petrou are sitting together at the table in the kitchen herb garden when Aja and Lina leave for the day. The two girls wish her a good afternoon, but they don't see him, when she is sure that they must. Which startles her – how could they not?

And knowing what she's thinking, old Petrou smiles at her.

"There, you see. Just you and me."

And they don't even hear him, thinks Electra, when they're so close; just a few steps away.

Only Ariadne, coming out after the girls, seems to sense something. A shiver, a settling of the shoulders; her lips tightening, her eyes darting around. Uncertain, and clearly uncomfortable. And with just a nod to Electra, she leaves on her moped for Anémenos.

"Why can't everyone see you?" Electra asks. "Why just me?"

Her companion watches Ariadne ride away, then turns to Electra and smiles benevolently. "They see me who need to see me. Whoever I want to see me. Wherever I want; and when, and how."

"How? What do you mean, how?"

"What form I take. I can be old Petrou, I can be young Petrou. A man, a boy. Anything… to suit the circumstances. We don't just look the way we looked when we died, you know?" And Petrou chuckles. "Which is just as well; when I went over that balcony railing I was wearing shorts and a vest. Whatever would you think of me, if that's how I appeared?"

She thinks about this for a moment, pours the last of the wine into her empty glass, and then says, "Tell me. If you know all these people… your father, your grandfather… Who else do you know? There?"

"Like here, and now. You see or know whoever you want to see or know. As long as they want to see or know you."

"Do you know the Admiral?" she asks, almost holding her breath. How wonderful that would be if he did; if he could tell her things… Though there might be problems with attribution, of course…

"I would not see or know this man. He is a Contalidis."

"Is that so bad, being a Contalidis?"

Petrou shrugs. "About as bad as it can be."

"And why is that?"

"The Contalidis are not friends. They sacked my father. The man from the olive grove. They sacked him when I was just a boy. So we went to live with my grandfather in Kalypti. And then he was betrayed."

For the first time in any of their encounters, Electra feels an odd sense of unease.

"Betrayed?"

"After that supply drop near Messinos, someone gave his name to the Germans. Told them he was a resistance fighter. The reason he was shot. My father, and all his friends. Everyone from around here. Anyone who knew him."

"But who would do such a thing?"

And Petrou gives her a look, as though she should know.

"So why do I see you? Why are you here?" she asks, when he doesn't reply.

"To protect you, of course. And to help you."

"Help me? Protect me? How? From what?" asks Electra, and finishes her wine.

But there's no answer from old Petrou.

In the time it's taken to tip back her glass and swallow the rest of the wine, he's melted away.

69

IN THE HOUSE of the Contalidis, the widow Ariadne Papadavrou has never seen anything.

No shadow, no form. Nothing. Ever.

But if she hasn't seen anything, there have been moments when she's… felt something; odd sensations she can't quite explain: like the weight of a hand on her shoulder, or its steering pressure at the small of her back; or something like a hand sliding around her waist; and, once, sitting at the kitchen table, even coming up between her knees, of all things. Which, when it happened, had made her jump up from her chair, cheeks flushing. Or there'd be a sudden draft of cold air in the Douka hallway as though someone had swept past her, as cold as the draft from an opened fridge door; or she'd catch a whiff of that thick sweet-smelling pomade that old Petrou used to bring back from Athens.

And something just like it had happened that very day.

Something odd, and unsettling.

She was passing Madam, lunching on a bottle of wine in the Douka herb garden – probably not the first of the day – when all of a sudden she'd felt a chill. A race of the shivers, and in bright midday sunshine, too. And that wasn't all. As she'd started up her moped, pulled on her helmet, she'd had this really strong sensation of being watched; of having eyes on her. Eyes that followed her all the way up the Douka drive, until she'd turned onto the Anémenos road and ridden off.

And as she pushes her moped onto its stand outside her house, and unlocks her front door, she feels unsettled still.

That sudden chill; that feeling of eyes on her.

In all the years she has worked at the house – for dear Theo and for his poor wife, Kalliopi; for Petrou in his time, and for the American who came afterwards – Ariadne knows it is only since the Contalidis reclaimed Douka that she has felt these things. As though the old boy is refusing to let the house go.

To the Contalidis, of all people.

He would roll in his grave at that.

And maybe that's what the old devil is doing.

She remembers when Theo moved back into Douka, after Petrou's nephew was forced to sell; all the problems they'd had. Starting with the doors. Slamming shut, if ever they were left open. Upstairs, downstairs… all day long; the sound crashing through the house like a crack of thunder.

Enough to rattle a cup in its saucer. And despite her best efforts, dear Theo always left them open, always forgot to close them. Kitchen, bedroom, salon… wherever he went. It wasn't until Minos Karoussis put spring-loaded closers on every door that the slamming ceased.

But it hadn't stopped there. After the slamming doors, it was the electrics that played up: lightbulbs blowing with a pop; the kettle, the radio, the toaster turning on or off by themselves. Or the water pipes rattling and gurgling; spitting and coughing whenever the taps were turned. For three years, there was always something going wrong; something to upset poor Theo.

And after the fire, during the rebuild, the accidents. A falling block of stone that crushed a foot; an unsecured length of scaffolding that swung loose and broke a workman's hip. Other mishaps, too. All of them the kind of incident one might reasonably expect on a building site; that's what everyone said.

But Ariadne wasn't convinced. It was Petrou, the mischief-maker, playing his games. And in her opinion, the injured builders were fortunate. It could so easily have been far, far worse…

Away with you, old man, Ariadne whispers to herself as she puts the kettle to boil; crossing herself, touching her thumbnail to her lips; wondering, as she spoons coffee into a tin *vriki*, if dear Nikos has noticed anything? Or if she's the only one. Not everyone, she knows, is as sensitive to their surroundings as she is.

And Madam? What about her?

Ariadne snorts at the thought. Some chance. Blunt as a stone, that one.

No interest in anything except herself.

Or the next drink.

70

WHEN ELECTRA picks up Nikos from the ferry the following Friday afternoon, he has a present for her. From Zafroudi's, in Athens. He gives it to her on the way home to Douka, almost absentmindedly, sliding the package from an inside jacket pocket and handing it to her as he negotiates the turns up to Akronitsá. He keeps his eyes on the road as Electra pulls off the ribbon and wrapping, tips open the lid of a long leather box. A fountain pen. A Montblanc Heritage. She holds it up, turns it in her fingers. Doesn't he know she already has one, she thinks?

"It's beautiful. Thank you." She leans across and plants a kiss on his cheek.

"For signing all those books," he replies.

Despite the duplication she is touched that he has bought her this gift – such an appropriate and thoughtful one, too – and tries to remember the last time he gave her something that wasn't associated with a birthday, or Christmas, or an anniversary.

But the pleasure soon fades, and gives way to a rising sense of anxiety. By the time they reach Douka, she is wondering whether he has done it to ease his conscience; to make up for something she doesn't know about.

And she remembers what her mother once said to her. Beware of men bearing gifts.

She shakes her head. She is being ridiculous. Paranoid. Another symptom to add to all the others. And hadn't Dr Paradoxis mentioned it as a possible side effect? Really, Electra thinks, whatever next?

But try as she might to shift it, the feeling persists.

And Nikos, she can tell, is not himself. He seems oddly distracted that Friday evening. She decides it must have something to do with the job in Corinth the previous weekend, but she knows not to ask. When he's anxious about work, it's best to wait until he brings up the subject himself. She wonders if it's money again. A sudden shortfall, contractors calling for payments due. It always takes him time to ask; out of some kind of pride, she imagines. And fear, of course. Her father may have died, but the directors and trustees of Stamatos Stone are no less rigorous in their demands.

They have finished their supper, Dimi is in the salon watching TV, and she and Nikos are sitting out on the terrace. It is a warm evening, a lowering sun like a blurred gold coin casting long shadows across the lawns, but already the heat of mid-summer is past.

"So how was Corinth?" she asks, taking the bull by the horns; deciding she might as well as start the ball rolling.

"A goose chase," he says, shaking his head. "A waste of time. A plot of land just west of Lechaio. A lovely site, but the developers wanted retirement homes like all the others. They looked at my plans as though I'd dropped in from another planet."

"Sometimes that's how it is. It wouldn't be the first time." It isn't meant as a criticism but she can see that he has taken her words in a way that she hadn't intended. "What I mean is, developers don't always…"

But he waves it aside. "It's okay. Nothing to worry about. You win some, you lose some."

And though she feels better for having brought it up, she can still sense a distance between them. Because she's said the wrong thing, or in the wrong tone, she can't decide. So she lets it go, and tells him about her week. About Dimi and his sailing classes at Vanti with Lysander and Kostis, and the blisters on his hands; and about her book, of course, and the discovery she's made that the Admiral probably did have an affair with Mantó Mavroyénous – or at least, she thinks he did.

Which seems to hit Nikos sharply. He sits up, looks suddenly uncomfortable.

"No, no. That's not possible," he says.

"Well, it's not confirmed; just a suspicion," Electra explains. "According to her biographer, Mantó's family took against the Admiral, tried to limit their meetings. But why? What else could it be? I mean, all that time they spent with each other. At sea… fighting together…"

Later they move inside, take over the sofa and TV from Dimi who's sent to bed, stretch out side by side. But half way through a documentary on the Pyramids, Electra realises that Nikos has fallen asleep. She leaves him be for a few minutes, comforted by his gentle breathing, then nudges him awake, and tells him to go to bed, too. Which he does.

Nikos's distant mood persists, and for Electra the two days that follow are fraught with the possibility of misunderstanding and filled with uncomfortable silences. Not even Dimi can quite break through to his father. There's clearly something on his mind, but for now she holds back. Either his mood will lighten after the coming week in Athens, or she'll try and have it out with him – whatever it is – the following weekend.

When Nikos decides to take an earlier ferry that Sunday, Electra is disappointed, but also a little relieved.

"It was not a good day, then," says Petrou. It is a statement, not a question.

Electra has just put Dimi to bed, and she is sitting at her desk with a Cointreau on the rocks, her favourite nightcap; intending to read through the last chapter she's written, before starting the next the following morning. It's a habit she has; reading the last few pages before going to bed. So she's ready for the next instalment. She's learnt that a good night's sleep always helps the writing; puts everything she's read into focus; gives her the energy and confidence to continue. Even with the Heripsyn.

But tonight the reading does not come easy.

"He was just a little out of sorts," she replies, not surprised to see Petrou there. But surprised, in a strange, unsettling way, that he should know about Nikos; how difficult their weekend has been. Was Petrou here with them, listening in? Maybe he was; maybe he always is. Always here, at Douka. Just as he was when they first arrived.

"He wants something, my dear," says Petrou, and his voice sounds just like her father's; soft and knowing, loving but hard.

But it's not just the voice, she realises, with a sudden chill.

What Petrou has just said is exactly, word for word, what her father had said to her on the day he met Nikos for the first time. At her uncle's birthday party, at the yacht club in Mikrolimano.

"And what do you suppose that is?" she asks Petrou. Which, she realises, is exactly how she'd replied to her father all those years ago. Those very same words.

And to complete the exchange, old Petrou does what her father did. A shrug, a knowing smile. As though the answer should be obvious.

So odd. So strange. So… confusing.

She closes the laptop, lays her hands on it, and feels suddenly a desperate weakness and vulnerability; realises that she is deeply, deeply unhappy. Just how she'd felt at the clinic in Lagonisi.

Lost, adrift… helpless.

She wants to cry, but knows she mustn't.

She wants to get better, wants to finish her book, she really does.

Wants to carry on loving Nikos and Dimi. And for them to love her back.

Always, always.

Oh please, Lord, let it be so, she prays.

But right now, sitting here in her study with Petrou, she begins to fear that things might have gone too far.

Gone for good. And all her fault.

"I know how it hurts," says Petrou.

"He was just so different. So distant, so… difficult," she says, stifling a sob; breath catching. "Like I didn't know him."

"He is a Contalidis."

She looks at Petrou. His expression is hard to read, but he seems concerned for her.

"What should I do?" she asks. "Tell me what to do?"

"You don't know?"

"If I knew, I wouldn't ask," she replies, sharply, a little irritated now; this is not the moment for puzzles.

Petrou smiles, tips his head. "Kill him, of course."

Which gives Electra a start. Sobers her. Fills her with a kind of shocked surprise.

Kill him? What in heaven's name is the man talking about?

"…Before he kills you," Petrou continues, before she can ask.

And then he isn't there anymore.

71

MAYBE IT'S because her conversation with Petrou reminded Electra of her father that he seems so close at the moment. A palpable presence. As close as he'd been in that dream, sitting on the edge of her bed. And after Petrou has gone, she thinks of her *Papou* Mikis with a deep and yearning fondness.

"We never really know who we are." That's what he had told her once. On the terrace at Apostólikou, the two of them together, waiting for his birthday lunch guests to arrive. The day he died. And she remembers that conversation now, as clearly as if it had happened only a few moments before.

"Not so long ago," he'd continued, "I began to realise that I wasn't a very nice person. I'd catch myself saying not very nice things, things I didn't really mean. To people I loved. Your mother, your sister, my brother…"

"Me, too," Electra had said.

"Yes. You, too, princess. For which I'm truly sorry. All those spiteful, nasty things I said. Getting cross all the time. But what worries me now, is whether I've always been like that, always been… difficult. And it concerns me, you know, that I might have been. And not realised it."

"You weren't, *Papou*," she had told him, sitting beside him, taking his hand. His smooth, soft hand.

"Well, that's as may be," he'd replied, the wrinkles round his eyes creasing into dark lines. "And you're kind to say it, my darling girl. But I can't be sure of it, you see, because, for the life of me, I just can't… remember. Like I was another person back then. Another Mikis. Someone I don't recognise now. Someone I don't know. It's all so… confusing."

And her father had sighed, a deep and mournful sigh, and squeezed her hand. "You see, *agapi mou*, we change. All of us. As we grow older, we become someone else, and we can't altogether remember what we were like before, what our life was like. That's what getting old means. Like a snake, shedding skins. And with each shedding, becoming someone else, someone new; whether we like it or not. Another person. Good or bad. And the worst of it is, there's nothing we can do about it. Nothing. Except start to worry, and try to say sorry, if we did not behave kindly, did not behave in a… loving way. Before it's too late."

Electra remembers that day, as clearly as she remembers his words. An old man sitting in his wheelchair, gently demented, but with moments of near lucidity. Like this one. When he came closest to the surface. Not quite altogether there, but almost. Just hours before he died.

"For instance..." he'd continued. "When you're old, *agapi mou*, you sometimes lose your balance and stagger. And you don't do that when you're young. Unless you're drunk." Which had made him chuckle. "Of course, we all of us accept that this will happen. The body ages, changes. Muscles weaken, eyesight and hearing fade... It's nature. It's the way life is. And we accommodate it. But so does the mind. Oh, yes. That changes, too. And sometimes it loses its balance, and staggers a bit... But that's not quite so easy to accept as the body beginning to falter. Or quite so easy to understand. Suddenly you can't quite recall what life was like before this... happened. Or even when it started happening." He'd squeezed her hand again, that smooth, beautiful hand. "It's like... like I see a photograph of me, as a young man, and I know it's me, but I know it's not me. Not now. Somehow... different." And he'd pursed his lips, and shaken his head, as though he couldn't quite make sense of it, or maybe explain it properly?

And that's exactly how Electra feels. That she's changing. Losing her balance. Not the woman she knew. And it's not just Electra in Athens, and Electra here on Pelatea. Two different lives. Two different people. It's deeper than that. She feels... somehow separate from everything; everything that should be familiar; suddenly out of place, and out of time. Unable to connect. It all made sense, yet nothing made sense. Which was how, at the end, her father had seen the world.

Is dementia hereditary, she wonders? Hasn't she read about it somewhere, that it's passed down from one generation to the next? In a newspaper or magazine, or had she seen it on TV? She wishes she could remember.

But surely, she argues to herself, she's too young to be losing her mind? Even if she'd had a go at it – back there at Lagonisi. The dread and the darkness; the sweats and shakes and chattering teeth. The end of everything. But she'd recovered, hadn't she? Come back from the edge; from that black, silent place she'd made for herself.

But that was different; what is happening to her now is not like that. This is more a sense of things going on that have nothing to do with her; that are not of her making. Or rather, things over which she has no control.

Like Petrou... Coming and going as he pleases.

There one minute, gone the next.

And it's not just Petrou. Or Nikos.

It's other, smaller things, too. Like her hearing, and her sense of smell; so much more highly tuned than she'd admitted to Paradoxis. And so much more powerful than she remembers. Enough to unsettle her. Around the house she's started to detect the soft groan of timbers and the sharp creak of heating glass; the settling of stone and the drying shrink of plaster. She can smell it, too. The wood, the stone, the plaster. Even glass, with a scent like cold, still water. And beneath those scents, always the sooty smell of smoke, and the sweet perfume that signifies another visit from Petrou. And in the silences, after he has gone, or when the girls have left and Dimi is playing in the garden or asleep in his bed, she sometimes fancies she can hear a soft whispering, like a draft sliding beneath a closed door. Not quite a whistle, but close.

And all these changes are making her anxious.

Was it ever like this before? This… acuteness.

Like her father, she can't quite recall.

And the worrying about it only makes it worse.

If not for the Heripsyn, Electra wouldn't have slept that Sunday night. But she does sleep, deeply. And she dreams. Of course. But when she wakes she can't remember anything. Because she wakes up with only one thing on her mind.

Why would she want to kill Nikos?

And why he would want to kill her?

As she showers she finds it hard to think of the night before in her study, with Petrou, as anything but a dream she can't quite recall.

But she knows, too, that his visit was not a dream.

Petrou was there in her study, and he did say those things. She heard him.

'Kill him… Before he kills you.'

And while she can't possibly think of any reason to entertain such foolhardy thoughts, she also knows that Petrou wouldn't have said those things without a very good reason.

Because Petrou is real.

Or rather… not quite real.

But certainly someone real enough, right now, to be a part of her life.

Someone she can trust.

Someone, she believes, who understands her.

Someone who wants the best for her.

When, increasingly, no one else seems to.

With Dimi spending the following day with Lysander and Kostis in Navros the day is hers, and from the moment she gets back to Douka she is certain that Petrou will make an appearance.

And explain himself.

But he doesn't.

So she writes. Line after line, paragraph after paragraph, page after page. The words coming from nowhere; pouring out of her.

The life of the Admiral. Standing on the rising, falling prow of his ship, sea spray splashing over his face, seeping into his beard. The briny scent of the ocean in his nostrils, the wind in his hair, his hand salty and sticky from the rope he holds.

Sailing to meet the enemy.

72

"ELLA, HI. It's Ana."

"Hi, Ana. How are you? How's Ilias, and Mina?"

It's a few days later, and Dimi and Electra have just finished lunch. One of Dimi's latest chores around the house is clearing the table, when the girls aren't there to do it for them. Rinsing the plates and bowls and cutlery, and stacking them in the dishwasher. A little discipline, Electra had said to Nikos when she'd introduced this initiative a few weeks before. It will do the boy good. Even if Nikos didn't seem convinced. So, when Electra reaches for her mobile and Dimi hears Ana's name, he scuttles away from the table before Electra can call him back.

"I'm just phoning to let you know that we've found somewhere," says Ana. She sounds breathless with excitement. "You know, how we were looking?"

"But that's wonderful. Where? What?"

"Tah! Just the most dreamy, magical place you can imagine. Up in the hills above Mandiraki. A little old farm that Ilias heard about. An hour's drive from Kolonaki, would you believe – door to door? The owner needed a sale, and we gave it to him. A steal, Ella, you wouldn't believe."

Electra can imagine the kind of steal that Ana is talking about, and she feels an odd mix of pleasure for her friend, but also a certain discomfort, disapproval. *Steal* really is the word, and now is not the time to be taking advantage when someone is down. Or maybe it is. Typical Ilias, she thinks. And her old friend Ana, just along for the ride.

"And the views," Ana rattles on, excitedly. "You get the sunrise over Nea Makri, and if you hike a few hundred metres up from the farm, there's this kind of saddleback ridge where you can watch the sun go down over Athens. You won't believe it… Just spectacular."

Electra can't quite picture Ana hiking anywhere, but she doesn't say anything. She must try to feel pleased for her friend.

"So, when do you move in?"

"When the house is built."

"I thought you said it was a farm?"

"Well, that's what the realtor called it; and the owner, of course! But you wouldn't want to spend the night in it. I mean… it's barely habitable. How someone could live like that… Tah! So what Ilias and I were wondering…"

She wants something. Electra recognises the pause, the wheedling tone that follows it.

"…Well, we were thinking if, maybe, Nikos might like to visit and take a look? Tell us what he thinks? See if ConStav can come up with something? I mean, money no object kind of thing. But don't tell Nikos I told you that, or Ilias for that matter. He'd throw a fit. You know Ilias. But enough about us. How are you? Did you get my flowers from Dendro's? I thought they'd go so well with the cymbidiums you've got in that salon."

"They were gorgeous," Ella replies. "You shouldn't have. I mean, you only stayed a night. Not even twenty-four hours."

"Tah! It was so fun!" And then her voice changes, lowers. A note of concern. "But your darling Nikos seemed to me a little down. Is he okay? Everything fine?" The same wheedling tone, but different this time. A searching kind of wheedle. It's as if Ana had been with them that very weekend, when Nikos really had been out of sorts. As far as Electra can recall, he'd been much brighter when Ana and Ilias came to stay. The perfect host, as usual; even if he didn't think much of their guests. There was no love lost between Nikos and the Doukakis. Whenever Electra told him they'd be meeting up, he'd give her that *If-I-must* sigh of his; or roll his eyes.

"Well, I didn't say anything at the time, you understand…" Electra begins, knowing she's got to say something.

"Yes?" A hungry yes.

"But Nikos had just been to see his father at the hospice, before coming to pick you up at the ferry."

"Oh," says Ana. As if she'd been expecting something else, something a little more… significant, thinks Electra.

"He's not very well at all, poor old fellow. A series of small strokes, and then a really big one. He's not really there, at all. Just stares into space, or seems to see things, and looks terrified all the time. It's very sad… And Nikos, well it's hard on him, you know?"

"I'm so sorry to hear that, I really am," says Ana, sounding not so much sorry as disappointed. But then, as Electra knows, illness, disease, and death are not subjects close to her friend's heart. Not things Ana likes to think about, or talk about. Particularly other people's problems. "But do let him know about the house, won't you?" she continues, breezily now, with a brisk *let's-change-the-subject* tone to her voice. "It would be such fun, wouldn't it?"

"Why don't you or Ilias call him?" says Electra. "Make it a little more formal. Nikos would appreciate that." Or rather, don't leave it to me to mention it to him, or he'll think I'm interfering… Because, she thinks, this is exactly what he might need after the disappointment in Corinth.

"Well, why don't I do just that?" says Ana. "What fun. And I won't say a word about mentioning it to you. I promise."

Electra smiles; at least Ana understands the basics.

73

NIKOS IS driving across town to Thiseio for a quiet evening at home with Cossie when his mobile bleeps. When he sees who's calling, his mind goes off the road; and off his driving. Until a horn blares and a blur of colour flashes past, and he realises he's gone through a red light.

Ana, of all people.

He doesn't take the call.

But she calls again, not ten minutes later, as he's reversing into a parking spot off Iraklidon. Knowing he can't avoid it, he answers.

"Hey, Ana. How're things?" he says, trying to invest his voice with interest and liveliness; just as he usually does, but also to disguise his unease; his heart racing as much from the blare of passing horns as the memory of those sweeping headlights in Vouliagmeni.

"Good, good, thanks. And how's Corinth going?"

Was that some kind of reference, wonders Nikos, heart beating even faster. She can't possibly know anything about Cato Mirastós. Can she?

"Electra told me you were up there on some big development project."

"Not as big as we'd been led to believe, regrettably."

"Oh, I'm so sorry to hear that."

As though she really cares, thinks Nikos.

"Anyhow, to the point…" And Ana proceeds to tell him all about an old farmhouse she and Ilias have bought up near Mandiraki. "Electra said you wouldn't mind if I just called you up out of the blue, but Ilias and I would love you to take a look. If you have time, Nikos. What do you think?"

Such a horrible wheedling voice, is what Nikos thinks. But he feels, too, a reviving sense of relief.

"Sure, why not. Love to."

"Tomorrow morning? It's the only day Ilias can make. Please say yes."

Which he does. Having Ilias along will make all the difference. At least he won't be alone with her.

The following morning Ana arrives at his office in Pangrati forty minutes late. And there is no lumbering Ilias; she is on her own.

"Darling Ilias begs forgiveness, but something's come up and he has to go to Frankfurt, and then on to London. So it's just you and me. Shall I drive?"

Ana has come dressed for the country. A pair of blue jeans tucked into low-heeled suede ankle boots, a blue plaid shirt, and a zip-front leather jacket that shines with its newness. The start of her country wardrobe, Nikos decides.

Ana drives like she talks. All over the place. In a Porsche Cayenne that smells new; and definitely is new, Nikos confirms, with just 1,500 kilometres on the digital display. He wonders how long this one will last, its transmission purring as they float over potholes and climb out of the city. And all the while Ana chatters away: the demonstrations in Syntagma that keep them awake at night; the price of food, of domestic help; the refugees on Lesbos. "Why don't they stop coming, and stay where they are?" she asks, not really expecting an answer. "I mean, if they think it's any easier here they've got another think coming. I mean, we're suffering here, too, aren't we?"

He's only grateful that the conversation doesn't stray towards Vouliagmeni; Ana swearing she saw him, and wasn't there someone with him? And who could that have been?

The farm is at the end of a weed-strewn track, a low single-storey building terraced into the slope; four red-roofed sections that drop with the incline like a set of steps, the roof on the lowest building in line with the foundations of the upper block. On their drive up into the hills Ana had told him that the place was a mess; needed a complete overhaul – something new, something exciting, something that shouted out ConStav. She could see the features, she said. *Architectural Digest*, *Arki-Tek*, *Vogue Living*, *Elle Country*. "Don't you know someone at *Arki-Tek*?" was as close as she came to Vouliagmeni. But it hadn't worried him. Electra had told them all about the shoot when they came to stay. Ilias had loved the story about Gert and the orchids. "Fucking krauts! It's because of them we're in the state we are."

But if Ana had led Nikos to believe that the farm was a mess, he can't quite see it. The four buildings may be in poor repair, but the structure is sound and there's a gorgeous pastoral feel to the place; utterly peaceful, tranquil, save the excited summer buzz of insects which makes Ana tread carefully along the path to the house. It reminds Nikos of the basilica on the road to Kiourkati; ancient, empty, but alive, and he feels the same kind of visceral response.

Which is a pity, he realises. When it comes to the work ConStav does, city properties are one thing, but out in the country, like this, it's altogether different. In short there is nothing he could do here that an interior designer couldn't manage. And nothing he would want to do that might disturb or compromise such a magical setting. The ridge above them, the low slope below them, pine tops and distant farmland; and away to the north-east a fractured coastline and the misty shapes of distant islands.

As Ana shows him the property, from building to building, exclaiming at the bulging plaster walls and warped floorboards, the broken shutters and dangling wires where fixtures have been removed – brushing off imaginary dirt from her leather jacket – Nikos can feel the building's integrity, a timeless character that almost reaches out to touch him. Like Douka, there is history here: the long covered porches that front each section, each one wide enough for a dining table and a dozen chairs here, some loungers or a nest of cane-weave sofas there; its magnificent beams, blackened and split with age; its stone slab flooring worn to a shine; and its half-panelled walls scored with scratches and shadowy stains – of family pets, of children passing, generations of them. Yet all Ana and Ilias want to do, as far as he can establish, is tear the whole place down so they can enjoy the sunrise from a single multi-storey concrete box through floor-to-ceiling glass… As if they'd ever be up early enough to see the dawn.

But he goes along with her plans, her 'vision', because he knows he has to. He might hate what they want to do, but he's enough of a businessman to know that Vassi would have a fit if he found out that Nikos hadn't done as much as draw up some preliminary plans. They had overheads, Vassi would tell him, and the kind of money Ana and Ilias might be persuaded to part with would fill the gaps between the big projects, and get them some very useful press coverage. There was also the Doukakis address book to consider. And Nikos has to admit that the prospect of getting one over on these two self-satisfied money-grubbers does provide a certain satisfaction.

It is only on the way back to the city that Ana stops talking about herself, about Ilias, about the refugee crisis and how little money there is around – having agreed to a preposterously high estimate for initial plans and implementation from ConStav – to ask about Electra.

"I'm so worried about her, Nikos. She's so thin. And shaky. Those hands! She sits on them, did you see? And she hardly ate a thing the whole weekend. Is she seeing a doctor? Is she on medication? Is there anything I can do?"

To which Nikos supplies the relevant answers. The stillbirth has taken it out of her… The breakdown has been difficult… The recovery is slow, but progress is being made.

If only, he thinks.

"Sometimes it must be so hard for you," says Ana, glancing at him.

All the time, thinks Nikos. Especially now, with Cossie.

"And so lonely," she continues. "Having to be here in the city all week, and all by yourself. You must come to dinner, or stay if you want. And if you ever need someone to talk to, I'm here for you…" she says, and taking a hand off the steering wheel she reaches out to lay it on his knee. Where it remains, long enough for him to feel its weight and its warmth through his jeans; to know that it is more than just a comforting touch.

If someone else can have you, then so can I.

Is that what she's thinking, Nikos wonders?

Is that the price she'll make him pay for her silence?

When she drops him back at his office, Ana gives him a peck on the cheek and tells him to behave himself. As the Cayenne slides away into traffic,

Nikos tries to recall if there had been a twinkle, or a hardness, in her eye as she said it?

74

AFTER NIKOS leaves for the office one morning, Cossie can hold herself no longer. Runs for the bathroom, drops to her knees, and throws up into the lavatory bowl with such a head-spinning, throat-scalding force that she's left slack, panting, and acid-mouthed.

Oh God, she thinks. *Oh God, how much longer must I suffer like this*?

It is a month or more since Cossie discovered she was pregnant. Two weeks after another missed period, a week following her return from Douka, and just days after she'd learned about Gert, she had crouched right here for the first time; elbows on the toilet seat, cradling her head in her hands. And known that something had changed. And it didn't have anything to do with Gert hanging himself from a beam in his studio.

Her doctor confirmed it.

But I use a cap, Cossie had protested.

Her doctor had spread her hands. Sometimes these things happen, she'd said with a kindly smile. For whatever reason… whether we like it or not.

It took no more than a few minutes for Cossie to decide what she was going to do about it. Flagging down a cab rather than jostle her way through the subway or stand strap-hanging on a crowded bus, she knew as she closed the cab door and settled into its springless, stifling interior, that she was going to keep her baby.

His baby. Their baby.

She didn't quite know how or when or where she was going to break the news to Nikos, and she had absolutely no idea how he would react. Or what might happen to her and the baby if he cast them aside – which he might; he was married after all. But her mind was made up. She was going ahead with it, regardless. She was going to have this baby.

And whether he liked it, or not, it seemed only fair that he should have the same choice as her. His decision.

Whether I like it or not, she'd thought.

If only I didn't love him so much.

Later that day, back in her apartment, before Nikos came round, Cossie pulled down her jeans, peeled off her t-shirt and stood in front of the bathroom mirror. Turning to left and right, as though one profile might be different to the other; smoothing her hands over her belly, over her breasts. Could she see any change? Could she feel any change? She thought not, but she knew it wouldn't be long.

She hadn't meant to break the news on their weekend away at Cato Mirastós. As they drove out of the city and hit the coast road, she'd decided to forget it, to put it out of mind. She knew she'd have to tell him sooner or later. But not then, not that weekend, their first together, as they set off on Nikos's mystery tour. She would tell him the following week.

And then, of course, it had just happened.

A combination of things, she supposed. Wanting to be sick that first morning in the hotel, but for obvious reasons not wanting to do it in front of him. Waking before him, pulling on a gown and hurrying down the hotel corridor to the landing bathroom as quickly and as quietly as she could manage.

And then, on the hotel stairs, coming down for breakfast, that German woman on a walking holiday had stepped aside to let her pass, and smiled what looked like a knowing, complicit smile. It had startled Cossie, to think that somehow this woman might know; that maybe she was giving out signals she wasn't aware of.

Had her friends noticed? Her colleagues at *Arki-Tek*? Had Nikos?

But the straw that broke the camel's back, that decided everything, was the basilica. Their climb up through those pine woods, swishing across that grassy meadow hand in hand; and then that beautiful little church, standing alone in its circle of pines. Christor Pantokritor. Its coolness, its stone-smoothed age, its empty echoing silence; it was like being in a womb, she'd thought. And it was that single, unsought, unexpected thought that had made her hurry from the basilica while Nikos lit his candles, as though she was looking for somewhere to be sick.

And that's where he'd found her, on the basilica steps. Coming to sit beside her, clasping her to him. His kindness, and his gentleness… It was all too much. And she'd just blurted it all out. Stammering, crying, reaching for breath; not knowing what he would say, what would happen next.

Cossie was sure she held her breath after the word 'baby' came out of her mouth. She had no way of knowing, couldn't quite remember, but it was as if time – and everything else, including breathing – just came to a standstill. And would stay like that until Nikos said something.

She'd felt for him, of course. It must have been such a sudden, paralysing shock. She'd had time to think about it, to accept it, but for him there had been no such opportunity to prepare.

And he had been… brilliant.

That smile he gave her; that helpless teary grin – without him saying a single word – had made her love him more than she could imagine ever loving anyone.

And when he had finally spoken, the words he'd chosen had melted her heart. "*What shall we call him*?"

But for all the closeness, then, and the caring and the gentleness that has followed, the only thing Cossie doesn't like to share – even now – is her desperate rush for the bathroom. The sound of her sick splattering against the porcelain; the rasping, gouging sounds that accompany each shuddering discharge.

Now that he knows about the pregnancy, she shouldn't feel too bad about it, too embarrassed, she supposes; there will surely be worse to come. But she knows, too, it's as much for her, as it is for him. The way she would prefer it.

Which is why, every morning, she waits until Nikos has left the apartment before stumbling, hand to mouth, to the bathroom.

75

IT WAS a shock. No other word for it. Completely… unexpected. Out of the blue. For a moment or two, sitting on those steps outside the basilica of Christor Pantokritor, Nikos hadn't quite been able to take it in.

Had someone else made Cossie pregnant? Was there someone else in her life? Was she telling him something he hadn't realised? Another man?

Those were the first jumbled thoughts that came to him.

But then he realised that the child was his, theirs. There was no one else. How could there be? And in the time it took him to comprehend this new development, Nikos embraced it, without condition, whatever the consequences; thrilled with a new world of possibilities, a bright white light shining on a life that had become, with the exception of Dimi and Douka, a dark and dreary existence with a woman who, increasingly, he no longer recognised, and no longer wanted to spend his life with. A woman, he had come to realise, whom he didn't, had never, loved. And as he and Cossie made their way back to the car, across the grassy meadow and down through the pine woods, he'd felt himself bursting with such an unexpected delight that he wanted to shout out his happiness from the hilltops, to share his great good fortune with anyone who might care to listen. He simply couldn't ever remember being so happy.

But at no time during their affair, from their first encounter in the King George Hotel, had he ever actually thought about a baby. He'd assumed she was on the pill, or taking some other precaution, to prevent any possibility of conception. She was young, her own person, with a good career ahead of her, none of which, it had seemed to him, she'd want to jeopardise with an unwanted pregnancy. But now that it was happening he couldn't have been more elated. It seemed, somehow, to make their relationship more real, more important. To compound this, he thought of the redhead in marketing, and all the other women he'd slept with during his marriage to Electra. If any of them had become pregnant, it would have been a disaster.

But not Cossie.

Cossie was different.

Before Cossie came along, he might have thought that he and Electra would grow old together, dividing their time between Douka and Athens. Electra involved with her writing while he worked away with ConStav, discreetly playing the field when and if the opportunity arose. A shared life together, but each with their own separate lives. That was how it worked, Nikos knew;

how most of his married men friends behaved. Even the ones who loved their wives. And he had been happy and comfortable enough to accept that.

But the loss of their second child, and the horror that had followed, had slowly but surely blighted any confidence or hope he might have had in a future together. Not to mention the fact that they would never have children again.

Electra was like a dying fire, he decided. A dead fire. It wouldn't matter how much he fanned the embers, they would never come back to life. Not a flicker, not a spark, of what it once had been.

Just… cooling ashes.

Which was why Cossie meant so much to him.

And so, so much more now.

If it were possible, the pregnancy made him love her more than he could imagine loving anyone; abetted by an overpowering desire to protect and nurture both Cossie and her unborn child, and to plan for their new life together. Not even Electra's announcement of her pregnancy with Dimi all those years ago had had such a profound effect on him.

Out from the shadows, and into the light.

There was only one problem. A real problem. He might hide an affair, but it would be difficult to hide a child.

As final and deadly a consequence, for him, as an execution.

Divorce.

It wouldn't even be messy – not with an Athenian involved.

Knowing Electra, knowing the Stamatos family, it would be swift and surgically ruthless. And thanks to the beady business eye of Electra's father, and his abiding suspicion of islanders, Mikis Stamatos had made sure that his daughter was well-protected – even if, as a Stamatos, she didn't need to be.

Which meant that any divorce would come with a hefty, and ruinous, price tag. He'd lose Douka, have to move out of the house on Diomexédes (given to them – in Electra's name, of course – as her parents' gift to the newly-weds), and face the prospect that his future with ConStav was all but doomed. He had no doubt that Electra would happily pay off the company's diminishing, but still extant, bank loans, and end up as the main shareholder, bringing in some new protégé to continue his work. And he knew that she'd love every minute of it; had no doubt that this was the kind of hand she would play.

Whatever it took, he knew she would destroy him. She was a Stamatos, after all. It was in their blood; what they did. And he knew it better than most.

Or rather, he began to think, she might once have destroyed him.

Because things were different now; their circumstances had changed.

Electra had been through a devastating breakdown, had serious alcohol problems as a result of it, enjoyed a questionable relationship with prescription drugs, (recreational, too, he knew), and, judging by Dimi's account of week-day life at Douka, Electra was not the most caring or diligent of mothers. Too wrapped up in her work to spend much time with the boy; palming him off on Aja or Lina, or Lysander and Kostis, or any other friends she could think of. And when the two of them were together, spoiling him one minute, then snapping at him the next, until the poor lad didn't know where he was with her. Nikos had even seen her slap him once, hard and sharp, when she caught him scratching his jellyfish stings.

And that wasn't all.

"Did you know she talks to herself?" Dimi had told him.

"She does?"

"When she thinks there's no one around. But not quite talking to herself. Sometimes it's like she's having a conversation with someone."

"Like how?"

Dimi had frowned. "Like she asks questions. In her study, when she's supposed to be working. Sometimes in your bedroom, or out by the pool. It's weird."

"Maybe it's what writers do," Nikos had said, not quite certain he believed it. "Thinking out loud. Maybe she's talking to the Admiral. Looking for ideas. Or reading out passages from the manuscript to see how they sound. Or probably she's just on the phone."

Or not.

Thinking about it now, Nikos realises he can turn all this to his advantage.

A fit mother?

Perhaps, or perhaps not.

It is, at the very least, an argument he can make and, additionally, an angle he can cultivate, even encourage. Drive her just a little more mad. Have her sent back to Aetolikou. Take control of their assets – some kind of power of attorney – and only then seek a divorce.

Which might, in the circumstances, be a route worth considering.

But whatever he does, however he does it, Nikos knows he will have to act quickly.

Two-months-pregnant doesn't last forever.

76

NIKOS KNOWS he is not a quitter. Never has been, never will be. He's worked hard to get where he is; studied, grafted, and come through a winner. Top five in his class at Metsovio; a promising job with a well-established firm of city architects within weeks of his graduation; the wits and the will to survive; and just enough money to cut out a path for himself. Add to all that the Contalidis looks, charm, and smile, and he knows there's nothing he can't do if he sets his mind to it. Knows, too, that there are no limits to his drive and ambition.

If proof were needed, he has only to look to the past.

If you can kill a man and feel no remorse, walk away and brush your hands of it, then you can do anything.

Because that's what Nikos had done, one wind-whipped winter night, aged twenty-seven. When something seemingly insurmountable had stood in his way.

A planned event; simple, straightforward, uncomplicated. No room for error. Every possibility accounted for. The perfect design. What had made ConStav the company it was. Clean and lean.

It was just before midnight when Nikos slipped into the old family home. He could hear Petrou, somewhere upstairs, moving about, knocking into things; a slurred curse. Drunk again. Like all the other nights that Nikos had watched from the grounds. Almost to the minute. The perfect moment.

Climbing the stairs, silent as a cat on concrete; moving through familiar shadows, down the corridor to a light spilling from an open doorway. The old drunk's bedroom, with its stale stench of unwashed bedding, scattered clothes, and sweet pomade.

And there he was, Petrou, in baggy cream shorts and a grey armless vest, with his back to Nikos, tufts of black hair sprouting on stooped shoulders. Staggering into the bathroom, a bottle in his fist.

Which was when he saw Nikos in the bathroom mirror, coming up behind him; fast, no hesitation, catching the hand with the bottle, pushing against his back, knocking him off balance as they danced towards the window; the open shutters, the balcony railing… Just heaved over, arms and legs flailing; the bottle flung from his hand, smashing onto the terrace below. Like the body that followed it.

Had murder ever been so simple? thought Nikos. Leaving the house, melting into the trees, finding his car and driving away.

Three days watching. Eleven minutes in the house.

And it was done.

You're only a thief if you're caught, thinks Nikos now. And as he pictures what the future might hold for him and for Cossie and their unborn child, he wonders if he could do it again?

Wonders if he should do it again?

The woman he married; the mother of his child.

Such a terrible thing to do; inconceivable, surely?

Yet so many problems solved.

And a new life beckoning.

It was just Petrou all over again.

Or was it?

77

THEO CONTALIDIS spends most of his day in an armchair at his bedroom window. Or in a wheelchair in the hospice gardens. Or in a noisy day-room, where they sit him in front of a television. But he has no real sense of time passing. Just things happening. Day after day.

In the morning he wakes up, and each evening after supper he is settled into his bed, with a pill to make him sleep. What happens between these times is just a gentle, undemanding routine that is oddly familiar. Whatever they make him do – sitting him at his bedroom window, wheeling him around the garden, spooning food into his mouth, taking him to the toilet, bathing and washing and shaving him – he knows they have done it before; that he has done it before. And he feels safe and comfortable in that knowledge.

If he has no clear understanding of the present, however, old man Contalidis has an increasingly vivid sense of the past.

The far-off distant past.

A fine house to live in, a young wife he loves, and a child he adores. A child, he decides, who bears more than a passing resemblance to the middle-aged man who occasionally comes to the hospice to visit him. He has no idea who this man is, but he is familiar, because he looks so like that little boy.

Which comforts Theo.

And then there are the women.

Two of them.

The younger woman, thin as a sickle blade with a hard, thin face and bruised deep-set eyes, who brings him bags of fruit, and tells him stories of the house she lives in, and her son, and her husband. None of which he knows anything about; the stories told in a high, brittle voice that grates on his nerves. Like seashells breaking. And she's always stroking his hand, the burned one, as though she doesn't realise how sensitive the skin is. How it pains him. Or maybe she does?

But then there is the older woman.

And this one he feels he does know.

In her widow's weeds and thick stockings and heavy clumping shoes. A slick of greying hair drawn back from her face and tightly bound in a bun.

So familiar. Something to do with the house and the woman and the little boy he remembers from his past. She calls in more frequently than the other woman, and she stays a lot longer. Always in the afternoon, never the morning, wheeling him around the garden, or sitting with him in his room. Most of the time she is silent, as comfortable in his company as he is in hers. And when she does speak, she speaks quietly, softly, of the distant past he so enjoys hearing about. How Madam liked to wander round the garden with her trug, picking flowers, herbs, and vegetables; dressed in her favourite green apron and that wide-brimmed straw hat. How the little boy was such a scamp, and do you remember when he broke all those glass panes in the greenhouse?

And old man Contalidis can see it all. Rising out of the mists of time. Bright and sharp and alive. The straw hat with its tattered brim; that little rascal of a boy with his short trousers and tousled hair; the trug, the flowers, the orchards, the vineyard. Those wonderful, far-off days…

Where have they gone, he wonders?

And where is that place?

It is this old lady who sits with him now, in his room, knitting contentedly, the needles tapping out a rhythmic, comforting click and clack. Just that soft, lulling sound. No words; no need for them. They are thinking the same things, he knows. Both of them back in that distant world; both remembering the golden days of their shared past; and the secret that binds them.

And then she puts down the needles, rubs the aching knots from the joints in her fingers, and asks about his other visitor. Does he still come?

He knows whom she means, of course.

He's told her about it, he's sure. Just as he'll tell anyone who will listen.

Not so much visitor as presence; a deeply disturbing presence that frightens him.

Someone he knew, but someone he can't put a name to now.

Someone whispering in his ear, making his heart race and his skin chill and his scalp pucker.

And though he understands what his companion asks, he can't quite manage to give her an answer. Instead he turns and looks at her, red pouches beneath coal-black eyes; one cheek smooth and pink, the other lined and wrinkled and grey. He tries to nod, but he knows it hasn't worked. More of a shake, really.

Which makes the old lady frown.

He wants to say yes, but doesn't know how. Can't quite form the word.

But he does want her to know that he has had visits; lots of them.

Finally, he manages as much of a grimace as he can muster, and she reaches for his hand, his good hand, and smiles, and tells him not to worry. There is nothing the visitor can do to him. He is safe.

But he knows that she is wrong about being safe.

He is not safe. No one is safe.

Alone or not, he knows always to be on the look-out. At any moment, he will see that shadow, will hear the whispering, feel the hate, and sense the terrible threat.

Without warning he will have company. Unwelcome company.

The devil himself, come for revenge.

It seems the old lady has been there with him for just a few brief moments when she starts packing away her needles, and fetches her coat from the hook behind the door.

He understands that she intends to go, that their time together is over. However long it's been, he can't tell. But he's enjoyed her company. Silently sharing their past together, as they always do.

As usual, she takes his hand and kisses it; strokes the hair on his head, and tells him she'll be back soon.

But he knows she won't.

Very soon there'll be no need for visits.

78

COSSIE is sitting in bed, watching Nikos lean down to pull on his shoes, when his mobile starts to bleat. She watches him reach for it, swipe the screen and hold it to his ear. There's a resigned look on his face, so she knows it's Electra. But calling very early, Cossie thinks.

Which is when she sees the change in Nikos's expression. No longer resigned, but suddenly stunned. A softening, as though every muscle in his face has ceased to function; the skin paling. Everything drooping: cheeks sagging, lips turning down, eyelids lowering; like a balloon deflating.

Whatever it is, it's bad news. Has something happened to Dimi? Has Electra found out about them?

Cossie has no idea what Electra is saying, though she can make out the scratchy sound of her voice. All she hears is what Nikos says:

"Oh, God…"

"No. No, I'm glad you called…"

"When was it?"

"Yes, I understand."

"You were quite right."

"I'm leaving now."

And then he hangs up, lays the phone on the bed beside him.

He sighs.

"My father died last night. In his sleep. A heart attack, they say."

If she hadn't been pregnant, maybe Cossie wouldn't have missed Nikos as much as she does. But she does miss him. Desperately. No snatched lunches, no evening drinks or candle-lit dinners to look forward to, no warm loving man to share her bed. And for the first time since taking up with Nikos she realises how… empty, how… aimless her life is without him.

She still has her friends, of course, and her colleagues at *Arki-Tek*, and during the week, when she's not with Nikos, or at weekends when he's on Pelatea, she's relied on them to fill her time, doing what they've always done – gossipy drinks after work, Saturday shopping sprees, dinner parties, clubbing.

But since falling pregnant, and having to keep it to herself, she's become aware of a growing distance between them; and how the pattern and pace of her old life, and her priorities, have changed. It's different now. She no longer smokes, drinks only a very occasional glass of wine, and she tires easily. She's more contemplative, too; more introspective. She's also started to worry that, like the German woman in Cato Mirastós, one of her friends might read the signs, realise what has happened, and recognise the condition she is in. And though she would dearly love to share her news, to tell her friends, she knows she cannot. Not yet.

So, to a certain extent, Cossie keeps to herself while Nikos is on Pelatea for his father's funeral. It is only the second time they have been away from each other for quite so long, and the days drag by. All she has is the memory of him; a shifting sense of his presence. Sitting beside her on their tiny balcony in Thiseio, curling up with her on the sofa, taking her to bed. Where she misses him the most. And when she thinks of him like that, making love to her before they go to sleep or when they wake in the morning, or in the shower, soaping her breasts, pressing up hard behind her, she can't help herself wondering whether he is doing the same with Electra? She has never asked him about this, and never would. But it doesn't stop her thinking about it – when Nikos goes home for the weekend; where he is now, for the funeral; at night, when he and Electra go to bed…?

So many times she wants to call him and hear his voice, or leave a message, or text him. But, of course, she can't do that. Electra might pick up his mobile, or Dimi… The only time they speak or text is when he makes the call; when he judges it safe to do so. Just in case. A kind of unspoken understanding.

And, of course, he does call her. At odd times of day when he can do so without risk. Late at night, mostly. Outside. When she can hear the familiar buzz of those insects, or the croaking of frogs by the upper cistern, and sometimes the brief rattling of a breeze through palm fronds. His voice always guarded, a cupped-hand voice; sometimes as low as a whisper, so as not to be overheard. And while it is comforting to hear that voice, so close, in her ear, the sound of his breathing, it is never enough. Makes her miss him more. His touch, the warm muscly scent of him, the pressing weight of him. Because Cossie is keenly aware that her appetite for him, for making love and lusty sex – up against a side-street wall covered in torn posters, across the boot of his car, in the sea at Cato Mirastós, wherever the spirit moves them – has increased dramatically since her pregnancy. There is no question, being pregnant really has changed her; in ways she couldn't have imagined.

She has never ever been a girl to hang back, and she has had many lovers. But sex with Nikos is an altogether different item. And suddenly she can't seem to do without it, without him; wanting him to be there with her, thinking about him all through the day, and night. Snapshot images that make her ache with longing. The way he unbuttons his shirt, slowly, button by button, one after another, all the way down, before sliding it off his shoulders; or crossing his arms to peel off a t-shirt; or standing naked at the bathroom mirror, tilting his head when he shaves, grunting softly, contentedly, as the blade slides across his skin; the tanned lean line of his body, wide shoulders, narrow hips, tight little buttocks; and that whirlpool circling of silky black hair round his navel which she likes to trace with her fingertip… And she thinks, too, of course, of his cock. Holding it in her hands; so warm, so alive, so capricious. Licking it, kissing it, feeling it press against her cheek, or thigh, or stomach, or back; feeling its heat and its hardened length slide into her.

But just as often, she gets to wondering. Exactly what is going to happen? How will things play out?

Two or three months pregnant doesn't stay two-or-three-months pregnant forever. Time moves on. The days and the weeks pass…

Sooner rather than later, as the baby starts to show, everything will change.

Just as Cossie has never called Nikos when he's at Douka, or talked about Electra, nor has she ever asked about what he intends to do about the baby. She hasn't had to. He's told her, in no uncertain terms. Which fills her heart with love for him, and excitement, and the deepest, purest joy. That the man she loves more than anything else in the world loves her in equal measure. And wants to be with her, not Electra. To live with her, the two of them together, out in the open; to bring up their baby together, as a mother and father, and do all the things a family does. Which means, he tells her, that he will ask Electra for a divorce; that he and Cossie will move in together; her place to begin with, but something bigger when the time comes. When they need more space.

He's also been practical. And realistic, and honest. Not just how he wants them to live, but how they're going to manage it. The big one: money. She makes a reasonable living from her job at *Arki-Tek*, and her prospects are good. And given the magazine's *laisser-faire*, *crèche*-friendly attitude to members of staff bringing in their children, there's no reason why she should necessarily give the job up. She can surely do both? And though she knows that a lot of women simply stop thinking about work when they have a baby in their arms, she is determined that that woman won't be her. She may be a mother, and have a baby to love and care for, but she wants to be independent, too…

And Nikos is happy with that; has told her she can keep her job, or find another, or give it all up… whatever she wants.

Her choice; he is there to support her whatever decision she makes.

But for all his protestations, for all their idle day-dreaming and nest-building, Cossie knows there will be difficulties. Whether she continues to work or not, Nikos should be able to support her. ConStav, she knows very well, is becoming a big name in architectural design – the go-to company for clients who want something just a little different – and his salary is considerably higher than hers. Plus, he owns the company… Or a part of it.

But… when it comes to divorce there will have to be a settlement with Electra. She may be a Stamatos, and wealthy enough not to care, but Cossie knows there's no way she's going to let Nikos off lightly; especially when she finds out who his lover is. Which means that Douka and the house on Diomexédes will have to be sorted. Maybe Electra keeps Diomexédes, and he can hang on to Douka? Come to some arrangement over its worth; what he might have to pay her if he wants to keep it in the family? Which is what she, Cossie, would like more than anything. Some little place of their own in the city, and Douka. Such a grand and wonderful house. For Nikos, for herself, and for their child. The next Contalidis. And anyway, why would a recently divorced woman in her late thirties want to hang around on an island when her home town's calling? Because Electra will always be more Athenian than islander.

But then, why wouldn't she, thinks Cossie? When she can have both. Just to be spiteful. To make him suffer. And her, of course.

Nikos not such a juicy catch after all.

But for now, at least, the funeral will have put all that on hold.

It's unlikely, Cossie decides, that Nikos is going to ask for a divorce when he's burying his father.

Or maybe he might, she thinks? The end of an era? Might as well combine the two. Father and wife. Bury them both. Two birds…

Which makes Cossie shiver when she thinks about it.

All the various twists and turns to come. All the possibilities.

Exciting, of course. But frightening, too.

That vast, dark unknown.

And sometimes, when she drifts off to sleep or opens her eyes in the morning, alone in her bed – or rather the two of them, her and the baby – she can't help wondering what she can do, what she might be capable of doing, to secure their future together; their child's future? What she can… contribute. To let her man have the things he loves, the life he wants? Unencumbered.

All the things she wants, too.

Yes, she decides, pregnancy really does change a girl.

79

POLICE-CAPTAIN Kyriakos Mavrodakis, with a new third star on his shoulder boards, is not a happy man. A small, but familiar ache has started up in his left hip. He straightens his shoulders and, with a wince of discomfort, eases his weight onto the right leg. In just a minute or two he knows that the ache will start to fade, but not completely. Standing too long, he thinks. By a lamppost, on the corner of Platia Agios Stefanos. Watching his second-in-command, Police-Lieutenant Evangelos Tsavalas, his Police-Sergeant Thanasis Lambros, and three of his deputies patrol the barriers holding back the crowd of mourners who, in the last hour, have filled the square. A sea of shifting black. Most of the town, by the look of it; come to pay their respects to old man Contalidis. What concerns Mavrodakis is their increasing number, and the need to keep open the access road for the cortège.

Already an hour late. Those damn Contalidis. Keeping them all waiting.

At least the crowd is peaceful, thinks Mavrodakis. No shouting, no jostling; just the gentle swell and surge of bodies pressing closer. And only a low murmur from them, and their shuffling feet, to break the silence. So low he can actually hear the chatter of sparrows and the darting rush of swallows slicing through the air above him.

Thirty or more cars, so far, have drawn up at the church steps. The great and the good of Pelatea. Island officials like the mayor, Aliki Laskari, and his deputy, Demis Vonas; various members of the Chamber of Commerce, and the tourist board; staff from the hospital and hospice; the Contalidis family doctor, Fotis Paradoxis, with his scarved top hat and fat wife, Thea; and family friends like the Vistalis, the Lountzis, the Karvounis, the Christidis, the Paxinous, and those two old English queens from Pecravi who'd caused such a stir when they set up house together. All in black – suits, ties, hats, veils, gloves, shoes – save the white shirts of the men. Handshakes, hugs, kisses, mournful smiles. Most of them will be seated by now, and cool, too, out of the heat. Lucky them, thinks Mavrodakis, feeling the sweat trickle in the small of his back. No shade out here, and closing on midday. If the cortège doesn't arrive soon, he'll need to find somewhere to sit, to take the weight off his aching hip.

All this bloody standing around; waiting, waiting…

And all because of the bloody Contalidis.

God, how he hates them.

And then, with a puff of relief, he hears the distant clatter of hooves and the grating of steel-rimmed wheels on cobbles, rising in volume as the horse-drawn hearse turns into the narrows of Katriakis Street and approaches the square. Heads turn, the crowd parts, and four prancing purple-plumed black horses appear, drawing the glass-panelled carriage with its ebony casket. With much head swinging, bridle jangling, and impatient snorting, the horses pass through the police barrier and are reined in at the bottom of the church steps, with one of Dimitidis's chauffeur-driven limousines pulling up behind it.

While the pallbearers work the casket out on its runners, and shoulder it between them, Nikos, Electra and Dimi Contalidis step from the limousine. Nikos buttoning his jacket, tossing back his hair; Electra straightening her skirt, reaching for her son's hand. The three of them falling into line behind the pallbearers as they climb the steps to the church.

Which is when one of the wreaths, a ring of woven white lilies, slides off the coffin and bounces down the steps like a runaway wheel, slapping into the side of the waiting limousine and spinning to a stop. The chauffeur, old Mikaeliades, retrieves it and hurries up the steps to the pallbearers. It's not possible to put the wreath back on the casket, so Nikos Contalidis takes it from the chauffeur and hands it to his son to carry.

At the top of the steps Archimandrite Paulos blesses the coffin as it passes him, and an altar boy swings his thurible, its chains rattling, a thick smoke rising from the perforated lid of the censer. And after the coffin comes the family, greeted with further blessings. Nikos, then the wife, thin as a rake, and the little boy.

Down in the square, Mavrodakis waits till the church doors close before pulling off his cap and making his way through the crowds to Kafeneion Kristos. For a smoke and a beer and a chat with Manolis, Yannis, and Costas, but more than anything for the desperate relief of a barstool. He knows that his second-in-command, young Vango, will keep things organised in the square, that Lambros and the deputies are on hand to help, which gives him an hour before the service comes to an end; time enough to cool off and chase away the pain in his hip before heading back to the church steps to resume his duties.

80

THE FUNERAL was lovely, Nikos tells Cossie, when he calls later that day. Such a wonderful send-off. So many people attending the service at Aghios Stefanos in Navros. The church packed, the congregation spilling out onto its steps and into the square below. So many people gathering together to pay their last respects, and bid old man Contalidis a sad farewell. So many tears, such sorrow. It would have made Theo so happy.

"And now you're old man Contalidis," Cossie teases him, to lighten his sadness – she can hear it in his voice, low and wistful – and, though she can't see it, to make him smile. Which she's sure he does. "Now you're the big man."

"Only with you beside me," he tells her.

"You and me against the world."

"There's no world against us, *agapi mou*," (how she loves it when he calls her 'my darling'). "It's all there for the taking."

Which fills her with a wonderful calmness; a sense that nothing can go wrong.

"Do you know one of the things I love about you?" she asks. "It's not the biggest thing," she continues, with a chuckle, "but it's important. It's who you are. Or, what I mean is, it's a part of you. A big part. Your unbelievable confidence, your optimism. Your unshakeable faith that everything will be okay. Even when everything looks so horrible, so threatening. Facing the future, you always see the positive."

It's as close as Cossie will come to talking about what her pregnancy, and his acceptance of it, may cost him. She's telling him, in a roundabout way, that she knows the price he'll have to pay; and that's she's grateful he's strong enough, and determined enough, and loves her enough, to see it through.

And as she says it, she wonders what he will have to do, what he will have to suffer, to make it happen, to secure their future?

And, once again, she wonders what she can contribute?

What she might do, to help?

81

ELECTRA is feeling guilty. And exuberant. It's a strange mix. Since the funeral she's been working so hard on the book that she has given almost no time to Dimi; dropping him off in Navros so he can go sailing or fishing with Lysander and Kostis, or letting him stay overnight with the Lountzis, or watching him scamper off with his little gang from Anémenos and Kalypti: Dio, Pani, Karo, and the rest of them. And even when the two of them are together, her mind is on the next word, the next paragraph, the next chapter.

She has no doubt that this burst of energy and creativity is the result of her new medication; taking the Phaladrin that Dr Paradoxis had prescribed, but then following it up with a full dose of Tropsodol. And a few drinks, of course. The perfect cocktail. What harm could it do?

Of course, she'd had to work at it; getting that balance of booze and pills. And it hadn't been easy. For the first few days she'd felt drained and washed out, tempted to go back to doctor's orders. But gradually this unforgiving exhaustion had given way to a sudden rush of confidence and light-headed delight. Not to mention a matching productivity; fingers flying across the laptop keys. And with her September deadline looming, anything that interrupted this surge of output – even Dimi – made her tense and irritable. The day after Theo's funeral she'd even told Nikos that there was no point in him staying at Douka on her account (and getting in her way, though she didn't say that). He should get back to the city, back to ConStav, rather than mope around the house feeling sorry for himself. Which he had done, more quickly than she'd anticipated.

Which was good. Back to the study and the Admiral.

And Petrou.

"Did you know he was adopted?" asks Petrou, one evening.

"Who?"

"Ioannis Contalidis."

"Adopted? The Admiral?" Electra stops writing, looks up. Petrou has been sitting in the reading chair for twenty minutes, but has said nothing. What he says now stops her in her tracks. There has been no mention, no suggestion, in her research that this might be the case. "How? Why? From whom?"

Petrou waves a hand, raises his shoulders. It's a gesture she is getting used to.

A small matter, nothing to concern her. Of no interest.

But, with a sly little grin, he tells her anyway.

"A slave girl. They had them in those days, you know; the traders, and the captains, and the admirals. Captives from their pirate raids, made to work in the house, the fields; made to entertain their owners if needs be. And the Admiral's father, Aris, was no exception. A dozen or more kept here at Douka, at the first house built on this spot, near where the storehouses stand now. And it was there that Aris would go, at night, to satisfy himself. This one, that one… A different one whenever he wanted."

Petrou smiles at her astonishment.

"So anyway," he continues. "It happened that Aris's wife, Kyra, was unable to have children. For years they tried, and no issue. So, when one of his slave girls fell pregnant, Aris took the child and gave it to Kyra."

"And the mother? This girl?"

Petrou shrugs again. "She was a slave. Of no importance."

Electra is stunned, reaches out to close the laptop.

And then, "Such things happened," Petrou continues. "Then. Now. All the time. Take Kalliopi, Theo's wife. As empty as a leaking barrel. Did you know that? I can see that you did not," says Petrou, and he chuckles.

Electra can hardly speak. "Theo?"

"Took a village woman to bear him a son. To give to Kalliopi. Everything arranged. Paid for. To have an heir. Your husband. The man who killed me."

Electra starts to laugh. Not at the news of the Admiral's adoption, and nor necessarily at Nikos's adoption. What makes her laugh is the suggestion that Nikos could kill. Has killed. None other than the man sitting in the chair across from her.

"And how, exactly, did my husband kill you?" she asks.

But Petrou waves the question aside. "It is of no importance now."

"So why do you say these things to me?" she asks.

"To warn you. To protect you."

"I don't think I need to be protected."

"Oh, I think you do."

Upstairs in his bedroom, Dimi can't sleep. He feels unsettled, out of sorts, and not even *Temple Run 2* holds any attraction. So he gets up from his bed, opens his bedroom door and goes downstairs. The lights are off in the salon and kitchen so he goes to the study, wondering how his mother will react when he tells her he can't sleep. Chances are she'll think he's been playing on his i-Pad or messaging friends, and get impatient, tell him off. But he hasn't done any of those things… He just can't get to sleep. Tossing and turning, punching his pillow, hot and bothered. It would be different if his Dad were there; he'd go and find his Dad first. But *Baba* is back in Athens now, at their home on Diomexédes. Which is where he will be soon. Back at school, with his friends again. But for now there is only his mother at Douka.

As usual the study door is closed, but a line of light shows beneath it. He knows he must always knock when the door is closed, but as he raises his little fist, he stops, listens; and a chill steals over him.

His mother is talking to someone again. He is sure of it. Just questions, it seems. The thick wood door makes it difficult to hear actual, individual words. But he gets the sense of it. Just the tone. Questions. But no answers. No other voice.

She must be on the phone, Dimi thinks, like his father had said, and forgetting to knock he turns the handle and pushes open the door. But his mother is not on the phone. She's sitting at her desk, elbows planted either side of her closed laptop, chin resting on looped fingers… And it looks to Dimi as though he's interrupted a conversation, that she's talking to someone in the room.

But there's no one there; he can't see anyone.

Just an odd smell; sweet and citrusy.

It reminds him of his grandfathers, Theo and Mikis. A bit old, a little musty.

"Mama," he says, wiping his nose with his gripped pyjama sleeve. "I can't sleep."

And as he speaks, Dimi is surprised to find that he is trembling, actually shaking; and afterwards he decides that it was this shaking and trembling, as though he had a fever, that had made his mother more sympathetic than he might have expected. Given that he had not gone to sleep, as instructed, and that he'd forgotten to knock. Because rather than chide him she rises from her desk, and comes over to comfort him; then takes him upstairs, to her bed, where he doesn't want to be, as though it is a spoiling treat.

For the next three days, Petrou makes no appearance. The chair in her study remains empty, no matter how many times she looks up to check. It is as if he is testing her, making her think. Leaving her to do what she does best. On her own account.

So she does her research, starting with the adoptions.

Since there is nothing she can do to source any reliable records from the time of Aris and Kyra – though she does confirm what Petrou had said about slaves – she flicks through the books she has used to research the Admiral's life but finds nothing substantive. The closest reference is the comment "that Greek bastard, Contalidis" made by a Turkish captain at Chios. But that, she supposes, would not have been surprising – bastard or not.

More important, however, and far easier to check, is Petrou's assertion that Nikos had been adopted. Copies of their birth certificates – her's, Dimi's, Nikos's – are kept in the safe in the library, and it is here that Electra finds what she's looking for. A completed form.

A son: Nikos Leonidas Contalidis.

Father: Theophiles Diomedes Contalidis.

Mother: Kalliopi Mena Contalidis (née Efstathiou).

As she puts the documents back in the safe, Electra decides that while it may be possible that the Admiral had been adopted, there is nothing to suggest that Nikos was. As an historian, she trusts official forms and written notarised evidence, even if – as a woman, a Greek, and a Stamatos – she knows, too, that established evidence is sometimes not necessarily worth the paper it is written on. But it is enough.

What she does wonder about is why Petrou should tell her such things? And whether he is lying, just to be mischievous, or actually telling the truth? As for the warning that he is there to protect her, well that is patently ridiculous. Whatever could he be protecting her from?

But after three days' absence, such questions are put aside as Electra plunges back into her work, and her life of the Admiral draws to a close.

82

THAT FRIDAY Nikos calls from Tsania to warn Electra that he's missed the last ferry and that he's waiting for Manolis to pick him up. When he finally arrives at Douka, much later than usual, he goes straight up to his son's bedroom, even though the boy is sleeping; to see him, to kiss him goodnight.

Much to Electra's tight-lipped irritation.

Because even though Nikos doesn't mean to wake Dimi, just kneeling by the bed and stroking his son's hair is enough to make the boy stir, open his eyes, delight sleepily in his father; hug him tight, and beg him to read a story. After she has spent hours putting him down, just so she can have Nikos to herself after a week away.

When Nikos finally comes down from Dimi's bedroom, they sit together on the terrace, watching bats flick against the still starlit sky. Nikos seems happy to be home, but for some obscure reason Electra feels combative and irritable.

"If something terrible happened," says Electra, as he pours more wine, "if you found yourself in an impossible position, do you suppose you could kill?"

"Of course," says Nikos, almost without a thought. "In war, for my country, for myself… to survive. And for you, as well. Dimi, and you. If either of you were threatened. Wouldn't you?"

Electra is taken aback. At the promptness and certainty of her husband's reply, and the fact that she hasn't asked herself the same question.

Could she kill? Would she be able to shoot someone? Stab someone? Orchestrate a fatal accident?

She shudders, but admits to herself that, like Nikos, she would certainly do anything to protect her son. Sacrifice her own life; yes, even that.

Then she pauses, wonders if she would do the same for her husband? She frowns, tries to think of a likely scenario, where Nikos is somehow threatened and needs her to intervene to save his life.

And suddenly there is Petrou's voice in her ear.

That long low, whisper. "Of course you wouldn't. Why would you?"

"Dimi? Certainly," she says. "No question. But you? Well, I'm not so sure. Sometimes I think a knife in your back would be a very pretty thing. I mean, the next time you wake up Dimi after I've spent hours getting him to sleep… Yes, I could very easily reach for the knife drawer."

And they both laugh, as they are meant to, and the conversation moves on.

Like other Friday nights, Nikos is tired and goes to bed before Electra. She follows soon after, thinking maybe he might be waiting for her, or close enough to consciousness to be stirred from his sleep. She knows she hasn't been the best company, and thinks perhaps she should try to make up for it. But his bedside light is off and his breathing deep and even. She closes the bathroom door before switching on the lights, brushes her teeth and thinks of the choo-choo train. Then washes down a Heripsyn as she sits on the loo. Killing the lights, she opens the bathroom door, crosses to the bed and slides in quietly. Curls up against him, strokes his hair, kisses his neck; but then, when there's no response, she turns her back on him.

Maybe tomorrow, she thinks…

And as the Heripsyn starts to work its magic she tries to remember the last time they made love; or when Nikos had kissed her without it accompanying a hello or goodbye.

She's asleep before she can come up with an answer.

83

ON SATURDAY Nikos and Electra have guests. A dinner party: Alinos Christidis, a dentist in Messinos, and his wife, Phaedra; an English couple, Peter Cornwell and Donald Christopherson, who have a villa on the headland between Anémenos and Pecravi; and the Lountzis, of course, Iakavos and his wife, Marika.

Peter and Donald arrive first, both in their fifties and both retired from the British theatre; Peter, an actor, and Donald a stage manager. Peter brings a scented candle from Jo Malone for Electra, and Donald gives a bottle of single malt Scotch to Nikos. Nikos hates whisky, and has a number of Donald's bottles hidden in the cellar, which he doles out as birthday and Christmas presents to ConStav staff and contractors (who probably like it as little as he does, but who make a show of being delighted; just as he does whenever Donald visits.)

The Lountzis and Christidis, who've come the furthest and will be staying over, arrive within minutes of each other, bringing their various children, three boys and a girl, aged nine to twelve, whom Dimi pounces on. They will not be seen until bedtime, with Lina and Aja kept on to help with the dinner, promising to keep an eye on them.

Drinks are served on the terrace, and when dinner is ready Nikos shows his guests through to the dining room. The blue Murano table top shimmers in candlelight, and the wall sconces throw out flickering shadows. They take their seats, the best Contalidis wine is poured, and Lina and Aja serve the first of four courses while the conversation covers the usual dinner-table ground: the economy, Brussels, *Mutti* Merkel whom everyone hates, and all the latest island gossip…

But gossip and Merkel aside, what each of their guests will remember later is Electra's haunted look that evening; the slurred voice, the gaunt features; her eyes flicking everywhere as though her attention has been caught by something only she can see. What they will also recall is the care and attention that Nikos lavishes on her – the smiles, the tender touches, the praise for her book, the way she runs Douka, and what she has done with the old place.

The two wives, Marika and Phaedra, are touched by his concern, and their hearts warm to him – such a kind, devoted, caring man – while their husbands, Iakavos and Alinos, are quietly astonished, and impressed, by his selfless loyalty. Once these two men had been bowled over by the woman at the end of the table, a little intimidated, too – her wit, her glamour, her city chic – but now they feel only a sense of wonder at how Nikos can bear this decline; such strength and stoicism, the sacrifice he is making.

When they go to their rooms that night, the two couples talk in whispers, of Nikos and Electra, and how bad it seems.

Poor Electra.

Poor, poor Nikos.

And as he runs his hand over Electra's bony hip, and pulls her towards him, to begin what he can no longer avoid – taking her from behind to avoid the sour smell of wine on her breath and the bitter taste of it on her lips Nikos knows that this weekend he is laying the foundations for an alibi.

When he leaves Douka the following day, he can see the way forward.

Only a few last pieces of the jigsaw to place.

84

THE LATE Petrou, as Electra likes to think of him, always appears in a different outfit. Black or grey or dark blue trousers, usually with buttoned flies, that might once have been part of a suit but now never match his choice of jacket, as though he has pulled on the one and tugged on the other without bothering to check. The jackets themselves are dated and drab. Dark, shadowy tweeds and indistinct stripes, as well as the plainer weaves, all with smooth shiny patches on the lapels, all stoop-shouldered and creased at the elbow, with curled pocket flaps.

The only items of clothing that appear the same are his shirts – always white, always buttoned to a stubble-frayed collar, cuffs grimy and threadbare; black woollen socks loose enough to show a band of blue-veined shiny shin; and his black leather shoes, dusty, scuffed and laceless, just like his grandfather's at Epione.

And always there, that barber-shop smell of pomade; sweet, almost citrusy, but lined with a strange undernote of patchouli or sandalwood that Electra can't quite identify. Whenever he appears, and for a short time after he leaves, there is always that scent. Pleasant, if a little sickly.

That Sunday night, after Dimi has left with the Lountzis for a reciprocal stay-over and Nikos has returned to Athens, the late Petrou joins her on the stairs as she comes down from her bedroom. She's showered, and is dressed in pyjamas and dressing gown. She can't see him but she senses him, smells him, on the stair behind her, as though Dimi is following her down for a jaunt, like a game of grandmother's footsteps.

By the time she reaches the study he's already sitting in his chair, working a set of coal black *kombolói* through gnarled, bony fingers. The same *kombolói* that his grandfather worked at Epione.

"Do you pray?" asks Electra, as she sits at her desk and pulls the laptop towards her, nodding at the beads.

"Ghosts don't need to pray." And he chuckles.

"What do they need?"

"Always the same thing."

"And what is that?"

"A second chance."

"A second chance at what?"

"To put things right. To settle accounts."

"So ought I to be frightened?"

"Not you, my dear. Not of me."

"And why is that?"

"Because the debts are not yours."

"So whose debts are they?"

Petrou sighs, "Dimitrios Contalidis, for one. Your husband's grandfather. You never knew him, but take my word for it he was a nasty piece of work. Killed his elder brother so he could have Douka for himself."

Dimitrios? Dimitrios? In her mind's eye, Electra runs through the portraits on the upper corridor. And then she has him. In a high winged collar and pinned cravat, sitting at the Admiral's desk. If looks suggest character, then maybe Petrou is correct, for Dimitrios has beady black eyes, thin lips, and an arrogant tilt to the head. A man, she imagines, who could never be wrong, whose word was law. Stubborn, impatient, intolerant. But not a killer, surely? Not the kind of man who would kill his own brother?

"And what did Dimitrios do to you that he owed you this debt?"

"I told you. He sacked my father from Douka, and then betrayed him to the Germans. We were left with nothing."

"But Dimitrios is long dead."

"And beat me to my revenge. But there is always his grandson. The man who killed me."

"Not that again. Nikos?" Electra tips back her head, starts to laugh. "No, no, no. Nikos wouldn't hurt a fly."

But when she looks back at the chair, it is empty.

Petrou has gone.

While Electra and Petrou talk that Sunday night, Nikos parks his car on Iraklidon and begins the short walk to Cossie's apartment on Efestiou. It is a warm night but he shivers, digs his hands into his pockets.

Is Electra getting better? he wonders. Or is her condition worsening? Judging by the evidence – her continued weight loss, her skull-like, haunted features, the shortness of temper, the reported talking to herself – Nikos would have to say he can see no conclusive improvement. And as he unlocks the apartment block door with the key that Cossie has given him and presses the button for the lift, he realises with a familiar and rising sense of detachment that it is time to act.

After this last weekend he has had enough.

Now, or never.

Two-or-three-months-pregnant won't be two-or-three-months-pregnant for much longer.

At some dark hour of the night, Electra senses footsteps in the corridor, hears the soft click of the bedroom door handle, and bare feet on Mexican oak.

Small, sticky footsteps… Familiar.

Dimi.

"I had a bad dream," the boy whispers, sliding beneath the covers, burrowing into her embrace, shivering. "I was frightened."

"Then you'd better stay here, *agapi mou*."

It is only when Electra wakes the following morning, finds herself alone in the bed, that she remembers Dimi is staying with the Lountzis.

Just a dream, she thinks.

But the boy had been so real, if a little cool to the touch.

And she feels a chill of premonition race across her skin.

Mystery

(Μυστεριο)

85

WHEN THE gardener, Joannou, arrives for work at Douka that Tuesday morning, he hears, over the tap-tapping of the lawn sprinklers and the early simmering buzz of insects, a familiar gurgling and sucking sound from the swimming pool. He sets down his wheelbarrow, and climbs the steps to the top terrace.

A towel, he thinks, left in the pool by Dimi; blocking one of the filtration ducts. It won't have been the first time.

But it is not a towel.

And as he crosses the terrace to the pool, Joannou remembers from the previous week that Dimi is spending a few days with his friend, Andreas Lountzis, over Eressos way. So Dimi will not be to blame.

Which leaves...

As Joannou draws closer, he makes out what looks like a spill of colour in the far corner of the pool, at the deep end. Like petrol, shifting with a blue coiling irridescence.

But it is not petrol.

Instead, it appears to be some kind of thin material. Silk, or cotton. A greeny blue. Spread out just beneath the surface. And amidst its patterned swirl of colours Joannou can see, as he draws near, what looks oddly like a thin bony ankle.

And then a wrist. Part of an arm.

Not a towel, blocking the filter. A body.

Which makes his heart start to race; though he is not immediately aware of it.

Joannou goes to the pool and kneels at its edge. He can see at once that it is Madam, but he is not sure what to do. It is clearly too late to help her. The back of her head is just a few centimetres above the surface, blonde curls gathered in watery tendrils that show the scalp beneath. But her face – her mouth and her nose – is under water.

There is no doubt about it.

Madame Contalidis has drowned.

Madame Contalidis is dead.

Joannou lives closest to Douka and is the first to arrive. He knows that Elias and Dilos, Lina's father and brother, will be there at any moment, and that Babis from Kalypti, as usual, will be late. So he goes to the terrace steps, sits, rolls himself a cigarette, and waits. He has no mobile phone, and doesn't feel comfortable about going into the house to call for help.

It is too late anyway. There can be no help; there is no coming back for the body in the pool.

When Elias arrives he will know what to do. Or Ariadne.

Joannou lights his cigarette, remembers to cross himself, and then looks at his watch. One or the other will be here soon.

86

POLICE-CAPTAIN Mavrodakis knows Douka. Doesn't need directions when the call comes in.

Douka. Again.

Mavrodakis may be Athenian, but he has been on the island long enough to remember.

Petrou first. And then the fire.

He takes the wheel of the Kia Sportage, second-hand from the Serious Crime Unit in Athens. White, with a blue stripe along its flanks and a bar of lights on the roof. Dented, worn bodywork, rusting door sills, with a hundred thousand kilometres on the clock and frayed seat-belts whose buckles only reach their housings after much violent tugging. His second-in-command, Police-Lieutenant Evangelos Tsavalas, takes the seat beside him and starts to give directions.

Islander. Athenian. It never changes.

"Thanks, Vango, I know the way."

And he does. Out of Navros and along the coast road, under a scattered mackerel sky, past graffiti-carved ears of ficus cactus and a grey shifting sea. It's not yet hot, but Mavrodakis knows it will be. That strange, stuffy September heat that can't seem to make up its mind if it's autumn yet, or still summer.

At the end of the sand-strewn blacktop Mavrodakis turns to the left and follows the road between browning stumps of maize and twisting groves of olive. Up through Falanistis and Calamotí, on to Avrómelou and Akronitsá, before swooping down along the Anémenos road.

Douka, and that Contalidis, thinks Mavrodakis.

Too good-looking, too sure of himself, too… entitled.

He's never liked the man.

From the very first time they met.

Mavrodakis had only two stars on his boards back then, but he clearly remembers standing by the broken body of Petrou. Splayed onto the terrace in a jigsaw-shaped puddle of sticky fly-buzzing blood, while his predecessor, the recently retired Police-Captain Goulandris, explained to Contalidis what seemed to have happened. The old man drunk again, falling from the balcony, a broken bottle close by. Something like it was bound to happen sooner or later, he'd said. And now it had.

And Mavrodakis had watched Contalidis nod, seen the twitch of a smile.

So he's got what he wants at last, that's what Mavrodakis had thought. He knew the story; they all did. How Petrou had taken Douka from the family.

And now it looked as though the Contalidis would get it back. The last, stubborn obstacle removed.

But it wasn't just that twitch of a smile that alerted Mavrodakis. There'd been something wrong about the body; something that had bothered him back then. And continued to bother him now. If Petrou had tipped over the railing, there was absolutely no doubt that he'd have been a lot closer to the wall of the house than where he ended up. Either he'd taken a run at that bathroom railing like some crazed hurdler; or he'd been heaved over it to land where he did, nearly three metres out from the wall. If Mavrodakis had been in charge he'd certainly have taken it further than Goulandris. But two stars on your shoulder boards weren't three. Goulandris was the man in charge. Goulandris was an islander. And Goulandris knew the Contalidis.

And all the time, gathered around that crumpled body, Contalidis hadn't even noticed him, standing there beside Goulandris. Not a glance, not a nod. No acknowledgement. As if he somehow knew that Mavrodakis wasn't happy, and didn't dare catch his eye. Or maybe, more likely, it was just the two stars on his boards. The two stars, his short stature, his beard, his crooked teeth. Not worth the time of day.

But what was Nikos Contalidis doing there anyway? Mavrodakis had thought. How come he was on the scene so quickly?

Staying with the Christidis, apparently.

But still.

Then there had been the fire at Douka. An accident, of course; it could have been nothing else with old Mr Contalidis. A group of them standing on the lower terrace, looking up at the house's smoking shell, the air sooty, sharp and acrid. Goulandris, again, Contalidis, and the fire-chief, old Athanasios Latsos. Mavrodakis, still with two stars on his boards, had found a charred photo album in a fall of blackened stone and had brought it to Contalidis. He'd taken it without a word; not even a look or nod of thanks.

And it had been no different at the old man's funeral, when Mavrodakis had stood by the road barriers placed on the streets leading to Aghios Stefanos. Watched the mourners gather for the funeral service of Theo Contalidis. Seen the son and heir help his wife up the steps of the church, exchange words with the Archimandrite Paulos, and then, when the service was finished, pass him by without a word of thanks. For everything he and his men had done to make the event go smoothly.

No, Mavrodakis doesn't like Contalidis.

Never had. Never would.

87

THE HOUSEKEEPER, Ariadne Papadavrou, leads them to the swimming pool. Tall, gaunt, and strangely unmoved, she stands aside while Mavrodakis kneels at its edge.

"Joannou didn't want to move her," she says. Watching, waiting.

"They can bring her out now," says Mavrodakis, getting to his feet, sucking at his crooked front teeth to cover the wince from his hip. He looks around the terrace, sees an empty bottle of Contalidis wine on a table, and walks over to it. No glass, just the bottle, and a saucer. The crumpled remains of a joint lie in the saucer, beside a marquetry box. He opens the lid, tips a finger through its contents. Tight little green buds, a scatter of leafy cuttings, rolling papers, cardboard filters. He smiles at the housekeeper, who has followed him to the table, and wonders whether she left the box for him to find rather than spirit it away, to save her mistress' reputation?

Madame Papadavrou raises a disapproving eyebrow.

No love lost, he suspects, recognising the signs.

And turns to see the Douka gardeners retrieve the body from the pool.

Water from the sodden bundle splashes onto the tiles; limbs hang loose, unmuscled. As carefully as they can, as modestly, the four men arrange Madame Contalidis's body in a growing puddle that darkens the stone. Then step back, not sure what to do with themselves, where to look.

In terms of weight, Mavrodakis observes, just one of the men could have managed the task. The body is just a crumpled pile of pale kindling. Bony limbs, barrelled ribs, sharply-pointed shoulders, elbows, knees; he's seen more meat on a supermarket chicken. Wrapped in what looks like a blue cotton sarong, a pair of light green bikini briefs beneath it. Nothing else.

He steps forward and the men make room for him. He squats down, uses a finger to lift a sodden loop of hair from the face. The eyes are closed, the lips blue and parted, water trickling from the mouth. Everything he would expect from a drowning. Save a darkening abrasion at the point between temple and forehead. Skin broken in four or five parallel grazes.

Accident? She'd drunk too much wine, smoked too much weed, and fallen into the pool, hitting her head as she did so?

Or suicide? Deliberately drinking herself into a near oblivion and wading into the pool, letting the water take her?

Or something else? Mavrodakis wonders.

From the Anémenos road, he hears the rising wail of an ambulance.

It is enough, he decides.

Maybe this time.

"So you're saying the doors were locked when you arrived for work?"

"That's what I said," says the housekeeper.

"From the inside?"

The Police-Captain is sitting at the kitchen table, the ache in his hip fading, Madame Papadavrou standing by the stone sinks. She has poured herself some water, holds the tumbler in both hands. A worker's hands, Mavrodakis notices, the fingers bent and swollen. He wonders what it would take to have her join him at the table? He knows it isn't going to happen. Out on the terrace, Vango is taking a statement from Joannou. The body of Madame Contalidis has been loaded into the ambulance, and is on its way to the hospital in Navros.

"Locked tight," says Madame Papadavrou. "Windows, too. No way in if you didn't have a key."

Windows, thinks Mavrodakis? Who closes all the windows when you're at home? On a hot day, a warm night?

"And the door keys? Madam's keys?"

"All inside."

"And were the keys in the locks?"

Madame Papadavrou shakes her head. "No need for keys inside. You just push a button in the handles if you want to lock up. Last thing at night." She goes to the door, shows him. "No keyhole – see? And in the morning, when you want to go out, all you have to do is turn the handle and the locks release automatically. When anyone leaves the house empty – Mr Nikos, or Madam, or the girls and me – we always double lock from the outside. There's a keyhole in that handle."

"And you can tell, when you unlock from the outside, if the door has been locked from the inside?"

The housekeeper tightens her lips, gives him a patient look.

"When you lock the door from the outside," she explains again, "you give the key one turn counter-clockwise to lock it, and unlock it. If it's been locked from inside, you turn the key clockwise."

Mavrodakis nods, takes this in. He can't quite make sense of it.

"And this morning, when you tried?"

"Clockwise, like I said. The front door, too." She takes a sip of water. "Which means they were both locked from the inside."

"So who has keys?" he asks.

"Mr Nikos has a set, of course. Madam, also."

"And staff?"

"I do. And the girls, Lina and Aja, in case they get here before me. They have one between them."

"The gardeners?"

The old lady shakes her head. She might look aloof, cold even, unfriendly, thinks Mavrodakis, but she must have been a beautiful woman once. Tall, and slim, with a long neck rising out of a round lace collar, coal-black eyes, finely pointed nose and full lips that lines and wrinkles do nothing to conceal. She should wear pearls, thinks Mavrodakis, and he wonders what she would look like if she smiled. He doubts she does too much of that.

"Any spares?"

"There, by the fridge, for the kitchen door. And there's a spare front door key in a drawer in the hallway table."

"And Madame Contalidis's keys?"

"On the ring with her car key. There." She points to a set of keys on the work surface beside her.

"And you say that Madame Contalidis was alone in the house?"

"Since Sunday evening, when Dimi left to stay with a friend, and Mr Nikos returned to Athens."

"When did you last see Madame Contalidis?"

"Yesterday. We left just before lunch. Me and the girls."

"And she was by herself?"

"She was working, in the study. We didn't want to disturb her. She wouldn't have been pleased. When the door is shut, you know not to bother her."

"So, you didn't actually see her?" Mavrodakis tries to make it sound friendly; not pointed, sarcastic. He doesn't want to offend the housekeeper.

But it's clear she takes offence. A little, anyway. She ruffles her shoulders, works her long neck in its lace collar. "We heard her. Speaking to someone. She was on the phone."

"And her state of mind?"

Madame Papadavrou shrugs. "The same."

"Meaning?"

"Madam has not been herself for some time."

"The breakdown?" Like everyone, Mavrodakis has heard about the family tragedy; remembers her, like a frail old lady, being helped by her husband up and then down the steps of Aghios Stefanos for the funeral service. And now, this bundle by the pool.

"Mr Nikos brought her here to help with her recovery. A change of scene. Away from the city."

"And has it helped?"

Another shrug from the housekeeper. "You can see for yourself," is all she says.

"So how do you suppose Madame Contalidis found herself locked out? With her keys inside. When there was no one else in the house."

The old lady gives Mavrodakis a look that says *You're the policeman, you tell me.*

He knows he's not going to get much more from her.

"Does Madame Contalidis have a mobile phone?"

The housekeeper looks around. "In her study, I expect. Or bedroom. She's always losing it. Never can remember where she put it." She gives an impatient shake of the head and her mouth tightens, producing a tiara of tiny wrinkles on her top lip.

"And when you found out about the body in the pool, did you contact Mr Contalidis?"

"I called him immediately, before contacting you. Left him a message to call me."

"His land line, or cell phone?"

"His mobile first, then their home in Athens, and his office."

"And you called from here?"

"On the kitchen phone."

"But he didn't answer any of your calls? He wasn't at home, in the office, or near his mobile?"

A look from the housekeeper.

"And he hasn't phoned back?"

Another look.

Which is when the phone by the fridge begins to bleat.

88

IT IS LATE that Tuesday afternoon. Mavrodakis is in his office at Police Headquarters in Navros when Vango knocks to say that Mr Contalidis is here to see him.

"Show him in," says Mavrodakis, getting up from his desk and straightening his tunic. He squares his shoulders, prepares himself. He might know Contalidis in an official capacity – from Petrou, the fire, and the recent funeral – but they do not mix in the same island circles, and he knows that Contalidis will not recognize him. He is correct.

"Mr Contalidis, thank you for coming in, and my condolences on your loss. And your father, too, of course."

They shake hands, and his visitor looks around the room: the desk, hat stand, two prints of Navros harbour crowded with the masts of merchant ships, a wall-sized map of Pelatea, and a Greek flag hanging in a corner, its blue and white stripes oddly entwined. When he is done with his inventory, Contalidis takes the chair that Mavrodakis has indicated.

Contalidis is as striking as Mavrodakis remembers. The fall of curling black hair, greying at the temples now; the long, lean body; the effortless way he crosses his legs and clasps his hands in his lap; the casual but well-tailored clothes – cream linen jacket, white cuffed shirt, black jeans; feet bare in tasselled suede loafers. He seems distant, somehow; not quite all there. Which, Mavrodakis supposes, is not so remarkable. The man has lost his wife. The mother of his child. So many things for him to deal with; the formalities of death, arrangements to be made. And his father just recently deceased.

Poor man. It rains, it pours, thinks Mavrodakis; taking his own seat, leaning forward, arms on desk, hands clasped.

"I do hope you won't mind, but there are just a few questions I need to ask. I'm sure you understand?"

"Of course, please. Anything." The voice is sharp and business-like, almost cracked; just another process for him to get through. His eyes, though, are clear, Mavrodakis notices. No tears spilled, no red rims. Just a few hours after learning about his wife's death.

"Your wife was not in the best of health, I understand?" Mavrodakis begins, clearing his throat, settling his shoulders.

"Ella, Electra... had a breakdown, following a stillbirth. We thought it better that she made her recovery here, on Pelatea, rather than in Athens. And she had her work, of course. She'd started writing again, and was finishing her book. A family history."

A family history, thinks Mavrodakis. Yes, indeed.

"And how was the recovery going?"

Contalidis sighs. "Not as well as we would have hoped."

"We?"

"Well, the doctors and I."

Mavrodakis puts on a suitably sympathetic look, nods, and then says, "Just for the record, would you mind telling me your movements during the last forty-eight hours? Since your return to Athens, on, I believe, Sunday afternoon?"

Contalidis looks startled.

"It is simply procedure," Mavrodakis assures him. "The way we do these things. Just a formality, you understand."

Contalidis frowns. "Well, if you must know, I was in Athens, working. I'm there from Sunday evening, sometimes Monday, to Friday afternoon when I come home to Douka."

"So you returned to the city on Sunday evening, spent the night at your home on…" Mavrodakis checks a notepad. "Diomexédes? Is that correct?"

"Diomexédes, that's right."

"And yesterday? Monday?"

"I was at the office. ConStav, in Pangrati."

"And you left the office, when?"

"Around five, to check out a new site, and afterwards I went home."

"To Diomexédes?"

"Correct."

"Apparently, Madame Papadavrou phoned you this morning at your home and your office, land lines and mobile, but was unable to reach you."

"Stupidly, I left my mobile at the office, and the phone at home is always playing up."

"So you got Madame Papadavrou's message this morning?"

"When I got into the office, yes. So I called, and…" Contalidis takes a deep breath, holds it as though to steady himself; then lets it out, low and slow.

Mavrodakis gets up from his desk and goes to the window, looks down at passing traffic. "You understand there will be an autopsy," he says, without turning.

"No," he hears Contalidis say. "I didn't know that. Why?"

"To establish cause of death."

"But she drowned…"

"She had been drinking," says Mavrodakis, coming back to his desk. "And she appears to have been smoking cannabis…" He gives Contalidis a look, raises his eyebrows, flashes a questioning smile.

Contalidis looks cross. "And she falls into the pool," he says, neatly avoiding the mention of drugs. "Probably unsteady on her feet."

"There was a cut to the head, an abrasion." Mavrodakis watches Contalidis carefully. The man is working his wedding ring with calm, steady fingers. Round, and around, and around. Eyes down, eyebrows up. "So we need to establish if it was an accident, or suicide. Or possibly something else."

Contalidis looks up, frowns. "Something else?"

Mavrodakis spreads his hands. "Just to remove all doubt, you understand? Also, did you know that your wife was locked out of the house?"

"No, I didn't." And then, "How would I?"

"The housekeeper, Ariadne Papadavrou, said that the house was locked when she arrived. From the inside. Doors, and windows too. No way in. And your wife's keys were in the kitchen. She would have been out there all night. Locked out."

"So she would have called for help."

"Her mobile was in the house. In her study."

His visitor thinks for a moment, shakes his head as though he can't explain it. And then, "Well, you must understand that Douka is a new build, Captain. After the fire, you know, we had to start from scratch. Just a shell to work with."

As if I didn't know, thinks Mavrodakis. Just like his housekeeper; the same air of bored tolerance. Two of a kind, they are.

"So, of course, there have been problems," Contalidis continues. "There always are. Snags. Glitches. The wiring, plumbing. One thing or another. It happens all the time. I can only assume the locks must have jammed, or something."

"Both? Front and back? At the same time?"

Across the desk Contalidis looks at a loss; then brightens, as though able to provide the slower-witted Mavrodakis with what should have been an obvious solution. "Well, look. If someone locked the doors from the inside, then whoever it was would still be in there, wouldn't they? I mean, it has to be some kind of locking failure. There's no other possible explanation."

So many things going wrong, thinks Mavrodakis. What a trial for the poor fellow. Not just the door locks at Douka, but the wiring, the plumbing; and then the phone in the house on Diomexédes. Everything playing up. Letting him down left, right and centre. How does he manage?

But time to move on, he thinks.

"As well as the cannabis," Mavrodakis continues, leaning back in his chair, not prepared to let the subject drop. "…I'm assuming your wife was on other medication?"

"Yes, she was. To aid her recovery."

"And this medication was prescribed by…?"

"By Doctor Fastiliades, at the Aetolikou Clinic."

"That's on the mainland?"

"Yes, it is. At Lagonisi, between Athens and Sounio. It's where my wife was treated."

"And you have a doctor, here on the island?"

"The family doctor, Fotis Paradoxis. A good man."

"So, Mr Contalidis. I would like to speak to Dr Paradoxis, as well as Dr Fastiliades, if that's acceptable? And I would also like a list of contacts for your wife. Friends, family… An address book? Her phone? Oh, and passwords, codes, for her phone and computer, if you know them?" Mavrodakis smiles. "If you wouldn't mind? Just to get an idea of what might have happened, her state of mind; if there is anything anyone can remember that might be significant. I'm sure you understand?"

"If you think it necessary." His tone has turned curt.

"Who knows, Mr Contalidis? But at least we'll be able to clear everything up. A few days, a week or so. Nothing more, I'm sure."

And they talk on. A few more minutes. Just the formalities. When he has what he needs, Mavrodakis thanks Contalidis for his patience, for his time; and getting up from his desk he shows him to the door. "By the way," he asks, "have you been to the house?"

"No," says Contalidis. "I came straight here. As requested."

Mavrodakis nods. "Good, good. For the time being I've secured the property as a potential crime scene, so if…"

"Crime scene?"

Mavrodakis spreads his hands. "Just a precaution, Mr Contalidis. Until we have everything we need. Everything sorted out. So, if there was someone you could stay with for the next day or two…?"

89

THE AUTOPSY report on Electra Theia Contalidis arrives on the desk of Police-Captain Mavrodakis twelve days after her death. And the high-priority Forensic report he's requested, after much arm-twisting with an officer in Budget Control at Police Headquarters in Athens, arrives just a few minutes later. Both reports rattle out of the office printer, and are brought to him by Vango.

These two reports may have taken longer to reach him than he had hoped, but for Mavrodakis the time has not been wasted.

He has been a busy man.

Around Navros; around Douka; around the island.

And on the mainland.

The day after the discovery of Electra's body, Mavrodakis returns to the house at Douka with Police-Lieutenant Tsavalas. Using the spare house-key, kept on a hook by the fridge and given to him by Ariadne Papadavrou, he unlocks the kitchen door – one turn counter-clockwise – and the two police officers go in.

On the journey there Mavrodakis has told his second-in-command what he wants him to do, and as soon as they are in the house Vango springs into action. There's a sense of expectation on the younger man's clear, wide-eyed face. Mavrodakis hasn't said anything to him, but Vango knows that something's up. That this is not as straightforward a case as it may, at first, have seemed.

"Anything out of the ordinary, anything that catches your eye," Mavrodakis calls after him. "Just walk around, open drawers or cupboards, by all means; but nothing too intrusive. Use your eyes. And don't forget your gloves, eh?" he calls out a little louder, taking his own from his tunic pocket and snapping them on.

The moment he's alone, Mavrodakis looks around the kitchen. A plate with breadcrumbs on it and around it, and a butter-smeared knife. Lunch, or supper? A wine cork on a corkscrew. An empty coffee mug. The housekeeper's water glass. Everything as it was the previous day when he'd left Douka with Madame Papadavrou, advising her that there would be no need for her or the girls to return to the property until notified to do so.

While Vango sets to in the house, the first thing Mavrodakis does is pick up the house phone by the fridge and dial the Contalidis number on Diomexédes. Six rings and the Ansaphone clicks on. Contalidis's voice. Direct, but friendly. There's a bleep for the caller to leave a message. Mavrodakis says nothing, counts five and puts the phone down. Then he uses his own mobile. Dials the same number. And once again he is put straight through. He's done the same from Police Headquarters, after Contalidis provided him with a list of telephone numbers. With similar results. Finally, he calls the Athens Telephone Exchange and asks if any faults have been reported for the Diomexédes number. After holding for nearly fifteen minutes, filling the time with a cursory inspection of kitchen cupboards and drawers, opening the fridge, running his eyes down the shelves, he is told by the Exchange that there is no record of any faults being reported.

From the kitchen Mavrodakis makes for Madame Contalidis's study. The room is surprisingly cold for the time of year, and it feels as though no one has been there for months. There is an odd citrus-like scent that reminds Mavrodakis of dying flowers, and it is strangely dark, too, given the wide sliding glass door that opens onto the rear courtyard. Across this wall-flowered, gravelled space, is another sliding door. The library. Or rather, the rest of the library. Because the room he is in is crammed with books. Open and closed, and bookmarked with Post-It notes. Books everywhere, filling the shelves, stacked on the floor, and piled around the edge of her desk. A sleek slab of pale wood in what Mavrodakis decides is a Scandinavian style, the chair a matching pale leather with padded chrome arms and a single swivel leg.

He pulls out the chair and sits where Madame Contalidis would have sat, their backs to the courtyard, and looks around; sees what she will have seen. A tightly beamed ceiling, a tasselled Persian rug that fits the room so perfectly that the room might have been built around it, the only lights in the room a small down-lighter in each corner, a desk lamp in slanting pale wood, and an arching brass reading light beside an old tapestried armchair. Placed on the seat of this chair is an oil painting of a young boy, recognisably a younger Dimi, head and shoulders; the canvas still to be framed and hung. Signed with the initials Y.F., and dated July 2013.

Apart from the desk lamp, the books, and a single framed photo of Nikos and Dimi, the only other things on the desk are an ashtray overflowing with cigarette butts, a half-empty bottle of Souroti mineral water, and an Apple laptop. Mavrodakis opens it, taps in the password that Contalidis had given him, and the screen lights up on a half-filled document page. Just where she would have left it. He leans forward and reads the last few lines:

> *"He was going to kill her. She was certain of it. Everything told her to be wary.*
> *Kill him, before he kills you, the old man told her.*
> *It was time to decide, time to prepare.*
> *Time to even the score, and clear the lines…"*

Mavrodakis raises his eyebrows. *Well, well…*

Scrolling back to previous pages he reads more fully. Admiral Contalidis is on Mykonos and having dinner with the freedom fighter, Mantó Mavroyénous. The man who wants her dead is another captain from the same island. Warring families. As usual.

Still…

Sitting back, Mavrodakis slides his gloved fingers over the keys, where her fingers would have moved. Stubby fingers, like his own. He'd noticed that when they'd pulled her body from the pool. Stubby fingers and rough, workman's hands. Then he leans forward and scrolls back through the document to the title page.

Ioannis Contalidis
A Life At Full-Sail
1756 –1848

And the by-line in a smaller font:

Electra Stamatos

Her family name, not her married name, muses Mavrodakis, and he wonders what Mr Contalidis would make of that?

Just as she would have done, he saves the document, then taps his way through other Desktop files. Nothing of interest. Ditto Bookmarks, Calendar, Notes and e-mails. He lowers the lid of the laptop, and pushes it away from him. Reaches for the single drawer set centrally beneath the desk. Slides it open and finds the woman's address book where Contalidis had said he would. Beside it, there's a worn leather journal with leather ties. He takes up the journal first; fine crisp pages covered with a spidery handwriting. Anything from a few lines, to a paragraph, to several pages; each entry under a particular day and date. But days and dates too far back in time to be of any significance. An old diary. Something to do with her research, Mavrodakis supposes.

The address book is smaller than the journal. Pocket-size. Sleek and expensive. A blue pig-skin cover, gold-edged pages incised along the leading edge with the alphabet in tiny red letters, the paper thin enough to roll a cigarette. Or a joint. The handwriting here is more definite than the writing in the journal but, instead of a uniform black ink, the pages are covered in pencil, blue biro, black roller tip; whatever came to hand. Names, addresses, and telephone numbers. Maybe a hundred names in all. Some legwork here, thinks Mavrodakis, and tucks the address book into his jacket pocket. He puts the journal back in the drawer and slides it shut. A whisper of smooth soft wood. He thinks of his own desk drawers back at police headquarters. Always a struggle. He's tried chalk and olive oil on the runners, but nothing seems to work.

And then, swinging round in the chair, Mavrodakis notices her mobile. On the edge of the nearest bookshelf. He picks it up, taps in the code and goes to 'Recents'. No calls in or out between 9:56 am and 1:42 pm two days earlier. So who, wonders Mavrodakis, was Madame Contalidis talking to when Madame Papadavrou heard her on the phone, since there is no land line to be seen? Was someone there? A friend? Someone calling by? Someone the housekeeper hadn't been aware of? Or maybe Madame Contalidis was talking to herself? Or reading aloud something that she'd written? Seeing if it sounded okay. Maybe that's how writers worked? Impossible to say.

When Vango returns to the kitchen an hour later, he's carrying a matchbox. Held between thumb and forefinger.

A matchbox with a scorpion inside.

Dead. Dried to a husk. The tail brittle but unbroken; still curled.

"I found it in one of Madam's dressing-room drawers. Must have been there months."

Who puts a scorpion in a matchbox, wonders Mavrodakis? And who would put it in Madame Contalidis's drawer? For her to open, and possibly be stung. Certainly shocked. And was it alive when it was put in there? Or dead? It wouldn't kill, of course. But still…

Taking the box from Vango, Mavrodakis adds it to the wine bottle from the terrace, the marquetry box of makings, and a number of other items that he has decided to bag up for forensic examination. Only then do the two police officers strip off their latex gloves.

"What a place," says Vango, standing aside as his boss closes the kitchen door behind them.

Mavrodakis hears the click of the lock engaging as he turns the key, counter-clockwise, just as the housekeeper had instructed, and removes it. He tries the handle. No play. The door is secured. He puts the key back in, turns it once, clockwise – no give, nothing. Tries it counter-clockwise, the lock disengages, and the door opens. He closes it again, locks it, pockets the key.

"I mean, it's not what you'd expect, is it?" Vango continues. "And those concrete floors? It's like the prison out at Korossos. And blue? Like… walking on water."

Mavrodakis grunts. "Some people think they can," is all he says.

"So, what are your impressions?" asks Mavrodakis, as they turn out of the Douka gates in the Kia and start the climb up to Akronitsá.

"Like I said," Vango begins. "It's not what you'd expect. Athens, maybe, but on Pelatea? Old on the outside, but inside it's like… space-age. Never seen anything like it. Not even some of those new villas out on Vanti Bay. But a cool place, no question. And some really nice stuff. The TV, the Hi-Fi. Top of the range, right? But a turntable? No one has turntables anymore, do they? And vinyl? All those albums."

"Some people say the music sounds better," says Mavrodakis.

"Maybe they do, but my Dad says different. Get a scratch on them and it jumps or goes schtick-schtick-schtick till it drives you mad, or you buy another one. That's what he says anyway."

"Anything else? Apart from the turntable."

"Well, you ask me, I wouldn't want to live there, that's for certain. Not in that house. I mean, great position and all. A really neat spot on the headland like that, and the beach and all, and the gardens. But it's not what I'd call a comfortable house. You know what I mean? Not a real home. It's all hard and edgy. Kind of… for show. Not snug, or comfortable."

Vango pauses.

Mavrodakis knows he hasn't finished, hasn't said what he really means. But knows the young man is not sure if he should continue. They're police officers, after all, and Mavrodakis is his boss.

"Go on," says Mavrodakis, by way of encouragement. "You were going to say…" As they breach the rise above Akronitsá, he slows the Kia for a wandering herd of goats. Their bells tinkle, and the rich urine-sweet smell of them comes through their open windows.

"Well, maybe it's just that old fellow, Petrou, dying there like he did, but for all the building work and everything they've done it still feels kind of… cold, you know, and empty. Spooky, even. Like there's been a lot of history there, a lot of things happening. Like once it was a real family home. But not so much now." Vango frowns, as though he knows he's not explaining himself properly. "I mean, there's nobody there, right? But it's like it's a house full of whispers. So quiet. So silent… but not. Like you've got company. Like being blindfold in a crowded room. If you know what I mean?"

Mavrodakis grunts again. "Quite the little writer," he says.

But he knows exactly what the young man means.

It takes the rest of the day to go through Madame Contalidis's address book. After matching its names and numbers with those on her mobile, and on the land line records he's called up from the local exchange, Mavrodakis has narrowed his list of the victim's closest friends to eleven names – whose numbers, mobile and land line, she'd called most recently and most often.

Discounting her mother, her husband, and the family doctor, Fotis Paradoxis, he's left with six telephone numbers. Three of them local, on Pelatea; three in Athens. Eleven names in all.

Three days after the body was found in the pool, and having been assured by Contalidis that news of his wife's death has been passed on to friends and family, Mavrodakis briefs Vango on what he wants the young man to do.

"There are three telephone numbers here. Three addresses. Six names in all," says Mavrodakis, handing him the list. "Alinos and Phaedra Christidis, in Messinos; Peter Cornwell and Donald Christopherson, on the Vorastivi road between Anémenos and Pecravi; and Iakavos and Marika Lountzis, in the Pelamotís hills above Eressos. They were all at Douka last weekend. Dinner Saturday night. Apart from Mr Contalidis, the housekeeper and the two girls, Lina and Aja, they were the last people to see Madame Contalidis alive. Find out what you can. How she looked, how she sounded. Anything significant. The Lountzis and Christidis stayed over, the Englishmen went home. They're gay, so don't be put off, okay?"

Mavrodakis knows that, like most islanders, Vango is uncomfortable when it comes to homosexuals.

"And remember, the Contalidis boy, Dimi, was staying with the Lountzis when it happened," Mavrodakis continues. "He's not there now, back in Athens with his father, but be careful what you say if the Lountzis kid is around. Also, have a word with the two girls from Anémenos. Lina and Aja. Take them out for a drink, that sort of thing. Informal. The same kind of questions. You got all that?"

Vango is writing it all down. Finally he nods. "Got it, boss."

The following morning Mavrodakis dresses in a light blue shirt, a cream linen suit, packs an overnight bag and takes the early morning ferry to Tsania where a rental car is waiting for him.

He is about to begin the real business of investigation.

90

MAVRODAKIS knows his way around the city. He was born in a fourth-floor walk-up on Thiomidias, three blocks back from the rail yards of Larisis, and grew up with the sharp sooty smell of burnt coal in his nostrils. Went to primary school on the same street, and a fenced high school in Peristeri, followed by three years' officer training at the Hellenic Police Academy in the northern suburb of Acharnes.

When he arrives in Athens he makes his way to the house on Diomexédes, on the slopes below Lycabettus. Not to make a call, but to watch. The Contalidis property is a corner plot, a narrow three-floor home with a basement garage and a white perimeter wall high enough to conceal all but the crown of a fig tree.

Once he's identified the Contalidis home, Mavrodakis drives past and fifty metres further on makes a U-turn to take an empty parking space across the road from the house. He switches off his engine, reaches for a toothpick, and starts work on his teeth as the residents of Diomexédes go about their business. Nannies pushing prams, housewives laden with glossy shopping bags that don't contain groceries, lycra-clad joggers weaving between 4x4 BMWs and Mercedes two-door sportsters.

It is no more than a few kilometres from here to that old walk-up on Thiomidias, but it might as well be on the other side of the world, thinks Mavrodakis. This is a different kind of Athens to the one he knows. As a serving officer in the Athens police the only time he had come here, to the residential streets of Lycabettus, it had been to provide an escort for a visiting statesman who was staying at his embassy not three blocks from where Mavrodakis now sits. No rape, no murder, no gang problems, no drug dealing… not so much as an overflowing waste bin on streets like these. Nothing of the real world touched this one, and the ones around it.

For more than an hour, Mavrodakis sits there. Picking his teeth, smoking. Watching the house. Eventually, he gives up. He starts his engine, and pulls out of his space, back past the Contalidis house.

Time is short, and he has other addresses on his list.

If Diomexédes is a world away from the Athens he'd grown up in and policed, he is soon to discover that the homes of Iphy Stavrides, Chrysta Hadsopoulous, and Ana Doukakis, the last people that Electra Contalidis spoke to on her mobile, are no different.

Iphy Stavrides is pale and red-eyed when she opens her front door to Mavrodakis, leads him in to her sitting room, asks if he'd like coffee. He tells her no; he just wants to ask a few questions about her good friend, Electra

Contalidis. So she sits opposite him, the size of an elf, curling up on a sofa that improbably makes her appear even smaller than she is. It's like talking to a child, he thinks.

"It is the most horrible, horrible news. Poor, poor Electra. And Nikos is shattered."

"You've seen Mr Contalidis?"

"Last night. He's here in Athens, came to supper with Vassi. My husband. Nikos's partner in ConStav," she explains, with a sad, brave attempt at a smile. Mavrodakis hopes she doesn't cry. He finds crying difficult to handle. Blood and guts are fine, but tears…

"And how was he?"

"Very quiet. It was hard to get a word out of him. Just… untethered, you know?"

Untethered, thinks Mavrodakis? Like a mad dog? They even speak differently in this part of town.

"Mr Contalidis tells me that you knew his wife very well?"

"Oh, so, so well. Years. Before Nikos, actually."

"And I understand it was a happy, successful marriage?" Mavrodakis understands no such thing, but it is a way forward.

Iphy Stavrides chuckles. "Like oil and water. An islander, an Athenian. History and money. But it worked. It shouldn't have done, but it did. Who would have thought?"

"And Madame Contalidis's breakdown? How did that work?"

"Oh, it was hard. For both of them, of course. Nikos and Electra had tried for ages for a second child. There had been miscarriages, problems. And then, out of the blue, she was going to be a mother again. They were both so thrilled. Like newly-weds. We all were. So, when it didn't work out, right at the end, well… It was very difficult. In no time at all, Electra went down. Down, down, down. Stayed in her room, drank. And then it got so bad that on their doctor's recommendation she was moved to the Aetolikou. It's a special clinic just outside Athens. Very good. The best."

"And Douka? It seems strange that they should move there so soon after the breakdown?"

"Maybe, but Nikos decided it would be good for her. And the doctors agreed."

And then she pauses, gives a worrying little frown. "But why all these questions, Captain? I mean, is this what happens after a suicide? What the police do?"

Mavrodakis has been waiting for this, and he has his answer.

"It is simply procedure, Madam. In cases like these, it is necessary to establish either suicide or, possibly, accidental death. For the documentation, for the hearing, you understand?" It is a line he will repeat many times over the next few days.

Iphy Stavrides nods, uncertainly.

"So what do you think, Madam?"

She frowns again, as though she's lost the thread.

"Accident or suicide?" Mavrodakis prompts.

"Well," she says, casting around, as though not happy to speculate. "Both are so horrible. Dreadful. But it must have been an accident. I mean I never, for a single moment, even at her lowest ebb, felt dear Electra was suicidal. And drowning herself? I can't even imagine how you might go about it. Such a… just so… difficult. And she was so thrilled with the house, so proud of it; and excited by her book, too. She was recovering, getting better, I'm sure of it. And there was Dimi, of course. She was devoted. She would never have done anything to harm, or hurt, or upset Dimi."

"Did you know she took drugs? Marijuana."

The question, the change of tack, takes Iphy Stavrides by surprise, and for a moment she doesn't know how to answer. It's clear she knows that Electra did smoke dope, and probably smokes it herself, thinks Mavrodakis, but she is also keen not to implicate herself. "Well, Captain. I don't know what to say. It's possible, but I'm sure I wouldn't know."

"You visited them, I understand. At Douka."

"Just the once, when they moved in. After the work was finished."

"And how was your stay there?"

Iphy Stavrides shakes her head. She looks suddenly uncomfortable, and Mavrodakis notes it. "Did Nikos tell you anything about it?" she asks.

"Just that you stayed. You, and your husband. The last time you saw Madame Contalidis, I believe."

"Yes, it was. And just the most terrible time. I was so horribly sick, you can't imagine." She chuckles lightly as though to dismiss it, to make it less than it was.

"Something you ate?"

She shakes her head. "No, no, not at all. Although, you know, that is the first thing you think. But this was something different. It was after we had all gone to bed, and I remember waking up an hour or so later and feeling… I don't know… This great weight on my chest. As if I was suffocating. And then… Well, I just couldn't stop myself. No time to reach the bathroom. Oh, it was just dreadful. And I eat like a bird. I mean, look at me. But I just couldn't stop. On, and on. Oh my, what a night it was. I really did think I was going to die."

"Did you like the house?" Mavrodakis is not altogether sure why he asks. But it seems a reasonable question, given what Vango had said.

She thinks about this. "As I said, it's a marvellous conversion. Really, something to see. And so ConStav. The same style, the same touch… And Electra worked so hard to make it perfect, you wouldn't believe. Which was good for her. Took her mind off things."

"But did you like it?"

She sighs. “Personally? To be honest, Captain; no, I didn’t. I mean, it’s beautiful to look at, and just divinely redone – such taste, such style. But… there was something not quite right about the place. I was glad to be out of there, to tell you the truth. I don’t think I could have stayed another night. And I didn’t.”

91

CHRYSTA Hadsopoulous is on her mobile when she opens her apartment door, glances at the badge Police-Captain Mavrodakis presents, and indicates that he should come in, make himself at home. He had called her after leaving Iphy Stavrides, and she had told him that she was off to a Book Fair in Milan that very evening but could spare him ten minutes if he could get to her without delay.

Which he has done.

While Miss Hadsopoulous continues with her call, to a publisher about proper accounting, circling a finger in the air as though she couldn't wind the conversation up soon enough, Mavrodakis has time to take in his surroundings. A fifth-floor balconied apartment maybe ten minutes' drive from Diomexédes. Horribly untidy, scattered with books and manuscripts wherever he looks; the dining-room table loaded with even more paperwork, and little else apart from empty cartons for pizza and Chinese take-aways. It is more an office than a home, but the view of a three-quarter profile Parthenon, a glaring columned white over a stepped slope of tilting rooftops, makes up for any lack of comfort or homeliness. But like so many things, he thinks, so much better from a distance.

"Jesus, you wouldn't believe what those publishers try to get away with," she says, when the call is finally terminated, tossing the mobile onto a sofa and then plumping down beside it, immediately seeking it out; something to hold. Like a child with a comforter, thinks Mavrodakis. A literary agent… they must be married to the phone, he supposes.

And Chrysta Hadsopoulous certainly suits his idea of an agent.

There's a flinty aggression about her. Sharp features, no make-up, and a knotted mess of blonde hair that shows dark roots. And her clothes are more about comfort than style. A pair of baggy blue shorts that do nothing for her legs, in need of a shave and mottled with tiny bruises, and an oversized tie-dyed t-shirt that exposes a slope of freckled shoulder. That's it. And barefoot, the nail varnish a little chipped. Scraggy, he thinks.

"And writers aren't much better," she continues. "They both lie with such astonishing abandon. Because the publisher's mislaid a payment, or the author's missed a deadline… whatever. No one should ever believe a fucking word either ever says."

"And your role?" says Mavrodakis, to keep the conversation going the way it is. Relaxed or rushed are good. When people tend to say things without thinking.

"Easy! Make the publisher find that fucking payment, and make the author hit that fucking deadline."

"And how was Electra Contalidis?"

"Scatty as shit. But she's a Stamatos, so does she care?" Miss Hadsopoulous runs fingers through her hair, and grits her teeth. "And now she's fucking died! Can you believe it? I mean, really… I'm sorry and all, but what the fuck?"

"Was she a good writer?"

"Not a natural. She had to work at it. Took herself a bit too seriously. I mean, she's writing history, okay, but it's not a fucking textbook for school kids; you've got to juice it up a bit if you want to sell big in the grown-up market… And she couldn't quite get a handle on that. Oh, and very needy. Did I say? But no surprise there. They all are, writers." She picks up her phone and waves it around, "'*Oh, my darling, the book is just so good. I love it. You're so brilliant. They're going to go mad for it, I promise.*' Believe me, it's just so *fucking* exhausting. I say bestseller about as many times a day as I say fuck!"

"Is her book finished?" Mavrodakis remembers the laptop on her desk. Title, by-line. Four hundred pages.

"She promised me she'd have it done this month. So if she hasn't finished… well, that's it. Advance repayable; and commission, too, if I know Massalia Press!"

"When did you see her last? Here, or at Douka?"

"Douka. End of June? July? I stayed a couple of days to take a look at the manuscript, and then hightailed it back here. Island life is not for me. Don't know how she did it."

Mavrodakis knows he doesn't have to say anything. He just frowns and tips his head.

Chrysta Hadsopoulous takes her cue. "Well, she's a city girl, right? I mean, Pelatea isn't Santorini and it sure as hell isn't Mykonos. Pretty, sure. But, oh lordy, so fucking dull, dull, *dull*! She took me on this expediton while I was there, to some ancient sanctuary or other. Just a pile of old stones, and not a single one standing; sent me trudging round these caves. God, the things I have to do. And it's not like Nikos was going to light up her life. I mean, good-looking guy, I'll give him that. And, okay, he's lasting well… But sometimes, Jesus, she must have felt like sticking a knife in him. I certainly would've."

Another frown from Mavrodakis, another tip of the head.

"Look, for all Electra's faults, God bless her, for all her needines, she was a clever girl. Bright and sharp and sassy. There are stories out there, I can tell you. When she was single. Left a trail of bloodied corpses, she did. But Nikos? Okay, a good family, sure. Lots of big deal history there. But brains are in short supply. Good at the drawing board, some great ideas, architect stuff. But off the construction site, away from the screen, there isn't much there. If he picks up a book it had better have pictures, if you know what I mean?" She cocks an eyebrow at Mavrodakis. "I've met him a couple of times, and that's all that's registered. Charm and looks. If it hadn't been for the boy, Dimi, they'd never have lasted. Believe me. But enough for her to commit suicide? Nah! You ask me, she drank a little too much, smoked too much weed, and just… took a tumble. God-*fucking*-dammit!"

92

AFTER TWO bottles of chilled Fix beer and a pricey plate of late-lunch *mezes* in a bar in Kolonaki, Mavrodakis makes his way to the home of Ana and Ilias Doukakis. A large two-floor belle-époque mansion in a single line of such houses, just eight in the block. Standing in their own walled and lawned enclosures, with their backs turned to the high rises of Kolonaki and just a narrow tree-shaded avenue separating them from a slope of parkland.

A maid in starched white apron and black dress opens the front door and shows him to a sitting room. Madame Doukakis will not be long, she tells him. The room is large, with a marble fireplace filled with flowers and flanked with breakfront bookcases, a line of French windows leading to a shaded terrace, and the two remaining walls hung with an extraordinary collection of modern art – daubs of oily colour, squares and triangles, pill-sized and plate-sized dots. Not the kind of room to come to with a hangover, thinks Mavrodakis, making himself comfortable on a long leather sofa, the coffee table in front of him nothing less than a length of riveted airplane wing. Stacked with financial publications at one end, and Taschen design books at the other.

"I'm so sorry to keep you waiting," comes a honeyed, apologetic voice from behind him.

Mavrodakis heaves himself to his feet, turns, and sees a woman in pleated white tennis skirt, low-cut white t-shirt, and trainers, coming towards him, reaching out her hand. Her legs and arms are long and tanned and muscular, the straight-cut edges of her black hair swishing as she walks. A walk, Mavrodakis notes, that sets up a complimentary movement in the open top of her t-shirt, her breasts like two bald heads trapped in white cotton and jostling for attention. To see her play tennis, Mavrodakis decides, taking her dry, cool hand, must be a most distracting pastime. She is a good deal taller than him, and he suddenly feels small and grubby.

Maybe she senses his discomfort, for she gives a little gasp as she releases his hand. "But oh my, Captain, what lovely, lovely eyes you have. Mine are contacts, of course, but yours are just the real thing. I can tell. So blue, so gentle. Are you really a policeman? Tah! You can't be, surely not?"

Mavrodakis is instantly disarmed, a puppy in her lap. Under that delicious overhang. Get a grip, Mavrodakis. Get a grip, he thinks to himself.

Madame Doukakis pulls off her wristbands and tosses them onto the airplane wing, drops onto the sofa and crosses her legs with an easy, teasing languor, adjusting the pleats of her skirt to lie enticingly at mid-thigh. She is radiantly, alluringly sexy. And as he takes her in, all those lithe lines and pulsing curves, the tight skin and plump lips, the fresh tanned bloom of her, Mavrodakis knows she knows it. To fuck this woman, he thinks, would be a dream. And he knows she knows he thinks it.

"So," she begins, patting the sofa beside her. "How can I help, Captain Blue Eyes? What do you want to know?"

For the third time that day, Mavrodakis explains the need to establish cause of death. Accident or suicide. Just a few routine questions. Procedure.

"Call me Ana," she says.

"So, er, Ana, I understand that you have known Madame Contalidis for some time?"

"Tah! She was the dearest friend," Ana replies, smoothing the fingertips of one hand over the top of a thigh, the other hand playing with a strand of hair. "School, university… way back! We were like sisters. Sidekicks. Gunslingers, the pair of us. What we didn't do together… Tah!"

The 'Tah' is like a kind of spit, Mavrodakis thinks. A short exclamatory gust of breath through the teeth. He's never heard anything like it before.

"But it has to be an accident," she continues. "Maybe a little too much to drink. She does like her wine, does Ella. I mean, she did. Or maybe," with a twinkle in her eye, "a little too much to smoke – if you know what I mean?"

And then, leaning forward, the bald heads colliding and jostling with a joyous and mesmerising motion, "But how is poor Nikos bearing up?" she asks. "He called the other day, the day it happened, told me the news. He sounded quite… forlorn." Ana gives the word a certain emphasis which makes Mavrodakis sit up. *Forlorn*? "Of course, it must have been a terrible shock, poor darling, but, well…"

"Well…?"

"Well, what I mean is, it's not exactly the end of the world, is it? A darling girl, of course, and I was quite devastated when I heard, and we'll all miss her dreadfully. But really, Nikos… well, let's not feel too sorry for him; I mean, when the dust has settled he's not going to suffer too much, is he?"

Not even the bursting swell of another pair of matching bald heads lining up beside Ana's would be enough to dilute Mavrodakis's astonishment at what sounds like it might be the casual disclosure of some significant fact he has so far not been aware of.

And Ana, seeing his puzzled expression, needs no encouragement.

"Well, I'm sure you know that Ella's the one in charge. She's the one with all the aces. Or rather, she was."

"The aces?"

"Well, Douka, for starters."

Mavrodakis frowns, scratches his beard.

"You didn't know? Tah! The whole kit and caboodle. That's how Nikos bought it. Stamatos money. It might be his ancestral home," she continues, with what sounds like mild disdain, the accent firmly on 'ancestral'. "But the place is hers. Ella's. Outright. Just her name on the deeds. Same with

Diomexédes. Though I guess that won't apply now, if you know what I mean? Both places will surely be his. Free and clear. Unless, of course, her mother has something to say about it. Or the Stamatos board. I mean, if Ella didn't actually leave them to Nikos in her will, he'll probably have to come to some arrangement if he wants to keep them. The Stamatos don't mess when it comes to their kids or their money. Believe me, I know.

"And it's not just Doulia and Diomexédes," Ana continues, as if she's on a roll, enjoying the sound of her own voice. "I remember a few years back, darling Ella mentioning that Nikos's company, this ConStav outfit, was having problems – cashflow, tah! So like dutiful wifey, she persuades Daddy to stump up some cash to see Nikos through. But Daddy's like Ella… I mean, a smart operator… only more so. So she gets a slice of ConStav too, doesn't she? I mean, didn't she? Which means, it's probably all back in his name now."

And then Ana pauses, as though she has suddenly, dramatically, realised what she's been saying. And how it might be taken, by a policeman, investigating her best friend's death.

"But heavens, would you just listen to me?" she says. "You'd think I'm accusing the poor man of murder the way I'm going on. You really must stop me, Captain. I was getting carried away."

As if Mavrodakis has any intention of stopping this woman's busy chatter.

"Well, see," begins Ana, warm and confiding again, leaning forward, cleavage swelling, fingertips reaching out to Mavrodakis's knee, but not touching. "Let's be honest here. Straight talk. I don't think old man Stamatos thought too much of Nikos. Probably reckoned his daughter could have done a whole lot better – which she could have, believe it. When she started up with Nikos, she was in real deep with that young senator chap, whatsisname? You know the one? Looked like a young Warren Beatty." She shakes her head. As though she can't quite remember the name, or it's a name not worth bothering about. Which for Mavrodakis is good, because he doesn't want Ana to get sidetracked. Now that she's started on Nikos, that's where he wants to keep it. Her tittle-tattle airhead gossip is nothing less than an investigating officer's dream. In every sense.

Just keep her going, he thinks. Get as much as you can. But softly, gently.

"So you don't think her father liked…?"

"Mikis? Not one bit," Ana interrupts, as though there is no need for Mavrodakis to ask such a question. Any question. It's as if she knows what he wants to ask before he's asked it, and she's only too happy to provide an answer. Gossip heaven, and with no tricky comeback. *But he was a policeman*, he can hear her saying. *I had to tell him everything, didn't I?*

Once again a frown is enough to spur her on.

"I mean," Ana takes a breath, continues, *sotto voce*. "When you've got as much as they have, the Stamatos clan, well you don't do that to a son-in-law, do you? Lend money on condition. Waivers and guarantees, all that sort of thing. Or maybe you do? Maybe they just didn't trust him."

"Do you?"

Ana gives a wince. As if Mavrodakis has touched a nerve. "Well, I do, and I don't. He is a bit of an outsider, you see. Not quite one of us, not really one of the gang. I mean, we've all known each other since we were knee-high, haven't we? And then along comes Nikos. So it can't have been easy for him, poor darling. Ella's family, for starters; like I said, Gina and Mikis were not the easiest people. And then, having to put up with us lot, too. Our little gang. And on top of it all, Ella getting so ill.

"But, well…" This time she hesitates, runs a thumb over her lacquered nails. "I don't like to bring this up, and it was a lot for him to deal with, but he did hit her once, didn't he?" As if Mavrodakis already knows this. "Once that I know about. Maybe there were other times, who can say?"

Mavrodakis stiffens. On high alert. But doesn't show it.

"But that's Nikos, for you. Island boy, in the big city. I suppose it's the way people like him deal with problems. They lash out."

"Do you know why he hit her? Did Madame Contalidis say?"

Ana waves a hand as though, on reflection, it's of no importance. "It was when she was ill, so, if you put it into that kind of context, maybe you could say it was… understandable. Excusable. I mean, poor Electra was dreadfully, dreadfully ill. And quite impossible to deal with, believe me. Getting paralytic, shouting, screaming, losing her temper all the time. And Dimi around, seeing it all. I suppose Nikos just snapped. But this was before she went to that clinic, so things obviously got a whole lot better when the treatment was over. Not that it was immediately obvious, mind you. But by then I'd say that Nikos wasn't too bothered, and had other things on his mind, some… extra-curricular distraction. I mean, Nikos isn't the idle type. Never was, either."

"Distraction?"

Ana gives him a look. "Well, you've met him, you know. Islander or not, he's a very good-looking man. And still looking good for his age. And Ella has… had been in such bad shape. So thin, so gaunt, so… distant." This last word comes with a sigh, but still carries the same kind of weighted attention and emphasis as 'forlorn' and 'ancestral'.

"Distant?" Mavrodakis rather likes these one-word questions. No need for much more. Just a touch of the spur to the flanks, and off the mare goes.

"Well, I'm sure I don't have to spell it out, Captain, but a man like Nikos – any man really – does need some fun in his life. If you know what I mean? And since the baby, he has had a very bad time of it. Not getting the kind of attention he needs." Ana gives Mavrodakis, Captain Blue Eyes, a very direct look, as though to make the point that she has said something very significant, and that she hopes he is paying attention, and is eager to hear more. "I mean, they talk about the seven-year-itch, you know. Like the film?

But like, sometimes the itch is just always there with some guys. It's, like, not just seven years. Could be seven days. Months. Who knows?"

Mavrodakis simply raises his eyebrows. Even this is enough.

"Well, let's face it, let's cut to the chase here. Nikos is a naughty boy. I mean, he's a man with his eye on the main chance. And I'm not just talking business here. On the look-out, if you know what I mean? And it's worth bearing in mind that before Ella he wasn't exactly a hang-back in coming forward." She chuckles, waves a hand. "So naughty. Even tried it on with me, would you believe? Tah! The nerve."

"He has girlfriends?"

"Well, one that I know about. There could be others, of course."

"You know her?"

"Seen her. Outside a restaurant in Vouliagmeni. Ilias and I were looking at some property around there…"

"And you saw the two of them together?" Mavrodakis doesn't want Ana moving off course by starting on about property. He wants the conversation to stay on Nikos. And this girlfriend.

"In his car, would you believe? The two of them, like snakes. All over each other. I couldn't believe it."

"And when was this?"

Ana shrugs, spreads her hands, dramatically enough to make the bald heads wobble.

But Mavrodakis isn't looking. He's listening.

"Let's see…" says Ana. "A month ago, I guess. Give or take. I was going to mention it to Ella but, you know, it was difficult. And it wasn't really my place…"

There's a spring in Mavrodakis's step as he heads to the underground parking lot where he's left his car.

Douka! ConStav! The girlfriend!

It changes everything. Or rather, it adds some considerable weight to the doubts that Mavrodakis has had after going to Douka, seeing the body, taking in the scene, and speaking to Contalidis.

He must find out who their lawyer is. See if he can take a look at the will. Or get some idea from the lawyer how Madame Contalidis's assets are to be dispersed. As surviving spouse, and the father of their child, it seems likely, as Ana Doukakis has suggested, that Nikos Contalidis will find himself well compensated for his wife's unfortunate demise. Her suicide. Or accident. If that is what it was?

As he turns out of the parking lot and joins traffic on Eximiou Street, Mavrodakis feels a pulse of excitement start up.

Just a hunch, at first. All those years ago.

But now… Now, maybe more.

At the first set of traffic lights, he pulls into the right-hand lane, waits for the green, and then heads back to Diomexédes

.

93

NIKOS CONTALIDIS has yet to show himself.

For more than an hour that morning, Mavrodakis had sat in his car and waited. And not a sign of the man. No suggestion that there was even anyone in the house. And after another hour sitting in his car following his meeting with Ana Doukakis, in almost the same spot he'd occupied that morning, there is still no indication that Contalidis will make an appearance.

Which is starting to frustrate Police-Captain Mavrodakis.

There is, as he knows only too well, a great deal at stake.

On a hunch. Not even that.

Just a grudge, really. Personal. His dislike of Contalidis.

And suspicion, of course.

Certainly not enough, by a long shot, for the detailed – and costly – forensic report he'd requested from Athens following what was, at first sight, nothing more than an accident, or a suicide.

Which had been pointed out by that officer in Budget Control. Was such an exhaustive high-priority forensic analysis really necessary, he'd asked? Were there any serious or reasonable grounds for such a request?

To which Mavrodakis had replied that, given the deceased was a Stamatos, it might be advisable for the Judiciary, and all those involved in the investigation, to make every attempt to cover every conceivable angle. So as not to provide any opening for possible legal recourse from one of the wealthiest families in the country if something was later found to be amiss. Or found lacking in their investigation.

And Mavrodakis would not be found lacking.

Not with the Contalidis.

Then, suddenly, there he is. Nikos Contalidis. Opening the front door, turning and bending down to talk to his son. The boy is standing in the doorway with a young woman who must be a nanny or babysitter. Contalidis kisses the boy's head, and then stands and says something to the woman, a girl really. With a wave, he trots down the steps and starts walking in Mavrodakis's direction.

Contalidis is no more than ten metres away from Mavrodakis, and is sure to recognize him if he comes any closer, when he stops, pulls a set of keys from his pocket and beeps the locks on a blue BMW just two cars away. With a glance up and down Diomexédes, he opens the door and climbs into the driver's seat, pulling the door closed behind him.

Sliding down in his seat in case Contalidis catches a glimpse of him in his rear-view mirror, Mavrodakis watches him pull out from the kerb and into the evening traffic. When he is a safe distance ahead, Mavrodakis does the same, making sure to keep four or five cars between them as Contalidis turns left out of Diomexédes and heads down into Kolonaki, skirting Syntagma to turn onto Mitropoleos. It is a little after seven and the worst of the rush-hour traffic is over. But it is still a slow, stop-start journey as Mavrodakis follows Contalidis through Monastiraki, swinging down past the Agora and Temple of the Winds where the traffic starts to thin and Mavrodakis is forced to drop back even further to avoid being seen. Just a few hundred metres further on, he sees Contalidis indicate to the right, and turn into Iraklidon. Boldly, Mavrodakis follows, passing the BMW as Contalidis reverses into a parking bay, before finding his own space just thirty metres on.

Staying in his car, he watches Contalidis climb out of the BMW, lock it, cross the road, and head up a side street. He waits until Contalidis is out of sight, then clambers out of his rental and hurries after him. Stopping at the corner and peeking round.

Contalidis is opening the glass door to an apartment block half way up the street, and in a moment is gone.

Mavrodakis hurries after him, slowing as he reaches the door, then strides purposefully past as though in a hurry to be somewhere. Fast enough not to be noticed or recognised if Contalidis happens to look back at the street, but slowly enough that a glance tells him what he wants to know. There is no one in the hallway. The only thing moving is the arrow indicating floor numbers above the lift doors. It stops on four.

Crossing the road Mavrodakis ducks into a shop doorway and looks up at the front of the building opposite. The fourth floor. A line of seven windows. Three windows on one side of a longer latticed landing window, three on the other. So, two apartments, and possibly two more at the back, looking over a courtyard or lightwell. But no way to tell which one Contalidis is in. Or whom he's visiting. No lights on yet; no movement behind the windows.

It has to be the girlfriend, Mavrodakis decides.

Because he wants it to be the girlfriend, needs it to be the girlfriend. The one Ana Doukakis saw him with in Vouliagmeni. Although, he concedes, it could as easily be an old friend Contalidis is visiting; someone to talk to following the loss of his wife; seeking solace, sharing his sorrow – yeah, right, thinks Mavrodakis, determined to keep a positive spin on it. Or a supper party, maybe, like the one he'd had with the Stavrides. It could be either of these, or any number of other possibilities. But Mavrodakis keeps coming back to a girlfriend.

Wanting it to be the girlfriend. Needing it to be her.

And if it is the girlfriend, whoever she is, she isn't poor. Mavrodakis knows this area. Rents for apartments like these may not be high by Kolonaki standards, but they won't be low either. So it seems fair to assume that the girl has a reasonably well-paid job.

Or maybe she's been provided with the apartment for services rendered?

By Contalidis? By other men?

Girlfriend, or mistress, or working girl?

Mavrodakis favours the former. Wants it to be the former.

After twenty minutes in the shop doorway, with not a twitch of a blind or a light being switched on, Mavrodakis returns to his car on Iraklidon and drives it round the block, coming into the side-street from the top end. Parking close enough to the doorway to keep an eye on it, but far enough away not to be seen when Contalidis comes out.

Opening his window, making himself comfortable, Mavrodakis settles down to watch; sees people walking up and down the street, passing the apartment block; some of them going in, and others coming out.

But no sign of Contalidis.

At midnight, after strolling past the apartment block a couple of times, as much to keep himself awake as to try to see into the fourth-floor apartment windows – which are now lit, but going off one by one – Mavrodakis decides to call it a day. He'll return to his hotel, set the alarm for five, and be back here by six the following morning.

94

IT IS COOL and light and quiet when Mavrodakis turns into Iraklidon the next morning.

And the first thing he sees – to his delight – is the Contalidis BMW.

The man has obviously stayed the night, and hasn't yet left the building. Five minutes later, Mavrodakis parks in exactly the same spot he'd left the night before, and once again he settles down to wait, breakfasting on a warm Danish pastry and Starbucks *macchiato*.

He doesn't wait long. By the time he's finished his coffee and Danish, licking his sticky fingertips one by one, and brushing out his beard, checking in the visor mirror for crumbs he might have missed, he sees the apartment block door open for the fourth time since his arrival. But this time it's not some unknown resident – three men in suits so far, heading off to work, and two elderly ladies. It is Contalidis himself, pausing on the doorstep to keep the door open for… a young woman. Nearly as tall as Contalidis, with a bundle of auburn curls held in check and drawn off her face by a bright blue bandanna. She is wearing a billowing blue Hawaiian shirt, black jeans and black espadrilles, and carries a large canvas tote over her shoulder. And if there was any possibility that Contalidis was being gallant for someone coming out behind him, holding the door for them, it is put out of question when he links his arm through her's, and gives her a peck on the cheek, before setting off down the street with her.

Mavrodakis is almost breathless with excitement. He was right. Not a friend to commiserate with; not a dinner party. Something else entirely; exactly what Mavrodakis had been hoping for. Contalidis was visiting a woman, and he'd stayed overnight. He's also wearing a white shirt – the day before it had been blue. So it's clear he keeps a change of clothes in the woman's apartment.

And though it's difficult to be absolutely certain, Mavrodakis has known enough hookers and mistresses in his time on the beat to know that the woman on Contalidis's arm is not one of their number. There is a youth and a freshness to her; a happy swing to her step. And when Mavrodakis sees the way she rests her head against Contalidis's shoulder as they walk, he can tell that this is a woman in love.

There can be no doubt.

All Mavrodakis wants now is to find out who she is.

And everything there is to know about her.

Twenty minutes later Mavrodakis has established that whoever the girlfriend is, she has a job.

A few minutes after Contalidis drops her off with a kiss and hug outside an office block on Panagiotis, Mavrodakis spots her through the floor-to-ceiling windows of a second-floor office space. Dumping her tote, settling herself at a desk and computer screen, then waving across the room at someone, saying hello.

The advantage Mavrodakis has now is that this young woman doesn't know who he is. He can get up as close as he likes – stand behind her in a queue, sit at the next table in a restaurant or coffee shop or bar, ask her for directions even – without fear of being recognized, or arousing suspicion.

So after Contalidis drives away, back to Diomexédes or the ConStav offices in Pangrati, Mavrodakis parks his rental and gets to work. It doesn't take long to find out what he needs to know.

In the office block's reception area he reads the floor-plan directory displayed on a framed board between the twin lifts.

Six floors. Nine company names. And on the second-floor, just one name. Art-Amiss Publications, with *Arki-Tek* Magazine in brackets. The name means nothing to him, but it doesn't take him long to link it with Nikos, and ConStav. *Arki-Tek*… Architect. Architecture.

Such an obvious way for the pair of them to meet. And she'll be a journalist, rather than a secretary, Mavrodakis decides. The way she dresses, the way she sits at her desk, chatting with colleagues, it's clear that she feels at home in her surroundings, that she enjoys a certain position – and it's not typing out other people's letters, or answering phones for them.

So he knows where she lives, he knows where she works, and he knows what she does.

All he needs now is a name.

So easy.

"A young woman with a blue Hawaiian-style shirt," he says at the reception desk, holding a piece of paper in his hand. He's scrawled a car registration number on it, and a made-up telephone number. "She dropped this outside. She came in a few minutes ago. She was wearing jeans, I think."

The receptionist looks perplexed. Maybe she's new, thinks Mavrodakis.

"I know who you mean, but…" She turns to the girl beside her, and repeats the description.

"That'll be Cossie. Costanza Theofilou. *Arki-Tek*, up on the Second," she says, and reaching out a hand for the piece of paper she asks Mavrodakis, "Do you want me to give it to her?"

"If you would," he replies, handing it over. He shrugs. "It may be important, you never know." And then he smiles, and takes his leave.

Not bad for twenty minutes work, he thinks, getting back in his car to wait for the next sighting.

Enough to be getting on with.

Costanza 'Cossie' Theofilou. 22 Efestiou Street, Thiseio. Twenty-nine, thirty… thereabouts. A journalist.

Mavrodakis has drunk two cups of coffee, eaten a muffin, and smoked three cigarettes before he sees Cossie Theofilou again, coming out of the building with his scrap of paper in her hand. She stops, reads it, then crumples it up and drops it in a bin. A moment later she squeezes between two cars and flags down a cab. He breathes a sigh of relief. The taxi's pointing in the same direction as he is; a U-turn on this particular street would have been a nightmare. All he has to do is find a gap in the traffic and follow the cab. Which he does.

Ten minutes later the taxi pulls up outside a narrow nineteenth-century townhouse on the upper slope of Praxiteles. Theofilou gets out, pays off the cabbie, and at the top of a flight of steps she presses a bell, waits a few moments, and then is buzzed in.

Not bothering to park, Mavrodakis cruises down to the building; brakes, leans over to read the brass plate on the door, and drives on.

It takes him a moment to register what he has seen, but then his heart starts racing.

It can't be. But it is. It must be.

Why else would a young woman like Cossie Theofilou make an appointment with Doctor Charis Kalatzakis?

An obstetrician.

Because she's pregnant.

Pregnant.

95

MAVRODAKIS spends three more days in Athens.

He speaks to a few other friends of Electra Contalidis whose names he had found on her mobile and in her address book. He goes to the Lycabettus Clinic where she lost her baby, and he speaks to her doctor at the Aetolikou where she was treated after her breakdown. He doesn't learn much more than he already knows, and the doctors and medical staff who looked after her are as evasive and unforthcoming as he'd expected them to be.

But what he does begin to understand by the end of his time in the city is that this poor woman, Electra Contalidis, was as good as lost. No matter how hard she tried to recover, no matter what drugs she was prescribed and took, whatever recovery methods were recommended, what care she received, Mavrodakis cannot help but believe that her life was effectively over when she left the city for Pelatea. As far as he can see it, she was simply a woman who had, ultimately, been unable to cope with her loss and its consequences.

And it was that inability of hers to effect any change or improvement that led to her death.

Like Petrou, it had just been a matter of time.

But not a suicide. Not an accident.

Like Petrou, it was murder.

Of that Mavrodakis is increasingly certain.

When time allows during those remaining days in the city Mavrodakis follows Contalidis and his lover, Cossie Theofilou. He waits outside their offices, he follows them through city traffic, and he watches them in bars and in restaurants; talking, holding hands, the pair of them wondering what the future holds. What they will do, now that Contalidis is a free man?

And all the time Mavrodakis wonders if Contalidis knows about the pregnancy. It doesn't show yet, but…

Has she told him? Maybe she hasn't?

Indeed, is it even his?

After all, she'd gone to that obstetrician on Praxiteles by herself…

But then he chides himself. Of course he knows, and of course it's his baby.

If she was keeping the pregnancy secret – because it was someone else's child, or because she didn't want him to know – well, she wouldn't look half so happy, so contented. Blooming. A belief confirmed his last evening in Athens before returning to Pelatea; at Restaurant Vrasidia in Piraeus, where he sees Contalidis put a hand on her belly, look at her in wonder, lean forward and kiss her.

And though they don't know it yet, only Mavrodakis, and the autopsy and forensic reports, stand in their way; cast a shadow on their hopes and plans for the future.

Because, if a crime has been committed, he, Mavrodakis, will make absolutely certain that the perpetrator, or perpetrators, feel the full weight of the law. Regardless of the consequences. The suffering and sadness it will cause. If, as he believes, it turns out to be Contalidis.

It is his job. His duty.

His chance to set the record straight.

And more than anything else, more than any other consideration, he owes it to the woman whose broken bundle of a body blocked a filtration duct in the swimming pool at Douka.

96

BACK IN Navros, Mavrodakis puts his feet on his desk as Police-Lieutenant Evangelos Tsavalas briefs him on the results of his investigation on Pelatea. While Mavrodakis has been in Athens, Vango has been following up the contacts his boss had given him.

"According to Phaedra Christidis, Madame Contalidis could be difficult. They've known each other for years, she told me, since Nikos married her, but she only ever felt really comfortable when Nikos was around."

"Difficult?"

"Icy, was what Madame Christidis said. They might meet up by chance here in town, or at a drinks party, or dinner, or something like that. All very friendly. But Madame Christidis never liked to phone her, socially, or just call in at Douka unannounced. Or in Athens. Her husband, Alinos Christidis, who I visited at his dental practice in Messinos, said the same. Nikos was their friend; Electra was just his wife. I got the feeling she was… tolerated. Not much liked."

"What about the Lountzis?"

"They were both at home when I visited. And both of them said much the same kind of thing. Nikos Contalidis, first. A great friend. But neither of them was as enthusiastic about Madame Contalidis. According to Marika Lountzis," Vango checks his notebook, "Madame Contalidis drank too much, and was always popping her pills. Like Chiclets, she said! Actually saw her tossing back a handful at her son's birthday party, which she didn't like at all. But not one of them – the Christidis, or the Lountzis – thought it was suicide. An accident, they said. Had to be. Because of the drinking, the pills. Sometimes they'd see her actually swaying, really unsteady on her feet… Too thin to take all that wine, was what Madame Lountzis said."

Mavrodakis isn't surprised to hear any of this. Not so much the actual information, so diligently recorded by Vango in his notebook, but how these friends ranked Electra Contalidis in the Douka/Pelatea pecking order: Nikos first; Electra a distant second. But then the Christidis and Lountzis were islanders, so it made a kind of sense. The two men from Pelatea, old school friends of Contalidis; Phaedra Christidis from Santorini, and Marika Lountzis from Alonissos. Mavrodakis has checked.

"Anything else?"

"It may be nothing, but Madame Lountzis and Madame Christidis both said how devoted Mr Contalidis was to his wife, how caring he was, and patient, when she could be so difficult."

Mavrodakis grunts. "What about the two girls, Aja and Lina?"

"Like you suggested, I took them for a drink on my way back from Pecravi. Informal, like. Nice girls. It was fun."

"And?"

Vango shrugs. "Madame Contalidis was the boss, they said, more than Mr Contalidis, but they had a laugh now and then. Bit tight, and superior; more Athenian than islander, Lina told me. Distant, too. Like, staring off, wide-eyed a lot of the time. As if she was in a trance, you know, or day-dreaming? Not really there. And not much of the please and thank yous, either, they told me. Always blaming them for tidying her things away when they hadn't – phone, keys, TV remote, things like that – and when she found them, never saying sorry. A fitness freak, too, always running, they said. And she liked a drink. Lot of empties she hid away, and then forgot about."

"And how were your gay friends in Pecravi?" Mavrodakis asks.

Vango looks taken aback, startled – as though they're no such thing. Then he sees his boss's smile, and flushes.

"Mr Cornwall, and his friend…" Vango checks his notes. "…Donald Christopherson. Both agreed that Electra was an angel. Very talented. A wonderful, natural interior designer." And went on to report how the three of them had met during the Douka rebuild and become firm friends. "Here, and in Athens; meeting up, shopping, lunching. Any excuse."

Mavrodakis can see that Vango is actually reading this from his notes, and can only imagine what the interview must have been like. A long haul. Everything written down; not edited, not remembered. That third star on his boards would take a long time coming for Police-Lieutenant Tsavalos.

"And how did they find her, her state of mind, at the dinner?"

"They both agreed she seemed a little…" He checks his notes again. "…A little… over-wrought. Not her usual self. But they both said Mr Contalidis was very attentive."

"And what did they think of Contalidis?"

"I didn't get the impression they knew him quite so well. They'd see Madame Contalidis every time she came down during the rebuild, and most weeks after she moved in. But as soon as he was home, most weekends, she went off the radar."

"Did they know why this might be?"

"I think… I think Mr Contalidis might have been a little uncomfortable with them. Being the way they are. Like, he was happy for his wife to see them when he was in Athens, but he wasn't that keen on them himself. But that's just a guess… I mean, they didn't actually say that."

"You mean you didn't actually ask?"

Vango reddens. "No, boss. No, I didn't."

After Vango leaves his office, Mavrodakis keeps his boots on the desk, ankles crossed, and ruffles his fingers though his beard. It's the way he thinks best; tugging and stroking his beard, seeing just the sky through his window.

Putting the pieces in place.

Motive? Inheritance, boredom, a pregnant girlfriend. Probably insurance, too. He'd have Vango check that.

Opportunity? The lost hours after Contalidis left his office on Monday, and went home alone without his mobile.

And what of Cossie Theofilou? Mavrodakis wonders what she'd say, if he asked her about Contalidis's movements that Monday night? Did he stay with her? Did he visit? Would she provide the necessary alibi? Would she lie for her lover?

So many questions. So many possibilities.

But right now, before he can proceed any further, Mavrodakis needs to know how it was done. Method.

How Electra Contalidis was murdered.

Because she has been.

He is certain of it.

All he needs to do is establish the identity of her killer.

97

A FEW DAYS later Mavrodakis finally gets his hands on the documents he's been waiting for.

The Autopsy Report. Subject: *Electra Theia Contalidis*. Procedure carried out by State Pathologist Sokratis Ouzounidis, at the Epidemios Department of Specialised Pathology at the Athens Medical School.

The Forensics Report. Subject: *Assorted Contents of the Contalidis House, Douka, Pelatea*. Investigation supervised by Doctor Illias Coriakis of the Hellenic Institute of Advanced Forensic Sciences, Glyfada.

Mavrodakis picks up the Autopsy report first; flips through the early pages. Name, gender, age, race; body weight, colour of eyes, colour of hair; visible marks on the skin – birthmarks, bruises, abrasions; stomach contents; weight of organs, state of organs… lungs, liver, heart…

And finds what he's looking for.

Cause of death: Drowning. Pre-mortem/active. Asphyxia, with signs of generalized hypoxia. Presence of water in lungs and stomach, with bloody froth in mouth, nostrils, and upper and lower airways; indications of laryngospasm, mastoid haemorrhage and cerebral oedema, with attendant damage to pulmonary surfactant and alveolar linings, leading to consequent diatom release. Evidence of sodium hypochlorite in said water samples, suggesting presence of chlorine, indicating immersion in swimming pool.

And then…

Toxicology: High readings for alcohol (stomach, blood, liver), in addition to fatal levels of Heripsyn and Phaladrin in blood and tissue samples.

An overdose.

Mavrodakis squares his shoulders, lets out his breath.

Not just a drowning, but an overdose.

And an overdose, he is certain, that had not been self-administered. It will take a coroner's hearing to formally establish that fact, based on the evidence he is able to provide.

But in the meantime…

Mavrodakis puts aside the Autopsy findings, and reaches for the Forensic report. The expensive, high-priority forensic report. The one he had to fight for.

Twenty or more items bagged, taken from Douka, and sent for examination. From the kitchen, bedroom, bathroom, terrace, studio. With a formal request for the most detailed fingerprint analysis that Forensics can provide. The latest technology. Mass spectrometry, with gelatin strips rather than powder to isolate proteins; a full molecular break down. The works. Nothing left to chance.

Which is why it has taken so long for the results to come through.

More than thirty pages; photographs of each item, and the various findings.

The empty wine bottle is at the top of the list.

According to the report, a single set of prints, belonging to Madame Contalidis, cover the bottle from neck to base; consistent with opening and pouring; or, as Mavrodakis had suspected, with drinking straight from the bottle, since there had been no glass on the terrace table. A suspicion confirmed in the report, which identified a pale lipstick and the victim's DNA on the bottle top. There were also, more significantly, traces of Heripsyn and Phaladrin on the bottle's interior surface, and in the few drops of wine left in the bottom. Which matched the toxicology findings in the Autopsy report. Top of the range medication, the forensic report makes clear, stating that though the Heripsyn is the stronger of the two, Phaladrin is also a serious sedative. The same drugs that Mavrodakis had seen in Madame Contalidis's bathroom cabinet; the first prescribed by Doctor Fastiliades at the Aetolikou Clinic following a nervous breakdown, and the second by Fotis Paradoxis, who'd told him that he had warned Madame Contalidis that alcohol should be avoided.

Just what Mavrodakis had hoped for.

It is now plain to see.

Because if Electra Contalidis were intent on killing herself, why would she go to all the bother of grinding up the pills? If the drugs had come in capsule form, like the Tropsodol he had found in her bathroom cabinet, there would have been no need for it. But pills? Like the Heripsyn and Phaladrin? Having to grind them into a powder, and then delicately tip that powder into a bottle of wine. Why not just toss back a couple of handfuls, and wash them all down with a glug or two of Contalidis wine? That's what most potential suicides would do. The same number of pills. The same lethal dosage. It wouldn't have taken very long.

Which is what Doctor Fastiliades had told him at the Aetolikou in Lagonisi, estimating the approximate number of Heripsyn pills needed to carry out a successful suicide bid, given his patient's weight and her drinking; and how many of them Madame Contalidis was likely to have had, stockpiling aside, in her possession at the time of her death. A monthly prescription, Fastiliades had confirmed, delivered to the pharmacy in Navros. Picked up by Madame Contalidis, regular as clockwork. Thirty-one pills. Given the dates, easily twenty-five remaining if she was taking them as prescribed. Certainly enough, the doctor conceded, to do the job; though, of course, he had seen no evidence to suggest that Madame Contalidis was planning on taking her own life. She had been recovering, he was sure of it.

The last time he had seen her, shortly before moving to Pelatea, there were definite signs of recovery.

But Mavrodakis knew there weren't twenty-five pills left. There were only three, in the bottle he had seen in her bathroom cabinet; small, white, oval pills that had left a chalky residue on the inside of the bottle. And just a couple of the Phaladrin – smaller, round, and pink – when there should have been a dozen or more, according to Dr Paradoxis. Easily enough pills in her possession to do the job.

So, if Electra Contalidis didn't grind up the pills herself, and then pour the powder into that wine bottle – why would she? – then who did?

Clearly, thinks Mavrodakis, she'd had company that Monday night. Someone had visited; someone had called by unannounced. Mavrodakis can see it no other way. Someone who had ground the pills into powder, then tipped it into the bottle when she wasn't looking. A dark green wine bottle, and no glass, so there was no possibility of her noticing any evidence of the fatal addition – no powdery residue, no tell-tale bubbling or discolouration of the wine. And taste? Well, if there was any difference, she clearly didn't notice it. Or was in no condition to notice it.

So, who could have visited that Monday night?

For Mavrodakis, there is only one contender.

It has to be her husband. Mr Nikos Contalidis.

According to the housekeeper, Ariadne Papadavrou, Contalidis had used his own boat, a Riva, to return to Tsania that last Sunday evening. Seaworthy enough to make the trip between Douka and the mainland in anything but the worst kind of weather, with easily enough range to make it there and back if he chose to. Mavrodakis has checked. And, most important, to make such a trip without anyone knowing. All Contalidis had to do was moor down by the beach, and walk up to the house, while the port at Tsania was busy enough for any departure or return to go unnoticed, unrecorded.

Either he steals in, knowing Dimi is not there, and adds the ground-up pills to the bottle without Electra seeing him do it (a little far-fetched, thinks Mavrodakis). Or, far more credible, he makes himself known; bustles in bright and breezy. A surprise. And then, when the time is right, he grinds up the pills he's taken from the bathroom cabinet, tips the powder into the wine, and watches her drink it.

And when the pills take effect, he simply picks her up and slides her into the pool. Holding her under, maybe, to make sure of it. Which is possibly why she has the abrasions on her forehead. Maybe she comes to, realises what's happening, and tries to retaliate? To save herself. Scraping her head on the side of the pool as she does so. Or maybe, she staggers and falls or, when he picks her up, he catches her head on the table or a chair?

Equally, he could have seen her start in on the wine, and then left her to it. It wouldn't have taken her long to finish the bottle, or for the drugs to take effect. Half a bottle would probably have done it. That she should end up in the pool and drown was neither here nor there. For Contalidis, it wouldn't matter where his wife's body was found.

An overdose. A deadly mix of drugs and alcohol. Suicide. That's what everyone would say. His wife was unstable, had had enough, had decided to end it.

But for Mavrodakis there is now only one certainty.

Electra Contalidis did not commit suicide, and nor was her death an accident.

Electra Contalidis was murdered. By Nikos Contalidis.

But then, Mavrodakis wonders, was Contalidis working alone?

Or did he have help?

Mavrodakis can't for a moment imagine that any of his friends on Pelatea – like Iakavos or Alinos, Phaedra or Marika – would volunteer their services.

But one name does come to mind.

Costanza Theofilou.

Maybe the two of them are in it together?

Both of them plotting. Accomplices.

Both with something very significant to gain from Madame Contalidis's death.

Mavrodakis frowns. But could a pregnant woman, bursting with new life, actually be capable of murder? Killing her lover's wife? Even aiding and abetting?

It doesn't take him more than a few seconds to come up with the answer, wondering how he could have been so naive?

Of course, a pregnant woman could kill.

Especially when the stakes were so high.

Mavrodakis reads on.

Now that it's been established that the wine contained powdered Heripsyn and Phaladrin, he's interested in fingerprints. On all the other items he'd sent in for analysis. Who touched what?

The matchbox, with the scorpion.

The box of grass.

The saucer used as an ashtray.

The plate in the kitchen.

The knife. The mug. The corkscrew.

A glass tumbler.

A ruler and pencils from Contalidis's studio.

His hairbrush from the bathroom.

His toothbrush.

Mavrodakis may never have had the opportunity, or the evidence, to prove Contalidis's involvement in the death of Petrou, but this time he's taken no chances.

And the tests have given him far more than he could have imagined.
But far, far less than he had hoped for.
Results that stop him in his tracks, that serve to shake his certainty.
Results that point in a totally unexpected and unforeseen direction.
Wing and a prayer territory.
Everything. And nothing.

When he reaches the end of the report, Mavrodakis drops the sheaf of pages onto his desk and turns in his chair to stare through the window, slowly scratching his fingers through his beard.

Trying to put everything together. Everything he's learned. Trying to make it all add up the way he wants it to.

Just a hunch to begin with; nothing more than a hunch.

Wanting it to be so.

But now? Now, he's not so sure.

After a few more minutes, working out his next move, Mavrodakis gets up from his desk, goes to the hat stand, and reaches for his cap.

"Vango," he says, striding through the outer office. "We need to make an arrest. Perhaps you'd care to join me."

"Who're we arresting?" asks Vango, jumping to his feet, and hurrying after his boss.

"A murderer," Mavrodakis replies, opening the Kia's passenger door, climbing in, and tugging at his reluctant seat-belt. "And a very clever one, Vango. Some people always seem to think they can get away with it."

"So where do you want to go?"

"Anémenos."

The street where Mavrodakis tells Vango to park is three blocks back from the end of the quay, where the hill starts to slope towards the white walls and blue onion dome of Aghios Spyridon. The road is narrow and cobbled, a small, stepped row of houses on each side; each of the houses with two windows either side of a front door; doors that open directly onto the pavement.

Mavrodakis gets out of the car and walks to one of these houses; the only house with two floors, with a moped up on its stand. When he gets to the door, he waits for Vango and then raises the door-knocker – a blackened brass dolphin – and raps it twice against the plate.

They don't have to wait long.

When the door opens, Mavrodakis smiles, tips a salute.

He doesn't have to introduce himself.

"I wonder if I could have a few words, Madame Papadavrou?"

98

A FORMAL interview takes place back in Navros. In Mavrodakis's office, not the interview room in the basement. There is a tape recorder on the desk, and Vango sits just inside the door.

In Anémenos Madame Papadavrou had invited them in, but Mavrodakis had demurred. It would be better, he said, if the interview could take place at Police Headquarters. Procedure, he'd explained with an accommodating smile. He was sure she would understand, and he would make arrangements for a lawyer to be present, if she wanted one.

"Do I need one?" she'd asked. "If it's just procedure?"

"It is entirely up to you."

"Well, if the State is paying. Better safe than sorry."

And so, by the time they arrive back in Navros, a lawyer is waiting for them; requested over the radio by Vango. It is Panos Kassos, whose duties as an island advocate rarely stray beyond basic notary roles: the registration of births, marriages and deaths, the drawing up and reading of wills, conveyancing contracts, border disputes, and occasional visits to Police Headquarters when requested. He is in his late fifties, paunchy, puffy-faced, with bright green braces showing under his jacket, and he is keen to get home for his wife's birthday.

"Let's start with a matchbox, and a scorpion," is how Mavrodakis begins when they are all settled.

The question makes Kassos frown; sitting beside his client at Mavrodakis's desk with little or no idea what is going on beyond the fact that the interview has something to do with the suicide of Electra Contalidis.

But the question doesn't appear to surprise Madame Papadavrou. She had said not a word on the drive to Navros, content to admire the view, but here in his office, sitting there at his desk, Mavrodakis can see that she knows exactly what he's talking about. Yet it doesn't stop her playing the dumb card.

Which, for Mavrodakis, is encouraging.

"Matchbox? Scorpion? Have you brought me all this way to talk about matchboxes and scorpions? Perhaps you'd be better off talking to dear little Dimi. He's the one who loves scorpions. Snakes, lizards; all kinds of creepy-crawlies."

Which throws Mavrodakis for a moment. Dimi?

But he recovers.

"Dimi didn't leave any prints on the matchbox," he counters. "But you did. Just the one set. No others."

The Contalidis housekeeper shrugs, makes no comment.

"Of course, a scorpion's sting wouldn't have killed Madame Contalidis," Mavrodakis continues, "even in her frail condition. But it would certainly have been painful. So why did you do it? Leaving it in her drawer like that."

Again there is no answer.

"I can only assume it's because you didn't much like her. Why else would you want a scorpion to sting her?"

The old lady shrugs again. Not liking an employer is hardly a crime, and she's clearly quite happy to admit it. "You're right; truth be told, I didn't like her. Not many do around these parts. But why would I think to do such a thing? She wasn't the easiest person to work for, but that doesn't mean I wanted to do her any harm."

Then she pauses, frowns. And a moment later her eyes widen, as though some memory has risen from the depths, and she starts to nod.

"But, of course… Yes, yes, I do remember," she says, with a twitch of a smile on her lips. "Why, that box must have been there for months. Yes, of course. I remember it now." She gives a dismissive *tsk-tsk*, that she could be so forgetful. "It was the day before Mr Nikos and Madam arrived at Douka; back in May it was. I saw a scorpion in their bedroom. And rather than leave it there, why I trapped it. In the matchbox. I had one in my pocket, emptied it out, and caught it. Not easy, of course. But I didn't want a scorpion scuttling about like that. And Madam so hated scorpions."

The housekeeper settles her chin on her chest, clasps her hands, and looks pleased with herself.

"So when you'd caught it, you put it in her drawer?"

"I suppose I must have. Without thinking. There was just so much to do, so much to get ready. And I wanted everything to be perfect for them. Coming back to Douka after all that time. It was a wonderful moment. To have him… to have them all back again. And young Dimi, too. Such a lovely, lovely boy. Such a fine Contalidis."

Madame Papadavrou may be chattering on now, hoping to cover what she knows is a slip of the tongue, but Mavrodakis doesn't miss it.

Such a small, easy slip to make. Confirming what he now knows…

But he doesn't say anything; doesn't pick her up on it. Not yet.

Instead he says, "You've worked at Douka all your life, I believe."

The change of tack seems to relax the housekeeper, as he knows it will, and she nods. Her expression says it all: *This is ground I know. This is not dangerous. No mistakes to be made here.*

"I was fifteen when I started at the house. With Mr Nikos's parents. Began in the kitchen, I did, brought in by my mother one weekend when the family had a full house; washing dishes I was. Such wonderful days they were at Douka back then. Oh, the parties; you wouldn't imagine. And

Madame Contalidis's birthday, it was. Such a beautiful woman. An Efstathiou, from Voutsis, you know. A good island family. Noble stock." She nods, as though that is enough to confirm the truth of what she says.

"And how did you get on with the family? With the Contalidis?"

"At first I didn't see them, of course. I stayed in the kitchen, or worked in the storehouses packing fruit, or pickling, or tending the kitchen garden."

"And worked your way up to housekeeper. A considerable achievement. You must have loved it there. To work for the family such a long time."

"At Douka it was never work. It was a pleasure. And the Contalidis were so kind, so considerate."

"So, when did you first meet them? If you worked in the kitchen, in the storehouses."

Madame Papadavrou's expression softens, as though at a fond memory.

Sitting beside her, the lawyer, Kassos, is starting to look bored. Still unsure where all this is going, but not all that bothered. Mavrodakis sees him glance up at the clock on the wall rather than shift his cuff to look at his watch. He thinks no one sees, but Mavrodakis does.

"I had been there a year or two," Madame Papadavrou begins. "I was in the kitchen garden, collecting herbs, when Mr Contalidis walked through and stopped to talk to me. Asked me who I was."

"Did he come to the kitchen garden often?"

"Now and again, I suppose. Though I'd never seen him there before."

"And what happened? What did you talk about?"

"He asked me about the plants, the herbs, and I told him. What they were called, what they did. In cooking, you know, and for medicines."

"And?"

"And the next thing I know, a day or two later, the housekeeper – Madame Trikoupsis, it was, back then – comes to tell me that Madame Contalidis wants to see me in the salon. Well, I was nervous, you know, and young. And it was the first time I'd been in the house apart from the kitchen. Oh, and what a house it was. I couldn't believe how beautiful, how grand. But I was frightened, too. I was sure I was going to be sent home. Fired, for I knew not what."

"And?"

"But it was not to fire me. Madame Contalidis wanted to know about the plants. Mr Contalidis had told her about our conversation in the herb garden. So she asked if I'd like to help her, in her own garden, when I had time to spare. And from there…"

"And when the Contalidis left Douka, you stayed on, I understand?"

Madame Papadavrou sighs deeply. "It was not a good time. Suddenly there was no money. A business thing dear Theo… Mr Contalidis… had set up, which had not worked out as he had hoped…"

Another slip. She knows it, of course, yet pays it no heed. But Mavrodakis does.

"And Mr Petrou bought the estate. Moved in, when they moved out."

"They passed him on the road to Navros, did you know? He was coming the other way. To Douka. He waved at them, tooted his horn."

"It must have been difficult. Saying goodbye to Mr and Mrs Contalidis. To Nikos."

"If I could have gone with them, I would have done. But there was no room where they were going. The old house, here in Navros. And we villagers had to live. We had to have jobs. And I wasn't the only one who stayed."

"And Mr Petrou? How was he? As a boss?"

"Not a nice man. Greedy. Tight with his money, he was. Tight with everything." She shakes her head, and shudders. "Suddenly it was a different house."

"Mr Petrou wasn't married; I'm right, aren't I?"

The housekeeper's features settle into a tight grimace of righteous disapproval. "No room for a wife in that man's life. Not him. Such an unnecessary expense, he'd likely have told you. And the drink was a far cheaper companion. Down in the wine cellar every day, he was. All that Contalidis wine."

"But you stayed?"

She spread her hands, gave Mavrodakis a *You-do-what-you-have-to-do* look.

"Was that when you became housekeeper at Douka? Or was it before?"

"Just before. When old Madame Trikoupsis retired."

"And you were working at Douka when Mr Petrou died?"

"It was me who found him. In the morning. On the terrace."

"An accident, wasn't it? I was there with Police-Captain Goulandris."

The housekeeper's eyes widen. "I thought I recognised you. Of course. Now I remember you. Did you have that beard then?"

"But an accident, wasn't it?" Mavrodakis repeats. He notes the lawyer is suddenly alert.

"Well, it wouldn't have been suicide, that's for sure. Old Petrou loved his wine too much for that, didn't he? Mind you, it would have got him in the end, all that drinking; and he must have known it. So, a kind of suicide, I suppose. The drinking, I mean."

"Were you surprised that Mr Petrou's nephew took over the estate?"

"Everyone was. We didn't know anything about a nephew. Not until the reading of the will." She turns to Kassos, and he nods.

"You had thought the Contalidis family might buy it back?"

"We all did. We all of us hoped. Of course. Everyone."

"And once again you stayed on? With the nephew."

Kassos leans forward. He can see that Mavrodakis is heading somewhere with these questions, but he's not sure where; just knows that he has to slow things down, get a grip on the situation. For his client's sake, if nothing else. If, indeed, she is a client.

"I can't quite see, Captain, where all this is supposed to be going?" he begins. "Or what Madame Papadavrou is doing here? All these questions… Unless…"

"Simply filling in the gaps, Mr Kassos. For the hearing," says Mavrodakis, interrupting the lawyer. He knows what the man is going to say. Unless he, Mavrodakis, wants to charge his client with a crime… But he doesn't need much longer. A few more questions. And then it will be done. "Just establishing some background, you understand. So," he continues, turning back to Madame Papadavrou. "Where were we? Oh, yes. The nephew. You were housekeeper to him, were you not? Another four years?"

Madame Papadavrou nods.

"And then comes the Crash. And the house is up for sale again. And sold to Nikos Contalidis. For his father to move back in."

She smiles for the first time, or as close to a smile, Mavrodakis imagines, as she ever gets. "This Crash was bad, of course. For everyone. For the country. Such troubles, *tsk-tsk*. But here at Douka, it was good."

"It must have been wonderful when old Mr Contalidis returned."

"Oh, such a day, you can't imagine. His face was a picture. Such delight, and so good for him. At last, back home again."

"And then, of course, the fire."

The housekeeper shakes her head. "We none of us thought he'd recover. So terribly burned he was. And at his age, too."

"And you were the one who pulled him from the flames?"

She nods.

"So late at night?"

Madame Papadavrou gives him a look. But she has an answer. Something Mavrodakis didn't know. "He was getting old by that time, and not so good at looking after himself. Which was when Mr Nikos asked if I wouldn't mind staying at Douka, to keep an eye on his father. So, I was offered a small apartment in the converted storehouses, where I used to work when I was younger."

"Your husband had died a long time before. Is that right?"

"Just eighteen months after we married. Lost at sea, he was." She crosses herself, touches her thumbnail to her lips. "Pavlos Papadavros, may the good Lord bless him."

"And no children?"

"No children, no."

"You didn't marry again?"

"There was no one… None to come close to Pavlos. And in Anémenos back then, well, it was second string or widow's weeds. I settled for the weeds."

"Now, after old Mr Contalidis came back from Athens, after his treatment for the burns, he stayed in the hospital here in Navros, is that right?"

"That's right. The house was still a ruin. And the poor man needed considerable care."

"And after a series of small strokes he was moved to the hospice?"

Madame Papadavrou tightens her lips, nods sadly.

"And at the hospital, and at the hospice, I understand you were a regular visitor?"

The old housekeeper looks surprised. Then shuffles her shoulders, as though she's been found out and feels uncomfortable about it. "There was no one else really. With Mr Nikos away in Athens…"

"But Madame Contalidis always visited. When the family moved back to Douka. At least once a week she would call in. Bring him fruit, the staff said. Talk to him. She was very caring, I understand."

Madame Papadavrou says nothing, but Mavrodakis knows what she's thinking. Caring, be damned!

"But, then," says Mavrodakis. "We shouldn't forget that you enjoyed a much longer, and more significant, role in his life than Madame Contalidis." He pauses. "And I don't mean as housekeeper. Because old Mr Contalidis was much more than your employer. Was he not?"

Madame Papadavrou draws in her breath slowly; seems to stiffen, glances at her lawyer.

Kassos gets the message. It is time for him to do something; even if he's not sure what.

So he leans forward, covers a clearing of the throat with his hand, and starts to speak…

But Mavrodakis cuts him short. He is too close now.

"Do you remember those fingerprints of yours on the matchbox?" he asks, lightly, as though he's decided to change the subject.

The old lady doesn't answer. Just the raising of an eyebrow.

"Well, you see, the interesting thing about fingerprints is that they don't just tell you who someone is. Establishing identity, and so forth. Seeing if someone has a criminal record. Nowadays, they do much more than that. Oh, yes, a great deal more."

Over Madame Papadavrou's shoulder, Mavrodakis sees Vango lean forward in his chair. Elbows on knees, hands clasped, not wanting to miss anything. Almost mesmerised by the proceedings.

For a moment there is silence in the office, and then the sound of a motorbike racing past. The rising whine of its approach, a high-pitched scream as it passes, and a gradual diminishing as the rider draws away, throttling down. When it is quiet, Mavrodakis begins again.

"In the old days, the police would dust for prints. Graphite powder, or some such, applied to surfaces with a fine bristle brush. The kind a lady might use for her make-up. Back then it was all we could do. But times have changed, and now, in special cases, we can lift and preserve not just the lines of the print, but also any residual fluids that might be on them. Sweat, for instance. From the…" Mavrodakis leans forward, picks up the Contalidis forensic report from his desk, flicks through the pages. "Yes, here we are: '*sweat secreted from the eccrine glands*'. Eccrine glands, eh? Whatever next?" Mavrodakis closes the report, puts it back on his desk. "And in certain cases, with specialised equipment and methods, our top forensic boys are sometimes able tell from those tiny, tiny traces, whether the print belongs to a man or a woman – something to do with levels of amino acids, I believe…"

He spreads his hands in wonder, as though such arcane scientific processes are as astonishing, and foreign, to him as they must be to Madame Papadavrou, and Kassos, and Vango.

"There's more, too, would you believe? Because these fluids can also tell us what the owner of that print might have touched before leaving it; what they might have eaten; and even whether they're taking any medication. If they're smokers, or drink a lot of coffee, or use cocaine, or smoke marijuana. Quite extraordinary, don't you think?"

If Mavrodakis had been expecting a response, he is disappointed.

So, he continues, "For instance, I know from your fingerprints, Madame Papadavrou, that you eat a lot of garlic…" He chuckles, shakes his head. "Would you believe it? Not from the prints on the matchbox, of course. Those prints are too old for conclusive testing. No, these are your prints from a glass tumbler. The one you were drinking from in the kitchen, remember? When you were explaining how the doors locked. And as well as the garlic, I also know from those prints that you take Rheumasol, a prescribed medication for rheumatism. Just from the tiniest drops of protein contained in the fluids from your fingerprint."

Kassos is frowning. He doesn't know whether to interrupt or not. Because, despite his role as Madame Papadavrou's counsel, he is caught up in the story that Mavrodakis is telling. Wants to know more.

As for the old housekeeper, she has raised her eyes from Mavrodakis and has settled them on the map of Pelatea behind his desk. It's as if, somehow, she senses where all this is heading, what is coming.

But Mavrodakis knows that that's not possible.

She cannot possibly know what he is about to say next.

Or where he is trying to lead her.

"Interestingly, our forensic boys found a match with your prints. From a ruler and some pencils in Mr Contalidis's studio. And from his hairbrush and toothbrush. Not a print as such – there were none of yours on any of those items. The match was a DNA match. Did I mention that a fingerprint could provide that kind of information? Well, it can. And it did."

Mavrodakis leans forward at his desk, clasps his hands.

"Which confirmed, Madame Papadavrou, that Nikos Contalidis is not just your employer. That he is, in fact… your son. By Theo Contalidis. For his wife, Kalliopi. For her to bring up as her own."

The silence is pure, still as stone. Not a breath. Nor the creak of a chair.

"Does Mr Contalidis know that you are his mother?"

Madame Papadavrou doesn't move, doesn't blink. And then, just a tightening in her jaw as she swallows, and from her eye a tear spills down her cheek. Followed by the merest shake of her head.

And Mavrodakis knows that he is close. Now that the truth is out.

But he says nothing; waits.

He needs more. Much more.

"She was not good for him," the old housekeeper begins, without any further encouragement. "She was such a terrible weight, that woman. I could see it in the poor man's eyes. The sadness. Such despair. And when he was starting to do so well… There she was, just… holding him back. Making his life a torment."

"So you killed her. That Monday night."

He says it quietly. Not a question, just a statement of fact. As if he knows. So there is no point in her denying it.

He can only hope it's enough. There is nothing left after this. Nowhere else to go.

Across the table Madame Papadavrou sighs, draws a breath, and then, "Yes. I did." She raises her head, points her chin. Proud of herself; proud of what she has done. For her son. Her sacrifice. The least a mother can do.

"And would you mind telling me how you killed her?"

Madame Papadavrou sighs again. "That Monday I knew she would be alone. Nikos was away in Athens, and little Dimi was staying with friends. So I went to the house and she was already drunk. As usual. Out by the pool. Staggering around, she was, almost naked. Talking to herself. Gibberish. Like old Petrou. And when she saw me coming towards her, saw what I had in mind, she called out for Nikos. '*Nikos, I need you*'. But it was too late for that. There was no Nikos to help her then. Just the two of us. The moment to settle accounts. And it was so easy. Easier than I'd imagined. Hardly any struggle."

Kassos, the lawyer, has regained some sense of composure, realises what is happening – what has happened – and reaches out a hand, puts it on his client's arm, starts to tell her that she should say nothing more…

But Madame Papadavrou shakes her head, waves him aside. It is as if, now, she wants to let it all be known; sees no reason to hold anything back. What's done is done.

"This was not the woman for my Nikos," she continues. "She didn't deserve him; didn't deserve his care and his love. Drinking like she did, taking all those drugs… And Dimi? What kind of a mother was she to that darling little boy?"

"Dimi. Your grandson."

"My… grandson. Yes."

"So how did you kill her?" Mavrodakis asks again.

And slowly, gaining a kind of strength with every word of her confession, the housekeeper, Ariadne Papadavrou, tells Mavrodakis everything he wants to hear.

Step by step.

From start to finish.

99

THE OFFICES of ConStav in Pangrati occupy ground-floor premises in an old textile mill. It reminds Police-Captain Mavrodakis, who has brought no overnight bag for this trip, of Douka and its interiors. The polished concrete floors, the shafts of direct and filtered sunlight streaming through panels of clear and sanded glass; the openness, the space. Worn city brick instead of Douka's faded island stone.

It is a little before lunch when he and Police-Lieutenant Kounellis, an officer from the Athens Police Directorate, arrive at ConStav. They are both in uniform; crisp, pressed, official; three stars and two stars on their respective shoulder boards. At the limestone-panelled reception desk, at the end of a vaulted tunnel of pale red brick, a young girl in t-shirt and striped dungarees gives them an uncertain but welcoming smile and asks how she can help?

"We are here to see Mr Nikos Contalidis," Mavrodakis tells her. "I'm afraid we have not made an appointment, but it is a matter of some urgency."

"I'm not sure that he's here," the receptionist tells him. "I don't think he came in this morning. If you'd care to wait, I'll call through to Mr Stavrides's office."

The two police officers stay where they are, while the receptionist makes the call. She explains the situation, then nods her head, smiles up at Mavrodakis and his companion. "I'll bring them straight through," she says, and puts down the phone. "If you'd like to follow me. Mr Stavrides will see you now."

She gets up from behind her desk and leads them to a set of sanded-glass doors, which slide open at her approach. The office beyond these doors is an open-space studio the size of a tournament tennis court, furnished with blonde wood desks that remind Mavrodakis of the one in Electra's study, and angled drafting boards, sofas and coffee tables, a bubbling fish tank, and, in the centre of the room, a raised display table with a cardboard construction model under spotlights. From the arched brick ceiling hang paddle-bladed fans and twisting mobiles, and from unseen speakers there's a soft rock 'n' roll soundtrack to accompany the buzz of chatter and ringing phones. It is not an office environment that Mavrodakis recognises, nor the people in it: a dozen or more men and women in jeans and t-shirts, chinos and button-down collars, tapping away at computer monitors or perched over the drafting tables, some of them glancing up as the two police officers cross the room.

When they reach the far end of the studio, one of two opaque glass doors slides open and Vassi Stavrides appears, introduces himself, and ushers them into his office.

"I understand you wanted to see Nikos. I am afraid he's not here, and won't be in for the rest of the day. Is there anything I can help you with?"

"It's Mr Contalidis we need to speak with," Mavrodakis explains. "Do you have any idea where we might find him?"

"Of course, yes. He called me this morning. He's at Evangelismos Hospital in Kolonaki. A friend of his took a fall, I'm afraid. It appears to be serious."

Evangelismos Hospital on Ipsilantou is as busy as anyone might expect of a general hospital in the centre of a city, but their police uniforms afford Mavrodakis and Kounellis an access others do not enjoy. Making their way to the front of the queue at the Information Desk, Mavrodakis asks one of the staff for a call to be put out for a visitor, Nikos Contalidis.

"Should I ask for him to come here?"

"If you'd be so kind," says Mavrodakis, wondering what other option made any kind of sense.

Nearly ten minutes after the call goes out – a tinny, echoing "Would Mr Nikos Contalidis please come to the Information Desk in Reception", repeated twice – Mavrodakis sees a set of lift doors open and Contalidis step out, pausing to look around. Which is when he spots Mavrodakis coming towards him. He frowns, looks uncertain.

Cornered, thinks Mavrodakis. And for a moment he wonders if the man might even try to make a run for it.

But he doesn't. He stands his ground, watching the two police officers approach. He is not as slickly turned out as the last time Mavrodakis saw him. His wavy black hair could do with a brush, his cheeks with a shave, and white shirt-tails and unlinked cuffs hang loose beneath a crumpled grey jumper. He looks like a man who has been up most of the night; a man who had come to Evangelismos in a hurry.

"Mr Contalidis, I would be grateful if you could come with us."

The man's frown deepens. A strange mix of anger and resentment, and then a flash of uncertainty, flit across his face.

"Come with you? What're you talking about, Mavrodakis? I can't possibly."

"I'm afraid you can, and you must."

"But my friend…" he looks back at the lift, spreads his hands. He doesn't know how to continue.

Mavrodakis spares him. "I'm sure that Miss Theofilou will receive the very best of care in your absence."

At Police Headquarters on Alexandras Avenue, Nikos Contalidis sits at a metal table in an interview room on the fourth floor of the sixteen-floor building. That Mavrodakis knows about Costanza Theofilou has clearly shaken him.

On the drive from Evangelismos, Mavrodakis had watched Contalidis in the rear-view mirror: hands on the seat either side of him, to steady himself on the turns; silent, staring out of the windows. But it wasn't a blank look. His mind, Mavrodakis knew, would be racing.

If the police know about Cossie, then they'll clearly be taking a closer look at Electra's death. That's what Contalidis was thinking.

A man with a pregnant girlfriend and a dead wife cannot fail to find himself a person of interest. A first port of call for any investigating officer.

And that is what Contalidis is thinking now; sitting side on to the metal table, legs crossed, foot tapping, hands clasped in his lap. Ordering his thoughts, preparing himself. And trying to look relaxed. Unconcerned.

Mavrodakis has seen this a thousand times, in a hundred rooms like this one. A suspect getting his story straight. Getting his ducks to stand in a row. For Mavrodakis, it is the kind of behaviour he has learned to expect from a man with something to hide. And Mavrodakis is certain that Mr Nikos Contalidis, sitting there at the table when he and Police-Lieutenant Kounellis come into the room, the man in the crumpled jumper and shirt cuffs, really does have something to hide.

"I hope Miss Theofilou wasn't too upset at your having to leave her," Mavrodakis begins, pulling out a chair and sitting down.

At the hospital Contalidis had asked to say goodbye to her, and Mavrodakis had accompanied him to an Obstetrics ward on the third floor; watched from the corridor as Contalidis leant over the bed, presumably explaining to her that he had to be away for a bit, but would be back soon. Like Contalidis, the woman in the bed – looking up at him, reaching for his hand – was not the woman Mavrodakis had seen walking down Efestiou with a swing to her hips and a spring in her step just a week or so before. Now she was as pale as the sheet that covered her. Listless, broken.

"I hope it's nothing serious," Mavrodakis had said, knowing it had to be, in the lift going down to Reception.

"She fell," is all Contalidis would say.

"How fortunate that you were around to help her," said Mavrodakis, as the lift doors opened and they stepped out.

Contalidis had shot him a look, but said nothing.

And he is still not saying anything. Not a word. Nothing. A shake of the head when offered coffee. Mavrodakis can feel the hatred and resentment pulsing off the man across the table from him.

And uncertainty, too.

Perfect ingredients with which to commence an interview.

"So, Mr Contalidis, as I said in the car, following our receipt of your wife's autopsy report, we are now obliged to look more closely into the circumstances of her death. Suspicious circumstances to say the least, wouldn't you agree?"

None of this elicits the least response from Contalidis.

"For which reason, if you don't mind, I will be recording this interview." Mavrodakis leans forward and switches on the tape recorder he has brought with him. The red light wavers, then steadies, and after giving the day and date and place, and naming those present he begins. "Having already stated that you do not have any need for legal representation, perhaps I could start by asking where you were on the night of your wife's death? Say, between six o'clock and midnight on Monday, September 11th."

Contalidis sighs, as though he knows he must show willing. Whether he likes it or not. Any other behaviour would only appear suspicious. But his tone is still combative.

"You know that already," he says, uncrossing his legs, repositioning his chair to face Mavrodakis. Down to business. "I told you. I was here in the city. I left the office around five, to check out a potential site, and then went home."

"To Diomexédes?"

"To Diomexédes, yes."

"Not Douka?"

"Not Douka, no."

Mavrodakis nods; scratches his beard, runs his tongue over his crooked front teeth.

"And not with Miss Costanza Theofilou?"

"Costanza is a friend. So there is no misunderstanding, you should know that she is a journalist with the design magazine, *Arki-Tek*. She has written about my company for that magazine, and recently organised a photo shoot at Douka. That is how I know her. Just that. Professionally, and, subsequently, as a friend."

It is clear to Mavrodakis that Contalidis is confident that he can get away with this explanation; that it is watertight. Indeed, the statement is so smoothly delivered it is as though he has practised these lines, this denial. In case he was ever confronted by his wife, Mavrodakis wonders? Possibly, he thinks. But he knows, too, that Contalidis wouldn't be half so confident if he knew that Mavrodakis had seen the pair of them strolling down that street in Thiseio; that Mavrodakis knew that he kept a change of clothes at her apartment; that he was in the habit of spending the night there.

But a lie is a lie, even if that lie is understandable in this kind of context: a married man, albeit a widow, refusing to acknowledge an affair. But Mavrodakis also knows that the time has come to disabuse Contalidis of such considerations; to put him on the back foot. To test that confidence.

A lie is a lie.

And in any police interview, a lie is a very good place to start.

Add it to resentment and hatred, and that splinter of uncertainty, and Contalidis is on very thin ice.

Which is good.

But Mavrodakis is also on thin ice, and he knows he needs to play his prey very carefully indeed. It has been a long time since that dismissive moment on the Douka terrace, gathered around a blood-puddled Petrou; at the Douka fire eight years later; and, most recently, manning the police barriers around Aghios Stephanos. And he doesn't intend this one last chance to slip through his fingers.

"I think, Mr Contalidis, the time has come to set the record straight, don't you? So let us be frank, shall we? Miss Costanza may well be a friend, but she is also your lover, is she not?"

"No, she is not."

"Then I am sure you can explain how you came to spend the night with Miss Costanza just a few days after your wife's death."

"I can't explain it, because I didn't. You are mistaken."

The same, confident denial.

Despite his own uncertainty, despite the risk he's taking, Mavrodakis feels a lick of excitement. He has been waiting a long time for this moment, and for what is to come; to catch the man out, and see him squirm.

"And would I also be mistaken in suggesting that you were seen outside Thanos restaurant in Vouliagmeni, kissing the young lady in question?"

There is no doubt that Contalidis is startled by this disclosure. He takes a moment or two before responding, but his reply is accompanied by a sly smile.

"Ah," he says, eyes narrowing, but twinkling too. "Now I understand. You've been talking to Ana Doukakis."

Mavrodakis says nothing, just spreads his hands.

"Well, let me put you straight about Ana Doukakis. She may have been a friend of my late wife, but if she is your source for such a monstrous allegation then you should know that she is a gossip and a trouble-maker. And that throughout my marriage she has done everything she can to undermine my probity… my suitability as Ella's husband. Jealousy, I would imagine; a determination to cause mischief and damage, having made advances towards me on a number of occasions, advances which I rebuffed. She would not have liked that."

Contalidis is angry now – making himself so, Mavrodakis suspects, to add weight to his lie – and still imagines himself in control. Because by discrediting Ana Doukakis as forcefully as he has, he is suggesting a very plausible defence should the matter ever come before a judge. His word, against hers. And Mavrodakis is in no doubt that Contalidis would lie under oath, putting any prosecution in a difficult position.

"So, Madame Doukakis is mistaken when she says that she and her husband saw you with a woman – presumably Miss Theofilou – at Thanos restaurant?"

"That she saw us? No. She is not mistaken. But there was no kissing. Nothing of the kind. That she should say such a thing is simply… malicious.

And typical. How dare she? I took Costanza to the restaurant to thank her for the shoot she organised at Douka. Simply a professional courtesy. She did an amazing job. It was the least I could do."

He reckons he's got it covered, thinks Mavrodakis. That half admission. Yes, I was in Vouliagmeni, and yes, I was at Thanos with Costanza Theofilou. Because he can't deny it. Wouldn't dare. Because he knows that Mavrodakis can easily check with the restaurant to find out if he had been there. And with whom. If he hasn't done so already.

"So Ana Doukakis is… mistaken about any kissing?"

"Quite mistaken," counters Contalidis.

Mavrodakis nods. "Of course, of course. But, you know, if it were just the one source, Mr Contalidis, if it were just Vouliagmeni, I would have no option but to treat it with the same kind of suspicion, the same… scepticism. But there have been other sightings, too."

Contalidis widens his eyes, and the twinkle starts to fade.

"For instance, a very credible witness saw you one morning arm in arm with Miss Theofilou on Efestiou Street, after you had spent the night with her; and at a bar called Acteon on Alexandrou in Metaxourgeio; and at the restaurant Vrasidia in Piraeus. All these sightings, and several more, I might add, in the days following your wife's death."

Contalidis pales, the colour draining from his face. This is not what he had expected.

Time to move it along, thinks Mavrodakis. No time for the man across the table to gather himself, to order his thoughts.

"As you know, your wife, Electra Contalidis, drowned. But it was not suicide, and it was not an accident. She didn't fall, or slip, or stumble into the pool. Or drown herself. Someone pushed her into the pool and held her under. And I'm sure you'll be delighted to learn that that someone is already in police custody."

Contalidis is a picture. His eyes open even wider. His lips part. And Mavrodakis knows exactly what's going through his mind. If someone has been taken into custody, then he is clearly off the hook. That whatever his relationship with Costanza Theofilou, it can have no possible bearing on the situation. His wife has been murdered, and the police have apprehended the person who killed her. That's all there is to it. Nothing more. It is also clear, from his astonished response to the news of this arrest, that Contalidis had not been at Douka when Madame Papadavrou attacked his wife.

"Someone killed her? And you've arrested them?"

Mavrodakis nods, smiles, spreads his hands.

"Who?" he asks. "Who did this? Who have you arrested?"

"I'm sure you'll understand that I am not at liberty, at this moment, to divulge such information."

"Then… then what am I doing here?" asks Contalidis. "What has all this to do with me?"

"Because the person we have arrested, and charged with your wife's murder, was not working alone. Albeit, unwittingly, of course. Isn't that so, Mr Contalidis?"

The game has changed again, and Contalidis knows it. One minute he thinks he has the upper hand. And then, suddenly, he's under pressure again; back in the hot seat. He doesn't know what is happening; doesn't know what to say, or how to react. Which is exactly what Mavrodakis wants.

"I don't understand…" he begins, more alert than he has been; eyes narrowing again, leaning forward on the table.

"Oh, come, come now," says Mavrodakis. "Of course you do."

Contalidis raises a hand, spreads the fingers, "This is ridiculous," he says, and starts to chuckle, as if the whole thing is some outrageous joke; but a joke taken too far. He turns to Kounellis, as though to share the joke, but Kounellis does not respond. Sitting in his metal chair by the barred window. Arms crossed, legs crossed. Just an observer.

"But let's move on, shall we?" Mavrodakis continues. "Let's talk about your two homes. On Diomexédes, here in Athens; and on Pelatea."

Mavrodakis sees what's going through Contalidis's head. What now? What now, for God's sake? That's what he's thinking. Where is all this going?

Which is exactly how Mavrodakis wants it.

"Tell me, Mr Contalidis. How are you in the kitchen, around the house? Domestically, I mean."

"What on earth has this got to do with my wife's murder?" Contalidis is frowning, perplexed.

"Do you cook, for instance?"

Contalidis tips back his head, and sighs impatiently. "My wife cooked. She was very good. But we also have people who help us with these things. Here in Athens when Electra was ill, for instance. And on Pelatea, there's Madame Papadavrou, and the house girls, Aja and Lina."

"So you don't cook? Can't cook?"

"When I have to, I can manage. The basics, if you like. Like most men; fathers, I suppose. I can knock up pasta, a salad, manage a barbecue. That sort of thing."

"Would you, for instance, know how to use a food mixer? A pasta machine? A pressure cooker? Coffee grinder?"

"If I had to, I suppose. It can't be that difficult."

"But not that often? Not on a regular basis? In other words, you wouldn't say that in the normal course of events you'd take an active part in the kitchen?"

"Like I said – only when I have to." Contalidis tries the chuckle again. He might not have any idea where this is leading, but Mavrodakis knows he's starting to feel more relaxed, a little more in control.

For now, thinks Mavrodakis; for the next few moments.

But only if he, Mavrodakis, can pull off the bluff.

"So, let's get back to the autopsy findings," Mavrodakis begins. "According to the pathologist's report, your wife…"

"She drowned. I know," says Contalidis, his confidence returning. "You said. Someone you've arrested for her murder pushed her into the pool and drowned her."

"Quite so, quite so. But it wasn't just drowning. Your wife had been poisoned first. An overdose. Did you know that?"

"Poisoned? An overdose? And how would I know something like that?"

Mavrodakis pays no attention to the question. "A mixture of prescription drugs that your wife was taking. Very strong sedatives; sleeping pills, if you like. Heripsyn and Phaladrin, to be precise."

"Well, I know my wife took Heripsyn. To help her sleep, after her breakdown. But I'm not familiar with the other one. Phaladrin?"

"For your information, the Phaladrin was prescribed in June by Doctor Paradoxis on Pelatea. So tell me, who would have known about these drugs that your wife had been prescribed? Apart from her doctors, that is."

Contalidis spreads his hands. "I have no idea. As I said, I knew about the Heripsyn, but I can't say who else might have known."

Mavrodakis can see that Contalidis is becoming uncomfortable again.

"Well, the point is that somebody did know. And they took those pills from her bathroom cabinet, ground them up and tipped the powder into a bottle of wine. The bottle of wine that your wife was drinking on the night she died. Easily enough pills to guarantee her death. A devastating overdose, according to the toxicology report." Mavrodakis pauses, frowns. "The interesting thing is that the person we currently have in custody denies any knowledge of those pills; the tainted wine. All this person has admitted to is hitting your wife hard enough to knock her down, and then drowning her. But why bother to do that when she's already been poisoned?"

"Are you saying there were two killers?"

"That's how it appears."

"Well, maybe my wife took the pills herself, intending suicide. And then this intruder, this person you've arrested, for whatever reason, decided to kill her."

"That's a possibility, I grant you. Except for a couple of facts. If you're going to commit suicide, why crush up pills into a powder, add them to your wine, and then drink the wine? When all you have to do is swallow a handful or two. Just over twenty Heripsyn, according to Doctor Fastiliades, and just a few of the Phaladrin. A deadly amount. And the other thing is that, according to the person we've arrested, your wife called out your name when she realised that she was in danger. Did I mention that?"

"No, you didn't."

"Odd that, don't you think? Calling out your name when you're in Athens. It's as if you were there, in the house, and she was trying to alert you; calling out to you for help. Help that you were never going to provide."

"Well, to be accurate – help that I was not able to provide, since I wasn't there."

There's a sudden click from the tape machine, and the red light goes out.

Mavrodakis smiles at Contalidis, holds up a finger, and proceeds to eject the tape, turn it, and put it back into its slot. Closes the cover. Presses 'Record', and the red light flickers back on.

"I choose my words carefully, Mr Contalidis," Mavrodakis continues. "Help that you were never going to provide. Because you were there, weren't you, that Monday night at Douka? Maybe not when your wife called out your name, minutes before she was attacked by someone else, but earlier that evening, certainly. Because you were the one who ground up the pills, and poured the powder into the wine." Mavrodakis grunts, shakes his head. "Two people, separately, on their own initiative; both intent on killing the same person, and at the same time. Extraordinary."

"I have no idea what you're talking about. This is absolutely ridiculous." Once again, Contalidis turns to Kounellis, as though seeking support or agreement. It is a wasted effort. Kounellis says nothing.

Mavrodakis sighs. He knows the moment has come to play his card.

It is now, or never.

Ace, or joker.

"I'm sure you don't. But I do. I know exactly what I'm talking about. I'm talking about fingerprints. Not on the bottle of wine, of course. You'd have wiped that clean. If your wife were the only person in the house, then her prints could be the only ones on it. No, I'm talking about the pestle and mortar. The one by the toaster? That lovely white Parian marble. Because not only did our forensic boys find traces of Heripsyn and Phaladrin on both items, they also found fingerprints. Your fingerprints."

It is a lie. The lie. No such prints exist. No such traces were found. The pestle and mortar hadn't even been sent for testing. Not yet, anyway.

But Mavrodakis is sure that that's how the pills were crushed. There, in the kitchen. By the toaster. The question is, did Contalidis wipe the pestle and mortar clean, like the bottle of wine, or was he wearing gloves throughout his preparations? In which case he'll see the bluff for what it is.

"My prints are probably all over the kitchen," Contalidis replies. "I live in the house, for God's sake. It would be odd if you didn't find them."

"Even though you don't, by your own admission, do much in the way of kitchen chores. But anyway, that's beside the point," says Mavrodakis, waving the matter aside; knowing now that Contalidis had not worn gloves that Monday night at Douka; that he'd almost certainly used that pestle and mortar to crush the pills; and had done no more than wipe the bottle clean.

So far his bluff has worked.

All that was needed now was one last tap of the hammer to the nail head.

One final play.

"Because," Mavrodakis continues, "the real point is that when fingerprints are properly and scrupulously analysed, using the most up-to-date scientific procedures, which we have done, they do a great deal more than simply identify the owner of those prints. Oh yes, indeed. For instance, there are certain fluids on a fingerprint that can provide the most extraordinary information. Did you know that?"

Contalidis frowns. Like Madame Papadavrou, he has no idea where this is going.

Mavrodakis savours the moment. The look on the man's face. The confusion. The discomfort. And a dawning fear.

Because the man across the desk from him is beginning to suspect that he's not going to like what he hears next. Something he hasn't prepared for.

"When someone handles explosives, for instance, there will always be traces of that explosive on his or her fingerprints. Like an ink stain, if you like." This time it's Mavrodakis who turns to Kounellis, and Kounellis nods. "And those fingerprints on that pestle and mortar – your fingerprints, Mr Contalidis – show unmistakeable traces of Heripsyn and Phaladrin. Neither of which, interestingly, were found in the analysis of your wife's fingerprints. No trace of them at all. Possibly not so surprising, I suppose, given the time she spent in the pool. But still…"

Contalidis doesn't move. Seems to freeze.

"So you see, I do know you were there, at Douka. Grinding the pills, pouring the powder into the bottle. And only then taking your leave, once your wife had started in on the wine, without her knowing you'd gone. Before she called your name, before she was pushed into the pool and held under." Mavrodakis tips his head, pauses… smiles. "Before Madame Papadavrou came calling."

Contalidis jerks back, as though hit by a fist.

"Ariadne? The housekeeper?"

"The very same. The trusted family retainer. All those years, serving the Contalidis. And serving them still."

Jaw clenching, brows tightly furrowed, Contalidis is silent now; searching for a way out.

Mavrodakis holds his breath. Has he done enough? The pills, the powder, the pestle and mortar, the bottle of wine.

So close, so close…

But will Contalidis have an answer?

Will he try to bluff back?

Because if he does, all will be lost.

And Contalidis will walk away. Back to Costanza Theofilou, and a new life together. Free and clear.

The seconds tick by, and then, across the table, Mavrodakis sees Contalidis swallow, shake his head.

Just like his mother.

The tiniest movements. But no tear.

It is all that Mavrodakis needs.

"Ariadne Papadavrou. Would you believe it?" Mavrodakis blows out a breath of air, gives a fair impression of Ana Doukakis's 'Tah'. "And the poor woman didn't need to do a thing, of course. Didn't need to lift so much as a finger. What she wanted to do had already been done. By you. Maybe an hour or so earlier. The time it would have taken your wife to finish that bottle of wine. But Madame Papadavrou didn't know that, did she? So she hits your wife on the side of the head, pushes her into the pool, and holds her under. Until there were no more bubbles, that's what she said."

Across the table, Contalidis lowers his head and his shoulders slump; the fight gone out of him.

And Mavrodakis leans back in his chair, and clasps his hands behind his head; feels a warmth spread through him.

A deep and comforting warmth.

A final, satisfying resolution.

By the skin of his crooked teeth.

But he hasn't finished.

"Oh, by the way, there's one more thing you won't know. About Madame Papadavrou, your housekeeper at Douka."

Contalidis just shakes his head again. He doesn't know how to respond. What to do, or say.

"Something the forensic report turned up. Fingerprints again. And something your housekeeper confirmed."

Finally, Contalidis looks up. Dead eyes, slack features. He hasn't the words, but the question is there.

Mavrodakis smiles; unclasps his hands, leans forward over the table. Takes his time.

"You'll be interested to learn that Madame Papadavrou, the woman we currently have in custody, is your mother."

100

IT IS DONE. Case closed. Everything matches: every small piece of evidence, every word, every single perspective and possible interpretation allotted its space and attention. Formal confessions. Signed statements. Guilty pleas entered. To be judged accordingly.

A single murder, but two killers. Mother and son. With the same motive: to rid themselves of an unwanted family member. Taking advantage of the same opportunity: the victim alone in the house of the Contalidis.

And neither killer, it transpires, aware of the other.

There is a sense of contentment – both professional and personal – as Police-Captain Mavrodakis takes his cap from the hat stand and leaves his office in Navros. He might not have been able to pin Petrou's death on Nikos Contalidis, but he's made up for it. He's got the man for something.

And it is enough, he supposes.

But his contentment is tinged with disappointment, too.

A certain… unease.

It hasn't quite ended as Mavrodakis would have liked.

Not as complete and watertight, as he would have wanted.

There's still something that nags at him.

Something that's niggled away since his visit to Douka that September morning.

It is only a short walk to his home in Navros, but his hip is playing up and he knows he must hurry. An early rain has started to fall, splashing into the summer's dust, leaving dark wet coins on the pavement, smacking onto the polished peak of his cap, and soaking into his shoulder boards. From somewhere far off he hears a low groan and grumble of thunder.

Everything in place. Everything as it should be.

And yet…

And yet… Those locked doors at Douka the morning after the murder?

Mavrodakis has thought about those doors a lot, but has come up with no convincing answer. He might not like Nikos Contalidis, and certainly wouldn't trust him further than he could throw one of the man's tasselled suede loafers. But his explanation for those locked doors at the house at Douka is the only one that seems to carry any weight.

The only one that seems in any way plausible.

A glitch.

A snag.

Just a problem with the locks.

Like the plumbing, the wiring…

And for Mavrodakis, fumbling for his own keys in the rain, feeling a chill as the first whisper of autumn settles on Pelatea and swirls around his uniform collar, he has to accept that it can be the only possible explanation.

Even if he's not altogether happy with it.

If it wasn't a glitch…

If it wasn't a snag…

Then who could have locked those doors from the inside?

Printed in Great Britain
by Amazon